Books by B.

Visit BVLarson.com for more information.

Death World

by
B. V. Larson

ISBN-13: 978-1511691390
ISBN-10: 1511691395
BISAC: Fiction / Science Fiction / Military

An excerpt from: *The Rise of Earth's Legions*

Earth's military changed forever when the Galactic Empire informed us of our status as proud members of their grand regime. Up until that time, the human species had wrongly assumed we were alone in the universe, and that our miniscule planet-bound concerns were all that mattered. The true state of affairs was not understood in the old days. We had no idea we were part of a vast political organization that laid claim to fifty billion of the stars in our galaxy.

After that blissful moment of formal annexation, humanity stood both humbled and enlightened. A turbulent period followed, during which certain stubborn nations and individuals were corrected in their thinking. Within a decade, however, those of us who survived came to embrace our new status in the cosmos.

Comforted by the realization Earth was part of a massive brotherhood of alien worlds, we were given a series of fantastic gifts. The first of these was security. Each province, such as our own Frontier 921, was patrolled by a Battle Fleet charged with the twin duties of local enforcement and expansion. Another boon came in the form of trade with countless alien worlds. Wealth and technology untold can now be purchased from any world in the Empire with Galactic Credits.

These gifts do not come without a price, however! Our great patrons, known collectively as the Galactics, tolerate no transgressions. The breaking of the smallest of their infinitely wise laws results in immediate, harsh correction. Perma-death of the perpetrator is the usual punishment meted out, but it is by no means their only option. At times, an entire family unit, organization, locality or even the source species itself is found collectively guilty for having fostered a criminal—in which case they're summarily removed from existence and forgotten.

Since our annexation, Earth's role in the Empire has always been military in nature. It was discovered early on that our best trade good consisted of mercenary troops. We formed the legions to serve this need for our alien brothers. More recently, we've become an enforcement arm for the Galactics themselves. Earth's military, therefore, is of vital importance to her economy as well as her security.

Our forces consist of two major groupings. Hegemony is a planetary organization dedicated to homeworld defense. Contracts with foreign worlds, however, are dealt with by a loose-knit brotherhood of independent legions.

Listed here are a few of the most famous (or infamous) legions from Earth's pantheon:

Hegemony
Emblem: The Blue Globe.
Although it is called a legion, Hegemony is actually far larger than all the independent legions put together. The organization is Earth's primary military authority, responsible for planetary security as well as the task of oversight for the smaller legions as they perform off-world missions.

As our role has recently shifted from performing purely mercenary tasks to local provincial defense, it's quite possible that Hegemony will someday devour the rest of the legions. However, there's been a good deal of resistance to the idea from the legions, various military leaders and even the public at large. The legions enjoy loyal patronage, almost like sports teams, among the general population. Talk of their dismantlement has resulted in lost elections for numerous politicians.

In addition, there's still some validity to an independent command structure. Due to the vastness of space, it's virtually impossible for a centralized government to fully control any military force deployed on a distant world. This reality means any task force must be capable of operating in an unknown environment with the freedom to make on-the-spot decisions for months or even years at a time.

The fact that deployed legions often cause incidents that come home to haunt Earth later is the topic of countless debates, but for the time being, the smaller legions remain independent.

Victrix
Emblem: The Crossed Swords.

Victrix was Earth's first formally commissioned legion. They brought home Galactic Credits after successfully performing an off-world mission for the Skrull in their home system. For this and many subsequent actions, they will be forever remembered and revered. Without their initial forays, two of which were completed before a second legion was even deployed, we all might have perished as financial failures—a crime that isn't tolerated by the Empire.

Germanica
Emblem: The Head of Taurus, the Bull.

Germanica has long been known as the legion most requested by the richest of clientele. They serve with distinction and even grace. There is no legion that is as professional in appearance and performance. Every despot among our neighboring worlds who requires an escort, a display of wealth, or merely a color-guard, asks for Germanica.

Vile rumors of corruption among the legion's officers must be mentioned here. Germanica's leadership has hotly denied the allegations for many years. It is this author's suspicion that such slander is the inevitable outcome of envy, a sin that lurks in the hearts of all lesser men.

Iron Eagles
Emblem: The Double-Headed Eagle.

The Iron Eagles have a varied history. The third of Earth's legions to be commissioned, they've fought in many difficult campaigns. Historically, they were regarded as among the most professional and capable of the legions. If a corporate ruler was in danger of losing his birthright to a gaggle of rebels, he would often summon the Eagles. In modern times, some say this legion has become more indolent and choosy with their missions, even refusing the hardest assignments. All in all, however, they still have the reputation for being the best fighting unit Earth has.

Teutoburg
Emblem: The Oak Leaf.

Teutoburg is a legion with a questionable past. Their tribunes have faced more charges of corruption, misconduct and unsanctioned alien dealings than the top officers of any other legion. A quick look through imprisonment records finds the odds that any given leader of this organization will eventually be convicted of a serious crime is nearly one in three.

On the other hand, it must be mentioned that Teutoburg has served Earth well on countless occasions. They pride themselves on never refusing an assignment or failing to complete their missions as described. Detractors point out that it is not their effectiveness that is questioned, only their unorthodox methods.

Solstice
Emblem: The Rising Sun.

Solstice would not normally be worthy of mentioning here as their performance has been far from stellar in years past. They have, however, been recently redeemed. Along with Legion Varus, easily our most infamous and questionable formation, they were instrumental in the procurement of a metal-rich planet circling Gamma Pavonis.

This author agrees with the common wisdom that Solstice did the majority of the fighting and dying on Gamma Pavonis, otherwise known as Machine World, and thus deserves the lion's share of the credit.

4

Varus

Emblem: The Wolfshead.

Some historians would argue that Varus shouldn't be mentioned at all alongside distinguished legions with valorous histories. However, despite their reputation for slovenly conduct, questionable ethics and behavior bordering on the criminal, this author feels no list of our legions could be considered complete without their inclusion.

Whatever one thinks of them, their impact on history is undeniable. The legion has participated in numerous critical campaigns. They've affected the fate of every human being that draws breath today, for good or for ill.

At the dawn of the current era, during which the local Battle Fleet was recalled from our province to the Core Systems, Varus battled with the saurians of Cancri-9, unofficially known as Steel World. This led to a falling out with the saurians who had been, up until that time, our best clients. This new rivalry between Earth and Steel World has never abated since.

Rumor has it we most recently came into direct conflict with the saurians on Machine World, our newly acquired metal-rich planet. Again, Legion Varus was involved.

Perhaps greater than these famous disasters was the inclusion of Dust World as Earth's second legally colonized planet. Legion Varus was on the scene again, by providence, claiming the new territory even as they helped trigger a new conflict with the Cephalopod Kingdom. This case exemplifies the dichotomy Varus represents: We gained a few thousand exiles who'd been marooned on a desert planet, but we did so at the cost of a new conflict with the cephalopods. Some hypothesize that this dispute will grow into an open war that may eventually lead to our extinction.

Misunderstood waifs? Or devils with hearts of coal? This author, like so many others, suspects the members of Legion Varus are a little of both.

"The poisoned fig tastes no less sweet."
– Livia Drusilla, 14 AD

-1-

After living on Machine World in the Gamma Pavonis system for months, coming home to Earth felt like a vacation in paradise. On my homeworld the skies were blue, the air was clean, and it was blissfully warm even in the dead of winter. Machine World, by comparison, was a frozen Hell. The land was permanently overcast and devoid of organic life. Instead of water, methane filled the seas and fell from the sky in flakes, forming alien snowstorms. The electromechanical beings that "lived" there could be friendly, but they weren't very bright, and their natural hunger for metals drove them to aggression when they encountered armored humans. In short, I didn't miss the place at all.

My hometown was Waycross, in Georgia Sector. My parents owned a small plot of land there near the Satilla River. I'd taken up residence in a dimly-lit shack on their back acreage. It had a portable fridge, creaky floorboards, and a sagging couch to sleep on. It wasn't much to look at, but I called it home.

Anne Grant, a legion bio I'd had a thing for over the years, spent a few happy days with me in that shack after our return to Earth. But one gray afternoon she said her goodbyes and drove back up to Kentucky. I knew I'd miss her, but I felt comfortable about our parting. She was one to be remembered.

Seeing that yet another girl had come and gone from my life, and possibly feeling wrong-headedly sorry for me, my parents took me out to dinner the same night Anne left. They

knew myself. They had enough damned DNA to build a whole new James McGill if they'd wanted to.

My mom was crying again. I tried to comfort her, and I transferred all the pictures and movies I had to her tapper. I don't think this helped much. She looked at them, but she still wasn't happy.

When she'd settled down, we had lunch, then I went back to my shack. I walked back home like a hound dog who has just experienced a good solid kick in the hindquarters. As far as I could tell, I'd done the worst job possible of breaking the news to her, and she'd reacted in the worst possible way.

James McGill had struck again.

That evening, my dad tapped on my door. I let him in and faked a smile. He managed a flickering one of his own.

"What's up, Dad?"

He stared at me for a few seconds. "You have any of that rot-gut beer left?"

"Sure do."

I put a cold one into his hands and popped one open for myself.

He took a slug before talking. "Your mother is freaking out."

"Yeah…I'm sorry about that. I didn't mean to break it to her that way."

"It's not about how you told her. It's about the news itself."

"She's always hinting about wanting to be a grandma," I said. "I thought she might be happy after she got over the surprise."

"Really, James?" he asked. "Our first grandchild is on another planet, and you thought she'd be happy? We're not getting any younger, you know. You might not have noticed, but we're aging—you're not, but we are. We don't have forever to wait."

Thinking about that, I frowned. It was true. A mercenary in the legions, a man who stuck with it, could live a century or more without aging. Centurion Graves, for example, was somewhere around seventy to a hundred years old, but he looked like he was around thirty-five, tops.

That sounded great when you were a kid, and it was. But your family, the people who weren't in the legions, they kept on aging. On every campaign I flew out to the stars and usually died out there in some fashion. Using the alien revival systems, the legion rebuilt a new body and mind for me from stored data. Since they didn't bother to do body-backups often, I usually came back physically younger than the age I'd been when I'd left Earth.

But back home everyone plodded along through a normal, quiet life. My parents had been aging all this time. I'd seen it, but I hadn't really thought about it until now.

"Mom wants to see the baby—is that what you're saying?" I asked.

"Of course she does," he snapped. "How can you be so smart and so dumb at the same time?"

He was angry, and with good reason, so I didn't object. Besides, it was a question I'd often asked myself. Instead of responding, I took a big hit of my beer and got up to get a fresh one. I offered him another one as well, and he took it.

"She's already pricing out a fare to Dust World," he said a few minutes after we'd each consumed another brew in silence.

"What? You're kidding me."

"No, I'm not. It's going to cost me a year's pay."

Alarmed, my mind was racing along new paths. Della had told me she was married. Not only that, when I'd last visited Dust World, there wasn't really anyplace for tourists to stay.

"Dad...you should probably try to stop her."

"I don't know if I can do that."

"But Dad, Dust World...it's not like Earth. Most of the planet is a deadly wilderness. The people there, well, they don't think like we do."

"Obviously not. Couldn't you have used some kind of protection, boy?"

"Sorry Dad, she took me by surprise."

He snorted in amusement and shook his head. He usually didn't drink much, and he was on his third beer already. I put another one in front of him on my floating coffee table. After a moment of thought, he cracked it open.

"You know what your mom's talking about?" Dad asked me. "Already?"

"What?"

"Moving out there. Emigrating. Hegemony has a new government policy, you know. If you buy a one-way ticket out there and promise to colonize, you can go for half-price. That's a quarter the price of a round trip. We might be able to afford that if we sell this place."

My eyes widened another notch. "But..."

"That's right," he said. "I'd be going with her. Now you know why I'm drinking every beer you put in front of me."

I was beginning to understand. My mom was a hard one to dissuade once she got an idea stuck in her head. I was the same way—but this was crazy.

"You can't move to Dust World," I said. "That's nuts. The place is like a giant Death Valley. Even worse than that."

"I know. But most of the colonists are settling on the other planet in the system, the ocean world."

My eyes widened. "That's where the squids were wiped out! That's an even worse idea. The squids still think they own that planet. They might show up any day and eradicate whatever humans they find squatting there."

My dad shrugged. "They might do that here on Earth, too. In fact, most people think it's only a matter of time. If the Empire doesn't send the Battle Fleet back to Frontier 921, we're all toast someday soon. Maybe your mother is right. Why not see the child before that happens?"

"We're building our own ships," I said in a confident, boastful tone. "We're building up Earth's home fleet every day. And our ships can take theirs, two to one. I've seen them do battle."

"Imperial warships can, not Earth's ships," my dad said. "People keep making that mistake. Galactic ships from the Core Systems are built by aliens who know what the hell they're doing. An Empire-built ship can take down cephalopod ships easily. Every news vid shows that. But our homegrown designs are totally different. Have you seen them? Big balls of puff-crete laid over wire ribs—our ships look like crap, and

13

they're untested. Some experts say they'll pop like balloons in battle."

My dad was right, of course. Hegemony *was* building ships as fast as they could, but our initial designs resembled lopsided dog turds floating in space. The ships were constructed more like barrels with guns sticking out than anything else. The hulls were formed with puff-crete layered over a titanium gridwork to give it shape and something to stick to. The process reminded me of the way people built in-ground pools. Concrete with rebar buried inside like metal bones. The new Earth ships were slow, heavy and ugly. Could they fight? That was conjecture.

With remarkable speed, my dad and I finished the entire twelve-pack I'd been saving in my fridge for the weekend. After that, we were both in a markedly better mood. Cracking jokes, we walked back to the house together where we found my mom watching another video of Etta. She'd managed to find a clip of the baby taking her first steps.

We sobered up immediately. My dad and I exchanged glances.

"I'll talk to Della about this, if she's still on Earth," I told him.

"If she's on Earth, wouldn't Etta be here too?"

"No. Dust Worlders are different. They raise their kids as a group. Della joined the legion, but she didn't bring Etta with her."

My dad shook his head. "They sound like they don't think the way we do."

"True enough," I said. "But listen, *if* it's possible to go out there, I'll help with the return fare. You guys wouldn't make it as colonists on such a harsh planet."

My dad gave me a hug, and I stared over his shoulder at the big screen in the living room. Etta had sandals on, but her feet were still black with grit. None of the colonist adults around her seemed to care, or even to notice, that she was dirty.

I stepped back outside. Standing in the dark with gnats and mosquitoes buzzing near, I tapped a fateful message to Della. I didn't know if she was on Earth or not, but as soon as I hit *send* and the little twirling icon began to rotate I felt my heart speed up a notch.

The note I sent said simply: *Della, we need to talk.*

The wait was longer than usual. I'd begun to think she'd left Earth and gone back to Dust World after all. Hell, she might well have ditched life in the legions entirely and gone home, calling the whole thing a bad dream.

But she hadn't. My tapper screen stopped twirling, and a tiny chime sounded in the dark. She'd gotten my message.

-2-

A day or two later, in the middle of the night, I heard someone in my room.

Della had never responded to my message. She'd gotten it—that much I knew. But I couldn't tell if she'd read it or not. She had that information blocked, as most people did.

To tell the truth, I'd done my best to forget about the whole thing. I knew my mom was still tense about the situation. Every time I saw her, she asked me questions I couldn't possibly answer.

How tall was Etta now? What did she weigh at birth? Were there complications during the delivery? What was the name of this husband fellow, this faceless stepfather who was supposedly caring for the child while her crazy parents were off getting themselves repeatedly killed on alien planets?

In answer to all these queries I could only shrug and shake my head. She growled at me every time I did that, accusing me of a dozen forms of idiocy and negligence. I took it all in stride. I knew she was upset—and with good reason. Della and I were far from ideal parents.

A sound in my room alerted me to the presence of an intruder. It was the crinkle of loose paper on dirty carpet. I knew the sound well as I often made a similar noise every time I crossed my littered floor.

My big-knuckled fist twitched reflexively on the neck of the bottle of Kentucky bourbon that was still in my grasp. I'd fallen asleep with the bottle in my hand because I'd run out of beer yesterday.

For all my faults, I'm a legion-trained Veteran who's been physically assaulted more times than I can count. Such experiences never fail to change a man. I think, in truth, I was never fully asleep anymore. Some part of me was always awake, watching, listening for the smallest hint of danger.

The part of my brain that was still operating set off alarm bells tonight, and I released the bottle with a sudden splaying of my fingers. The bottle thumped down and the contents began to glug out onto the carpet—another in a patchwork of innumerable stains.

That same hand flew upward with unerring aim. My fingers found a throat, and they squeezed.

My eyes cracked open, and I coughed. The action caused a tiny line to be cut into my windpipe. Someone had a knife at my neck.

"Drop the knife," I said to the intruder. Blood ran down my neck, warming it in twin lines.

For a brief moment, the intruder and I struggled in the near blackness. I wasn't about to let go of that throat. Sure, the knife-wielder might well kill me—but it would take a few seconds for the life to run out of me. You ever seen a pig with a cut throat? Often, they wriggle for a long time before they stop twitching.

The neck my fingers were wrapped around didn't feel all that thick or strong to me, and I figured I could probably squeeze my assailant half to death before I lost consciousness.

I was okay with dying for a good reason. Sometimes, putting a good scare into an attacker gave them pause the next go-around.

Sure, I was probably the one who was going to take an unscheduled trip through the revival machine by the end of this fight. But my murderer was at least going to know it hadn't been easy.

For about five seconds, the two of us grunted and strove. Then I heard a sound that surprised me. A thump and a metallic clatter. My attacker had dropped the knife—it was gone from my throat, no longer sawing there.

17

But I didn't let go of my assailant just yet. I groped with my other hand and clicked on the light.

Della's pale face grimaced at me. She looked pissed off. I let go of her and sat up. She gasped and rubbed at her throat. There were finger marks there that would bruise up by morning.

"If it was anyone but you, James," she said, "your head would be lying on the floor."

"You should have knocked," I replied. "Normal people on Earth do that—you know about knocking, right?"

"I like to be in control when I enter an unknown situation," Della explained.

"That's not a good enough reason to sneak into a house and put a knife in someone's face, girl."

"If you'd only relaxed and let me control the situation, you wouldn't be bleeding now."

"I'll have to try out that theory next time I come over to your place."

We both took deep breaths and tried to calm down. It took longer for Della to settle down than it did for me. She had a bit of a temper.

Della and I had always had a strange relationship. She was paranoid, and so was I. We'd killed one another on several occasions. When a person has a history like that with another person, there are always trust issues afterward.

"Why did you send me that note?" she demanded.

"Because I wanted to talk to you."

"I know that. About what?"

"Etta—and my parents."

That surprised her. She blinked and frowned thoughtfully. "I thought it was about Turov and Claver. About some new scheme you'd hatched to take over the world with those two."

"Now hold on," I said, "I'm no rebel. I just tend to accidentally get involved in the plans of others."

She chuckled. "Yes, and then you screw them up. All right then...tell me what your parents want with Etta."

"They want to see her, of course. My mom's talking crazy about going out to Dust World on her own."

18

I explained the situation at length. She seemed baffled by some points, such as my mother's extreme desire to meet her one and only grandchild. But at the same time, she seemed pleased that they were taking such an interest.

"Maybe I should have brought Etta to Earth to be cared for by them," she said thoughtfully. "That had never occurred to me."

"That's an idea," I said.

Della shook her head, frowning. She picked up her knife and sheathed it while I watched her hands carefully. Della and I had killed one another just about the same number of times as we'd made love. I didn't like those odds, so I always kept my eyes open when I was with her.

"I don't think I'd like to raise a child here, on Earth," she said at last. "It's too different. Your people are soft and lazy, James."

"Not me."

She looked up at me and laughed. "No," she admitted. "Not you."

"So that's what I wanted to ask you about," I said. "I wanted your permission to visit Etta."

She gave me a baffled look. "Permission? No permission is required. You and your parents are blood-related. You have the right."

It was my turn to look her over in appraisal. I realized, at that bleary moment, just how little I knew about how she would respond in different situations. In a way, I'd picked the most culturally diverse person I could possibly have found to mate with. That hadn't been my plan, but that's how it had turned out. Hell, she wasn't even from Earth. We spoke the same language, but that was where the similarities ended. A girl from any continent on my home planet would have been more comprehensible to me than Della.

"Okay then," I said. "So you wouldn't mind if we traveled out there to see Etta. But there's another party involved. What about your husband?"

Her eyes flicked to my face, then dropped away. She shook her head. "Don't worry about that."

"What? How can I not worry about it? He'll have thoughts of his own. I'm sure you realize that. He might not appreciate seeing me and my parents. You have to warn him, or send him a note at least. What's his name?"

"Don't worry about it."

"Why not?"

She looked up at me again, troubled. She heaved a sigh and sat on my couch. I sat beside her, puzzled.

"My husband," she said finally, "he doesn't exist."

"He doesn't...? What?"

"There is no stepfather, James. No marriage."

"You lied?"

"I didn't lie. I'm not a liar."

"What would you call it, then?" I demanded.

She looked uncomfortable. "I don't like to be called a liar. I'm a scout, an honorable member of my—"

"Look, let's forget about that. Who's taking care of Etta if there's no stepfather? Is your father doing it?"

"The Investigator?" she asked incredulously. "No, he's much too busy guiding my people for such a trivial thing."

"Who then? Don't tell me she's out eating rockfish on her own."

She squirmed. "Natasha. Natasha is doing it. She wanted to help—she volunteered."

That left me scratching my head. "Okay," I said. "Natasha is caring for Etta—oh."

"What?"

"Now I understand why you lied. You told me about Etta back on Machine World, but at that point you hadn't confessed about Natasha yet. So you made up the stepfather story to cover for Natasha. But then later, you told me about Natasha's copy. Why didn't you confess then?"

"A scout does not lie—at least, we're not supposed to."

"I see. You had to cover up one lie with another. That's the kind of thing I understand. I get into trouble that way myself sometimes."

Della stood up angrily. I couldn't help but admire her body as she struck a sleek pose without trying. I don't think I'd ever met a woman who was more fit and graceful. She wasn't like

20

an Earth girl that worked out all the time—it was all natural with Della. She was like a feral cat, possessing a body built of tight muscle through natural means.

"I don't see why I even came here," she said. "All you offer is insults."

She took a step toward the door, but I gently caught her hand. She stopped and frowned back at me.

"You'd best let go," she said.

"That's why you kept coming to my bed back on Machine World, isn't it?" I asked, hanging onto her lightly. "You weren't really married—but you couldn't tell me. I shouldn't have rejected you back then, but I didn't know the truth."

"What's done is done. Mistakes were made. Now, I must go."

My mind worked with unusual speed. I only had one move left, I could tell that. Then I'd have to let go of her hand before she cut mine off for me.

"Don't worry," I said, "your honor is safe with me."

I could tell by the look on her face that was the right thing to say. Some people think I'm as off-key as a hound in a firehouse, but with women, I've often managed to turn a bad situation around at the last moment. We all have our gifts.

Della smiled. The whole mess between us had been about her honor. She'd been lying about one thing or another since I'd met up with her again on *Cyclops*, and it had been grating on her. By assuring her I wasn't going to run around talking crap about her, she was instantly relieved of her greatest fear.

She sat back down on my couch decisively.

I'm not going to claim I'm a master of timing, but I *am* an opportunist. I rarely pass up women who are smiling and within easy reach, for example. I put my hands on her gently, and she didn't resist.

We were in a lip-lock inside of five seconds. I had to mentally congratulate myself. Della had been converted from a murderess stalking me in my sleep into an urgent lover inside half an hour.

But it wasn't all my doing. That's just how things tended to go between the two of us. There was no middle-ground.

21

Things progressed quickly. She bared her breasts and then her teeth as we made love. I'd seen that last part about the teeth before, and it'd always freaked me out a little. She turned animal when we had sex—every time. I can't think of any other way to describe it.

Afterward, I inspected my bloody throat in my bathroom mirror. Damn, that girl had come closer than I'd realized to severing my carotid. I put a band aid on the wound and gave a long whistle. I was impressed.

I was glad she hadn't pressed her sharp blade into me another few millimeters. A morning meet-and-greet with my parents would have been awkward if she'd killed me the night before.

After I washed all the blood off, we curled up on the couch together. We slept in a warm tangle of limbs until the gray light of dawn cut through my tattered curtains.

-3-

The next day went much better all the way around. My mom was thrilled to meet Della, who even had a few fresh pictures of Etta from Dust World that none of us had seen. Della seemed touched by my mom's honest desire to make a connection with her granddaughter. I gathered that her own people had only feigned polite interest in the kid.

On Della's planet, Earth's one and only colony world, family units were much less bonded and tight. Della's family were important people she respected—but they weren't anything like what any kid from North America Sector would think of as doting relatives. They were more like your family doctor: a friendly, caring person who you grew up around, but who maintained a certain professional distance from you and your problems.

The conversations we had with Della concerning Etta and her life were strange ones. My mom did her damnedest to keep a smile fixed upon her face. I could tell she all but wanted to shout at Della, demanding to know what she'd been thinking when she'd left her baby behind on some hellish desert planet alone. Managing to control herself, she kept her cool and worked every bit of charm she had on this newcomer who had her granddaughter's life in her hands.

The whole thing made me feel a bit bad. I'm not the kind of man who's a worrier. I go with the flow most of the time, and if the world isn't bothering me, I don't bother it. As a case in point, the women in my life had never dominated my thoughts. I'd always floated from one to the next, not taking any relationship too seriously.

But things had changed. Knowing I had a kid living on a rock circling a distant star was even working on my mind, I could feel it. The knowledge was affecting my parents, too.

"So, Della," my mom said, moving in for the kill after ten-odd minutes of beating around the bush, "what do you think about the idea of us all going out to visit the little darling?"

While she said this, Mom stretched out a hand to pour each of us a fresh cup of coffee. I could tell Mom was nervous. Her hand shook a bit while she poured. For all that, she didn't spill a drop.

Della hadn't touched her cup as she wasn't from Earth and she thought coffee tasted like used motor oil, but that didn't stop my mom from topping her off.

"I think it's workable," Della said in a neutral tone.

That was classic Della. Dust-Worlders weren't the type to run around doing a happy dance when they met a friend or a relative. They were an impetuous, somewhat paranoid people. I guess they'd spent too many decades watching the sky for slave-ships to be celebratory as a group.

Still, my mom was pleased by Della's answer because it wasn't a flat "no." Mom gave us both a big smile.

"It's a plan then," Mom said. "When do you think you'll be going back?"

"I hope to do so after the arrival ceremony at the spaceport. Legion Varus members are required to attend."

My mom gave me a frown. "What ceremony?"

"I meant to tell you about that," I said. "It must have slipped my mind. The whole legion, including Winslade's cohort of dragons, is going to stand on the parade grounds to welcome the first freighter back from Machine World. They're bringing in a load of titanium as I understand it—thirty thousand tons. Can you believe they got that much metal out of that mountain in a few short months?"

"It's the worker machines," Della said. "They work for metal, but they mine much more than they eat. Did James tell you about them?"

24

My parents gave her baffled looks. My dad leaned forward. "James likes to keep the details of his campaigns to himself."

Della nodded and looked at me, impressed. "Be sure, be safe," she said, quoting a Dust-Worlder proverb. "Even at home, you keep secrets? I'm learning from you still."

That was the perfect example of how conversing with Della often went. She didn't always get what we meant, and we didn't always know what she was talking about, either.

The real reason I'd neglected to fill in my parents on the Machine World campaign was because it had been bloody as Hell and…well…downright weird. But Della had assumed I'd stayed quiet out of a paranoid sense of caution and secrecy, as she might have done.

I decided it was best not to correct anyone and switched the topic instead.

"Are you guys going to go?" I asked my parents. "To the ceremony at the spaceport, I mean?"

"We'd love to," my mom said before my dad could do more than open his mouth. He closed it again and looked glum.

"It will be quite a drive," he muttered.

"No problem at all," Mom insisted. "Della, I didn't see any vehicles out front…?"

"I was given a ride by a man from Atlanta," she said. "He repeatedly requested sexual contact, but I refused as I found him unsavory."

My mom cleared her throat and nodded. "I see. Well…we'll have to drive you, then. When is the ceremony, James?"

"Uh…Thursday, I think."

As it was already Tuesday, my mom raised her eyebrows. "All right…you'll have to stay with us until then, Della. I have a guest bed all made up on the second floor. We hardly ever get any visitors who stay with us in the main house."

"No thank you," Della said. "I prefer to stay with James on his couch."

My parents fell silent for a second. Their eyes flicked back and forth between us. They knew I entertained various women in my shack from time to time, but this was different.

25

I expected my mother to frown disapprovingly, but she didn't. She smiled instead. "That's just fine," she said.

It took me a second to get it. Mom *wanted* me to sleep with Della. That felt strange on the face of it. Maybe she was already having some kind of fantasy that the two of us would get married. I could have told her the odds of that happening were slim indeed, baby or no. Hell, the woman had almost killed me in my sleep just last night.

The next few days were pretty nice, from my point of view. I had a girl sharing my room and my bed, and my parents were treating us like royalty. This was an unprecedented situation.

My folks didn't ask any probing questions, they never mentioned Anne, nor did Mom give Della a single disapproving stare. They tried to make things pleasant and comfortable for both of us and insisted we take our meals in the main house. The four of us spent a lot of time together.

All that said, Thursday could hardly come fast enough for me. Don't get me wrong, I love my parents. But despite the fact I look to be about twenty-two years old, I'm really pushing thirty, and I'd gotten used to having my own space.

On the day of the big parade, we rode up to Atlanta and gathered our equipment at the chapter house. The old tram could barely carry our rucks with all four of us in the cabin, but we made it to the spaceport and left my folks at the gate. They moved off to join the audience that ringed the spaceport fence.

Carlos was there, rolling up on his foldable alien-made unicycle. He'd bought it back before Hegemony had started confiscating Galactic credits and sweeping all our legion accounts of hard currency.

What surprised me wasn't the vehicle itself. It was the fact that he had a passenger riding with him. I recognized her, and I noticed she hugged onto him like she meant business.

"Kivi?" I called out in surprise.

Carlos steered our way and nearly ran us down. He only had partial control of his bike, being an alien contraption that wasn't entirely meant for a single human to ride, much less two.

After half-crashing to a stop, Kivi climbed off and slapped him lightly.

"You didn't tell me this thing would give me a butt-ache," she complained.

"Let me kiss it better," Carlos suggested.

They chased each other around for a moment while Della and I shook our heads.

When they'd at last settled down and come close, Kivi looked Della up and down. "Oh. You're not Anne, are you?" she asked, as if that thought had just occurred to her.

My gut felt that jab of hers. Kivi had always been moody, and this afternoon was no exception. If I had to put a name to it, I'd say Kivi's mood was "catty" today.

I glanced at Della, hoping that Kivi's jab hadn't landed. Unfortunately, Della seemed to have gotten the reference. She was frowning.

"I'm Della, a specialist, and your superior," she said.

Kivi smiled and lifted a finger. "Not anymore. I'm a specialist now, too. A tech."

"And I'm a bio in training," Carlos said. "Anybody want to turn their heads and cough?"

I clapped my hands together, making a booming sound. They all looked at me. As long as the girls were pulling rank, I figured I might as well pull mine. I was a legion veteran, and I outranked them all.

"Let's go to the rally point," I said firmly. "We've got to suit up and get our dragons out of storage. My briefing email said they're in the lifters."

Together, our group traveled across the seemingly endless expanse of asphalt to the waiting line of lifters.

The transport spacecraft were broad, squatty and built for utility more than looks. We marched up the metal ramp with a few dozen other troopers and an hour or so later we were lined up in our dragons beside the rest of Legion Varus. We were all standing at attention.

As the senior noncom, Veteran Harris held the Wolfshead pennant in his right gripper. It was an honor to hold the pennant. As a newly hatched veteran, I could only watch him and note his obvious pride.

Thousands of us lined up, unit by unit. Less than ten minutes after we'd completed our formation, the lifters took off and another set roared down to take their place.

More troops in armor with polished weapons marched from the ramps. They had pennants too, but their flags were from a rival legion.

"They're flying the Rising Sun of Legion Solstice," Harris said loudly. "Stand straight, look sharp. Don't shame me, people."

Legion Solstice had fought and died with us on Machine World. I had mixed feelings about their troops for personal reasons, but I saluted them along with the rest of our dragons. Solstice legionnaires were true fighters, if a little rough around the edges. I could only conjecture as to they thought of us.

Soon, over twenty thousand troops stood in long lines and squares all over the tarmac. We covered two square kilometers, maybe more. It was an impressive sight, and I felt glad to know my parents were in the crowd somewhere, watching us. They didn't often get a chance to see my legion presented with any kind of honor.

Standing on a stage in front of the two legion formations was a knot of officers and politicians. A gaggle of reporters with camera-drones clustered around them. I noticed only a few of the drones were panning the troops. Most were focused on the stage.

Imperator Turov spoke first. I wasn't surprised that she was there or that she was hamming it up for the cameras. She was a glory-hound that rarely missed such opportunities—in fact, she created them whenever possible.

"In a few minutes, history will be made," she said, her voice rolling out over the assemblage. She had an amp system set up, and some joker had cranked it up to full blast. "I welcome the eyes of Earth today. I, Imperator Galina Turov, have brought home a great bounty from beyond the borders of the Empire itself. As most of you know, I was in command of an expedition into uncharted space. After a hard-fought campaign, legions Solstice and Varus defeated no less than three alien forces on Machine World. Now today, at last, we'll see the fruits of that expenditure of blood and treasure in space..."

She went on like that for a very long time. The woman could make a speech, that was for sure. She made certain to mention her name and her command status in every paragraph as she waxed eloquently about the immeasurable wealth she'd brought home to Earth.

Finally, long after I'd stopped listening, a rumble sounded above us. The skies flared brighter. We craned our necks—despite the fact we were supposed to stare at our commanders and nothing else.

The freighter had come in. It was a big one as such ships went. A super-massive, they called them, a class of ship built to haul goods from star to star in quantities that could serve a whole planet.

"Something's wrong," Della said in my headset.

I frowned. She was right. The ship didn't look the way it should. That first flare—what had that been? Too bright for braking jets. I could see those now, blooming from the forward modules.

"She's in too close," I said. "She must have dropped out of warp too late. She should be parked in orbit by now."

Turov went on, seemingly oblivious. "There she is!" the imperator boomed. "Take note of our lifters rising to greet her. Thirty thousand metric tons of titanium—just think about it! Earth's annual production is less than a tenth of that, and a freighter like this one will be arriving every month from Machine World from now on—"

She broke off then as everyone present, thousands upon thousands of us, turned our heads up to the skies.

There was another brilliant flash of light. The effect was bigger this time, silent in space, but bright enough to make us squint all the way down here on the surface. The troops around me gasped and exhaled in amazement.

"She's listing," I said. "She's *way* too close. Dragons, activate your engines. Rev them. We might have to move fast."

"To where?" Carlos demanded. "There's nowhere to run. The lifters ditched us already. Turov thinks they're headed up to dock, but I say they're fleeing the scene."

"Quiet in the ranks!" Leeson boomed over the platoon chat. "We've got word from command that something's gone wrong with the freighter. She's coming in hot, and she's not stopping."

"No shit," Carlos said in a low voice.

I didn't even bother to shout at him. What was the point? We could all see it now. A ship as big as a skyscraper was bearing down on us. She wasn't even flying straight anymore, her nose was turning to starboard, and the whole ship was doing a slow barrel-roll.

People began to run in all directions, but I stood my post. Harris did, too. He held onto the pennant of Legion Varus, which flapped in a growing maelstrom of wind.

Harris looked over at me. "This is bullshit!" he said. "Did you do something to that ship, McGill?"

"That's right, Harris. I jury-rigged the engine myself."

The freighter broke up after that. I saw burning cubes of metal coming out of it at the end, I swear I did. They came down like a shower of meteors, spreading over the vast spaceport like shrapnel. They reached the ground ahead of the ship's tumbling, burning hull. The ingots of hard metal caused a thousand deafening explosions that knocked everyone off their feet.

People ran around screaming. Some threw themselves on the ground. Harris and I...we didn't bother. We knew we were screwed, so we watched the show wearing grim expressions. The burning ship came right down on top of us, growing impossibly large and loud during the final moments—that was a sight worth remembering.

My final thoughts as I died along with thousands of others were of my parents. I regretted having brought them anywhere near Legion Varus. If there was ever a bad-luck outfit in history, we were it.

Bringing my folks out here hadn't been the brightest thing I'd ever done, but it might well have been my last. A burning cube struck the tarmac a hundred meters away. The shockwave knocked my dragon flat, and I couldn't get it to stand up again.

As I died, burning in my dragon's cockpit, I thought about my mama. She'd never get to see her only granddaughter. That was a crying shame.

-4-

Eventually, I did manage to catch a revive. As you can imagine, there was quite a backlog of dead people in line ahead of me.

Coming back to life is akin to awakening from a dream that won't leave your mind. I could feel my memories…they were like cobwebs on my face. The past was a veil of hazy unreality.

Somehow, when I opened my bleary eyes again, I knew it had been a *long* while since I'd drawn breath—don't ask me how I knew, I just did.

"He's breathing," said a female voice I didn't recognize. "What are his scores?"

"Nine point one."

"Good enough. Get him off the table."

The first clear image that came in from my retinas was that of an orderly with a few days stubble on his chin. He gave me a grim smile.

"Welcome back, Veteran," he said.

"Where am I?" I croaked, gripping his shoulder for support.

"You're aboard *Minotaur*. We're in warp. Could you let go for a second? You're bruising my shoulder."

I peered at him and blinked, trying to absorb this information with my newly grown brain. Everything was still a bit fuzzy.

"How long have I been gone?" I managed.

"I don't know—about ten days, I'd say."

32

Ten days. I'd been nonexistent for ten days while the universe had marched onward. It wasn't as if I'd slept in a coma—I'd been as dead as a doornail. Ten long days were lost forever in time.

It was just this sort of thing that could eat at a legionnaire's mind if he let it. Fortunately, I wasn't the kind of person who dwelled on much of anything.

I stood, leg muscles trembling a bit, and slowly staggered toward the equipment lockers. I pulled a smart tunic over my naked, slimy body, and it began to worm its way over my bulk. My clothes were always stretched thinner than those worn by smaller people. It was a natural hazard endured by any man who was two meters tall.

When I was dressed I looked for weapons in the locker, but there were none.

"We're not in combat?" I asked.

The unfamiliar bio looked at me. I didn't recognize her even though she wore the Wolfshead patch of Legion Varus. At least I was with my own outfit.

"No," she said. "We're in pursuit of an enemy, however, and we might come out of the warp bubble at any time. You have time to recover, but you should maintain readiness. Those are Turov's orders."

Imperator Turov? Could she be on this ship too? Great.

Only half knowing what was going on, I was able to walk straight by the time I made it to my unit's module. My mind was working again, too.

A thought struck me then. A horrible thought. It hit just as I opened the hatch into my module's unit and was met with a chorus of shouted greetings from my comrades.

They were all there: Carlos, Kivi, Natasha and Leeson. Sargon was polishing a heavy weapons kit, and Della was talking to Harris. She gave me a smile and a nod when I stepped inside.

I would have smiled back, but a horror had just been released in my mind. I should have felt glad to see them all again—but I didn't. The thought in my brain, the terrible realization, didn't allow me to have any happiness.

"My parents," I said aloud to the assembly. "My folks were there, at the ceremony. Is there any word…?"

The enthusiasm of the group dampened immediately. Smiles turned to frowns, and most of them looked down at their work.

Della stared at me, troubled. Natasha dropped what she was doing and walked up to me. She looked me in the eye.

Every time I faced her lately, I couldn't help but think of her copy back on Dust World. Knowing that Natasha 2.0 was taking care of Etta for Della and I made me feel like I owed her something, too. It was a weird situation, and we all tried to ignore it most of the time so Natasha wouldn't get in trouble. If the Empire officials ever figured out there were two of her running around, well, one of them would have to be deleted.

"I'm sorry James," she told me sincerely. "Everyone in the crowd—they were killed. The whole spaceport was devastated. We lost thousands: visitors, politicians, reporters, troops and ship crews. It was a disaster."

"It was more than that," I said firmly. "It was an attack."

I stared at nothing. My parents were gone. Only military people and rich, important folk got revivals. The rest weren't copied and tracked in the data cores.

"You might be right," Natasha said. "Our entire unit has been revived over the last twenty-four hours. We haven't been told much yet but from what the techs are saying privately online, the consensus is the destruction of the freighter was deliberate."

We'd wiped. That's what she was telling me. We'd been standing around on the ground like a bunch of fools, holding onto flags and playing martial music while an enemy stalked us and wiped us out.

"That's why we're flying now, isn't it?" I asked. "Who are we following? The saurians?"

She shook her head. "I don't know yet. Centurion Graves will tell us more soon. He's with Imperator Turov and the Tribune now, getting the details. He'll brief us after that."

I wanted to put my face in my hands, but I didn't. Everyone was watching, and I was a veteran now—a man who wasn't allowed to feel anything when faced with loss.

34

Mentally, I corrected that thought as soon as I had it. I was allowed one emotion: rage. I could safely apply that to any enemy, at any time.

"Well," I said grimly, "when we catch up with them, they'll rue the day they came to Earth's skies whether they turn out to be squids, lizards, or something else entirely."

The group gave me a ragged cheer, and I moved to my equipment locker. Veteran Harris and Della came up behind me.

"Yes?" I asked, trying to stay civil. In the past, Harris and I had rarely seen eye-to-eye.

Harris cleared his throat uncomfortably. "I wanted to express my sympathies, McGill," he said.

I looked at him. "I didn't think a few civvie deaths could faze an old soldier like you."

"Well, we're talking about family. Family is different. And getting permed while attending a parade isn't the same thing as a legionnaire dying on the battlefield. What happened back on Earth was wrong. But we'll put this right when we catch them—whoever they are."

I nodded and watched him walk away. When he'd left, Della stepped close and put her arms around my neck. She had to reach really high to do that, standing on her tiptoes. She put her cheek against my chest and didn't say anything.

Awkwardly, I patted her on the back. Then she hugged me and walked away. That was it—grieving done Dust Worlder-style. At least she'd understood I'd suffered a loss, as had our daughter Etta, who would never meet her grandparents now.

I spent the rest of the day drilling my squad—but not in their dragons, because we didn't have any aboard *Minotaur*.

That was a surprise—a bad one. Primus Winslade's auxiliary cavalry cohort had been attached to Legion Varus. We'd been riding the best cavalry units we had left in the parade, but they'd naturally been destroyed along with our bodies. The spare units, the most battered dragons in the legion, had been sent back to Dust World for servicing before our next mission assignment. The long and the short of it was that we'd been reduced to an infantry cohort once again.

Disappointed but no less determined to find those who had permed my family, I readied my troops as heavy infantry. Someone had scared up enough breastplates and exoskeletons for that.

"At least we aren't down to running around in our panties with snap-rifles," Carlos said. "Sorry about your parents, big guy."

"Thanks."

"You think it was the lizards? I think they hate us the most. Or maybe it was the squids. Hard to tell."

"That's right, it's hard to tell."

My flat, expressionless answers got through to Carlos. Even he could tell I just wasn't in the mood for banter. He offered me a hit on a flask he had in his locker, against regs, but I passed. I was too upset to drink. It would rip up my fresh-grown guts right now, and I wanted to stay sharp for the briefing.

My tapper beeped about a half-hour into the exercise regimen, and my people sighed in relief. They seemed to think I'd been working them hard right after a revive, but I didn't care. We had to be ready for anything. That was my new motto.

The message on my tapper was from Centurion Graves. I'd been summoned to his office. I put my squad on break and left them breathing hard with their backs on the deck. None of them had complained, but they were more than ready for old McGill to take a hike.

When I reached Graves' office, I honestly expected the other adjunct officers and noncoms to be there, but they weren't. We met alone in his stark chamber.

Graves' office had always been neat and dimly lit. Today was no exception. Unlike other officers, he didn't adorn his workplace with pictures of comrades, defeated aliens, soothing forest holos or anything else. There were only four steel walls, a big computer desk, and Graves sitting ramrod straight in the middle of the room.

He stood up as I entered and gestured toward his desk. He'd cleared it of computer scrolls and had a star-scape displayed from edge to edge. "I thought you might have a particular interest in our destination this time out."

"You'd be correct in that assumption, Centurion."

Graves nodded. He tapped his desk, and the image shimmered in response. "This is Sol, ringed in green. Thirty lights out toward the core is Zeta Herculis—Dust World. See this new green addition? That's Machine World, circling Gamma Pavonis."

I followed along easily enough. As a star traveler, I'd had occasion to consult maps of the systems I traversed. Within the vast region of space known as Frontier 921, there were thousands of star systems, most of which were uninhabited. The hundred-odd systems that did support life had all been subjugated by the Galactic Empire.

But Graves' map showed more than that. He scrolled a little and zoomed out. A blue line appeared, then a red one. The two met in places, but not along a perfectly smooth border. Machine World was in one of those gray areas, right between the outer limits of the Empire and the red-lined territory, which I already knew delineated the Cephalopod Kingdom.

"This map..." I said, eying it with growing interest, "this is the best star-map I've ever seen, sir. Have the Mogwa finally supplied us with better intel?"

"Hardly," Graves said. "This is our own creation. This comes straight from Central. They've got a few thousand eggheads working on stuff like this down there. For once, they've earned their paychecks."

I had to agree. I leaned over and my hands touched the edge of the desk. The screen rippled where I touched it, but didn't change as I was careful not to give it any gestures it might take as a command.

"I thought the squids only had three hundred stars," I commented. "There must be a few thousand inside that red squiggly line."

"That's right, over two thousand stars are inside their territory, in fact. But you have to remember that they said they had three hundred *worlds*, not star systems. They meant inhabited colonies and conquered planets, not just sterile rocks in space."

I nodded thoughtfully. The Cephalopod Kingdom was dwarfed by the Empire. Even Frontier 921 by itself was larger than the squids' entire region of home space. But all the same, when compared to them, Earth's three occupied worlds were a joke.

"Sir," I said, "this is intensely interesting, but could you get to the part displaying our target world? I want to know who we're about to exterminate."

Graves looked at me for a second. "I understand you had a private loss back on Earth."

"That's right, sir. My family was in the audience."

"I don't want to give a man false hope," Graves said. "It's very unlikely anyone in the audience survived. As far as we can tell, those people were all permed."

I frowned. "That's what I figured. Is there any way to confirm who's among the dead?"

He shook his head. "Not now. We're in a warp bubble, and even when we come out of it, we won't be using the deep-link to talk to Earth. We're off the grid on this one. Communications blackout. You'll have to wait until we get back home."

Slowly, I nodded my head. "Let's talk about the enemy then. Who did this, sir?"

I looked at him with hungry eyes, but he shook his head.

"We honestly don't know the exact nature of the enemy. All we can do is follow this line into space."

A white line appeared, cutting across home space. One end started at Earth, and the other headed toward the red region on the map—cephalopod space.

"The squids," I said. "I knew it."

"We don't know that for sure," Graves said. "Not yet. Look at the angle of attack, for example. If it was a deep-thrust assault from the squids, why didn't they head directly back toward their territory?"

I looked, and I saw he had a point. The line we were following didn't go straight from Earth to the border and then on into squid space. It cut off at about a forty-five degree angle.

"I'm sure the techs have been working hard," I said, "but how do we even know we're on the right path?"

"We're not one hundred percent on that. Here's what happened: the freighter was hit by weapons fire after it came out of warp, indicating a ship had followed it. We received distress calls, and the word came down that they'd been boarded."

"Boarded?" I asked in alarm. "By who?"

"We don't know. Alien invaders of some kind. The freighter crew was knocked out almost immediately. The one thing we do know is that shortly after they came out of warp, they were attacked. A significant portion of the titanium cargo was stolen. The ship kept following its original course, but without pilots, it struck the atmosphere and blew up over the spaceport."

"Right. How did we get a trace on the enemy ship?"

"The second warp-signature was detected. The attackers went back into warp and slipped away. By definition, a warp bubble moves faster than light and is hard to trace. We were fortunate enough to get a course heading from sensors in its path after it had already left our system. We couldn't see where they were at that moment, but we could see where they *had* been as the light of their bubble moved away from Earth."

"I see. So, we extrapolated their course and attempted to follow. How many ships are in pursuit?"

"Just *Minotaur*. She was the only dreadnaught on station over the spaceport, so she responded immediately. She didn't have any troops aboard. We were all dead on the ground, but Nagata figured we could revive the legion on the run. No one else could load up and move out faster, so Varus got the assignment."

I nodded again, unsurprised. Legion Varus had never been blessed with luck.

"It sounds to me like we're chasing ghosts, sir," I said. "The enemy could come out of warp anywhere, change course, and we'd never know it while we're in warp."

"We've thought of that. We're coming out now and then, checking data, and continuing. So far, we've seen no evidence indicating they've deviated from their original path."

Frowning, I looked at the white line on the map. "So, where are they going?"

"Three systems loosely intersect this course. None of these harbor noteworthy civilizations."

"Are the stars in squid space?"

"No, all of the stars the course intersects are within the borders of Frontier 921."

Scratching my head, I stared at the data. Graves had added three golden circles around star systems that were strung along our course. None of them held worlds of significance.

"It doesn't make much sense, does it?" I asked. "If they *are* squids, why aren't they running to an occupied squid world? If they're not squids, why aren't they going to an inhabited world, like Cancri-9?"

"That's a puzzle, and we're working on it. But that's about all the time I have to chat, McGill. Return to your squad and carry on."

I hesitated before I left. "Sir? May I ask why you gave me this private briefing?"

"Two reasons," Graves answered. "One, I wanted to know how you were taking your loss. I'm impressed. You don't seem to be broken or irrational. You're pissed and ready for blood, sure, but that's more than acceptable."

"And the other reason?"

"I thought you deserved it. The rest of the troops will be getting the boiled-down version. This new intel—the star charts and the exact position of the squid worlds—that won't be common knowledge. Some of these details are technically illegal, in fact. Any Nairb would designate maps of stars beyond our provincial borders as classified, need-to-know data. But I knew you would be interested, and hell, you and your friends helped give us much of it."

I perked up at that. "The data-globe. The one Carlos and Kivi discovered in the squid tunnels back on Machine World. You got this intel from that find, didn't you?"

He nodded. "Another secret for you to keep locked inside that thick skull of yours."

"It's in the vault, sir."

"Good. Dismissed, Veteran."

I left Graves' office with a lot to think about. I didn't exactly feel better—but I didn't feel worse, either. I figured I had to accept that my parents were permed. They'd never had themselves copied onto a data disk. That was only for military and government people.

Like most of humanity, my folks were privileged in that they would only have to die once for their species.

-5-

Over the next week, our first destination star grew bigger and brighter by the hour. Our course didn't intersect it precisely—we had to deviate a few billion kilometers to reach the system itself. But that didn't mean it wasn't a hit. The raiders could have made a course adjustment. They could've been careless, in a hurry, or purposefully deceptive. Whatever the case, the brass figured they couldn't afford to skip this possible destination. If we slid on by, staying in our warp bubble, while they were hiding in this lonely system, we'd never find them again.

As far as I knew, following a ship that's traveling in an Alcubierre drive warp-bubble had never been done before by Earthlings.

We were very new to space combat. Among the Core Systems where a civil war still raged to this day, I could only surmise that alien captains were old hands at techniques like this. But humans were comparative rubes out on the frontier. For us it was all new.

Knowing it was my commanders' first time out didn't make matters any easier for me. Second-guessing their decisions was driving me crazy. I wished I could hound them up on Gold Deck. I wanted to be there, watching every instrument, privy to every briefing. I burned to find these raiders. They had to die.

42

We came out of warp near the target star, already on high alert. For all we knew, the enemy had the capacity to trace us as we chased after them. There was some evidence to support this; they'd caught our freighter handily enough.

Fully armed and standing ready in the lifters for a hot-drop, my people were tense but professional. The troops in my squad watched me closely and followed my lead. None of them were smiling or carrying on like Harris' people were. Instead, they were grim-faced just like I was.

The star was an M-class red dwarf. In our stellar neighborhood, about three quarters of the stars were red dwarves. It was the dimmest kind of star known that still burned.

There were planets around the target star, but they were cold rocks. Nothing to write home about. Still, if I were trying to set up a secret base, why not here? No one would care to do more than survey the place once and move on. It wouldn't be comfortable, but it would be safe.

We scanned and cruised around like a prowling shark for just over thirty hours. The wait was intolerable for me. I didn't sleep until the all-clear was sounded by the brass.

My squad mates smiled—until I hammered my fist in frustration on a bulkhead. They stopped smiling after that, and I left the module to take a walk. For them, the all-clear meant no fighting, no dying. For me, it meant no closure. No chance for revenge on Earth's attackers.

I felt the ship lurch back into warp again. We'd wasted our precious time, and now there were only two stars left on our projected course. In my mind, our odds of catching the raiders—or even properly identifying them—had just dropped by one third.

My troops sensed a darkness in me, and most of them kept their distance over the following days. Even Della didn't seem to know what to say to me. She wasn't in my squad, but she was in the same platoon. She gave me sympathetic nods but no comforting touches. I could have used a few touches, but she'd never been the nurturing type.

Natasha was different. She seemed more concerned than ever about my well-being. Of the entire squad—whom I drilled for twelve hours out of every ship-board cycle of twenty-four—she alone kept trying to reach me on an emotional level. Unfortunately, she did this by scolding as often as not.

"James," she said after we'd finished yet another obstacle run on Green Deck. "Don't you think you're working them too hard?"

"No."

"But everyone in the squad is—"

"Listen," I said, "I'm done with half-assing around during my training sessions. This squad has grown soft since we left Machine World. In my opinion, it started even before that—back when we began riding dragons instead of walking. Did you see how Centurion Belter's crew could run up a mountain all day? In their full kit? That's how we should look. We're heavy infantry now, not saddled-up aristocrats with our butts high and dry inside a dragon."

She nodded, pursing her lips. "You have a good point. We're out of practice playing the part of infantry. But do you think Harris is a sloppy veteran?"

"What's that got to do with it?"

"He's not drilling his people to death, James. He's doing no more than five hours of the physical stuff, and marksmanship for three more. That's the norm, right?"

Despite my good feelings toward her, Natasha was now beginning to piss me off. After all, I outranked her—but this conflict ran deeper than rank. She'd always been something of a mother hen to me, and sometimes I think she still believed it was her job to play the part of my conscience.

"You've given me an idea," I said. "Thanks, Specialist."

"Um...my pleasure, Vet," she said, her voice surprised and confused. I could tell she had no idea what I was planning.

I strode purposefully off Green Deck. I could feel her eyes on my back.

My first move was to okay the idea with Adjunct Leeson. He gave me a dirty chuckle when I described my proposal.

"That's *great*, McGill!" he said. "I didn't think you had it in you. Approved! Give 'em hell!"

My plan was thus set into motion. I didn't warn anyone about what was coming. Instead, just after lunch, I jogged my team up to Green Deck again. They groaned, but followed me gamely enough. They'd toughened up over the last few weeks.

Harris was there, as I knew he would be. He was using low-powered laser target rifles, having his troops nail moving targets. I marched up and stood behind him until he finished coaching a trooper on adjusting her sights.

"McGill?" he asked in surprise. "What do you want? We have this turf until 1400 hours. Get lost."

"Can't do that, Vet," I said. "I'm here to issue a challenge."

Frowning fiercely, Harris watched me remove a gauntlet and throw it on the ground at his feet. He put his hands on his hips instead of picking it up, however.

"What the hell...? Have you lost your mind, boy?"

"It's approved, Vet," I said. "Adjunct Leeson thinks it's a great idea."

"He would..." Harris broke off, and he couldn't help but glance around himself. My squad, panting from their run, had come up behind me and stood with grim looks on their faces.

Harris' own people had stopped shooting and were walking up to see what was going on. Everyone soon caught sight of the gauntlet on the ground, and they knew what that meant. Since ancient times, a challenge was a challenge. Harris couldn't refuse to pick up the gauntlet unless he wanted to look like a coward.

He scooped up my gauntlet with an angry flourish and threw it into my chest. I caught it and slipped it back on again.

"All right," he said. "Have it your way, kid. As the challenged, I choose the ground and the rules. I choose the mud-pit—with knives, nothing else."

I blinked. That hadn't been part of my plan. I'd envisioned a straight-up shooting contest. Most Varus full-contact exercises went that way. We were accustomed to stalking one another in the rugged greenery, playing capture the flag or last-man-standing. Usually, scores were kept with automated equipment that incapacitated "dead" soldiers. But this time, it was going to be for real.

"Knives?" I asked. Part of me began to question the wisdom of my challenge—but it was too late for regrets now.

"You chicken?" Harris demanded angrily.

"Nope. We accept. When do we go?"

"How about right fucking *now*, farm-boy?"

That was it. Negotiations had been concluded. Both squads began to hoot and rip off their clothes. We walked in two loose knots toward the mud-pit, which was located in the swampiest corner of Green Deck.

The mud-pit was about forty meters across and one meter deep at the center. In the deep section in the middle of the pit, every step a man took threatened to suck off his shoes. The effort was quickly exhausting.

"Strip down to your shorts," I ordered my squaddies. "No tops. Don't give them anything to hold onto. And try to stay out of the center of the pit."

My team shed their clothes and soon stood in camo shorts. They looked nervous, but game. I felt a surge of pride at that and also a pang of remorse. Not all of them would make it out of this alive. Their willingness to die at my orders gave me pause. Was my personal anger at the universe worthy of the pain and sacrifice they were about to experience?

As soon as these debilitating thoughts entered my head, I did my best to push them away. They wouldn't help me now. We were committed. Honor had to be served, and the best thing I could do for my squad was lead them to victory.

Lining up on the shore, both squads stood with knives drawn. Some were snarling, some were staring with determined expressions.

Experienced Varus legionnaires aren't like normal folk. We're killers. Everyone present had died at least a dozen times, and we'd killed many times our weight in enemies.

There's something different about a soldier who's seen so much death, but you can't understand the difference until you've see an experienced legionnaire face combat. Sure, we knew we'd catch a revive when this was over. But that didn't mean shit to our bodies or our minds. A revive was a copy, nothing more. This flesh we stood in right now—that was going to be torn up and spit out. That's what mattered to us, and we knew it was all too real. Our guts and our minds were churning.

Before we started, I noticed there were drones floating overhead. A few knots of officers and troops from other units had come out to watch in person as well. Word had traveled fast. We were about to put on a show, and I had the feeling the entire complement of *Minotaur* would be watching tonight.

Harris lifted his blade. It glittered, catching the gleam of a passing star that shone through the dome above. The heavens were displayed on that dome along with an added artificial sun that matched the one nearest to us in actual space. It was like standing in pale daylight—even though it was an illusion.

Harris held his blade higher, urging me to get started.

I looked over my troops. They were breathing hard and wearing grim expressions. Most of them were splashing mud over their bodies to provide less grip for our opponents. The women were bare-breasted, but nobody gave a damn about that now—we were about to fight to the death.

None of them needed encouragement or correction from me, so I turned back to face my enemy. That's what Harris and his crew were now—the enemy.

My knife rose into the air, matching Harris' blade and signaling we were ready. A roar left my throat, and I sprang into the mud, leading the charge. The opposing squad rushed to meet us, legs pumping up and down, brown muck flying high.

It was on.

-6-

Despite my orders to the rest of my squad, I moved to the middle of the mud. You see, I'm an extremely tall man. That meant that while the mud came to a short person's waist, it only went to just above my knees, giving me a distinct advantage in mobility.

I honestly expected to see Harris rush into the center and meet me, but he didn't. Instead, he sprinted around the rim where it was just deep enough to get his ankles sloppy. He went for my weakest fighters, the ones that were hanging back uncertainly.

Harris wanted to teach me a lesson—I realized that about ten seconds into the fight. He was a masterful warrior, but that didn't mean he liked to die. He'd deliberately chosen a grim scenario, one sure to result in horrible moments. He'd also chosen a setup that would play to his own personal strengths. He liked knives and hand-to-hand combat because he was deadly in close.

Harris met Gorman near the edge of the circular pool of mud, and Gorman went down after three cuts. Harris moved away with a bloody line across his chest but nothing more. Gorman was flopping and shivering in mud at his feet, trying to make it to the edge of the pit. If he could climb out under his own power—well, he might live. Harris danced past him and moved on to the next closest opponent, Kivi. She gave him a harder time, but he put her down pretty fast too. Crippled and making a lot of noise, she crawled for the edge holding in her guts with one hand.

In the middle of the pit, I had my own problems. Seeing me isolated, three of Harris' fighters rushed as a team to meet me. I stood my ground, ready.

Fighting with knives is different than fighting with swords or clubs, especially when you're stuck in mud. Reach is a critical factor. Although the three men who came at me tried to time it so they hit me at the same moment, one of them slipped and fell behind his two charging comrades. The other two— well, they didn't have the reach I did, and they couldn't move their mired feet as fast, either.

With my arm outstretched to its maximum length, I planted my knife in the neck of the leader. His eyes bulged, and he tried to get to me, even though he was dead on his feet. I applauded the effort, but retreated and let him die face down with bubbles farting up around his grimy head.

The second man came in before I could retreat and managed to score. He got a shot into my ribs—but there's a reason why we have ribs, they're built to deflect weapons and teeth from our inner organs. I was hurt, but the thrust hadn't punched deep.

He had his arms wrapped around me, and we did the bear hug thing, struggling to keep on our feet and roaring.

In return for the blade in my side, I brought mine down two-handed, driving it into the shorter man's skull. His eyes rolled up, and he slipped away bonelessly into the muck.

The third man, the one who'd slipped while charging with his two fellows, couldn't help but notice I'd nailed both his wingmen and was still standing tall. He turned and slogged away as quickly as he could. I didn't blame him.

Instead of following the runner, I moved to meet Harris at the edge of the pit, where he was now sparring with Carlos.

Whatever else Carlos might be, he's not a slouch when it comes to a hard fight. The two of them were in a clinch, each holding onto the other's knife hand and straining.

Carlos couldn't hope to win the struggle. Harris was bound to overpower him in the end, despite the fact he was bleeding now from a few wounds of his own.

What Carlos needed was a quick rescue, and I came up on the two of them from behind, planning on an easy kill.

Harris didn't give it to me. He got his foot hooked behind Carlos' ankle and sent him down on his back. A quick stoop, thrust, and Carlos was out.

I tried to slosh my way up to Harris before he could turn back around, but he must have heard me coming. He spun around and grinned with blood in his mouth.

"Why are we always meeting up like this, McGill?"

"At least this time it was my idea," I replied.

"See you in Hell, boy!" he shouted, and threw his knife at me.

It was a surprise move and expertly executed. The blade flipped once and drove right toward my chest. Our knives are sharper than simple steel, and I knew that if that point hit dead-on with that much force, I was going to be taken down.

Twisting with all the speed I had left in me, I took it in the shoulder. My right arm was numb after that, but I managed to grip my knife in my left.

Advancing, it was my turn to grin. Harris had disarmed himself.

But Harris didn't miss a beat. He stooped and grabbed Carlos' knife out of his dead hand. How had he managed to find it in an instant under a foot of mud? I don't know, but I'd always thought Harris was a man who could fight like the devil himself.

Around us, the wild roars and screams of battle had died down. Many of the combatants on both sides were dead or too injured to continue. Most of the survivors were busy dragging themselves out of the mud-pit. Only a few were still in the game.

Harris and I slashed and circled, shuffling awkwardly in the mud. I kept backing up, drawing him toward the deep section, which had been my original plan. To some degree, it worked. He snarled and fought to take me down quickly with lunges and thrusts, but I stayed in the fight.

My right arm hung, almost useless. My left was bleeding too, having picked up a slash somewhere along the line.

"You're the one who will bleed out this time," Harris said, grinning at me.

He was right, but I didn't bother to reply. The last time we'd fought with knives, he'd had the upper hand, but he'd lost too much blood and passed out. This time, it looked like I would suffer the same fate.

But I had a plan, of sorts. I kept retreating, drawing him into the deepest mud. He followed with a greedy light in his eye. He wanted to see me fall.

When I figured it couldn't get any deeper, I made my play. I reversed myself and came on hard, making wide, sweeping slashes. My arms are longer than an ape's, according to every schoolmate I'd ever scuffled with, and those slashes were hard to avoid.

Now, you have to understand something about Harris: he doesn't like to get hurt. He likes to win as cleanly as he can. His first instinct, therefore, was to fall back before my onslaught and look for an opening to dart into and finish me.

When he took his first backpedalling step the sucking mud pulled at his legs, locking him in, slowing him down. I switched tactics again, stopping the slashes. I made an my all-out lunge while he was off-balance, and I saw the shock in his eyes.

I'd planted my blade in his chest, stopping his heart. Even so, he got his knife around to stab me in the back. The move opened me up, but didn't quite put me down. Harris sank, slowly.

Roaring and grinning, I lifted my knife and whirled around, looking for fresh challengers.

At first, I thought there wasn't anyone left. About half the combatants were dead and floating. Most of the rest were lying on the shore around the pit, struggling to breathe.

Bio people had shown up from somewhere. They were like vultures when anyone died. They were tending to those who could easily be patched up and hauling the rest away to the recycling center.

Then I spotted a figure. She was relatively near, but I hadn't noticed her because she was as motionless as a tiger in tall grass.

51

It was Della.

My heart sank, and I felt a little sick. In my rage and frustration, I'd forgotten that she was part of Harris' squad.

She came toward me, realizing she'd been spotted. She watched me with predatory eyes and moved like a cat stalking prey. Somehow, even bare-breasted and covered in filth, she still managed to look graceful.

I let her approach. I didn't move except to follow her as she came close and began to circle. She stepped around me carefully, and I thought she might throw her weapon the way Harris did—but she didn't. She gazed up to me with deadly serious eyes.

Tossing my weapon aside to the edge of the pit, I stood still. She followed my knife with darting eyes. She looked at me in puzzlement and cocked her head.

Stepping close warily, she dared to speak. "What are you doing? Everyone is watching. Thousands of eyes are on us."

"I don't care. I can't kill the mother of my own child."

She licked her lips and stalked closer. I stood, watching her, wondering what she'd do.

"You're dishonoring both of us," she hissed.

"Why don't you just kill me then?" I asked her. "Are you afraid?"

Della kept her eyes on my hands, flicking her gaze from one to the other. I could tell she didn't trust me at all. This wasn't our first fight, you have to understand.

"A little," she said. "But the real problem is I don't want to kill you, either. Why did you start this stupid fight? What was the purpose?"

I heaved a sigh. "I don't know. When we came to that first star system, I was so ready to catch the raiders and kill them... I wanted blood. I guess I started this out of frustration."

"A stupid move. I should kill you just for that."

She came at me then, but her arms moved slowly. It was only a fractional difference, but I could see it. A play thrust, not even on target.

I caught her wrist and pulled her off-balance. A moment later I had my knee on her back and her knife-hand stretched out away from both our bodies.

"Yield," I said.

"I will not," she said angrily.

"You won't? Wasn't that what you wanted?"

"I won't," she hissed. "Not unless you admit I could have killed you."

I laughed. "All right, I admit it. I'm as good as dead on my feet. Happy?"

"Not at all—but I yield."

Getting an arm under her waist, I straightened and tossed her onto dry land. She landed on her feet and dropped her knife in the blood-soaked dirt.

The mud-pit battle was over. I walked wearily to the bio people who clucked their tongues and sprayed me with cleansers and nu-skin.

Della returned to her own squad, and I looked after her thoughtfully. She'd never passed up a solid opportunity to kill me before.

People congratulated me on the victory and even cheered me. I didn't feel like I deserved their praise, however. I felt spent and almost as frustrated as I'd been when I'd started this mission.

A few hours later, Graves summoned me to his stark office again. I went with my arm in a sling and my left eye swollen almost shut.

He wasn't smiling, and he didn't congratulate me when I got there. I stood at attention until he told me what he wanted.

"At ease, Veteran," Graves said at last. He walked toward me and looked me over. "You're in sorry shape."

"Nothing a few layers of fresh cells won't cure, sir."

"I don't mean your body. I'm talking about your mind. I thought you'd take your losses in stride—but I was wrong. You let your emotions make your decisions for you today."

I didn't say anything. We both knew he was right.

"Well," Graves said, "despite its questionable effects on morale, it was an effective training exercise. Mud-pit fights to the death? That's the sort of thing we usually reserve for recruits and candidates seeking promotion. Let's not have a fresh challenge from you next week, clear?"

"Clear. Nothing like this will ever happen again, sir."

"I don't believe that for a second."

Again, I said nothing. I don't like to lie without a good reason.

Heaving a sigh, Graves returned to his desk. "Here's something that might cheer you up. We've decided to pass up the second star system we were targeting. The techs have run all the numbers. They think the second star—a binary system— is very unlikely to be the raider's base. Odds are we'll find them at the last star in the line, which is right at the squid border."

He had my interest now. I shuffled to his desk where he had displayed the local stars. I tapped at the binary system we were supposed to pass by. It had the generic name of L-374. It contained an orange-colored K-class star circled by a smaller M-class companion. The last star in the line, the one we were to visit next, was yet another of the ubiquitous red dwarfs.

"Sir?" I asked. "We're really going to skip this orange star? Why?"

"Why skip L-374? Because Gold Deck says so. Remember Veteran, I'm not in command of this expedition—and neither are you."

"But what if we don't find them in the third system? What will we do then? If we have to backtrack to the K-class, they might have had time to slip away."

Graves shook his head. "We won't bother. If I had to guess, I'd say we'll check the last system and give up. Turov will turn us around and head home again after that."

"She'd give up? She'd actually be willing to go back to Earth empty-handed?"

He shrugged. "What else would you suggest?"

"I think we should keep searching until we find them," I boomed. Letting my voice rise more than I'd meant to. "There has to be a fourth star somewhere along this line... Somewhere else to look."

Graves studied me for a moment before speaking. "If you kept following this course—which we don't know is the correct one anyway—you'd enter enemy space. After passing through the entirety of the Cephalopod Kingdom, we'd come out on the other side, near the core of the Perseus Arm. *There* we'd find another star to check."

"It's that far, huh?" I asked in disappointment.

He put two fingers on his desktop and brought them slowly together. The map contracted. I could now see the line extended farther out. There *was* a fourth star, but it was pretty distant.

"McGill," Graves said. "I want you to give this up if we don't find them soon. It's not healthy, and worse, it's pointless. Use your brain, man. What are the odds the raiders came from so far out? We're talking about more than a hundred and seventy lights from Earth to get to that fourth star. It doesn't even make sense that an enemy would know about a freighter heading to Earth from Machine World at that distance."

Brooding and quiet, I stopped asking questions, and Graves soon dismissed me.

Frustrated and feeling like my greatest fears concerning this expedition were coming to life before my eyes, I left his office. I hadn't wanted this to turn into a wild goose-chase, but that's exactly what was happening. I could feel it.

There was only one other place to go, only one other person to talk to who could change things.

With a heavy sigh, I headed for Gold Deck.

-7-

Imperator Turov wasn't always the easiest officer to talk to. First off, she liked to put barriers in a man's way. Secondly, she was always busy doing something important or at least something that *seemed* important. Today was no exception to either of these rules.

There were no less than three adjuncts and a couple of centurions that I had to go through to meet up with Turov. The high and mighty one herself didn't have time for a lowly noncom, I was told this repeatedly.

Insisting I had something to say that only Turov herself was qualified to listen to got me pretty far—but that was only because they knew I'd had unusual dealings with her in the past. Eventually, I was faced with a final adjunct—a woman named Bachchan. She had an attitude as snotty as the rest of them. I told her my story all over again, concluding that Turov wouldn't like it if an adjunct turned me back. At last, she led me to a well-appointed office door. It wasn't the same office where I'd met up with Turov in the past, but I figured maybe she'd moved.

The lock buzzed open even before my fist rapped on the door. It melted away from my hand as I pushed it open. Stepping inside, I was met with another unpleasant surprise.

I was standing in Winslade's office, not Turov's. He was sitting behind his desk with his non-reg jackboots resting between a monitor and a cup of coffee. Working on a computer scroll, he waved at me with a skinny set of fingers, indicating I should approach but remain standing.

I did so, but after a moment I couldn't take the waiting around.

"Sir? Primus, sir? I'm sorry, I must have been led to the wrong office. I'll be going now. Didn't mean to bother you."

Winslade glanced up and gave me an unhappy stare.

"You're in the right place, McGill," he said. "That is, if it can be said that there is a right place for the likes of you."

"I don't understand, sir."

He set the scroll aside and removed his feet from his desk. Weaving together his fingers like a spider web, he leaned forward and gave me an unfriendly appraisal. I could tell I was a bug on a dinner plate to him.

"Let me spell it out for you," he began. "I'm in command of your cohort. In truth, even *I'm* too far up the chain of command to be talking to the likes of a freshly promoted veteran, and the Imperator is two steps above my station. The idea you should be allowed to waltz in here and meet with her in person on demand…it's preposterous. And it's going to stop today! If you have something to say to the Imperator, you'll tell me first. If I find it worthy, I may kick it up another level. But I'll warn you right now, that's highly unlikely."

Winslade had my attention now. I knew he didn't like me, and he didn't enjoy it when I went over his head and talked to Turov. But this wasn't about protocol or personal dislike. He wanted to know what I was up to. He didn't want to be cut out of the loop, as had happened in the past.

"I hear you, Primus. Loud and clear. I'll be going now."

I spun on my heel and managed to take two long strides across his thick carpet toward the door before he reacted.

"Halt! You haven't been dismissed, Veteran!"

Stopping, I spun back around, but I still didn't say anything. I stood at attention and looked at the wall.

"Tell me why you wanted to talk to the Imperator," he prompted.

"Because I think she's making a strategic error, sir."

A frown grew on his face. It was a wary look of displeasure.

"You've always believed you know better than your commanders how to run our legions, haven't you?"

"Not at all, sir. But sometimes, people don't have a clear view. They don't have the vision of the man in the trenches."

"Interesting. Let me see if I can interpret your vague hints. You've uncovered a scheme of some kind. You believe the Imperator should be given this information in person as it may affect her decisions regarding our current mission."

I gave him a startled glance. I didn't have any such information. I was planning on trying to convince her not to give up on finding the raiders too easily, that was all. But as usual, Winslade with his conniving personality thought I was holding back something more sinister.

"Ah-ha!" Winslade cried, banging a skinny fist on his desk. "I've got your attention now, don't I? Yes, McGill, even *I* can follow your clever machinations. Well, I'll have none of it. I don't want you pestering Turov. I've given the staff orders to intercede if you try. As you can see, they've been quite effective today."

Nodding and looking back at the wall, I paused for a second. "Am I dismissed then, sir?"

"No, you're not dismissed."

He studied me quietly for a few seconds. He was obviously waiting for me to volunteer information. I endeavored to make my face a blank mask and said nothing.

"Damn you, man," he said at last. "You're not getting out of here without telling me what this is about. But even if you don't want to talk, your motivations should be vulnerable to logical reasoning. Let's continue extrapolating down this path...if you wanted to tell Turov something crucial, why not send her a text? Can it be because you're well aware all your texts are carefully monitored?"

I gave him another startled look. He smiled.

"I see that you *do* know. That indicates you want to talk to Turov in person in order to give her a private message—and don't even try to convince me you're simply making another ham-handed romantic overture. I know that you've been far from lonely at night."

This entire discussion was getting off-track in an alarming way. Winslade seemed to have gone paranoid. Reading my texts? Having people provide him with reports on my dating life? The man was losing it.

"Sir, I'm in the dark about all that," I said honestly. "I'm just trying to help our commander achieve her goals. If you stand between me and the imperator—well, that's your business, but I wouldn't recommend it."

Winslade was suddenly pissed again. He stood up and began to pace. He clasped his arms behind his back oddly, with one hand grabbing the elbow of the other.

"Threats? You dare so much? You think you still have her ear and her eye, don't you? All right, McGill. You can go to the imperator and give her your dirty little report. But don't think I'm not watching. Don't think I'll allow you to keep rank-climbing and undermining my position year after year. I have *real* rank, and I have a growing record in the field. On top of that, let's not forget I'm still in your chain of command. I can make things unpleasant for you."

"Of course, sir. I must say it's been a pleasure to serve. Can I be on my way now?"

"Get out."

I'd been thrown out of any number of offices, so I knew the routine. I left without saying anything more. I didn't even glance back to see what he was doing.

When the door squeezed shut behind me, I met up with the sneering Adjunct Bachchan. She'd evidently been waiting for me.

"I'll take you back to your module, Veteran," Bachchan said. "This way, please."

"Uh...you might want to check with Primus Winslade on that point, first."

Frowning, she looked at her tapper, which beeped and displayed fresh orders. She looked up at me a moment later, startled.

"I'm to take you to the imperator?"

"Yes. As I originally requested."

Adjunct Bachchan didn't say another word as she marched me down a passage or two. We wound up in front of a pair of imposing doors. She looked more worried than annoyed now. When Turov was involved directly, she knew enough to stay quiet and keep her head low.

The office doors that led to Turov's office were impressive indeed. They weren't like any I'd ever seen on a dreadnaught before. Ornately carved with dark alien hardwoods, they depicted the heads of what looked like a species of bird that had been crossed with a demon.

I stepped inside, and the first thing I noticed was the carpet. It wasn't your typical military-grade weatherproof stuff. It was sumptuous. Red, rich…it felt like I was walking on velvet.

"What do you think of my new office, McGill?" asked a voice I recognized. I looked for Turov, but I didn't see her right off. There were hanging curtains, folding glass barriers and a variety of other decorations all over the place.

"Wow," I said, "this is really something, sir."

Imperator Galina Turov became visible then—sort of. She was lurking behind a semi-opaque pane of glass. I couldn't help but stare, as her lithe form was displayed in stark silhouette. What's more, it looked to me like she was walking around nude back there. She seemed to be toweling off her hair, like she'd just come out of the shower.

It took me a long second, but I finally realized this personal display couldn't be an accident. No one put a light bulb behind their shower curtain and stood between the two without a damned good reason.

"Sir?" I asked. "Should I come back another time?"

"Will your visit be any less annoying if it is postponed?"

"I'm not sure I can promise that."

"Then let's get this over with. Take a seat, James."

James. She usually didn't call me that. She only did so, in fact, when she was in an amorous mood, or drunk.

You have to understand that I'd had an inappropriate relationship with the imperator some years back. Most people, especially Winslade, still considered my familiarity with her to be improper.

She came out of her inner sanctum a moment later with her hair still hanging limp and wet. She had clothes on, but they didn't amount to a regulation uniform. She wore something like a sleeping jumper with rank insignia on the epaulets. It was the sort of thing officers wore to bed. But as usual, it was tighter than it was supposed to be. Smart clothes could be told to cinch-up if you wanted them to.

"Uh...is this your off-duty shift, sir?" I asked.

"Unfortunately, high level officers are never truly off-duty. Your visit is a clear exemplification of that reality. Now, before you waste any more of my time, get to the point. Why are you working so hard to see me in person?"

"Because I think you're making a mistake. I think you should check out all three of the systems where our enemy might have taken refuge as we originally planned."

"The raiders...of course. James, I know of your personal loss in this tragedy. I too, would like to hold the raiders accountable. But I have to be honest with you—we've lost them."

I blinked at her in surprise. "That's not how I understand the situation."

"We had one chance, really—that first stop. After that, the odds that we're still following the right course have grown very long indeed."

"But the techs did the math," I objected. "This heading should match that of the raiders. They have to come out eventually."

"Let's assume you're correct," she said, toweling off her hair while I watched. "We may have been going in the right direction initially, but we must admit to certain realities. Any raider with a modicum of intelligence should have used the last few weeks to come out of warp, switch courses and fly in another direction. They could have done that a week ago, for example, and we would never have known as we were in a warp bubble ourselves and thus blinded. They could be doing it right now in fact—and again, we'd never know."

"I understand that. But a ship's crew will normally take a straight path toward their destination while fleeing. We had three target stars they might have been trying to—"

"Not really. We never had three targets. That first one held promise. The odds were high we'd catch them there. But now, the probability is slim. It's simple mathematics. We drew a line

61

following their initial path as best we could. But our measurements couldn't be exact. Therefore, each lightyear we fly from the original starting point creates a cone of space, not a line, containing places they might stop. We're reaching the wide end of that cone, and there are a great number of destinations within it. So as I explained, that first binary system was our only real hope."

I felt a wave of frustration. She might be right, and in fact I sensed that she at least *believed* she was, but I didn't want to give up. Not yet.

"You're talking about the margin of error," I said, "about probabilities. Well, if it's hopeless, why aren't we abandoning the hunt right now? Why not simply turn around and go home today?"

"Politics and public relations forbid it," she said, setting aside her towel and walking languidly around her desk to my side of it. She put her butt up against the edge of the desktop and leaned back, resting her hands on the desk. "We must make it seem we've searched everywhere to satisfy the angry mob back home. We're going to return empty-handed in the end, and it would be best that we our take time before we admit failure."

"Look," I said, "Imperator, we have a lot of secrets between us, and quite a colorful past—"

"You think I'm going to listen to threats?" she demanded, interrupting. "Really, McGill? I hadn't thought you were so deluded as to think you could damage me at this point. I know about your little talk with Nagata. Don't think I'll be taken unaware."

Internally I was shocked, but I didn't show it. Equestrian Nagata had charged me with feeding him information on Turov. He wanted her taken out of the upper brass—presumably because she was after his job.

"I'm not making any threats," I said carefully. "I'm asking for a favor."

"A favor? What gives you the right to ask for such a thing?"

"We—we owe each other a great deal. All I'm asking for this time around is a break. If you're going to stop searching

62

after one more star anyway, make it the one we're passing by now. You said yourself the probability they'll switch course on us is growing every day. This binary system is inside the cone where they might make that move. Let's not skip it."

"That would make you happy?"

"I wouldn't say that. I'm only going to be happy if we find them."

"That I believe," she said, looking up at me thoughtfully. "What's in this arrangement for me?"

I tried hard to think of something, but initially I drew a blank.

"You mentioned Nagata," I said at last. "Maybe I could keep you informed on his actions instead of the other way around."

This made her eyebrows rise high. She nodded appreciatively, taking her butt off her desk and approaching me.

"I like the sound of that," she said. "The best agents are double-agents. You'd do that for me? Risk everything to feed me information about the witch hunt my enemies are engaged in back at Central?"

"If it will make you stop this ship—then yes."

She turned away as if considering her options. My eyes wandered, as I was sure she knew they would. They fixated upon her hindquarters almost immediately, which were tightly packed into her thin jumper.

She glanced over her shoulder and caught me looking. She smiled.

"I accept your offer, James. You will make regular visits to my office. You'll report three times a week—every other day. Do you understand?"

"Uh..." I said, looking down at her face and trying not to look even farther down. "Not entirely. What am I going to report on? Nagata is back on Earth."

She rolled her eyes and sighed. She reached back, grabbed my hand and put it on her rump.

"Are we clear now?" she asked.

"Oh...yes sir."

I was surprised, but I got over that very quickly. I stepped forward and began pawing at her. She leaned over her desk, and I removed what she had on, which didn't amount to much more than an ounce of sheer smart-cloth anyway.

We made love then, right on her desk. I really hoped she'd had good sound-proofing installed in her office walls, because she wasn't quiet about it.

"One more thing, sir," I said when we were finished. "Can I call you Galina?"

She thought about it for a moment, frowning. "No. I'd prefer that you didn't."

"Very well, sir."

I left after that, and I have to confess, I was smiling.

One could say I'd been abused by my superior. Sexually coerced, even. But then again, one could say that I didn't mind the abuse. Not one bit.

-8-

We stopped at the binary star system the next day. For some reason, I wasn't as keyed-up this time around as I'd been the on the first stop. Whether that was because I'd given up on finding the raiders or because I'd had a chance to blow off some steam, it was hard to say.

Leeson came to check up on me while I donned my battle armor. He put his hands on his hips and put a crooked grin on his face. When he spoke, his voice was low, rumbly and amused.

"You sly *dog* you!" he exclaimed. "I heard about Turov. What I can't believe is you managed to halt an entire expedition in deep space with a single office-visit."

I glanced at him and fooled with my helmet straps.

"Whatever you heard, sir, was exaggerated gossip. I will admit that the imperator has seen the light and reconsidered her options. I presented my case, and she made the call. Rumors that I went farther than that to change her mind…well, that's sheer speculation."

"You just marched up there to Gold Deck and did a little persuading, eh?" Leeson said, chuckling and leering at me. "What do I have to do to get a ticket to a lady's office on Gold Deck?"

Snorting, I shook my head. "I'd recommend taking up that question with her personal staff. She has one adjunct that's particularly accommodating. Her name is Bachchan."

65

Leeson nodded thoughtfully. "Adjunct Bachchan, huh? I might just look her up. Thanks for the steer, McGill."

"No charge, sir."

I watched him leave with a hint of a smile on my face. I truly hoped he did approach and proposition Adjunct Bachchan. She'd probably tear him up.

The target system didn't have a lot of planets, but there were some that were worth investigating. We came out of warp near the M-class star and cruised by her handful of dimly lit planets in the first hours. Then we turned the bow around and pointed it toward the K-class and glided in that direction.

More waiting followed. I felt stressed and ordered my squad to stand down. It would be nearly a full day's cycle before we reached sensor range for the bigger star.

I was anticipating failure. My mind was churning. I'd sold my soul to Turov already. How could I get her to continue the hunt when this system proved fruitless? In retrospect, I was wishing I'd held something back to bargain with. I needed to keep this search going, and I was running out of both options and time.

That night, I lay in my bunk stewing over my situation. I couldn't sleep. In the morning, we'd arrive at the K-class and either discover the enemy raiders, or more likely, nothing at all. Then I'd be right back where I started. How could I get Turov to fly to the next star?

And if I managed that, what if the third one was as empty as the first two? What was I willing to do to get the imperator to press on?

At about one a. m., I finally sprang out of bed, wide awake. I paced for a time like a caged tiger then threw on some clothes and headed out into the passages.

The ship was quiet but not dark. The night shift of Skrull crewmen were pacing the halls and keeping everything running. They glanced at me as I passed by, but said nothing. It wasn't their job to question the humans, who they thought were crazy anyway. They flew the ship—that's all. Sometimes I envied the spidery little aliens.

Adjunct Bachchan intercepted me as she'd done the day before. To my surprise, she was still on duty in the middle of the night. Maybe intercepting people who were coming to see Turov was all she did.

This time, however, she didn't sneer at me. She frowned and looked suspicious, but there was no more sneering.

"This way, Veteran," she said in an almost mechanical voice.

I followed her, not bothering to ask questions. She'd clearly been briefed and ordered to let me pass. She didn't seem happy about that, but she wasn't openly complaining.

When the door to Turov's office opened, I found the imperator to be absent.

"Wait here," Bachchan said.

I nodded and did as she instructed. A few minutes later, Turov arrived.

Again, I was surprised. She wasn't yawning and wearing a nightie. Quite the opposite, she was fully dressed and seemed stressed.

"What do you want now?" she snapped. "Haven't you done enough?"

"What are you talking about, sir?"

"The K-class—" she said, but then she broke off. Her eyes narrowed. She walked up to me and stabbed a finger into my chest. "You *knew*, didn't you?"

"Uh…knew what, sir?"

"Again with the dumb act? It won't work McGill—not this time. And to think I believed I was manipulating *you*…what I don't understand, is how you could have known…but you must have! You were emphatic about stopping here, suggesting we skip the last system in the line. Did you imagine I wouldn't remember the details?"

As often happened when conversing with officers— particularly Turov and Winslade—I felt I was being imbued with powers I simply didn't have. The question in my mind now was how to deal with this situation.

My first instinct was to play dumb, because that's exactly what I was. I had no idea what she was talking about, including why she was claiming I'd managed to trick her somehow. But I didn't want to play dumb. I was desperate, and I needed leverage. She could stop this mission at any time, but I knew that if she thought I was some kind of wizard, my odds of keeping things going improved. Therefore, I chose to pretend I had the upper hand.

"I'm often underestimated, sir," I said, giving her a confident smile.

Her lips pouted, and she made a hissing sound as she brushed past me. She moved to her desk and swept her arm across it, casting a dozen scrolls and a fold-up monitor onto the floor. The desk turned into a screen and displayed local space.

"There," she said, stabbing near the center of the system. "This K-class star has only a single inner planet. Mysteriously, life has been detected on its surface."

She looked back at me accusingly as if daring me to confess to a crime. I looked back in bewilderment.

"Okay," I said. "There's life—but there's plenty of life on different worlds. What's the big deal?"

"We checked the catalogs, and this system was scanned and deemed empty centuries ago by the Galactics. How do you explain this discrepancy?"

"Hmm…" I said thoughtfully, stepping closer to the display. "Looking at the planet, it doesn't seem remarkable. It's in the goldilocks zone circling a stable star. It's rocky, and although it's a little smaller than Earth, it appears to have an atmosphere and liquid water."

"I know all that," she snapped. "The point is it was listed as uninhabited and uninhabitable. Why? There are life readings down there! And that's why you led me here, isn't it? To find a world that shouldn't be? A secret living planet?"

I shrugged because I was pretty close to being out of ideas. Sometimes it's best to let imaginative people run with the ball for you.

She stared at me and made growling sounds. I could tell she was thinking hard. "You've given me provocative hints," she said. "I'm putting the pieces together. The only way this planet could be here is if someone altered the data. Someone must have hidden this world by deleting or changing the records. That means one of two things: involvement by the Galactics or some kind of criminal element."

"I find it highly unlikely that the Galactics would bother to do this to themselves. The Nairbs would have a fit if they found out."

"Right," she replied intensely. "It can only be a conspiracy. A purposeful error in the local star surveys. In any case, it doesn't matter. The criminals we seek must be here, waiting for us."

"Well then, let's go nail them!" I boomed.

She stared at me with hooded eyes. "Are you leading me into some kind of trap? This smells like one of Claver's schemes to me."

"Claver was back on Earth the last I knew, sir."

She looked at me oddly for a moment, and I had to wonder if she knew where Claver really was. Then she made a dismissive gesture, erasing my words with her hand.

"Regardless of where Claver might be," she said. "I know you two are working for Nagata. Don't bother to deny it."

"Imperator, let me assure you on one point: for the duration of this mission, I'll be working for *you*."

She bit her lower lip. She looked worried, and I could tell she wasn't sure who to believe in.

"Let's go over recent events," she said at last. "First, mysterious pirates show up over Earth and brazenly attack. Second, I'm sent out here to catch these pirates—but then third, when I deviate from the course recommended by Central, you do your best to dissuade me. Fourth, as if by divine intervention, the second star system you specified as the target turns out to be the correct one."

I watched the wheels turning in her head. I figured I had to say *something*. Heck, if I let her keep thinking on her own, she'd have me drawn and quartered by sunrise.

Taking a half-step toward her, I placed a hand on her elbow. "I couldn't sleep," I said. "That's why I'm really here."

She shook off my touch. "Don't. Seduction won't work this time, McGill. You'll have to do better than that."

My mind was in a state of confusion. By my way of thinking, she'd seduced *me* the first time around—actually, it had been that way every time around, if my memory served...

But a man doesn't get far with the ladies if he doesn't back off when signaled to do so.

"Sorry sir," I said. "Should I be returning to my squad? Should I prepare for action?"

Her slitted, suspicious eyes studied me. "I wish I knew what was really going on inside your brain, McGill."

"Sometimes," I said, "I'm uncertain myself."

"Dismissed. Get some sleep. We'll probably be in action within twenty hours. I'll make sure you're given a frontline seat when the fighting begins."

"Thank you sir, I'm looking forward to a shot at revenge."

She watched me leave, and I could tell she wasn't sure how to take my reference to revenge.

I'd hoped she'd feel that way. I knew it was always best to keep your opponent guessing.

-9-

It was precisely eleven hours later, down to the minute, when we finally spotted our quarry.

They weren't trying to hide, not really. They'd taken some precautions, but nothing our techs couldn't penetrate. Their radio network, for example, was set up to emit low-power, diffuse transmissions which looked like white noise, and the exhaust plumes of their ships weren't nearly as brilliant as those an Imperial ship might produce.

But then maybe that was because Empire ships had little to fear inside the borders of Frontier 921. These people were fugitives. They had plenty to worry about.

Primus Winslade gave us our mission briefing personally. He explained that we were the designated shock troops who'd been hand-picked for the honor of being the first ones dropped on the newly discovered planet.

I had to give Winslade a few points for style. He was making the best of the situation, one which I knew he couldn't be happy about.

"This is a rare opportunity," Winslade said, addressing the entire cohort from the forward wall of our respective unit modules. "We've lost our dragons due to the depredations of these criminals. Now, it's time for payback. We'll drop, engage, and exterminate. We're Imperial troops with a clear mandate. These creatures, whoever they are, broke Galactic

Law when they attacked Earth's freighter. At that moment, they all forfeited their lives."

Hearing these words, I frowned a little. Sure, I wanted to kill the culprits who attacked our planet and dropped burning metal bricks onto my family, but that didn't necessarily mean I was out to kill every alien on the world we were approaching. That would be like killing all the relatives of a murderer. Sure, the criminal deserved justice—but did his grandma have to die as well?

"As representatives of the Empire," Winslade continued, "you should feel no remorse in your hearts. No pity. No quarter. Remember, they gave none to our people when they attacked and disabled our freighter on its final approach. There were over thirty thousand casualties within moments."

Still frowning, I tried not to shuffle my feet or say anything. It required a concentrated effort, but I managed it.

"Here's how the invasion will unfold. First, we'll launch a full strike with our broadsides. The enemy has a large base, which we've located by tracing their transmissions. That base will be destroyed. The landing will then commence, with this cohort leading the way. It will be our mission to mop up any remaining resistance."

A cheer went up from the unit. I smiled proudly. There wasn't a coward among them. A few were more cautious than the rest, but no one shirked from a good fight.

"There are possible caveats to be considered, however," Winslade continued. "Events may not unfold as we plan. We're unclear as to the enemy's precise strength. We might be facing a strong space defense, for example, before we reach the planet itself. So far, it appears we have the element of surprise on our side. Imperator Turov elected to apply massive thrust with the smaller star to our stern, hiding our emissions signature in the glare of the red sun. From the enemy's point of view, we probably look like an unusual solar flare."

I gave a tiny nod in appreciation of the strategy—although I doubted Turov herself had come up with it. She'd clearly had the foresight to recognize a good idea when she heard one, no matter who had thought it up. As was her nature, she'd probably ordered the tactic to be employed then quickly took credit for it when she briefed her top officers.

"This ruse can't protect us forever, unfortunately," Winslade continued. "Cruising at high speeds, we're approaching the point at which we must slow down or slam into the target planet. After that moment, they may spot us and launch a counter-offensive."

You could've heard a pin drop after Winslade mentioned a counter-offensive. The troops had been all grim smiles and determination, but the idea that we might soon meet up with a defending enemy fleet, or at least a missile barrage, hadn't sunk in until now.

The last thing a ground-pounder wants to encounter among the stars is a fleet battle. Under such circumstances, we were no more than spam in a can, as the old saying went.

"We'll know the truth within eight hours," Winslade concluded. "Deceleration has already begun, and it will continue until we've reached the target. Everyone is to stay in full kit, ready to deploy when the word is given."

The briefing ended, and the wall of the module went dark. Afterward, Graves called his officers and top noncoms to a meeting. Under our feet, the deck was heaving and shuddering. We felt about an extra half-gravity of weight on our bones. The inertial dampeners couldn't contain all the fantastic stresses that physics was applying to *Minotaur* as we went into what amounted to a long, roaring skid toward the target world.

"Sounds like the brass has it pretty well in hand this time," Adjunct Leeson said, walking ahead of his veterans.

I glanced at Veteran Harris, but he didn't say anything. He looked kind of glum, but that was all.

Accordingly, I decided to give the adjunct what he expected. My natural skills with bullshit often came in handy when motivational statements were called for.

"Right you are, sir," I said loudly, without a trace of doubt in my voice.

Not to be outdone, Harris sucked in a breath. "The enemy are as good as dead, sir," he boomed. "They'll never know what hit them. Justice will be done, and this nest of thieves will be wiped out!"

"Damn straight," agreed Leeson without even looking over his shoulder.

We hit the hatch with outstretched gauntlets, and it retreated from our touch. Graves was in his office. After all three of his adjuncts, plus Harris, Johnson, me and a half-dozen other veterans filtered in, the room was a little cramped.

We gathered around the desktop display. Graves was tapping at it, sliding icons around and projecting colorful arcs.

The planet itself had a lavender-green cast to it. I wasn't sure if that was due to the atmosphere or the natural shade of the surface.

"This is it," Graves said, waving his hand over the map. "The planet is fractionally smaller than Earth, with a gravitational pull of about point-eight Gs. It has a breathable atmosphere, and although it's hot, it isn't unbearably so."

He paused to run his eyes over each of us in turn.

"That's where the good news ends," he continued. "There's life here—lots of it. We've got high oxygen levels, and as far as we can tell, the whole place is a massive forest. When I say massive, I don't just mean in extent—which is shore to shore on every continent. I'm talking about the growths themselves, which seem to be mega-flora."

Frowning, I looked around the group. A few of the others looked concerned at the centurion's statement. Others, like me, had no idea what he was talking about.

My hand went up almost before I knew I was raising it.

"What is it, McGill?"

"Sir? What exactly is mega-flora?"

"Plants. I'm talking about huge plants," Graves replied. "These trees, or flowers—or whatever they are—they're *big*. Very big. We're talking bigger than the redwoods of Earth for the small ones."

He let that sink in. Adjunct Leeson raised a gauntlet next, and he asked the question I was pondering. "Sir? Are we talking about a thick forest canopy? And if so, how are we going to get through it and down onto the ground?"

Graves pointed a finger at him. "Bingo, Leeson. We're going to have trouble. Two paths are open to us. The most obvious is to fly down in lifters and try to squeeze in-between the growths with careful piloting. The other approach is to simply fire down everyone in capsules and hope some punch through to the ground and make it out alive."

No one replied. No one looked happy with either suggestion, but Graves didn't seem to notice.

"I like the pod-drop approach, myself," he said. "It's quicker, even if it is dangerous. On the other hand, using lifters risks a long hang-time over the target, giving defensive batteries plenty of time to lock on and shoot us down."

Alarmed looks were exchanged. People frowned and massaged their chins.

Both invasion approaches sounded like suicide to me. Particularly the pod-drop method. I didn't like the idea of coming down in a bullet-shaped capsule and slamming into a thousand-meter tall oak tree.

"Of course," Graves went on, "a secondary concern when faced with a world loaded with mega-flora is the possibility of mega-fauna to go with it. Some of you may be senior enough with the legion to remember dropping at Barnard's Star?"

He looked around, but no one else appeared to recall that particular campaign. It had probably happened decades ago.

"No matter," Graves said. He smiled and chuckled in a rumbling fashion, as if musing on a distant memory. "That was a mess. We came down into a world full of marine life. The oceans weren't deep, only a mile or so, and the planet was dotted with islands. We'd heard about the big aquatic species, of course, but hadn't realized so many of them could come humping up onto land if they wanted to. Huge leviathans came after us the moment we landed. They gulped down recruits with an appetite that was almost insatiable."

He shook his head and sighed. "I was an adjunct back then. Those were the days. Anyway, we've found only moderate methane levels, indicating there *is* animal life, but not necessarily *huge* animal life."

The briefing went on, detailing our insertion plan. As Graves spoke, I began to grow an appreciation for the difficulty of our task. We simply didn't know what we would be facing.

Normally, when an Earth legion flew out on a mission, we at least came to the party with a solid conception of what we'd be facing. But not this time. This world wasn't even supposed to be here at all. The system was essentially unknown to us. We couldn't look it up in our databases. We had no maps, no data...

And we didn't have much time, either. There was only a few hours to go, and we had to make crucial decisions before we reached the target.

Graves made these difficult calls without a qualm. He gave us our orders after laying out his thin intel, his hopes, and his worries.

"We're going to try a combination approach," he said in summary. "We're part of Winslade's lucky cohort, so we're the guinea pigs. Half the cohort will be fired down into the canopy of this vast forest like a spray of bullets. The other half will glide down in lifters and try to penetrate the vegetation. In either case, we're to reach the surface any way we can. Depending on what happens to each group, the rest of the legion will choose the better option for further drops."

I left the briefing with a slightly queasy feeling in my stomach. I told myself it wasn't fear—but, as I've said, I can be a terrible liar. Even to myself.

-10-

As we made our final approach to the strangely overgrown planet, Imperator Turov couldn't resist the opportunity for one last speech while she still had her captive audience intact.

We were called to the module briefing area where our glorious leader was displayed on the far wall. The image had to be thirty feet high. Her dark eyes were a lovely almond-shaped, but they were disturbing at this level of magnification.

"Troops," she said, addressing all of us. "I have a treat for all of you—Justice!"

The camera view switched to *Minotaur's* tactical control room. I'd been in that chamber before and noticed it hadn't changed much. There were two primary operators who both had to engage the firing system at the same time to arm the broadsides. As we watched, they checked the final targeting data and gave our hovering camera-drone the thumbs-up.

"We've located a source of emissions on the planet surface which doesn't match any natural patterns," Turov said on voice-over as we watched the gunners work their equipment. "We've picked up radio transmissions, heat, and other energy-release readings. This region on the southern coast of the central continent must contain their base."

The camera shifted to an external view. We watched as the massive broadsides smoothly traversed and zeroed in. The big guns didn't look like they were aiming right at the planet, but when you're throwing fusion shells over a million kilometers, you had to take gravitational effects into account as everything began to curve.

"Locked on," Turov's voice announced.

A yellow, circular firing-reticle lit up on the planet. We were indeed aiming at the southern coast of the largest, central continent. Shrouded in clouds and covered in purplish-green vegetation, the continent was a big piece of land—maybe the size of Asia.

"And now, I'll clue in our criminal friends concerning our intentions. They will bear witness to their punishment—even as we mete it out!"

A red box lit up on the screen, and the word *transmitting* appeared.

"Alien criminals," Turov announced in an officious voice. "We have come to deliver justice to this world. Whether you know it or not, you're within the boundaries of the Galactic Empire. We are local enforcers in this province. We will now annihilate you in recompense for your attack upon local shipping."

We all watched, fascinated. Turov's speech was making it more suspenseful, I had to admit. I wasn't feeling any remorse for the enemy. This was their base. With any luck, the enemy raiding ship that had killed so many back home would be down there. We'd blast them all dead in one shot.

"We're broadcasting this announcement to you using every known form of communication," Turov continued talking to the unknown aliens, "including that of the Cephalopod Kingdom, just in case you're allied with them. Let it be known that we do not take this action for reasons of anger and revenge. We're merely applying the strict rule of Galactic Law to creatures that—"

Something happened then, and Turov stumbled in her speech. The screen, which depicted the planet as seen from our zoomed-in targeting systems, *changed*. It was a subtle change at first. A glimmer of shiny green appeared—not just at one spot but at a dozen of them all at once. They were objects, unknown ovoid contacts, appearing between *Minotaur* and the target world.

"What the hell are those things?" Carlos asked aloud.

I was his superior, and I should have cuffed him one, telling him to shut up during our top officer's speech, but I didn't. I was too dumb-struck and confused to do much of anything.

"I see there is a response," Turov said, regaining her composure. "Crew, take defensive action. It will make no difference how they try to squirm away from their fate."

Turov has always been long-winded. There'd been more than one occasion in our storied adventures together during which I'd wished she'd get on with the show. This time, like so many others, she decided to keep on talking.

"As I was saying, we take this action to correct a grave wrong inflicted upon us. After enduring your punishment, from which there is no escape, you must submit to the Empire and hope that they will be merciful. When the Nairb prefects eventually come here to see that justice is exercised properly, it's possible those of you who have survived this day will be spared. I make no promises, but with appropriate supplication and an attitude of servile—"

The green things, which were shiny and kind of egg-shaped, took action again. Instead of hanging around *Minotaur*, they plunged toward it.

Intercepting fire from a dozen point-defense cannons blazed orange sparks out from our dreadnaught to meet these incoming green eggs. They popped and burned—but more and more appeared behind them.

"We're under attack," Turov said irritably. I could tell she was annoyed that the enemy had managed to cut off her speech, which was just winding up to its climax. When she spoke again, her words came a little more quickly. "In conclusion, I say this to those who are about to be crushed: you're on the wrong track. The road to total destruction is paved by resistance. You will learn this lesson now. Weaponeers, fire the broadsides!"

The view from outside the ship disappeared as the blast-shields rolled into place and clammed shut. Then, the broadsides spoke at last.

Having been aboard dreadnaughts before when they unleashed the power of their primary weapons, I knew to brace myself.

The deck bucked up with the tremendous release of energy. Plenty of my fellow troops either hadn't known what to expect, or they'd forgotten. People were knocked to their knees or even onto their faces. The ship's stabilizers fought to keep the vessel on an even keel and after shuddering with sickening after-shocks, the automated systems seemed to manage the task.

But the shivering didn't subside completely. The ship was still rolling a little, quivering. It was as if we were releasing smaller projectiles, or...

"Those green pods," Carlos said, climbing back to his feet. "They're hitting us—right now! Landing on the hull!"

He was right. He had to be.

"Visors down," I roared to my confused troops as they picked themselves up off the deck. "Weapons locked and loaded!"

"Listen up," Graves said in my helmet. He'd engaged the unit-wide channel so I didn't have to relay his instructions: "We've been hit by unknown objects. They're sticking to the hull. We don't know anything more, but in case this is a boarding attempt, we're to report to the rim outside Blue Deck."

The "rim" was a region between two heavy hulls. The inner hull of the ship had an empty pocket between it and the outer skin. I hadn't spent much time in that region of the ship, except for a few training drills, but I was game for something new today.

"Stay together, squad," I ordered. "Follow me!"

Rifles in our hands, we clanked for the exit. On the big forward screen, I caught a final glimpse of Galina Turov. She looked pissed off—and maybe, just maybe, a tiny bit scared. Her haughty pronouncement of doom had been transformed into a battle by an enemy who appeared to be more cunning than she'd thought.

I wasn't any happier about that than she was. As I trotted through passages full of yellow flashers and blaring alarms, I couldn't help but wonder how this was going to go down. After all, it seemed to me that this enemy, whoever they were, had been at least one jump ahead of us every step of the way.

They'd shown up in our skies back on Earth, stolen part of a vital cargo from an Earth freighter, and managed to send the freighter crashing down into the middle of two assembled legions. Today, what had appeared to be a desperate attempt to escape our fleet had instead transformed into a trap to ensnare us.

The knowledge that our broadsides had already fired on them gave me some solace, however. The enemy may have miscalculated on that score. Those shells were arcing toward their base, and as far as I knew, they were unstoppable.

"That had to be the dumbest thing I've ever seen Turov do," Carlos said inside my headset on a private channel, "and I've seen them all."

I didn't really have time to talk to Carlos, but he had me curious with that statement. "What do you mean, Specialist?"

Carlos was my squad's resident medic on this mission. A bio specialist of the lowest grade, he'd been assigned to our combat unit to patch us up. On the surface of things, that sounded logical enough. He had good fighting skills, and I was pretty sure they'd tested him and determined that he would suck at any other function a bio normally performed. I couldn't easily imagine him running the revival machines, performing surgery, or even providing long-term care for the moderately wounded.

Because of this, embedding him in a combat unit as a medic seemed to be a no-brainer, but I had my reservations. I didn't relish being patched up by my old friend, despite his new stripes and training.

All that said, I still wanted to know what he was thinking about Turov.

"I mean that she broadcast some long speech at the aliens instead of just firing on them," he explained. "That was a mistake. Maybe they didn't even know we were hostile. Maybe they weren't sure where we were in space. We probably had the element of surprise going in, but *noooo*, she had to go and make a speech and blow all that."

81

"You might be right," I admitted, "but what's done is done. We have orders. Let's follow them."

I cut off his channel and opened my squad chat. "All right, listen up. I want everyone looking sharp when we come through this hatch into the rim. Remember that there's no pressure in there. Not much in the way of gravity, either. Turn on your magnetics and keep buttoned up. Look around for anything like a breach, and sound off if you see anything."

We reached the hatch, and I opened it after taking a breath. A whoosh of escaping gas rushed past me like a small storm. There was an airlock, but it wasn't an efficient one with pumps and pressure-equalizers. All it did was limit the amount of air it farted out when you opened the side that led into vacuum.

We rushed into the airlock and sealed the hatch behind us. The whole squad fit—just barely. Harris' squad was next in line to go through, and they watched us with grim expressions and tight grips on their weapons. We swung the second, massive hatch open which released a gush of air into the rim between the hulls.

In between the two hulls were the ribs of the ship. These titanium bones ran beyond the limits of our sight, above and below us. Each rib wrapped around the belly of the ship. They were huge, imposing, and curved with the ship's contours.

"Tactics, vet?" Sargon asked me. "With my belcher, I mean?"

"Use your weapon as you see fit, weaponeer," I said. "This area is kind of tight—only about ten meters between the hulls with lots of structural girders and the like. We'll be on patrol, but you never know when you'll run into a surprise."

I saw him cranking his weapon aperture to a medium setting. I approved. It's what I would have done. Widening the muzzle a bit turned his weapon into a shotgun rather than a rifle, but without making it as broad and uncontrollable as a fire hose. I'd spent years as a weaponeer myself, and when I didn't know what I was going to be aiming at in a tight space, I broadened the scope so I would at least make sure I didn't miss.

Off toward the stern was another knot of troops. My HUD told me it was the third squad from my platoon. Adjunct

Leeson had seen fit to fight with them instead of with me, and that was just fine in my book. Sometimes, an officer in your midst on a patrol mission could be more of a hindrance than a help.

We moved as a squad to the location that Graves had pinpointed on my tactical display. The position was depicted both inside my helmet and on my tapper. When we reached our post, we dispersed taking what cover we could, and latched our clamps and cords onto the girders. Then, we waited.

The waiting was far from peaceful. The ship often vented gases into the rim—blasts of unknown origin that equalized pressure from inside the ship into this no-man's land in-between the hulls. The ship also lurched and wallowed at random intervals. I knew the pilots were trying to maneuver and avoid danger. I could only hope they were being successful.

"Unit," Graves said several long minutes later. "We've got word from Gold Deck: we're to expect boarders. Repeat, the hull is being breached in a dozen spots. At first, they clustered their attempts to penetrate near the jacket that encircles the engine core. That was too thick for them, apparently, and they've shifted tactics. They're now attempting entry all over the outer hull looking for the thin spots. It won't be hard for them to find a weak point."

A single question was burning in my mind, and I took this opportunity to ask it. "How are they getting in, sir? How can they drill through even a single meter of titanium that fast?"

"They aren't drilling," he said. "The word is they're using concentrated acid. The shielding around the core was dense and full of lead. But the rest of the skin is relatively thin. The acid is eating holes in *Minotaur* like a hot flame applied to wax."

Acid? I gave my head a shake. The enemy had an acid that ate metal like nothing? How had they gotten it up here in sufficient quantities? And what were those shiny green egg-things, anyway? Pods full of acid?

There weren't any answers forthcoming, but we were about to have company. Even as I cradled my rifle and tried to look everywhere at once, Kivi shouted behind me. I craned my neck and levered myself around to see where she was pointing.

83

"There it is!" I shouted. "We've got a breach! Centurion Graves, we've got a breach. I see liquid running inside the hull near my position. It looks like the titanium is dissolving into bubbling, smoking mercury."

"Keep your head straight, McGill," Graves replied. "We've got reported breaches in a half-dozen spots. Hold your position and repel the enemy. Graves out."

-11-

All our questions about what we were facing answered themselves over the next few minutes.

Because the ship rotated to provide simulated gravity through centrifugal force, we were standing on the inside of the outer hull. Melting metal bubbled up under our feet. The enemy burned their way into the ship as we watched, and we soon learned it was best to stand well-clear of any breach we spotted.

When the acid came through, it produced a vapor that looked poisonous. I was glad I had my visor clamped down. If the zone had been fully pressurized and my visor open, the gas might have killed me. It spread quickly due to the low pressure inside the rim, and soon formed a fog that filled the entirety of my visual range.

"If a spot starts to bubble under your feet, get out of the way," I needlessly instructed my squad. They were already climbing the girders and hanging there like nervous monkeys in trees.

There were two regions bubbling before the first one burst and showered droplets of molten metal everywhere. A few of my troops were in the splash zone.

Curses erupted immediately. Sargon, unfortunately, was one of the troops showered with droplets.

"I caught a few, vet," he reported. "Bad luck, I guess."

"Bad luck," I agreed, eyeing him. His kit was smoking. We were wearing armor that was pretty thick—but not as thick as the ship's hull. How long could he hold out before it ate through to his flesh?"

"Sargon, I want you to retreat to the airlock," I said. "Get out of that armor and get a new suit issued by the techs."

"Vet—I'm good, really," he said. "I think the effect is dissipating. This armor is layered with polymers, not just metal. Maybe the acid can't—"

That was as far as he got before the patch of the hull that had turned into a stewing, smoking mess popped completely open. We were well back from it by then, and no one was hit by the splash this time. But that didn't mean we weren't in danger.

A dark, greenish shape wriggled through the liquid metal. It was smoking and probably hissing, but we couldn't hear that through our thick helmets in the near-vacuum.

The shape loomed up until it was taller than a man, and just for a second, I thought I saw something that resembled a misshapen head. Beads of metal ran from it like thick sweat.

A gush of energy was released by our side a fraction of a second later. Sargon had fried it—whatever it was. Fortunately, although these things were able to melt metal and wriggle through a bubbling mass of acid, a bolt of plasma burned them just fine.

The thing shuddered and thrashed, but Sargon kept the trigger down on his belcher for a full second. Converted largely to ash, the invader slumped and stopped moving.

"Holy shit!" Carlos exclaimed. "What the hell was that thing?"

"There's another one!" Kivi shouted. Sargon swung his belcher around, but it had yet to recycle and dissipate the heat-buildup after such a long burn.

We all unloaded our rifles on the second invader. Our new morph-rifles were more powerful than those of light infantry. We'd configured them into their assault-weapon form, increasing their rate of fire. At this range, any loss of accuracy didn't matter much.

We hammered the second monster with accelerated explosive shells. Again, it demonstrated tremendous vitality by not dying right off. We must have put two hundred pellets into the thing, blasting it apart, before it stopped struggling.

Approaching cautiously, Carlos poked at the mess with his rifle butt.

"Strangest damned critter I ever saw," I said, keeping my distance in case it wasn't quite dead.

Carlos squatted next to it. "I just took xenobiology—and this thing is weird," he announced. "This isn't a normal creature of meat and bone. It could be some kind of construct. See these strands? They're cellulose, I'm sure of that much."

I was impressed not only by Carlos' newfound knowledge, but also his newfound balls. He'd walked right up to a dangerous monstrosity and poked at it.

Examining the fibrous stuff he was talking about, I nodded.

"Looks like corn silk," I said. "Burnt corn silk... What kind of an alien is stuffed with that?"

We didn't have any answers so I reported in that we'd encountered two aliens and killed them before they could fully enter the ship.

"Good work," Graves said. "But we have a problem. Not all the units were as successful as we were at repelling the boarders. Some have gotten through the secondary hull and are loose inside the ship. We're being recalled from this zone. I want all three platoons to withdraw back to the hatchways. Retreat by squads, and prepare to enter Blue Deck itself. We're to search-and-destroy any invaders you find there."

"Are the bio people under attack, sir?" Leeson asked on our shared unit channel.

"That's right. The enemy got through somehow. There are reported fatalities on Blue Deck. Our revival machines might be their target. This unit is to join the rest of our cohort and defend the revival machines at any cost. Graves out."

After relaying our new instructions and hustling back to the airlock, we piled inside. Everyone was grim-faced, and I could see sweat on their cheeks through their visors.

Facing an unknown enemy in space is difficult. The freaky possibilities work on a man's mind. The stars have produced countless variations of life, and a legionnaire never knew what form his next murderer might take.

While the two hatches clanged and gasses hissed past us in a gush, I had to wonder which squad had failed to hold the line in the rim zone. Had they been overwhelmed or just unlucky? I was glad it wasn't my team. So far, we hadn't suffered a single casualty.

But beneath those thoughts lurked a new worry. The enemy seemed to know what they were doing. They'd tried to get into the engine core first and failed. Now, they were going for Blue Deck. Could they be aware of the strategic value of our revival machines?

If they got through and destroyed our equipment on Blue Deck, every death afterward would be a permanent one until we returned to Earth—*if* we returned at all. That thought alone was enough to make any legionnaire sweat.

The bio people had always been paranoid about their technology. They were like jealous lovers who'd been cheated on a dozen times. They hid their secrets from everyone—even other members of their own legions.

Accordingly, Blue Deck was a fortress. This region of the ship was all on one horizontal level, but it was more complex than that. It was built in concentric rings, each layer protected by thick walls and hatches that could keep an army at bay.

When we got to the sealed inner region of Blue Deck proper, we were in for a shock. By that time, our entire unit had hooked up into a single force. We jogged down the passages to the main entrance, running in armor that clattered and boots that rang on the deck plates.

The passages were wide here, ten meters across or more. But the hatchways that led into Blue Deck's inner regions were even more imposing. They were huge, round portals with massive metal hinges and gears that looked like they belonged on a bank vault.

The shock came when we reached the portal itself and saw it had been badly damaged. Sagging down and lying partially on the deck, I thought at first its hinges had been ripped loose by some kind of terrific force—possibly an explosion. But then I saw the hinges themselves and realized that the enemy had made good use of their excreted acids. They'd melted the hinges away and left the hatch lying askew. A pall of gray vapor writhed in the area, and I knew right off I didn't want to get a lungful of that.

"Squad, double-check your visors," I ordered.

"Good idea, McGill," Graves said. "Unit, halt! Secure visors! Harris, take your squad forward and secure that hatchway. Approach with caution."

Harris gave Graves a single sour glance. His lips were twisted up in an expression of resigned disgust. He wasn't a man that liked to go into chambers full of unknown aliens—or at least he didn't like to be the first in line.

Despite his obvious opinion of his orders, he moved his people up gamely enough. Leapfrogging through the hatchway, each trooper took a defensive firing position and waved forward the man behind him. They were inside in seconds, sweeping the area.

"The immediate entrance area is clear, sir," Harris reported back.

"Press on," Graves said. "Leeson, get the rest of your platoon in there to back him up."

Veteran Johnson and I were sent in next. Right about as I stepped over that smoking molten metal and onto Blue Deck proper, I began wishing I hadn't lost my dragon back on Earth. I'd have much preferred marching through this hatchway inside an armored vehicle with heavy weaponry.

Once inside, Harris broke left, I broke right, and Johnson took his squad directly up the middle toward the next hatchway which led deeper into Blue Deck. Leeson went with Johnson while Graves and the other two platoons hung back at the original hatch.

Graves was playing it safe this time, I noted. Not just safe with his own skin—he'd never cared much about dying—but careful with the lives of his troops in general. I had to figure his caution was due to the fact the revival machines might be out of the game. Each loss could now be a permanent one, and he didn't want to lose more people because he'd rushed us into a trap.

At first, we found nothing but corpses. Bio people lay on the decks in contorted positions. They were orderlies and specialists, mostly. They were in various states of death all along the gently curving inner passages.

"Looks like they put up a good fight," I said.

"Veteran McGill?" Kivi called. "Come look at this."

I trotted to her position, and she showed me a smoking trail gouged in the deck.

"Looks like one of the invaders was wounded and dragged its acid-leaking body this way," I said. "Ready for action, people! Pop that door open—it's got to be hiding inside that storage compartment."

Kivi was the closest, and she didn't shirk her duty. She stepped up and shouldered the damaged door open.

A pall of vapor swirled out into her face. In the middle of that smoky wreath, an appendage of some kind stretched after her.

"Shit!" she shouted, backpedalling.

Now, I'm not a squeamish man, but this reaching limb made my hair stand on end. The alien appendage looked like a brownish-gray claw with hard black nodules all over it. But that wasn't the strangest part. What really got me was how *long* it was. That limb had to be longer than any man's arm I'd ever seen. It just kept reaching and reaching, as if it was telescoping somehow after Kivi.

She backed over a dead body and went sprawling. Sitting on her butt, she got her rifle up and sprayed fire at the approaching horror. The monstrous limb terminated in a spray of seven grasping fingers, each of which were as thick as Winslade's wrist.

Orange fire burst from the muzzle of her gun, and she was joined by several other troops who were close enough to help.

The monster shuddered but didn't stop coming. Pieces of it flew off, snapping and splintering. The flesh was white inside, kind of like wood, but there was too much liquid flowing out for it to be *real* wood. Slippery thick fluid splattered all over Kivi and the other soldiers who'd rushed near.

"Use your force-blades!" I shouted. "Bullets are just pissing it off!"

The truth was worse than that. Kivi's armor was already smoking. Her visor was pitted and gray—it had been splashed with acid.

Still, she and the others managed to get their blades turned on, and they slashed off the grasping alien limb. It fell onto the deck and dripped and smoked—but it didn't squirm around. It was dead once disconnected from the rest of the monster.

I realized at that moment what this thing was: my first honest-to-God monster. I'd seen more than my share of aliens, but these things—they were different. They weren't *right*. There was no earthly equivalent that I could compare them to.

We tore the monster apart, blasting it with bullets and hacking off its limbs. I ordered Sargon to hold back with his heavy weapon. There wasn't room for a safe, direct blast. I could only imagine what would happen if this thing unloaded all its acid at once in our direction.

At the last moment, before it died, it surged toward us. Dragging itself out of the doorway into the passage with a wild heave of its limbs, it made a clacking sound and threw itself into our midst.

Kivi was its goal. I could see that right off. She tried to get away, and I felt a pang. I shouldn't have let her sit there and fire at the thing that had attacked her. I should have had someone pull her to her feet and drag her out.

Grimly determined, the monster hugged her and sort of squatted over her. Prongs of some kind stabbed and scrabbled on her armor while she struggled and cried out.

We all laid into it then. After about twenty seconds of blasting and beating on the thing, we took it down at last.

It was a good effort, but we were too late to save Kivi. She lay on her back, coughing and writhing. Her faceplate was cracked and fogged up. Her armor looked like it had been run over by a truck.

"Are you burning?" I asked her, kneeling beside her.

"Some," she said, her voice choking. "It's the smoke—I can't breathe. The acid penetrated my faceplate."

"Drag her out of here!" I ordered. Carlos and Sargon did the honors, taking her back to Graves in the main hallway.

We swept the rest of the passageway and declared it clear. Carlos reported back to me after that—and the news wasn't good.

"The vapor killed Kivi, as far as I can tell," he said. "The smoke was poisonous."

I nodded grimly, and we pressed ahead. The other squads had had similar experiences. It seemed like the aliens preferred to leave their kind behind when injured. The wounded monsters holed up and lay in wait for humans to wander by. Was that part of their tactics? Did these things even have natural behavior? I had no idea.

Each time we met up with resistance, it was a single alien. They fought to the death with relentless fury, using whatever they had left in them to do as much damage to us as they could.

Still, we cleared our zone over a ten minute period. Other units were doing the same all over Blue Deck.

Then, finally, Graves brought the rest of the unit in to support our platoon. As Leeson and Johnson hadn't had much contact with the enemy, and no casualties, he ordered them to take the lead and press on toward the second hatch.

That's where we found a full nest of creatures waiting for us.

-12-

Johnson's squad was ambushed and mauled just moments after rushing past the acid-burned hatch.

This time, we didn't encounter a lone, wounded monster left for the humans to find and exterminate. There were at least a dozen of them. The enemy was waiting on each side of the entrance in hungry groups.

Johnson's weaponeer got off a burning shot, but the man had cranked his belcher for a wide-angle cone of fire. It simply wasn't effective. To kill these aliens with a belcher took a focused, hard-hitting beam set for a full-second burn. I guess Johnson hadn't gotten the memo on that one.

The weaponeer managed to singe several of the enemy, but all that did was send them into a rattling frenzy. The aliens were left with cooked skin, but they were far from dead.

Surrounding Johnson's squad, their long, smoking arms reached out and plucked away rifles, arms and even heads. Acid streams squirted next, hosing down the clumped troops.

The purposeful spraying of acid—that was a new one. Up until now, we'd faced only wounded, weakened creatures. They'd only splashed us with acid when they were torn up. That's when the acid leaked out like splattered blood. But apparently, when these monsters were intact, they possessed the power to eject their foul caustic liquids with accuracy and at will.

The fight was over within thirty seconds. Johnson's squad had advanced through the hatch, and most of them died horribly. Harris and I watched, unable to help since we couldn't fire down the passageway into the open hatch without hitting our own troops in the back. If we rushed in, we'd be so crowded in the cramped space we'd join the victims.

What was left of Johnson's squad fell back, with Leeson and a few others making it back to our line. Leeson had been embedded with Johnson, and he'd gone in with the squad and made it back out.

With one eye burned away, Leeson was dying in my arms. Like the others from his ill-fated group, his armor was riddled with smoldering holes, the flesh bubbling beneath. He tried to tell me something, but I couldn't make out the words.

I looked at Harris, who was making a gesture behind Leeson's back. A throat-slitting gesture. I got it then.

Leeson was asking me to kill him.

I took out my sidearm and put the muzzle into his faceplate. Leeson looked grateful—but then he passed out and slumped. Carlos checked his vitals immediately.

"You can put that away, McGill. He's gone."

I holstered my weapon, feeling a degree of relief. I'd put down men in agony before, or those who were in danger of being captured. I'd never enjoyed it.

"2nd Squad, advance!" Graves said from behind me. The centurion's voice was even and seemed unconcerned.

Harris was in charge of 2nd Squad. He didn't look happy. Not at all. "Sir?" he asked. "Shouldn't our platoon get a break? We just lost our adjunct, and a whole damned squad with him. After all—"

"Harris," Graves interrupted. "You're in command of your platoon now. We've been proceeding with caution up until, but our orders have changed. We've been directed to get to the revival machines within the next five minutes and report. Your squad has the most experience with this enemy at this point. You're going to get in there and clean them out for me."

"Well sir," Harris said angrily, "if this is so important, might I suggest Winslade bring his skinny ass down here and personally help out?"

94

Everyone looked at Harris, but they didn't say anything. This was an unusual display for him. He rarely back-talked Graves or otherwise bucked the chain of command publicly.

Even Graves seemed a little surprised. The centurion stepped forward and eyed Harris coldly.

"Chicken?" Graves asked.

"No sir, not at all. I don't mind dying. I've done it more times than I can count."

"Sure," Graves said. "When you know you'll come back, you're all balls... All right Harris, fine."

His eyes scanned the rest of us in the vicinity. "McGill? Show Harris how it's done."

"Yes, Centurion," I said with a heavy heart.

Graves nodded approvingly, looking me over. He pointed to the smoking mess of burnt bodies and alien matter that had slimed-up the entrance to the center of Blue Deck.

"Penetrate that enemy position and defeat them in detail, McGill," Graves ordered me. "Harris, consider yourself under McGill's command for the duration of this action. Go!"

Harris' mouth twisted up like he smelled a dead skunk. Graves knew what he was doing. He'd put me in charge of Harris to shame him.

But it was more than that. Harris was my senior, and he'd long had a problem with my rapid rise in the legion. In my opinion, that was due to a mixture of envy and outrage. As he'd often pointed out, I was likely to go off-script. Only in a legion like Varus, which respected results above all else, could I have gotten away with so much.

Slapping a fresh magazine into my rifle, I waved my squad forward. As I did so, I gave my head a little shake. I had to get my brain into this game if I was going to survive the next few minutes.

Thinking fast, I put up my fist before we reached the mess at the hatchway. Two squads behind me halted. I couldn't charge in and repeat Johnson's mistakes. I went down on one knee, and my people huddled up.

"Okay," I said. "We don't want to repeat Johnson's mistakes. He rushed in there and got himself ambushed. We have to lure them out to us."

"How the hell are we going to do that?" Harris snapped.

I didn't look at him. I focused on Della instead.

"You're fast on your feet," I told her.

She studied me with big eyes. She didn't even nod in recognition of the compliment—it was true, she was fast and agile, but she didn't want to admit it. I figured she already had some idea where I was going with this.

"Trot up there with a grav-plasma grenade," I told her. "Toss it in, and run back before they can grab you. Then race back to our lines. Your mission is to piss them off enough to chase you. When they come out, we'll blast them."

Della licked her lips once. "Is this because of the mud-pit?" she asked me.

"No, girl! You're honestly the slipperiest trooper in the unit. Don't worry, you'll make it."

Harris, Carlos and the rest of us watched her pop out a grenade, roll it between her fingers, and then nod. She ran off like a gazelle after that. She was in heavy armor, same as the rest of us, but she moved like she was in gym-class.

"She's powered up her exoskeleton to full," Carlos said. "She must have. No weapons output, no shielding, but plenty of speed."

I nodded appreciatively. "Yeah, that sounds right."

"That's crazy," Harris said, frowning. "If they catch her, they'll burn her fast."

I knew it was true, but I figured Della could play it her own way. She was the one doing the dying, after all.

Kneeling, I took careful aim. All around me, a dozen others took up firing positions, altering their weapons into rifle-mode. We aimed at the hatchway, which was still wreathed in a haze but not hidden behind roiling coils of smoke as it had been earlier.

"Crazy," muttered Harris again, watching Della with me.

"It's her death, and her call," I said to Harris.

He frowned fiercely at me but didn't say anything else. Among legionnaires, it was a generally accepted premise that if a trooper took a suicidal assignment, they should be allowed to die in their own damned way. That's because we'd all died multiple times, and we felt a soldier had a right to make certain decisions when the end was near. This unofficial rule was part of our legion culture, I guess you could say, like allowing a condemned man a last meal, or giving him a choice between a firing squad and hanging. It was ingrained in us, part of our code of honor.

Della reached the hatch and crept up to it from the left side. She was slinking low, almost on her knees. In her hand was a live grenade.

"I said five minutes, McGill," Graves buzzed in my helmet. "Not five hours. You've already blown about three minutes screwing around."

"Taking action now, sir," I reported back.

Della didn't just toss in her grenade. She sprang through the hatch into the dark interior. I cursed under my breath and aimed just over her head, hoping to catch the reaching arm of any alien that tried to scoop her up.

A blue-white light flickered.

"She tossed in the grenade," Harris said. "Ready-up, boys. If she's got one on her tail, we'd best blast them both down together."

I tensed, wanting to order him to give her a chance—but I didn't. A quick death for Della might well be a blessing under the circumstances.

For about two seconds, nothing else happened. The grenade was on a timed burn and was gathering power for a single convulsive implosion. Grav-plasma grenades drew in everything around them then spat that material back out as shrapnel. Even water could be used as a weapon.

In the last second, Della sprang back out of the hatch and sprinted to the left. One bizarrely long arm lunged after her, then another.

The grenade went off, releasing a shockwave and a shower of alien blood and body parts. The debris had been weaponized, and although I doubted it could kill the aliens, I had no doubt they felt it.

Flailing and scrabbling, the arms moved with greater speed if less purpose. After a moment of confusion, during which Della sprinted back toward us, they got moving. Sure enough, they surged through the hatch chasing after her.

"Fire!" I roared, and we all opened up. One rank of troops was down on their bellies in front of me. The second rank stood above, firing over the heads of the first rank. That way, along with our weaponeers, we had an impressive amount of destruction flying downrange into the enemy charge.

Della threw herself onto the deck and crawled. She was as fearful of being caught by a stray round as she was being snagged by an alien claw.

The aliens had really taken the bait. They charged us in a single mass. We blazed at them with everything we had in return.

Up until now, most of the fighting had been pretty one-way. The enemy had possessed all the advantages and delivered all the surprises.

This time was different. We tore them apart. They never made it across the thirty meters or so that separated our position from theirs. When it was all over, eleven alien corpses lay shredded and oozing on the deck.

Della reached our line, panting but alive. She had burning acid-spots on her boots and leggings, but she was safe.

I stood up and strode forward. Sargon was on my right and Carlos on my left. We advanced into the hatchway, but found nothing there that still lived—alien or human.

"Hatchway secured, Centurion!" I announced to Graves.

"Well done, McGill. Your platoon is relieved. Adjunct Toro, take point. Column, advance!"

Harris wouldn't meet my eye. After Toro's fighters moved up, Harris marched after me, marshaling his own troops with his usual butt-kicking flare. Was he a little harsher on his squad than usual? I don't know—with him, it was hard to tell.

Della came up to me after we'd passed into the inner region of Blue Deck, and we began taking stock of things. It was pretty much a mess in there. The bio people were present and accounted for—at least their dead bodies were. We met no further resistance.

"Why'd you send me in?" Della asked when we had a second to relax.

"I told you. You're the fastest. You've got the moves, girl."

She looked at me intently. "You've barely spoken to me since we left Earth," she said. "You're blaming me for the death of your family, aren't you? That's unfair, James."

My head cocked to one side, and I frowned at her in honest confusion. "I what? No—that's not it at all. I don't blame you. I blame the bastard raiders who live on this planet. They killed my folks, not you."

"I've been reading psychology books since I came to Earth," Della said. "I wanted to have a better understanding of our cultural differences. I believe you're exhibiting a classic example of displacement."

I almost laughed, but I knew that rarely went over well with upset women. "Displacement? Hardly—I place all blame squarely on the enemy. That's it, case closed. Listen, Della, I don't know much about psychology except that it's mostly horseshit. Don't get all caught up in that stuff."

"I accept that you believe your statements to be true," she said. "But that doesn't mean that they are."

So saying, she walked away.

Left wishing I could scratch my head through my helmet, I stared after her. In my opinion, she was making things more complicated than they had to be.

I'd been avoiding her a bit, sure. But that wasn't because I was mad at her. I was a man whose attentions tended to wander. That was the plain truth—but lots of people seemed to have trouble with that fact and liked to make it complicated.

-13-

In the very heart of Blue Deck existed the protected guts of our medical technology: The revival chambers.

Inside each room was a single machine. Serviced by a gaggle of lab coat-wearing professionals, these machines were the most valuable resources our legion possessed.

The revival units themselves were...well...strange. They were part electronic, part biological, and part something else I couldn't hope to understand. These machines had the power to grow a biological entity within their guts like intelligent wombs that could control their output consciously.

The priesthood of bio people existed primarily to service the machines—to charge them with protoplasm, bone meal and power. In a modern human legion, we didn't really heal the sick and mend the injured. We recycled them and rebuilt them from scratch. It was easier that way.

The machines could reproduce a person by turning raw biological materials into a living being. After a period of time that varied somewhat—always more than ten minutes but never more than a half an hour—the machines could churn out a new human being that was a clone of a previously killed soldier.

There were two astounding tricks to this technology as I understood it. One was their ability to restore our minds as well as our bodies to their original state.

They did this by reading stored data. When I'd first joined the legions, that data had been stored on a tiny silver disk like a coin. But now, it was constantly updated on my tapper. Embedded in our bodies, tappers continuously recorded our mental engrams and the state of our synapses and neurons.

What was a tapper, after all, other than a built-in, semi-biological computer? Just like any mobile computer, tappers had a relatively small storage capacity—only enough to store a few quintillion bytes of data. That was enough, however, to record changes in our neural network rather than the entire thing. They monitored our brains for tiny alterations. Combined with the originally stored engrams in the mainframes, the revival machines could be used to rebuild our memories and personalities.

As if all that wasn't enough, the second amazing capacity of the revival systems was the speed with which they operated. Hell, a human woman took nine months just to grow a baby, and the average infant only weighed a few kilos. How could these machines work so fast?

According to the speculation of our best science people, these wondrous alien devices could accelerate time within their confines and thus gestate a full human in an unbelievably short period.

With these combined powers, it was easy to see why they were so valuable. Imported from the Core Systems and paid for with hard-earned Galactic credits, there were few devices I was aware of that cost more. Only starships, like *Minotaur* herself, were more expensive.

With the critical goal of securing the revival machines firmly in mind, we penetrated the innermost layers of Blue Deck. Each meter of deck we stepped over in the core chambers was packed with death. All the bio people we found were dead. Some of the revival machines were damaged too, but apparently the aliens hadn't found them threatening enough to destroy. I was glad for that.

When we broke through to the innermost chambers, I found Anne Grant personally. She was a bio who I'd had an affair with on my last campaign. She was slumped over her revival unit, trying to protect it with her body as a woman might defend a helpless child.

Her back was a patchwork of burn-holes. Acids had penetrated her smart-cloth uniform and sizzled into her flesh. Her fair skin was still smoking in places.

"Dammit," I said, prying her clutching fingers from the maw of the revival machine and placing her gently on the floor. As I closed her eyes with my fingers, someone eagerly clanked past me to inspect the machine.

"I think this one is okay," Carlos said, tapping at the console.

The revival machines were semi-biological, as I said, but they had an electronic data interface grafted on, so humans could work with them.

Carlos breathed hard as he checked the diagnostic data.

"I've got yellow bars on the fluid levels," he said. "We'll have to fix that. And the free-floating nucleotides are all bound up. We'll have to dump this batch and do a full reset—but Vet, I think we're in business."

I glanced up at him. I was still kneeling over Anne.

"Don't worry about her, man," he said. "Didn't you hear me? She's coming back. I'll bring her back first, if that's what you want."

Heaving a sigh, I shook my head. "Let her rest for a bit. She had a bad death, I can tell. Get some other bio out to run this contraption."

"You've got it. You feel like helping me?"

"No," I said, and I strode out of the chamber.

I'd personally operated the revival machines in the past, when I'd had to, but I wasn't like bio people. They practically worshiped these alien contrivances. I didn't even *like* them. They were disgusting and, if the truth be told, a little frightening. I'd always eyed them the way soldiers had eyed a surgeon's tools throughout time. Bone-saws and sharp scoops designed to remove flesh purposefully—these things were instruments of the Devil in my opinion. And the revival machines were the worst of the lot.

That said, the alien machines had also come to mean life itself to every legionnaire. We guarded them more closely than we guarded our own lives because they effectively made us immortal.

I left Carlos behind because I knew what he was going to do. The dead would be used to reprocess into the living. We recycled our own corpses to form fresh ones in the guts of our wondrous, horrific machines. Like I said, they were disgusting…and a little creepy.

I didn't want to watch Carlos feed my former girlfriend into the blades to regrow her again. I'd seen enough of that kind of thing. Compared to the work of the bio people, our combat missions were nice and clean. All we did was kill people—we didn't grind them up and process them like raw sausage.

Graves caught up with me outside the chamber. He had a glimmer of a smile on his face. That was a rare thing for him.

"McGill," he said, "you did a good job back there at the hatch. I knew you could take out that nest of aliens."

"Thank you, Centurion."

"I just reported in to Winslade. We're the first unit to make it this far in, but more support from the cohort is on the way. The other cohorts are patrolling the rim, the engine room and Gold Deck. There were numerous breaches, but none so critical as ours. Winslade is very happy."

I thought about that and nodded. I knew what Winslade was probably doing right now. If I had to guess, I'd say he was on the net chatting with Turov, taking personal credit for our hard-fought victory.

Graves watched me and chuckled. I could tell he knew what I was thinking.

"You're thinking about Winslade, aren't you?"

"Yes sir," I admitted.

"It's almost sad to watch you grow up, boy," he said. "You're not the wide-eyed country bumpkin you used to be."

"This can't just be a social call," I said, eying him back. "Your orders, sir?"

"You're right again, McGill. I'm here to ask for a little more of your magic. I want you to cheat."

Blinking, I shook my head. "How's that, sir?"

"Bump my troops up in the revival queues. We took this deck back solo, and we saved Winslade's and Turov's bacon whether they want to admit it or not. I say our people should breathe again first. To hell with the automated queues and priority systems."

I nodded. "I'll try, sir."

"Just do it. I know you've hacked the machines before—among other things."

He left me then, and I stared after him. Just how much did he know about my unsanctioned editing of official equipment?

Shrugging, I walked into each of the revival chambers one at a time and fiddled with the controls. Carlos and the other bio people that were filtering in from other units squawked at me, but I ignored them. I had orders from Centurion Graves, and I informed them they could take up the matter with him.

They grumbled, but no one went out to find Graves and complain. They knew better than to try.

-14-

Several hours later I sat in a lifter, riding down toward the planet. The final stages of our approach to the target world had gone smoothly. There'd been no further attacks from space—but few of us thought this battle was over.

We watched as the shells reached the target world long before our invasion forces did. Turov made sure to funnel the video of the strike to everyone's tapper. I had to admit, it was a morale-booster.

The combined explosions of a full broadside were always a shocking spectacle. Each warhead packed a multi-megaton wallop. At first, all you saw was a brilliant flash of light, as if a new sun had somehow ignited itself on the surface of the planet. Then the light kept growing in pulsing waves as more warheads detonated. Finally, the light dimmed and turned orange while shockwaves spread like brilliant raindrops splattering into a puddle. Then, even the shockwaves vanished, consumed in a looming cloud. To me, the cloud didn't look like a mushroom. It looked more like a bulbous gray growth from out in space.

"The broadsides have done their work," Turov announced confidently. She'd begun broadcasting again after the invaders were pressed back, and we'd buckled up for the final approach.

Sitting in a lifter and craning my neck back to see the imperator displayed on the ceiling, I marveled at the woman's gall. The alien boarding effort had almost been successful, but she made it sound like a glorious victory.

"The identified base on the enemy world has been obliterated," she said with pride in her voice. "They attempted to board but were repelled with contemptuous ease. The attack was an utter failure. By the time Winslade's cohort reaches the ground, we will have revived every lost soldier."

Carlos rapped on my breastplate with his gauntlet. "Hey look," he said, "the new guy puked."

I glanced down, and I saw it was true.

"Lau? Pull it together, trooper," I chided.

Lau looked sheepish and nodded. I frowned back at him. Last year on Machine World, he'd been in a light unit. Maybe they'd promoted him to the rank of regular and put him in my heavy unit too early.

"Too bad they didn't project Turov's face down on the deck," Carlos remarked. "Lau's puke would have nailed her."

I had to chuckle at that. Carlos was often irritating, but every once in a while he was funny too. It almost made it worth having him around.

"All of you shut up and listen to Imperator Turov," I ordered my squad without conviction.

Dutifully, they all gazed back up at the ceiling again, where the imperator was still droning on.

"We'll take what's left of this planet for the Empire," she said. "The result is inevitable. To help speed the effort, our techs have made a full study of these aliens. It has been determined that the invaders were a form of biological construct. They aren't very intelligent, but they're still dangerous when they get in close. My advice to the infantry is to keep them at range. Such creatures will not stand a chance against a large formation of our troops employing focused fire."

I had to admit, she had a point there. It was one thing to get surprised by a grabby alien in a storage closet. But when you put armies up against one another in the open—well, ranged weaponry always won out because you could put all your fire onto a single point and break an enemy before he could get close.

106

"The results of the upcoming conflict are a forgone conclusion," Turov continued. "We don't know who made these plant-creatures and sent them at us, but it doesn't really matter. In the end, they will fall to our legions. After that, things will get even worse for them. They'll be utterly destroyed by the Imperial fleets that will follow. Our part will be done by then. We'll have added another conquest to the Empire's infinitely long list of victories. These creatures may not yet understand why we're here or how futile their efforts to resist us truly are, but they will learn! The Empire will not be denied. Justice must…"

She went on like that for a long time. I fuzzed out pretty quickly, as I always did when someone made a speech.

When the lifter lurched and began to shake a few minutes later, indicating we'd touched the top of the troposphere, I was relieved. Surely, Turov had to stop pep-speeching us now.

"As a final gift," she was saying, "I want to leave the brave soldiers of Primus Winslade's cohort with this glorious thought—"

"Ah jeez," I whispered. The woman was still going.

But at that precise moment she stopped talking. She turned her head, frowning off-camera.

"Just a moment," she said. "There's a disturbance—what's that?"

Someone talked to her, but we couldn't see who. After a few seconds, she turned back toward the camera, sourly.

"There appears to be a little life left in the alien constructs that violated this ship's integrity earlier. Do not worry about us. Stay focused on your mission. The other half of your cohort is now being launched from orbit in pods. We're watching this two-pronged attack closely. If the lifter touches down without incident, it will be designated the best approach to a full-fledged invasion. If, on the other hand, the pods make it down and the lifter doesn't, theirs will be the preferred method of insertion into—"

She broke off, jumped a little, and glared off-camera. Carlos and I exchanged quizzical glances. What the hell was going on now? More green pods from space? We'd figured the alien invaders were wiped out.

107

"I'm sorry," Imperator Turov said, returning to her audience. "Tribune Drusus is now telling me that we have confirmed invaders in the engine section. Apparently, they've been burning their way through the thicker hull and radiation shielding since their initial attack. The shielding was so thick it took many hours to melt the hull and achieve access. They're tenacious beasts, I have to give them that. But have no concern! They will be defeated, just as they were on the prior occasion. I have no doubt—"

Again, Turov paused and looked around. The camera tilted a little then righted itself. Turov had been jostled, there was no other explanation.

For some reason, I felt a trickle of sweat in my armpits. I wasn't even on *Minotaur*, but this didn't look good.

"When they hit us before," Carlos said, "the whole ship never shook once."

"I know."

"I bet I know what's going on," Natasha said, leaning in close from my other side. She was a tech specialist I knew well, possibly the best friend I'd ever had.

"Talk to us," Carlos said.

Natasha began to explain, and I considered stopping her. Sometimes, grim news was bad for morale, but I didn't because I wanted to know the truth myself.

Natasha, being a tech and one of the best, always seemed to know what the hell was really going on before I did. Techs communicated privately, and even if she didn't get the best information from her buddies, she was good at divining the truth from observable phenomena and using her logical mind.

"The invaders might have breached the core directly," she explained. "Think about it, they've probably been melting their way down into the engine all this time—for hours. What happens next all depends on where they broke through. Some might be coming out in the engine room, causing a lot of damage, killing engineers. In that case, they could be defeated and repelled just as they were before. *But*, if they came out right inside the reactor itself..."

"What?" Carlos demanded. "What then?"

Natasha shook her head. "They could rupture the cooling jacket. They could release the heat and radiation from the core. There could be an explosion—which would disrupt the entire ship."

My eyes flicked back up to the ceiling, but Turov had vanished. The signal had gone dark.

"Hmm," I said, running my eyes over the metal roof of the deck. "Did she say anything before shutting off the transmission?"

"You weren't listening, were you?" Carlos said with a dirty laugh. "She said she would reconnect when we landed. She was going to personally oversee the defeat of this second boarding attempt."

I looked to Natasha, who nodded in confirmation.

"Unit, this is Graves," said a gravelly voice I knew too well. "We'll soon lose contact with *Minotaur*. We're in the upper atmosphere now, and we're in for some turbulence until we reach lower altitudes. When we reach the ground, I'm sure we'll hear the rest of the imperator's glorious speech."

A few dared to groan.

"Hey," I said to Natasha. "Do you have one of your bugs planted upstairs?"

She'd been watching her tapper. She looked at me and nodded. She piped her feed over to me, and Carlos craned his neck to watch.

Natasha was a bundle of technological surprises. One thing she liked to do was release a buzzer, a tiny spy-drone, into the air of any ship we were flying in. By directing it to a portal, in this case one in the upper decks which were reserved for crewmen and officers, she was able to get an external view of space.

I watched the transmission with interest. The mysterious overgrown planet loomed, filling the image with its purplish-green vegetation and fluffy white clouds. As I watched, the steamy atmosphere of the target world consumed us.

"Turn it back into space," I said, "get a shot of *Minotaur*."

Natasha worked her controls, and the camera angle shifted. By sending the buzzer crawling up the glass, she was able to get a clear image between two droplets of condensation.

"There," she said to me. "I've zoomed in as far as I can. A buzzer's cameras aren't really designed for long-distance shots."

I saw a silvery-white tube surrounded by the blackness of space.

"Is that *Minotaur*?"

"I sure hope so," she said. "If it's not, we have more company in this system than we thought."

"The ship is venting something," Carlos said. "You see that?"

Squinting, I could barely make out what he was talking about—then I saw it clearly for a moment. A plume of gas was jetting from the aft modules.

"Doesn't look like much," I commented.

Natasha chewed her lower lip and stared. "At this scale, that plume is better than a kilometer long—it's almost as long as the ship itself."

I looked at her in alarm. "That sounds pretty bad. We have to tell Graves."

"What the hell for?" Carlos demanded. "All that will do is get the buzzer swatted—or us. Get away from me, McGill. I never saw anything."

He scooted as far from me as possible and stared in the opposite direction. Natasha continued to watch the grainy image on her tapper until it was shrouded by the gray clouds that had begun surrounding our lifter as it descended. We were bouncing around now, deep in the troposphere.

Ignoring them both, I contacted Graves. I felt I might have information that could affect his command decisions. Commanders needed input to make the right decisions.

"This had better be good, McGill," Graves answered.

"Sorry sir, I have to report something. *Minotaur* appears to be venting from her aft modules. I believe her engines have been damaged."

"How the hell—are you hacking into command chat again?"

"No, sir."

"Well then, shut up. We know about it. Brace yourselves, we're trying to find a break in the megaflora, and when we do, we'll slip down into the lower ecosystem of this planet. Be prepared for anything. Graves out."

The channel closed. I turned to Natasha, who looked scared.

"They know about it," I told her. "The officers are in contact with *Minotaur*, and they're doing what they can."

She nodded and looked at the floor.

"What's wrong?" I asked.

"I'm scared, that's what."

"We've faced death before. Don't let it get you down."

She looked at me for a second then she leaned close. "James," she said in a low voice, "I don't think there are any revival units aboard this lifter."

"Why wouldn't they bring at least one?" I asked in alarm.

"Think about it: Why would the brass send something so valuable down with a ship that they half-expect will blow up during the descent?"

I blinked then frowned. The more I thought about it, the more worried I became.

The trouble was she could be right. They normally sent lifters on landings with a revival machine to support the cohort. But this mission had been deemed a dangerous experiment. If they lost a lifter and a cohort—well, that was one thing. But a revival unit? The brass didn't like to lose those. Not at all.

And that meant...

"We can't recover," I said aloud.

Natasha looked back at me. Her face had reddened as if she was holding back tears. Natasha was probably the smartest person in the unit, but she wasn't the toughest.

I extended my hand toward hers, and she clasped it.

"You've got it now," she said in a hushed tone. "If we lose *Minotaur*, they can't revive us. And we can't revive them. We'll be stuck down there on the surface, assuming we survive this landing, with only one life left to live."

Giving her hand a tiny squeeze, I manufactured a smile.

"Don't worry," I said. "Legion Varus has wiped before, and we'll wipe again. We've faced death, even perma-death, countless times—and we're still here!"

111

My words had been meant to be supportive, but judging by the look on her face, I hadn't cheered her up at all.

-15-

We found our hole in the upper canopy of the megaflora. Natasha showed me this on her tapper, which was still getting vid data from the lifter's upper decks.

Down in the hold, the soldiers around me were in a grim mood, but if I had to wager, I'd say the mood among the officers upstairs had to be even worse.

This planet already looked like a bad one to me. I'd only visited five planets before, including Earth, but I'd never seen anything like what they were calling "megaflora."

"Are those *really* trees?" I asked Natasha. "I mean—they've got to be a kilometer or two high and a couple hundred meters thick as well."

"They're not exactly trees," she said, studying her screen. "They have spongy-looking pods on top. And look at the coloring, there's almost as much purple as there is green."

She was right. I could see purple, green and various shades of brown. The growths were definitely alien. No one would confuse them with Earthly trees. But their structure was still familiar. The lower portions were knotted and thick—clearly what we could call the roots. The center was dominated by a massive trunk in most cases. The upper regions were where things looked the most unusual. The roof of the forest, to use a familiar word, was tightly packed with stuff that looked more like a crown of broccoli than a treetop.

Of course, the imagery filtering to us on our tappers wasn't perfect. It was choppy and fuzzy. The monstrous growths we were seeing didn't even look real—they were just too big. The plants even had hazy clouds floating between the trunks like the tallest of Earth's buildings.

"What I don't get is how we managed to get through that canopy at all in the lifter," I said. "I don't see any holes in the forest roof other than the one we came in through."

Natasha glanced at me. "There was a hole because we put it there. The burn marks and the size of the opening indicate we blasted it into existence with our broadsides. I'm almost certain of that."

I nodded, getting the point. We'd blown a hole in the forest then dropped the lifter into it. It made sense, and it also put us close to our target area.

Shortly after gliding into the forest and finding a relatively open spot on the ground, the lifter landed. We were between two roots of a particularly massive growth. The roots were like folds in a mountain.

"We made it down alive, anyway," I said.

Carlos clapped me on the shoulder, and he was grinning again.

"That was a good call, Vet," he said. "I would have put my money on the drop-pod people, but I would have been wrong."

"What?"

"I'm saying it was a good idea to come down with the lifter instead of the drop-pods."

Blinking at him, I frowned. "I didn't have anything to do with that decision, Specialist."

He raised his eyebrows in surprise. "No? I figured you'd gone up to Gold Deck and offered Turov a freebie if she gave you your choice."

I try not to smack Carlos around too much, but sometimes I can't help myself. I clamped onto his neck with my gauntlet and gave him a shake. My fist thumped into his breastplate, but that didn't even leave a scratch.

"Why are you such an ass, Carlos?" I demanded. "Aren't you ever going to grow up?"

114

"They keep resetting me back to the day I joined up. That means I'm permanently immature—and it's not my fault."

I let him go and stood up. The lifter had cycled down the engines and the go-lights had flipped to green. The big ramp was opening up, and it was time to move out.

Fortunately, I wasn't among the first squads to deploy. Graves' entire unit was, in fact, slated to be the last to leave the lifter.

We didn't waste any time checking our weapons, shouldering our rucks or staring at the exit. Sometimes the first few minutes on a new world were the worst of all.

"Look alive, people," Graves said in our ears. "Don't push, and don't screw up. We don't have any intel on this planet other than the confirmed fact that it's hostile."

"No shit," Carlos muttered.

We watched tensely as the first platoons hustled off the lifter ahead of us. My heart pounded, and I watched Natasha as much as anything else. She was reading incoming data on the planet we'd just invaded.

"Breathable atmosphere," she said. "But I'm getting a lot of biologicals in the air. Pollen, spores, traces of unknown pathogens."

Experimentally, I lifted my legs and stomped my feet back down. "Gravity seems pretty close to Earth's."

"I'm reading about eighty-one percent of normal," Natasha said. "That's nice for sore feet."

"Nice for giant tree-growths, too," I said. "With lower gravitational pull, it has to be easier for these plants to get taller."

She nodded in agreement.

Eventually, we were ordered to disembark. We gathered in a loose formation on the ground, taking up a flanking spot alongside one of the giant tree roots.

"I don't hear anything—except for us." Carlos said, messing with his audio inputs. "No birdsongs, no jungle-cat roars. Just silence."

I listened, and I had to admit he was right. I'd been in plenty of forests in my time, and I'd never visited a quieter place.

Natasha prowled around reading instruments while Carlos pecked at the tree roots with his medical instruments. I didn't stop either of them. I was hoping one of them might come up with something interesting.

"Listen up, people," Graves said at last, gathering the unit. "We've landed just a kilometer north of the big hole we blasted in this forest. Our readings aren't giving us any data on enemy positions, but those invaders up on *Minotaur* had to come from somewhere. Let's spread out and search the region by squads. If you make any kind of contact, report in. Otherwise, come back to camp under the lifter within an hour's time."

Only one unit stayed with the lifter to protect it. The rest of us split up and began exploring the immediate vicinity. None of us were supposed to leave sight of the lifter, just in case.

Among the knot of officers in the middle of the defensive unit, I spotted Primus Winslade himself. I pointed him out to Carlos as we climbed on top of an over-sized root.

"Figures," Carlos said, following my gaze. "Winslade isn't going on patrol. He'll sit back here and sip wine until we bump our noses into something. Then he'll call for help, screaming."

He was probably right, but I ignored Carlos' complaints anyway. I watched as Winslade moved to talk to Graves and the other centurions. Something was up.

After a few minutes of huddling and talking in low voices, Graves overrode our channel and made an announcement.

"Platoon leaders, join me in the lifter," he said.

Graves then followed Winslade up the ramp into the shadowy interior of the lifter. A half dozen other officers gathered behind him.

Carlos nudged me.

"What?" I demanded.

"You better get going," he said.

"What are you talking about?"

"Leeson's still dead. Last time our platoon had a leader, it was you. That means you're up, dummy."

Squinting at him, I was too surprised to smack him one. For one thing, he was technically right. The way legion chain-of-command worked, if there wasn't an adjunct handy, command was handed down to a veteran. Normally, the most senior veteran was given the honor, which would have been Harris. But Graves had specified me for the job back aboard the ship.

Legion soldiers died a lot. Because of this, we often had holes in our ranks until people were revived. In the past, prior to revival systems, new commanders would have been sent out to the front, or units would fold into one another to form full strength formations. But with our revival technology in play, death was usually just an inconvenience. Lower level officers automatically moved up the chain to replace their superiors until the dead man returned to take over his job again—standard routine.

Shrugging, I walked toward the ramp. At the bottom of it, I felt a heavy gauntlet slam down on my shoulder. It didn't hurt as my epaulets were over a centimeter thick, but it was irritating. I swung around with a frown.

Harris glared at me. "Just where the fuck do you think you're going, McGill?" he demanded.

"Up this ramp. Graves just summoned the platoon leaders to a conference. Didn't you hear?"

"I heard. I heard, all right. He was talking to *me*, you fool. I'm your senior by a decade. Don't think for a second you've got the right to play this kind of game with me."

"You're right, Vet," I said. "I don't mean to play any games. Maybe we should clear this up with Graves right now."

Turning, I stepped up the ramp again. Harris caught up to me with a growl and yanked on my arm.

You can ask anyone, and they'll swear I've got a slow fuse. But this planet was hot and steamy. Too much heat always put me into a bad mood. I could feel the humidity coming right through my armor, making my skin prickle. It was like being inside a car in a jungle—sure, you might have air conditioning, but systems like that were never perfect. My body *knew* it was standing in a sweaty sauna. The little bit of cool air that was pissing on my skin in a half-dozen spots didn't do all that much to relieve my discomfort.

The long and the short of it was that I just about punched Harris. He knew what I was thinking, too. He'd grabbed me once, and I'd taken that in stride—but both of us knew that grabbing me twice was too much.

He could tell I was on the verge of jumping him, so he dropped his hands from my arm. That was good for both of us. I took a deep breath and forced a smile.

"You've got something to add, Harris?"

"I sure as hell do. We'll clear this up right here, right now. Call Graves."

"You call him," I shot back.

We stared each other down for a second. Harris liked to hide from officers. He tried to never be the man to bring them a problem. But I wasn't going to be tricked into being the whiny guy with a question for the boss—not this time.

With a growl, Harris brought up his tapper and opened a channel to Graves. I was right there, so I overheard everything.

"Centurion, sir?" Harris said, his voice as perky as he could muster. "There's a small misunderstanding, sir."

"Specify, Harris. I'm busy."

Harris cleared his throat. "Sir, McGill and I were wondering which of us should be attending the command meeting in the lifter as Adjunct Leeson's replacement."

Graves hesitated. "Yes...right," he said. "I did put McGill in command, didn't I?"

Harris frowned fiercely. I could tell he'd expected an immediate decision in his favor.

"Sir," he said, "perhaps we could both attend, if that would be more convenient."

"It wouldn't be. It's too crowded up here already. My orders stand. Send McGill. Graves out."

Harris' mouth hung open. He stared at his tapper in shock.

Right then, I felt bad. Sure, Harris and I had never been best buddies, but we'd fought to the death back-to-back more times than we'd killed one another. He was the senior man. I suddenly felt that I shouldn't have pushed for this—that I should have backed down and let Harris have his day in the sun without me horning in.

"Vet," I said. "I'm sorry about this. I didn't mean to make a big deal of the situation. Why don't you just go up there and tell him I'm helping an injured soldier on my squad?"

Harris eyed me. His jaw muscles were bulging, and his lips were squirming. I could tell he was upset and didn't know how to react.

"That's a nice gesture," he said, "but the Centurion has given a command. I'm not like you, McGill. I follow orders. Get your ass up there and attend that meeting."

Turning away, I left him there at the bottom of the ramp.

"I hope the whole damned lifter blows up and kills the lot of you!" Harris shouted after me as I disappeared into the dim interior.

I chuckled to myself as I made my way to the upper decks. Now that was the Harris I knew so well!

When I reached the conference chamber, it turned out I was the only noncom in the room. I barely made it inside before the hatch in the floor glided shut and locked. I frowned at that. Was this a secret meeting?

Winslade stood in front of the central tactical display. Lifters were equipped with a decent battle simulation computer, so they could operate as a headquarters for land or space-based forces in a pinch.

"I'm not going to soften this," Winslade said. "We've got serious problems. Critical decisions must be made immediately."

These dramatic words surprised me, so I decided it would be best to stay as invisible as possible. I stood in the very back, leaning up against the curving hull. I was so far back, the ship's walls pressed against my helmet.

Looking around the room, I frowned. Hadn't Graves said something about it being cramped up here? Well, it wasn't. The chamber was designed to house all the officers in a full cohort. Lifters carried a thousand troops, and the officers were supposed to use the primary chamber of the upper decks as a meeting area.

The odd thing was the room was mostly empty. With only half the cohort with us, there was half the usual number of officers. I could have snagged a comfy chair, if I'd had the balls to.

Did that mean Graves had wanted me up here and decided to let Harris down easy with an excuse? Or was this just his way of slapping Harris around for complaining about his orders back when we were in the face of the enemy on Blue Deck?

I didn't know the answer, so I tried to push these thoughts from my mind and listen closely to Winslade. He tended to be overly dramatic, but he seemed to be serious today.

"That's right," Winslade said. "I think we've lost the rest of the legion. *Minotaur* hasn't blown up or lost orbit, but she's dead as far as we can tell from the ground. There's no response to any transmissions we've made requesting their status."

That was a punch in the gut for me. I'd had no idea things were that bad. Sure, there'd been venting from the engine core...but all of them? Dead?

"Primus," Graves asked, "is this speculation, or is it confirmed?"

Winslade eyed him. "Confirmed. Their computers acknowledge our requests, but nothing other than preprogrammed responses have come back. The Skrull crew must be dead as well. Only the AI remains active, and it's of limited usefulness. What we have gotten from it amounts to statistical data showing onboard conditions. The engines are disabled, and the atmosphere aboard is deadly—where it exists at all. The regions that remained pressurized are toxic. The radiation levels are serious. Even in suits, any survivors must be in dire straits."

Graves considered. "So, we've lost ninety percent of our force. What about the troops that came down via drop-pods?"

"Most of them made it. Better than sixty percent, in fact. They'll be gathering into units and proceeding to our position over the next twenty hours."

"Ninety-three percent of the legion lost," Graves said, shaking his head. "I have only one more critical question, sir: Do we have a revival unit on this lifter?"

Winslade smiled. "We do. A single unit. So far, it's automatically queued itself up with cohort losses and those of us who were confirmed dead during the drops. Now people, I need input. What's our strategy?"

Right about then, despite the fact I was in a mild form of shock, I had to admire Winslade. He was arrogant. He was sometimes petty and always dramatic. But here he was again, doing the right thing. He knew Graves had five more decades of experience fighting in space than he did. He wanted to live, so he was asking for help. He was flat out admitting he needed it. That made it harder to hate the man.

Graves took in a deep breath. "Let's talk about our revival strategy first. We should keep reviving our own people until we have firm knowledge of *Minotaur's* state. We don't want to duplicate personnel here on the surface if they're not confirmed dead in space."

Winslade nodded. "Agreed. How do we proceed tactically?"

Graves turned to the central display. A few others huddled up with him. All of them were centurions, so I hung back.

They talked for about half an hour. In the end, it was decided that we'd have to scout the enemy base. Supposedly, it had been annihilated by our broadsides, but that hadn't been confirmed.

After we'd dealt with the enemy on the planet, we had to come up with a way to recapture *Minotaur*. Without that ship, we had no way to get back home.

But taking her back...that sounded like it was going to be a tall order.

-16-

Leeson popped out of the revival system and began to hassle me almost as soon as he was able to draw breath. He couldn't do it very well as he kept having coughing fits.

"What's this I hear from Harris about you usurping my platoon, McGill?" he demanded.

I looked him over speculatively. "Sir, you're swaying a bit. Maybe you should catch your breath."

"Oh no," he said, shaking his head and going into another coughing spasm. "That's how it starts. That's how a man finds himself replaced. I'm not falling for that—especially after what you did to Harris."

"Adjunct, all I did was follow Centurion Graves' orders."

"Yeah, right. Sure. You want me to believe you're just some kind of country slap-dick, right? That there's not a scheming thought in your mind? Forget it, McGill. I'm not falling for that one."

"Your orders, sir?" I asked, suppressing a sigh.

"Just stay the hell out of my way. Those are your orders. No—hold on. I've got a better idea. I want you out on patrol. *Deep* patrol. See if you can find some of the stragglers from the drop pods. Barring that, maybe you can find yourself a sweet way to get killed."

I spun around on my heel and headed out of the lifter. Angry but resigned, I gathered up my team and we took a hike in the brush.

"What was the officers' meeting about, James?" Natasha asked me.

Not knowing what to say, I just shook my head and grunted. Sometimes, that works.

We were almost out of sight of the lifter, a thousand paces into the forest. No matter what anyone said about megaflora, I couldn't help thinking of this place as one giant forest. Sure, the trees looked weird, and they were as much purple as they were green and brown, but they might as well be trees. They had trunks, branches and thick flowering sprouts on top. Their crowns were so distant overhead, however, they looked like mountains seen through a haze of cloud cover.

I turned around and stared back at the lifter where Graves and the rest of them had remained.

"Look at that," I said. "That lifter looks tiny in this forest. The trees dwarf it like a toy."

Natasha looked back as did a few others. One of them was Carlos. He turned me a suspicious eye.

"So how come we're out here marching around in the undergrowth instead of camping with the rest of the cohort?"

I shrugged. "Harris complained, that's why."

"That bastard. He's worse than Winslade in his own way."

"Now, now," I chided. "None of that. He's nowhere near that bad."

"You still haven't answered my question," Natasha said at my side. "What happened in the meeting?"

This time I stopped dodging and laid it out for her. She was smart, and her face was squinched up with worry by the time I finished explaining.

"So…we're screwed?" she asked.

"Well and truly," I admitted. "The only good news is that Winslade brought along a revival machine."

Carlos hooted at that and joined us. "You know why he did that, don't you? He never leaves home without a revival machine in close proximity. I bet that thing is programmed to spit him out the second he croaks."

"Could be," I admitted. "But in this case, his caution has benefited us all. We can take a few losses and still keep going."

"A few losses?" Carlos demanded incredulously. "Have you somehow failed to notice we're as good as wiped right now? This has got to be the biggest fiasco we've ever been part of."

"Nowhere close," I said, shaking my head. "Remember back on Tech World? It was down to Galina Turov and me alone at one point. Everyone else was as dead as a mackerel on a dock—including you. Now *that* was a fiasco."

That shut Carlos up for some reason. He frowned, not liking talk of his nonexistence, even though it'd been temporary.

Natasha stepped close to me again. "What are we looking for?"

"Survivors from the pod-drops. Those sorry bastards did even worse than we did."

"What else did the officers say in the meeting? What's their plan?"

"They were talking about reviving people: What order, who should go first, who they could be sure was really dead, that sort of thing."

She nodded thoughtfully. "I know what I would do."

"What?"

"I'd revive the crew of the freighter. They might know what happened back on Earth. They might know who our enemy really is."

I halted and frowned at her. "Who our enemy really is? What do you mean?"

"I mean I want to know who's making these plant-constructs and sending them at us in droves. And who came along and blew up the freighter in the first place."

Shrugging, I continued to march. "I don't know why it matters much. They did it, and we're here to find and destroy them."

"But they're putting up quite a fight, wouldn't you say? It would help a lot to at least know why they did it."

The more I thought about it, the more I came to believe she was right.

"Okay," I said, "but do we even have the freighter crew's data?"

"We do. I checked."

I chuckled. Of course Natasha had checked. She wasn't supposed to have access to the bio-database—but that sort of thing had never stopped her before. If she was curious about what a given computer knew, she would dig it up whether she was authorized to do so or not.

"So we have their data. How do we know the crew wasn't already revived back on Earth?"

Natasha hesitated. She looked over her shoulder to make sure the others in the patrol were out of earshot. They weren't—but Carlos was telling a loud story, and no one was listening to us at the moment.

"I happen to know that Turov was given the data with instructions to revive the crewmembers if she felt they might be useful."

We were coming into a dense region of undergrowth where huge waxy pods hung down from the nearest tree. They didn't sprout from the crown, but from much lower down, just above the gnarly roots.

The pods themselves were odd things—the color and general shape of a jalapeno pepper. Fresh, shiny and dark green. Just like poison.

I halted and poked at the nearest of them with my rifle. "You think these things are seed-pods or something?"

"Yes. Probably part of their reproductive cycle."

The pods were over thirty meters tall. They hung from fresh-grown tubers until they touched the forest floor. It was startling to think a seed could be so large, but it made sense. The adult mega-growths, after all, were a hundred times as big.

I stopped poking the pod and turned to Natasha. "This isn't an accidental conversation, is it? You want me to go back there and kick around the idea of reviving the crew, is that it? How do you think that's going to go over? Turov could have done it at any point on the flight out here—but she didn't."

"Exactly," Natasha said, looking up at me with a gleam in her eye. "That's a mystery, isn't it? Why avoid an obvious resource of data on an unknown enemy?"

"Hmm...I don't feel like reviving Turov to ask her about that."

"She's the last person I would ask," Natasha admitted. "But she's not around, is she? Remember the chain of command, James. Who's in charge now? Who has every right to sate their curiosity in this desperate situation?"

I stared at her for a second. "Winslade. Winslade is in charge."

She nodded, watching me.

Sighing and shaking my head, I could already envision my fate. She'd put these thoughts into my head. Shoving them in one at a time, until my mind was full. She'd known exactly what she was doing, too.

"You're a sneaky one," I said. "You're trying to get me into trouble again, aren't you?"

"Ninety-six percent of us are dead, at last count. I'd say you're already in trouble. We all are."

"Why don't you march into Winslade's office and tell him all this? Why don't you do it your damned-self?"

She laughed quietly. "I'm good at a lot of things, but I can't stir a pot like you can, James. No one can."

I opened my mouth, planning to agree with her, but right then we heard a sharp, cracking noise.

Frowning, we turned toward the pod that hung close enough to touch.

It had split open a fraction. As we watched, the crackling turned into a ripping noise, and a seam in the plant gave way, tearing with the sound of a splitting tree-trunk all the way up to the stem overhead.

Inside the split, which was now several centimeters wide, we saw movement.

-17-

Needless to say, my squad was surprised by the thing that tore its way out of the pod. Its appearance was disturbing—I don't know how else to describe it other than to say it was man-shaped. It looked like a gigantic, lanky humanoid with limbs of brownish green and skin like wet bark. There were no eyes or other obvious sensory organs, but there were fronds here and there hanging from the body. These pulpy, sickly-orange fronds ended in polyps that flopped and pulsated. I wasn't sure if they were organs, like lungs, or eyeballs, or what.

"Fall back!" I shouted, taking my own advice and stumbling away from the massive creature. "Don't fire yet, we don't know if it's hostile."

"Should I let it eat me first, Vet?" Carlos called out. "Just to be sure?"

The creature took two sweeping strides forward and stood in our midst. The fronds hanging from its body shivered and drifted up and down like bouncing hair as it walked.

"This is amazing!" Natasha said in a delighted voice. "I've never seen anything like it. How does it move? What kind of musculature does it have? I'm dying to find out."

"Keep backing up," I ordered. "Sargon, have you got a bead on that big bulbous pod on top?"

"Got it sighted, Vet."

127

About ten seconds passed, during which the newborn creature stood and swayed. The orange fronds hanging from it kept swelling and lifting higher like slowly inflating balloons.

"Did you see that?" Natasha asked. She was the only one staying close to the monster. She was walking around it in a circle.

"See what, Specialist?"

"One of those external growths—I'm sure it's tracking me. I'm getting the impression it's a sensory organ of some kind."

I saw it now. It *was* tracking her. The orange, floating polyps were drifting, but with more purpose. They'd locked onto Natasha, and when she walked around the standing monster, they followed her movements.

"I don't like it," I told her. "Back off, Specialist."

"It's shown no hostile intent," she insisted. "I'm going to try to get a sample. If it's a plant, plucking a low-hanging frond shouldn't—"

Now, I'm not a rule-follower as such, but Natasha's idea alarmed me. I knew her well, and she was the type that could only be brought to break rules and laws when she was curious or to help a friend. In this case, it was the former.

Before I could order her back yet again, she trotted in close to the two monstrous feet and plucked a frond.

It was only a small one, attached to what might be the monster's toes. In my opinion, it shouldn't have hurt any more than plucking a single hair out of a cat's paw might—but I was wrong.

The creature reacted as if stung. Torpid and confused before, it moved with sudden purpose. A hooting sound erupted from far above us. It was as if someone had activated a foghorn and left it on. Long, low and loud, a single note of noise rolled out over the forest and made our ears ring.

Spinning its vast bulk around with a speed that belied its behavior thus far, the monster dipped one of those seven-fingered hands toward Natasha.

"Fire!" I roared, having seen enough.

The squad opened up, lashing the trunk and legs with explosive pellets. Sargon's belcher had been craned to a medium-wide aperture, and he used it to burn away a dozen clumps of those strange, orange fronds. A few of the big ones even caught fire.

The creature went absolutely berserk after that. It missed Natasha with its scooping sweep of a claw-like hand, but then it switched tactics and began to stomp. Hansen died, then the rookie Lau. It went after Carlos next, but he dodged away and ran off, screeching and firing over his shoulder.

"Sargon, narrow that beam and take its head off!"

"Not sure it's got a head, sir!"

"You know what I mean."

Sargon fired, but just took a burning chunk out of the shoulder. The beast spun around and crashed onto the forest floor. Carlos was still running, almost out of reach.

That long, long arm shot out again. It caught Carlos as a man might catch a fleeing rat. Lying on its side, the monster lifted him to its upper body and seemed to study him briefly before popping him into its maw and crunching down methodically.

Carlos only screamed once before he died in those massive jaws. The hole was a little small, so the creature had to shove to get him in there, all the while chewing enthusiastically. I would have thought his armor would have saved him, but the creature exerted such great pressure on the breastplate it collapsed with a wet popping sound.

The creature's distraction gave Sargon time to take aim. The monster's slavering jaws and eyeless face gave it a slack, idiotic expression. It chewed with mechanical efficiency.

Sargon blew the bulbous head clean off. Before he did, however, I was treated to the sight of blood running down the sides of the tree-trunk face.

After being shot, it didn't die right away. We had to blast away every sensory frond and destroy its limbs one after another. Even after that, the burnt carcass still twitched and rolled around on the forest floor like a haunted log that'd been struck by lightning.

Breathing hard, I grabbed Natasha by the shoulder and spun her around. She was still examining the thing.

"Happy now?" I demanded.

She blinked at me uncomprehendingly for a moment. The odd thing was—she *did* look sort of happy.

"That was amazing," she said breathlessly. "I've never even read about anything like this. Do you know what this means, James? They aren't constructs. They're grown this way, by these trees. All this time I was under the impression that the creatures that attacked *Minotaur* were a form of genetically engineered bio-weapon. Something cooked up by a scientist like me. But I was wrong. The megaflora—they grow these monsters. I think they're a natural form of defense."

Peering at her then looking at the carcass, I had a hard time understanding her words.

"I lost three good people because you didn't follow orders," I told her. "That's what I know. You're on report, and you might be on your way to the brig."

"I'm sorry," she said. "Can I complete my investigations first?"

Giving up, I made a sweeping gesture with my arm toward the fallen monster, which was still flopping this way and that. "Be my guest, girl! Have at it. But the rest of you: if Natasha gets rolled on or squirted with acid, do not endanger yourself to save her. That's an order."

I stomped away to check on the dead and the wounded while Natasha busily poked and probed at the dead creature.

While she worked, I reported the encounter to my superiors. Graves came on a few minutes later.

"That's the second report we've had of pod-growth. What does Natasha think they are?"

"She says they're some kind of natural defense for these plants."

"Right… Makes sense. Bring samples back to camp—and you should be heading back soon. Darkness is coming, and the word is that there are more of these creatures moving around out there."

An hour later we dragged ourselves back to the lifter with samples of the monster on our backs. Natasha made her report to Graves while I stood near.

"The blood and digestive fluids are acidic," she said, "but not dangerously so. They aren't the same manifestation as the creatures that attacked *Minotaur*. Still, we have to assume they're related."

"But they're plants," Graves said. "Have you figured out yet what makes them move? What kind of musculature they have?"

"Think about them as something akin to a beetle or a crab," Natasha said. "What I mean is they have a shell, rather than bones. They have a tough cellulose exoskeleton, but they keep all the organs and muscle inside. They have an alien form of muscle, it's not like ours."

"So, do you still think the megaflora is growing them on purpose?" Graves asked. "As a defensive mechanism against us?"

"I'm almost certain of it. That's the only explanation that makes sense. These creatures weren't here until we landed, and now they've been growing and breaking out of their pods. What's even more interesting is their chosen physiology. In my opinion, they're mimicking human anatomy."

"Hmmm," Graves said. "Why?"

"I'm not sure, but I'm certain it's by design. The initial creatures that assaulted our ship were less humanoid. These are bigger but more like a man. Whatever shape they take, they're dangerous."

"You have my complete agreement there," Graves said, reviewing the video showing Carlos being eaten.

Graves turned toward me then. "McGill? What was the count of pods on that tree where you found this abomination?"

Hesitating, I at last shook my head. "I didn't take a firm count. I would say there were less than a dozen, sir."

Natasha raised her tapper and pointed to it. "I was taking streaming video the whole time. I count fourteen, including the one that we destroyed."

"Thirteen more monsters in the forest," Graves said thoughtfully. "That's my lucky number. Did you know that, McGill?"

"I'm not feeling so lucky today, Centurion."

Graves walked away and left me with Natasha.

"Seriously Specialist," I told her. "I need you to follow orders when we're under fire."

"When have you ever—?"

I halted her with an upraised hand. "That's not true. I follow the orders that matter—orders that are justified and which will save my fellows and my mission. You endangered all of us to satisfy your curiosity."

"Veteran McGill," she said, drawing herself up straight. "I don't think you're being fair. We discovered an amazing new life form. Don't worry about Carlos. He'll pop back out of the oven in a few hours."

Shaking my head, I turned to go. She wasn't getting what I was saying, and I was tired of repeating it.

"Just a moment," she said. "Aren't you going to go talk to Winslade?"

"About the revival queue? I guess it doesn't seem all that important to me after the events of the afternoon."

"James, the freighter crew may have information that's vital to the success of this mission. Let's not have all this turn out to have been a waste because I got curious."

She knew how to get to me. She knew I hated the idea of suffering and dying needlessly.

"All right," I said. "I'll give it a shot."

She nodded while I tramped up to the officer's deck.

As far as I was concerned, I was on a fool's errand. Winslade didn't even want to listen to me, much less take any advice I had to offer.

After I'd explained to the primus about the dead crew of the freighter and that we had reserved the right to revive them during this pursuit, he gave me an odd look.

"Claver," Winslade said. "You're talking about Claver, right? I knew you had a shady past with that snake, McGill, but I didn't think you'd go this far."

Blinking, I stared at him for a moment.

"What's Claver got to do with this, sir?" I asked.

"You're going to play it that way again, are you? The hulking ignoramus routine? It gets old, McGill. It really does."

"Uh…"

"Claver was on the freighter. You arranged that part yourself according to legend, helping him get the titanium delivery contracts."

132

"I don't remember anything about delivery contracts."

Winslade rolled his eyes at me. I hated that, but I waited for him to explain.

"How else did you expect Claver to cash in on the lucrative deal you helped set up for him if he wasn't flying cargo back and forth from Machine World? Didn't your best friend at least send you a text?"

I frowned, thinking hard. Claver had been given the right to trade titanium from Machine World but only to other parties. Not to Earth. We got our share for free.

"I'm confused, sir—" I began.

"To put it mildly."

"Well…I mean the last I knew of Claver he was on Earth. He was arrested, you know, and put on notice by Central. I didn't know he was released to go out to Machine World and do business."

Winslade crossed his arms and huffed. "Central arresting Claver? You're talking about Equestrian Nagata. That man has no idea what will stick and what won't. He's honorable, but stupid. Central wasn't going to let anyone hold Claver. Earth *needs* that titanium. Who better to get it than a snake like your friend?"

I followed his logic to a degree. Apparently, Claver had been authorized to transport and deliver titanium from Machine World. It wasn't surprising that I hadn't heard about that. I'd ducked out of legion politics as quickly as I could once I'd returned home to Earth. But now here I was, back in the middle of it all.

"But sir," I objected. "Claver was given the right to trade titanium with other worlds, not Earth."

"Right," Winslade said in a condescending tone. "Let's go over the logic of that statement, shall we? One trader was given the right to transport and sell some of the titanium to other worlds while the balance went to us. Now, how do you think the actual delivery went down?"

"I have no idea."

"I thought not. It's the same as the delivery of any product. Claver was already transporting the product to multiple customer worlds. Why wouldn't he make his delivery rounds in

133

a single ship—collecting a transportation fee from everyone along the way, of course."

"Of course," I said, finally catching on.

Claver was a slippery business man. If there was a profit to be made, a deal to be cut, he'd get it done. I could see how he'd used his position to lever delivery contracts with Earth in addition to other worlds. The metal was "free" technically, but it still had to be transported. It only made sense to have one transportation network from a supplier world. Why duplicate the effort?

"So," I said. "You're saying Claver was aboard the freighter according to the manifest, and he died when the ship slammed into Earth."

"He was probably long dead by that time. But your statement is accurate enough in the essentials."

"Well sir..." I said, "then I suggest we revive him."

"What a surprise. Let's hear your reasons, just for the record."

"Because, if there's one man in the cosmos who knows what the hell is going on out here, it's Claver. He may not want to tell us—but he knows the score."

Winslade chewed on his upper lip for a time. I tried not to watch.

"Agreed," he said at last. "He's the only one we can ask. After Turov and Tribune Drusus have been revived and given their blessings, we'll—"

"Whoa, hold on there," I said. "Let's back that up, Primus. I strongly recommend that we get Claver out right now, before anyone else."

Winslade frowned at me. "Whatever for? Are you trying to get me into difficulties with my superiors? I know you excel at that sort of thing."

"I do, sir, I do. But I want you to think about something: if Turov could have revived Claver at any point along this search into space—why didn't she do it?"

Winslade's eyes narrowed until they resembled those of a ferret. "You're right. Such primitive cunning—but it's undeniable. If she'd wanted to do it, she would have done it during the voyage out here."

"Exactly sir. And might I add that if she didn't want to do it before, she's not going to allow it once she's back in charge of this mission."

Winslade looked stressed. He began to pace. I could see the warring thoughts within his mind. He wasn't sure what he should do.

If he crossed Turov, it would cost him. But then again, he wanted to know what Claver might say. His own survival might hang in the balance.

"There is something wrong, here," he said. "I'll admit that. And another point has occurred to me: Did you know Turov wasn't too keen on this mission to begin with? She wanted to turn around and abandon the search after the first target world was missed."

"I heard something to that effect, sir."

Winslade eyed me with calculated respect. "You've got my mind churning, veteran."

"Yes Primus. I excel at that."

Winslade flicked his eyes down to his desk. He tapped on virtual keypad that appeared before him, and soon the revival queue as it stood now was displayed. He studied it, and made tsking sounds.

"This won't do at all," he said. "I'm going to go further than you suggested...I'm going to fully streamline the revival queue. I'll make sure the best possible use of our limited resources is achieved."

For a second, I blinked at him. Then I got it. He was going to reorder the queue, micromanaging the process. He would decide who lived again—and who stayed dead.

"I understand perfectly, sir."

"I wouldn't go that far," he said in a condescending tone. "But you understand enough to do my bidding. That will suffice."

-18-

We moved ourselves down to the revival chambers. After waiting around for a few minutes, we saw the bio specialist in charge leave the room. She gave us an up-down look, but didn't say anything as we both out-ranked her. When she hurried away down the passage, we quickly ducked inside.

Editing a revival queue isn't all that hard to do—especially not when the acting C. O. has given you the go-ahead.

I hacked my way past the login screen easily enough. Our first snag came when the system required me to enter a comment in a memo box justifying the change. Winslade and I looked at one another in concern.

"This input field is a new one," I said.

"Indeed. Someone has altered the data entry screens to add this requirement."

"Do you think it was the bio people? Or maybe a new firmware release from Central?"

Winslade shrugged. "It hardly matters. The pertinent detail is that the system is logging our changes, including who made them, when, and why. What's your answer, McGill?"

"Me?" I asked, aghast. "I'm supposed to put in the answer?"

"You're making the alterations. I'm a bystander. Technically, I'm not even here." So saying, he stepped away and looked into the distance. Maybe he thought his face might get into a vid recording, somehow.

My lips twisted up into an expression of disgust. Winslade was as quick and slippery as a snake in a grease-fire—and he was just about as ornery, too.

Cracking my knuckles, I typed in a spray of text and hit enter. Winslade turned around on his heel and came back to stand at my side.

"What did you enter?" he asked.

"Nothing special. Just some vague double-talk. I've heard it all my life, and it comes out naturally when convenient."

Winslade snorted. "Indeed. Well enough, then."

"Who shall we revive first?" I asked.

"Claver," Winslade said. "As you suggested earlier. Push him to the top of the queue."

I did so and locked it in.

"And what's next?"

"Take these names off the list," Winslade said, sliding a computer scroll in front of me. The list contained the names of everyone in the legion who outranked him, either by virtue of position or seniority. In particular he'd taken pains to remove senior brass from the list entirely, putting them on hold.

"Are you sure about this, sir?"

"Just do it, McGill."

I didn't like it, but I did it. I adjusted the queue and saved it. A few short minutes later a tapping sound began at the chamber door. Anne's face appeared in the foggy porthole. Maybe she'd been alerted somehow. Then I saw that the bio we'd chased off earlier was with her. Doubtlessly, the woman had gone to get Anne.

Anne was frowning at us like we were two urchins in her kitchen, sneaking cookie dough. I knew the look well. Two non-bio people were fooling with her most holy of holy machines. That wouldn't do at all for any self-respecting bio.

"They're getting restless," I said.

"Too bad. Do you have any other suggested edits, while we're at it? Who should come out after Claver? It can't be the brass—not yet. We have to have time to interrogate Claver thoroughly before anyone can take command and remove me from my position."

137

After thinking about it for a moment or two, I came up with an idea.

"How about prioritizing combat troops?" I asked. "We'll load up everyone who's died in this cohort first. That way, we'll have hours to talk to him while the rest of the cohort people are spit out."

"Excellent. There are operational precedents for that sort of thing. When under fire from local resistance, unit cohesion comes first. Front-line troops are often revived before top-level brass. We'll claim the situation was an emergency, and that the reordering of the revival process was necessary."

"As good a dodge as any."

"Do it. Make the rest of the edits and reactivate the machine."

"Uh...but sir, if I do that, it will abort the current grow. Can't we just let this one finish and then bring Claver out next?"

Even as I said these words, Anne's fist began hammering on the door. Her face was in the porthole again, one eye roving angrily.

"As you can see," Winslade said, "we already have our first objector. I want this over with. We must be ruthless and quick. Perform all your questionable deeds at midnight, McGill. Do them all at once, as fast as you can. Those are words to live by."

"If you say so, sir," I said. Gritting my teeth, I typed in the changes and engaged the confirmation code.

The machine began to burble and made sloshing sounds. The noises reminded me of a dishwasher switching into the rinse cycle. I hated to hear that sound.

After less than a minute, the maw yawned open and disgorged a half-baked person. The living corpse was gray and malformed. I'd expected it might be small, like a baby, but it wasn't. The machine apparently grew people differently than a normal gestation of an infant. It formed the cellular structure of an adult and kept refining the shape until it got it right. The thing looked like a slug with fat, curled-up arms and legs. The gray skin was covered in slime.

"That's got to be the foulest thing..." Winslade said.

Anne must have caught sight of our latest action, and she didn't approve. She burst into the chamber puffing with anger.

"What is the meaning of this act?" she demanded. "Who's responsible for aborting this grow?"

"Remain calm, Specialist," Winslade said. "You do it all the time when something goes wrong."

"But this was a perfectly good grow. You killed it!"

Truer words were never spoken. Partially formed lungs heaved and sighed. They rattled their last and the proto-person shivered in death.

"Recycle this mess," Winslade ordered. "Do not alter the queue as it now stands. Alert me when the next grow is complete."

He left then, with an imperious air. I had to admit, he knew how to give orders like a pro.

"I'm sorry, Anne," I said when he left.

"This has got to be your idea," she said.

"Not at all. Check the memo in the work order."

She did, and she frowned: "'Authorized by Primus Leonard Winslade, acting commander. Alteration request approved. Reasons: Classified.' What the hell is this?"

"That's what he had me type in," I said. "He was in charge. I just knew how to do what he wanted. Maybe he thought a real bio would give him grief."

"He was right about that. You wait until I make my full report. Winslade will wish he'd never been revived this time around. Turov will tear him apart."

Inwardly, I grinned. My ad-lib memo field was already coming in handy. I was fairly certain it would reap even bigger rewards later on.

"Aren't you interested to know why he really did it?" I asked.

"Yes, I suppose. Tell me."

I pointed to the queue. "Did you happen to notice the next name on that list—the next grow, who even now is gestating inside the guts of the machine?"

Anne looked, and she gasped. "Claver? Tell me this is some kind of mistake!"

139

Shrugging and shaking my head, I endeavored to look innocent. "I'm following orders," I said. "I didn't even know he was aboard *Minotaur*."

"Don't be a...never mind. Yes, James, he was on the manifest. We've had his data since we left Earth. He died on the freighter when it crashed into Earth. At least, that's when his death became officially recognized. We've had the authorization to revive him since that time."

"Why didn't Turov do it?"

"I don't know. It does seem odd. The machine sat idle for nearly a month. Why let him linger in death for so long? And why is Winslade bringing him back now, when we need this single machine to revive an entire legion?"

"Different commanders, different priorities."

Anne narrowed her eyes. "You know more than you're letting on, right? Never mind. Don't tell me. I don't want to get into politics. The only thing slimier than the guts of this machine is the twisted double-dealings of people like Winslade and Turov. I want no part of it."

I nodded and shut up. It was easy to keep quiet. After all, I barely knew what was going on myself.

But I intended to find out.

-19-

By the time Claver was coming out of the oven, things were heating up outside the lifter as well. We were back in Winslade's office where he was looking over incoming reports.

"My helmet's buzzing nonstop," Winslade complained. He glowered as he worked his tapper. "Those...*things* you discovered out there in the forest, how many do you think you saw?"

I shrugged. "Thirteen was the count. But that's only counting the production of a single tree. There might be more."

Winslade's expression changed to one of worry. "No weaponry, right? Just a pack of big, walking bipeds?"

Thinking about the monster I'd witnessed, its power and sudden fury, I didn't want to downplay how dangerous an army of them might be.

"We only fought one, but it had just crawled out of its cocoon. Even so, the damned thing killed one of my people before we brought it down... By the way, sir, did we bring any heavy weaponry down from *Minotaur* on this lifter?"

Winslade eyed me for a second. "There have been over a hundred sightings now. The confirmed reports number half that many—but the aliens haven't moved against us yet. They're maneuvering out there in the forest, just beyond our reach."

"I don't like the sound of that, sir. If they come at us, all at once and organized...well sir, in my opinion superior firepower may not be enough."

"I'll recall all our patrols," Winslade said after a moment's thought. "No one is to go more than a kilometer from the lifter. We'll force the aliens to march into a killing zone."

I watched in concern as he relayed these orders to Graves and the other Centurions. We had six full units of troops now, six hundred heavy infantry.

He hadn't answered my question about artillery. Maybe there wasn't any. Maybe Turov had wanted to make sure we survived the descent before she committed expensive equipment. If that was the case, we were more screwed than I'd thought.

My next move should have been to leave the revival room and rejoin my squad. They were outside preparing fortifications now, and if an army of those things was approaching, I needed to be with them.

But before I could excuse myself, Anne contacted us. "Claver is coming out now. James, would you come help me? I'm in the middle of a shift-change on orderlies."

Never having been a fan of this process, I marched down there to help. It was the least I could do. My teeth were gritted for the next few minutes while we delivered a naked, slimy Claver onto a steel palette. He shivered and mewed. It was almost enough to make me feel sorry for the bastard—almost.

"He's a good grow—if that can be said about Claver," Anne said, letting go of his eyelid. The eyeball underneath rolled away from us and he snapped that eyelid shut when he was able.

"I don't feel like a good grow," he said in a croaking voice. He kept his eyes screwed shut. "Can you turn off those lights?"

"No," Anne told him flatly.

Claver chuckled and coughed. "You get an 'F' in bedside manners, my dear."

Anne hauled him up into a sitting position. Claver hissed. I took his arm and looked meaningfully at Anne. "I'll take it from here."

She looked doubtfully from Claver to me then to Winslade, who was just arriving. Winslade had a grim expression on his face.

She put her hands on her hips and sighed. "If you're just going to recycle him again, why did you bother going through all this trouble to mess up my schedule?"

"Because," Claver answered, his eyes still squinched tightly, "they'll doctor the records afterward. A few bad grows, no ID assigned. Nothing to show I was ever here."

The funny thing was that Claver might be right. I'd suffered just such a fate a year or so back when people had wanted to question me. It gave me pause and made me doubt my actions. Was this revenge-related? Claver may have had something to do with the perming of my family, but I couldn't be rock-solid certain of that.

Sternly, I told myself we had to do what we had to do. Claver had caused a lot of deaths back on Tau Ceti before this—hell he'd even gotten a load of squids, Nairbs and saurians killed on Machine World.

Half-lifting him off the table, I helped him to the lockers where a smart cloth jumper was applied. It wrapped itself over his body, and Winslade made a flicking gesture toward the hatch.

"My office," Winslade said.

Claver perked up when he heard Winslade's voice. "Is that the venerable Primus?" he asked. "Or perhaps you've been elevated to the rank of Tribune by now?"

"To you, I'm God," Winslade said.

We left the revival chamber, abandoning Anne to her grim work. She looked after us fretfully. I knew she didn't like any kind of mistreatment. She especially felt protective of those she'd returned to life personally. Some part of her brain believed she'd mothered us all, I think.

We reached Winslade's office a minute later. Claver was still limping, and he'd only forced his eyes once or twice.

"Snap out of it, Claver," Winslade said. "We know you're a good grow."

"My eyes—they burn this time. You ever get that? Sometimes you can't take light at all. Can you dim the interior?"

Winslade and I exchanged glances. It *could* be true. Fresh-grown eyes were often sensitive, like nerves severed and later reknit. They sent odd signals to the mind until they settled in.

"It could be true, sir," I said to Winslade. "I've had trouble with my eyes at times."

Winslade gave Claver an appraising glance. I noticed Winslade had his sidearm in his hand.

After a moment of hesitation, Winslade reached for the light panel. But before he touched the pad and lowered the lights, he reversed himself and jabbed the muzzle of his sidearm into Claver's gut.

The prisoner made a woofing sound and coughed. His eyes opened wide, and he made choking sounds.

"Changed your mind, sir?" I asked the Primus.

Winslade pointed with one thin-boned finger at Claver's hand. I looked down and watched as Claver's hand retreated from my belt.

"He went for your weapon when I reached for the lights. You're overconfident with those big muscles of yours, Veteran. They won't do you any good at all with your brains splattered on the ceiling."

I nodded tightly. "Thank you, sir."

Winslade prodded Claver methodically with the barrel of his gun.

"Let's have a little talk, shall we?" he asked.

"What for? You've already made up your minds. Just record my confession or whatever you want and blow my brains out. My eyes really do burn. I'm ready to recycle right now."

"What happened aboard the freighter?" Winslade asked.

"We were attacked and robbed. It was piracy, plain and simple."

Winslade sighed. "Let's be more specific. Start with your personal story."

"He's just going to make something up," I commented.

"We'll get to the truth in time," Winslade said dispassionately, "but we might as well start with his fabricated version first. I find it's cathartic for some criminals."

Claver looked from one of us to the next. There was no pity in our eyes now. He'd lost all of mine when he'd tried to grab my gun.

"All right," he said, judging it was time to say his piece. "It was weird, actually. Pod-like things attached themselves to the ship as we left warp. They burned through the hull very quickly. The ship was a freighter—we didn't have much in the way of weapons or troops, just a few onboard marines. My entire crew was overwhelmed and killed. I died on the bridge giving orders."

Winslade nodded thoughtfully. "What killed you, specifically?"

"Some kind of gas got into the vents. We didn't have our vac suits on—stupid, I know. I think the fumes were created by an acidic fluid the creatures emitted."

"That's it?" Winslade asked his eyebrows lifting high.

"Yeah, that's it. To repeat, we came out of warp near Earth, and these pod creatures jumped us—then I died. I don't know what happened after that."

"You lost the shipment," I said. "The freighter crashed into the spaceport and killed about thirty thousand people."

"Thirty thousand?" Claver asked, impressed.

"At least. Many of them were permed. Two legions were in attendance to ceremonially welcome your death ship."

"What do plants want with metal in any case?" Winslade asked.

We both looked at him.

"That ship they used to follow my freighter and attack," Claver said, "it was metal, or at least it had some metal parts."

Winslade nodded. "I suppose some parts of a starship have to be metal."

"There you have it," Claver said with a helpless shrug. "It was a tragedy all the way around. You gentlemen have my utmost sympathy. If this briefing is over, I'd like to recover in my stateroom—"

Winslade's gun jabbed him again. This time, it was a hard poke in the ribs. Claver grunted and clutched a spot there. As I watched, it began to ooze blood and turn purple.

"As I said," Winslade commented in a languid voice, "it will take time to get to the truth. Fortunately, I have time."

Claver's eyes were wide open now. He looked like a caged animal. I did my best to look unsympathetic, but I was starting to feel he'd told his story. It sounded real enough.

"Varus bastards," Claver said. "What do you want me to say? If the truth isn't good enough for you, maybe you should just write it down for me so I can sign it. That would save us all a lot of time and trouble."

Winslade lowered his gun. Instead of aiming it at Claver's gut, he aimed it at his foot. "You have far too many toes, in my opinion. We'll begin removing the excess shortly. Every thirty seconds, I'll remove another, until we run out. Then, we'll stop for some blood-staunching and get to work on these fingers—I might have to reload as well."

There was steel in Winslade's eye, I could see it. He might be an arrogant prick, but he had a spine when it came to dealing out pain.

Claver saw it too. He believed, and he buckled.

"You prick," he said. "I was on the ship. I died there—just like I said. What else do you want from me?"

"I want to hear what you know about these creatures. Why might they be following you? Why did they attack you, and how did they come to be here on this world that was supposedly uninhabited?"

"I never said I was out here at all—wherever here is. I told you, I was on my way to Earth—"

Winslade nuzzled Claver's toes with the barrel of his pistol. Claver twitched while Winslade remained strangely expressionless.

"I'm getting bored," Winslade said, selecting a toe. It was the middle one on Claver's left foot. "Hold him, Veteran."

"They're called the Wur," Claver said suddenly. "It's a squid word, I believe. Basically, they're pod people. They come from beyond our frontier."

"All right then," Winslade said. "We're getting somewhere. Where are these creatures from?"

"I don't know."

146

Winslade walked angrily to his desk and brought up a star map.

"This is where we are now, Claver," he said, tapping the K-Class star labeled L-374. What do you know about it?"

Claver eyed the map. "Out there, huh? That planet is uninhabited."

"Wrong," Winslade said. "The planet was marked as uninhabited because that was true when it was last surveyed by the empire. But that was probably three hundred years ago, before the Industrial Revolution back on Earth. Can you explain the discrepancy?"

"Maybe. Three hundred years…that's plenty of time for the Wur to seed a planet."

A whisper of a smile played on Winslade's mouth. "I'm a little surprised," he said. "I honestly thought I'd have to remove appendages before you'd confess to treason."

"First off," Claver retorted, "I only talked because I know you're a cold snake that would actually follow through."

"And you were correct."

"But secondly, I have to ask, Primus, by what stretch of the imagination does my helpful information amount to treason?"

Winslade sucked in a breath through his narrow nostrils. He raised a skinny index finger to his nose and tapped it there. "You could not have this information without having dealt with this enemy. Clandestine interactions with a renegade alien species amount to treason—not just on Earth but by the laws of the Galactic Empire itself. Further, you withheld information concerning this enemy when first questioned. Let us call that a second count of treason."

"Let's not," Claver said. "Okay, you have me—or at least this version of me. Let's talk business. I want a signed immunity agreement. Then I'll tell you what else I know."

"I have another proposal," Winslade said, his eyes flashing dangerously.

At that moment, Winslade's tapper began beeping. I knew that sound. There was an emergency call coming in.

Winslade stepped away and consulted his arm. Mine began flashing and beeping as well.

We both looked up at one another at the same moment after reading the incoming priority message.

The giants from the forest—they were on the march.

-20-

About five minutes after I left Winslade to continue Claver's interrogation, I found myself manning a trench line we'd hastily dug with the aid of our "pigs."

Pigs were huge walking drones that buzzed and revved. They were still digging, carving up the soft dark loam of the forest floor into curling rolls of dirt. Using something on the front of the machines that looked like a plowshare, the earth was gouged and thrown up in the direction of the wild forest.

The hole behind me was over a meter deep. The dirt pile on the forest side formed a handy barrier we could rest our rifles on. Already the pigs had dug a double-ringed defensive earthwork that encircled the lifter that rested on its struts in the middle.

I didn't think our dug-in defenses were going to do us much good against the giant aliens, however. Unlike the techs driving the drones and most of our officers, I'd actually seen and done battle with one of these giants. I knew they would step right over these trench-lines—or worse, step down into them, crushing us.

So far, the pod creatures had yet to show themselves. My helmet-based tactical display indicated they were out there, but I couldn't see them yet due to what might be called "undergrowth" in this forest of immense proportions. Fern-like plants ten meters high were everywhere, blocking my vision and generally getting in the way.

149

"How is this even possible?" Carlos demanded of no one in particular. He'd been revived by the time we returned to the lifter, before Winslade and I had commandeered the machine that doled out life in order to revive Claver.

Fresh from a violent death, Carlos' voice seemed less confident than usual.

"How's *what* possible, Specialist?" I asked.

"How can these tree-aliens move at all? I mean, they're just plants, right? They haven't got any muscles! I don't get it."

Kivi spoke up right away. "You took xenobiology," she said. "Were you paying any attention? Our pigs don't have muscles either, but they can also move. Those machines back on Gamma Pavonis moved very quickly too."

"Yeah, but these things are freaking trees. It's not the same."

He had a point, and I didn't have an answer. Natasha came to my rescue.

"I've been running tests on the samples I took," she said. "We don't know everything yet, but as far as I can tell, they have something like nanotubes inside their tough exterior. You saw that material that looked like corn silk, right? That stuff contracts when stimulated. Each strand works like a thin muscle. Each of the thousands of string-like hairs are attached to two spots inside the tube-like outer structure. Working together, they cause the creatures to move."

"You're talking about nanotubes inside the trunk, right?" Carlos asked.

"The trunk and the limbs. They're the same. Those arms that look like branches to us are really tubes of flexible cellulose. Think about them as tough rubber hoses filled with strands of nano-fiber. It's a marvelous system whether it was designed, or it evolved naturally."

Her last comment sparked my interest. "You still think these things might be bio-engineered?"

"It's possible," she said. "We just don't know enough yet."

"Well," I said, sighting along my rifle barrel, "I think we're about to get schooled."

There was a distant movement, a shivering of the tallest ferns to the south. I focused on that region as it was directly ahead and part of our designated firing zone.

"They're creeping up on us," Carlos said suddenly.

There was a certainty in his voice that got my attention.

"Do you see something, Specialist?"

He never got the chance to answer. At that moment, Natasha reported in, updating my tactical screen. The techs had sent out a skirmish-line of buzzers into the deep forest to watch for trouble. She relayed the live feed to her commanders—including me.

Sure enough, the tree things were advancing toward us on all fours. They lit up on my helmet's tactical display with red arrows pointing down to their tracked positions. I did a quick count. There were about twenty contacts coming toward our unit's portion of the defensive line. There had to be more than a hundred circling the entire camp.

"Hold your fire until they break into the open," I said. "We want to hit them hard and all at once. If they come in a little closer, they won't be able to turn around and run."

"I don't like this," Kivi said, breathing hard over her microphone. "They're intelligent. The one that we killed didn't seem too smart—but this behavior, these things are coordinating. I don't think they're simple animals."

"Agreed," Natasha said. "They're clearly intelligent beyond the animal level. As to the behavior of the first one, remember it was a newborn. How smart were you thirty seconds after birth?"

They both had made good points, and I didn't like any of them. I'd hoped the enemy would be as dumb as the trees they resembled. The mere fact that creatures made of cellulose were creeping up on us as an organized group was, well, *creepy*. How did they communicate? Who was leading them?

I gave my head a little shake to get back into the game. The here and now was all that mattered. There wasn't time to have a scientific debate about the enemy. All we could do was wait for their charge.

They didn't take long to begin the attack. Almost as one, they rose up above the ferns they'd been hiding behind. I heard a ripping roar of gunfire as hundreds of soldiers opened up all around us. We were blazing away like there was no tomorrow—and with only one lifter and one revival machine, we might be right.

Thousands of tracing rounds leapt through the air from the squads around us. My reticle lit up indicating I was on target, and my team joined in.

The monsters were lumbering toward us. They were a little slow at first because they had to stand up from a hunched position and get their big legs moving.

The ten meter tall ferns of the forest came to the curved knees of the tree-creatures. I hadn't really noticed before, but now that Natasha had explained they were boneless shells full of thousands of strand-like muscles, I could see they didn't have joints. Their knees flexed in a curve rather than bending sharply in the middle. The effect was strange to witness, but it was also undeniably effective. They came at us at an alarming pace, tearing the ferns apart and brushing them aside. A combined warbling howl began as the charge became widespread. All of the creatures seemed to be letting loose at once. The sound could only be described as a battle cry.

Just one of these things could give you a headache, but a hundred of them? I wasn't sure my eardrums would survive it. Men put their hands to their helmets and shouted in pain, but the monsters were making so much racket that our own screams couldn't be heard. Our rate of fire slackened until it almost died out.

Fortunately, the aliens didn't keep the howling up for long. They were moving faster now, orange fleshy fronds bouncing like leaves all over their strange bodies. Giant ferns whipped at those lanky, striding legs. I even saw several of them leap, soaring over gigantic roots.

Our small-arms fire wasn't doing much. We fired into their mass but weren't bringing anybody down.

"Sargon, burn the closest one. Squad, all follow his target. Everyone hit the one that he lights up—hit it hard!"

At first, our automatic fire slowed. Then when Sargon nailed the leader, we all lashed it with a storm of bullets, knocking it from its feet. It went down hard, thrashing and rolling. The next two monsters behind went down as well, tripped by the fallen leader.

"Focus on those three. Mark your targets. Follow my lead."

I engaged a tactical option in my helmet's battle system I'd never had cause to use before in infantry gear. The option made the arrow over the head of my target blink rapidly.

That got my whole squad to target the same alien. We hadn't fought too many monsters that were so big we needed to use the system, but we needed it now. I'd used it before to coordinate fire on the biggest machines on Machine World, but I'd been driving a dragon then—and I wished I was driving a dragon right now. I'd have felt a lot safer.

We'd only brought down six by the time they hit our line. My whole unit, facing twenty of the enemy, was overrun. Graves came on the channel, giving us all direct orders in the final seconds before they hit us.

"Duck down when they step over you," he said in a remarkably calm voice. "Lie down in the trench. That way you'll probably avoid being crushed. When they stop the charge, do battle by squads with the nearest enemy. Fire at will."

The battle went into slow-motion for me after that. It was like I was living at a different pace. My heart was pounding, and my lungs were burning with rapid, panting breaths.

I fell on my back when the enemy hit our front trench line. A wave of dirt splattered my faceplate, obscuring my vision, but I was able to see the foot that had landed not five feet from me.

Someone in the line hadn't been so lucky—it was Natasha. A giant had stepped right on her, crushing her down with terrific force.

I let rip with my rifle, shooting the alien right in the crotch, but that only lasted for a split-second before it was gone. A few drops of milky fluid dribbled from the creature onto my armor, smoking white as the acid burned the metal.

Scrambling on all fours to Natasha, I was able to haul her out of the dirt. She was buried and helpless inside a huge footprint, but she was still alive. The earth and her armor had kept her from being crushed to death, but she had been pinned down. After freeing her, I turned back to the enemy.

They ended their charge as I watched. We were in the first trench not the second one, but this time we'd actually gotten the better end of the deal. The monsters that had overrun us stumbled to a halt. Some of them actually bumped into the hull of the lifter as a man might push off on a wall after a hard run. They doubled back and began going to work on the humans inside the inner circle of trenches.

Methodically, the aliens dug soldiers out of their shallow, scraped holes. All at once, I knew how gophers in a field must have felt when their homes were being stomped out of existence by a pack of grinning farm boys.

Fortunately, these "gophers" had teeth that could reach up to bite an enemy at range. I lit up a new target, the one I'd shot in the groin. Everyone who was able to fight blazed at it until it fell, thrashing. A flopping infantryman was in its hands, looking like a toy. Even though we took it down with concentrated, close-range fire, it had time to crush the man's helmet with its massive jaws. The headless body was then cast away, twirling end over end until it crashed down onto the upper hull of the lifter and lay there motionless.

"Unit," Graves said, still sounding like he was officiating at some kind of picnic, "I've been informed that the lifter crew is about to employ anti-personnel weaponry. Take cover—*now*."

For a moment, my mind froze over. Then I remembered what he was talking about. Our lifters had new equipment: anti-personnel turrets. Essentially, these weapons systems were pulse-lasers on rotating mounts. The weapons had been added after our troubles on Machine World. I'd been briefed on them, but I'd never seen them in action.

Looking over the scene, I thought it might be disastrous to employ such a tool now. We had every soldier left alive in the legion out here defending the line. The automated turrets didn't always know friend from foe, as I recalled. If they had a target, they fired, regardless of who might be behind that target or even in-between the target and the turret.

"Take cover!" I shouted to my squad, throwing myself into the trench again.

154

Others tried to follow me, but it wasn't easy for all of us to fit. The soft dirt of our trenches had been greatly disrupted. Much of the trench line had been filled in by the tread of multi-ton monsters as they charged over us.

Gazing out of my thin line of cover, I realized why the lifter people were panicking. The creatures were all over the ship, tearing at it. Metal chunks had already been ripped from the hull. In their combined fury and strength, they'd managed to shift the entire lifter, and it now stood at a cant of perhaps five or ten degrees. All around the perimeter of the transport, more and more aliens were rushing up, joining their frenzied comrades. They were about to tip the ship up and over.

The turrets rolled out of protective clamshells. Visually, the effect was like that of a large animal opening eyes that had been tightly clamped shut. There were five or six turrets within my field of view—too many for my comfort.

When the turrets began to fire, things got worse. As far as I could tell, they were killing men as often as aliens. For every monster that was lit up and blown apart, at least one of our own troops died in the flashing spillover.

Scrambling on all fours, I crawled up against the body of an alien and took refuge there. As I moved, I felt something catch my foot. I pulled hard and quickly broke free.

Dragging myself, sides heaving, I fell back against the trunk of the dying alien. It was still shivering with those fronds it had on its trunk twitching and squirming like dying snakes. But it provided shelter for me with its body.

Two of my troopers joined me in short order. One was Carlos, the other was Kivi.

"You hurt, boss?" Carlos asked.

"I'm fine," I said. "Keep down. We'll be okay."

Carlos gave Kivi a worried glance. We were all staying low, up against the fallen trunk of the alien. Carlos backed down the length of my body, toward my boots. He kept the body of the fallen monster against his shoulder as he moved.

"Just lie still, McGill," he said.

I felt something then. It was a hard tug on my foot. "What the hell are you doing?" I demanded.

"I'm doing my job, Vet. Kivi, get his attention."

Kivi's face came into view. I was lying on my back now, and my breathing was ragged. I felt a little funny.

"James," Kivi said, forcing a smile. "You're going to be okay. You took a hit, that's all. Just lie here and let Carlos do what he's been trained to do."

I knew it was good advice the second I heard it. But as my mama could have told you, I wasn't much for following good advice.

Heaving myself into a sitting position, I grunted and strained. I pushed Kivi away and stared down at my legs.

One of them was missing, just below the knee.

"Damn," I said. "Those frigging turrets. That was Winslade, I'd bet you a dollar to a donut. He ordered them to let loose with the turrets."

"I've almost got this," Carlos said. "But you've lost a lot of blood, Vet. You need to lie flat. Sitting up is sending more blood right out of your body."

"What good am I with one leg missing anyway?" I demanded. I tried to get up, but they both worked to stop me.

If I'm one thing, I'm a large, strong man. I bowled Kivi backward and pushed Carlos' face out of mine.

Lifting my rifle, I unloaded it into the nearest creature. The monster went down with a crash, but it wasn't just my doing. It was one of the last ones standing. Lots of people were firing at it. It felt good to see it fall anyway. In each of its alien claws, it clutched an armored corpse, as if it didn't want to let them go.

I looked around the battlefield, sweating and panting. I grinned.

"Looks like we wiped them out," I said. "Maybe Winslade made the right call after all."

Carlos came back to my side and gently tried to push me down. I felt myself sinking. I didn't remember him being that strong.

I kept on sinking after I was lying on my back. Spinning, too. I wanted to vomit, but I couldn't get anything to come up.

Carlos and Kivi were saying something, but I didn't catch their words.

Then, looking up at plants so tall that hazy clouds drifted between my eyes and their glorious crowns…I died.

156

-21-

While I was dead, a thought occurred to me.

No, it didn't *really* happen that way…but it felt as if it did.

Sometimes, when a man is revived, it seems like his mind has been dreaming while floating in a hazy half-existence between life and death. This was just one of those times.

The thought that was fixed in my mind as I breathed with fresh lungs, coughing and hacking, was that I'd been wronged. I shouldn't have had my leg blown off. It was the fault of my officers, and I wasn't happy about that.

My mouth worked the moment I came back, but my limbs were sluggish. I squinted as I opened my eyes. All I could see was bright white lights and shadows moving nearby.

I knew they were bio people. For some reason they seemed like ghouls to me today, and I wanted nothing to do with them.

"You can all go to Hell," I said in raspy voice.

"What's that?" asked a voice. I recognized it was Anne after a moment, but I didn't care. I was in a bad mood this time around.

"I said you're all assholes, and Winslade's the worst of your kind."

"You're not making any sense, James," she said patiently. "I can barely understand your slurred words."

Sitting up with a grunt and a deep breath, I found an orderly was poking at my neck with something.

"What's his Apgar score?" Anne asked.

"Nine, I'd say. He's a good grow by all the numbers—but his mind seems fuzzy."

"Give him a minute."

The orderly poked at me again. His face was too close to mine. He was looking into my ear for some shitty reason. I found him and his instruments to be intolerable.

I put my hand on his face and pushed. The man went over and back onto his ass with a satisfying crash.

Another face appeared in my limited field of view after that. It was Anne, and she looked pissed. Her arms were crossed under her small breasts, pushing them up a little.

"That's not an appropriate attitude, Veteran," she said.

I looked at her. More specifically, I looked at her breasts. They were plumped up by her arms, and I focused on them blearily.

"You've got nice ones," I said. "They look perfectly round, like apples."

She made an odd sound of disgust then. "Are you making a pass at me, James? The moment you come back? Are you serious?"

"Suppose I am?"

"Well, that has to be the worst pick-up line I've ever heard."

Despite myself, a smile flickered over my face. "I'm a little off my game," I mumbled.

"You sure are. Now, is there a reason why you're abusing my staff?"

I looked at the orderly. He was standing well clear of me, looking wary and irritated.

"Hey guy," I said. "You look like you're going to cry. Why don't you go pout somewhere else?"

Anne moved between me and the orderly as I began to climb off the table. Maybe she took my move as threatening.

"James," she said. "You're exhibiting aggressive behavior without cause. That's not good. Try to get a grip on yourself right now."

I finally grasped what she was saying. She had the right and the duty to recycle me if my brain wasn't working correctly. If

I'd come back physically crippled, I'd have been killed for that as well.

"I'm fine," I said.

"Sometimes," Anne said, eyeing me in concern, "a bad grow doesn't have a twisted limb or an organ failure that's easy to measure with a blood test. Sometimes, they come back with a twist in the mind. I'm hoping that's not your story, James."

"It's not. I'm fine."

"Can you tell me why you're angry?" she asked gently.

The truth was that her questioning was pissing me off. But that wouldn't have been a good thing to admit. Instead, I tried to remember why I'd come off the table so sure that I'd been mistreated.

The thoughts I'd awakened with were hard to grasp. They were already like dreams that faded the second you woke up. Often, a minute or two after re-birth, I couldn't recall what I'd been thinking about as I woke up.

But then, I finally remembered.

"I've got it now," I said. "The turrets—the officers screwed up."

"What do you mean, James?"

"They put the troops out in the forest instead of using our new defenses. They should have kept us back, under the hull of the lifter. They should have deployed the turrets before the giants even showed up. If they'd done that, only a few of us would have died. Maybe none of us would have. That's why I'm pissed off. Hundreds died for nothing."

Anne looked at me thoughtfully. After a moment, she nodded. "You have a point. We lost about half the force we had out there. I'm no tactician, but I can see why you aren't happy."

I sucked in another breath, and I felt better. I took a second to glance at the orderly.

"Sorry," I said.

"No problem," he responded. But I could see in his eyes that it *was* a problem.

I ignored him and moved to the lockers. I pulled on a uniform and left the revival chamber. As I did so, I could hear the orderly talking to Anne quietly.

"Are you sure he's okay?" the man asked.

"It's my call, and I've made it."

"Yeah, sure. Your call."

Feeling another mild surge of anger toward the nosy, whining orderly, I left the chamber before I could act on it.

Was something wrong with me? What part of the brain controlled anger? I had no idea. Could it be true they'd brought me back to life with new emotional problems that I didn't already have? Wonderful.

Usually, when troops were revived outside of battle, they headed for their bunks or maybe got a light meal. I did neither. I almost didn't know where I was headed until I got there.

The guards at the ladder that led up to the officer's deck let me pass after a cursory glance. After all, I'd blown past them with Winslade's blessing just a few hours earlier. They had no idea what I was intending to do.

Winslade was in his office, but he wasn't alone. The primus had a guest.

Claver was strapped to a chair in front of Winslade's desk. I barged in and stared. Claver's head was lolling strangely.

"What the...?" Winslade demanded. "Oh, it's you McGill. I thought you were still dead. Well, no matter. Did they send you to collect the body? That's what I requested. I thought you were an orderly. Such an inconvenience having them all so busy down there."

I was still staring at Claver. His head rested on his chest. His tongue protruded, and his eyes were open a fraction.

"You *killed* him?" I asked.

Winslade laughed. "Slow today, are we? Claver chose not to give me the information I wanted. I decided to reroll, as it were. Next time, we'll get more from him. I've learned a few things from this experience."

There was blood on the floor. Claver's blood. My eyes crawled over it silently.

Now, don't get me wrong—Claver has always been a card-carrying fucker of the first order. I'd once watched him cause thousands of Tau to die just because they inconvenienced him.

But that didn't mean the man should be tortured to death. What made it worse was knowing I'd suggested we revive him for questioning.

This same cruel cycle of life, torture and death, had been visited upon my person in the past, and I took a dim view of the practice.

"If there really is a Hell and there's any justice in this universe," I said, "someday Claver will be the devil's favorite."

Winslade cocked his head and narrowed his eyes. "You're in an odd, poetic mood today."

"But that doesn't mean," I continued as if he hadn't spoken, "that we should torture and kill even such a wretch as he!"

I looked up, meeting Winslade's gaze.

He knew then what I intended. He saw the emotions surging behind my eyes. A murderous lust burned in my twisted mind. An anger I couldn't hide any longer.

"What's wrong with you, McGill?" he asked. "Has something gone wrong with your revive?"

"I don't think so, sir," I said. "I think it's gone very right. I think I can see more clearly now than ever before."

Winslade nodded and sat on his desk nonchalantly as if he didn't have a care in the world. I didn't have a weapon—but we both knew that didn't matter.

"Your head is tilting to one side, and your left eye is blinking on its own," Winslade said. "Are you even aware of that?"

"What I'm aware of is your shortcomings as an officer," I said. "You ordered us to set up a defensive position too far out from the lifter. We should've been tightly circled under the vehicle's struts. Then anti-personnel turrets could have been deployed safely with us in reserve—instead of the other way around."

Winslade shrugged. "Tactical hindsight? Really? That's what this is all about? You think you know better than I do how to run a cohort?"

"Yes," I said flatly.

He frowned at me. "I shall have you arrested for this," he said. "But I want to hear more first. Let's hear what you *really* think."

"I think you're a sadist who sat up here toying with Claver instead of doing your job," I began, and it got worse from there. I told him everything I thought—hell, everything the whole legion thought about Primus Winslade.

He shot me before I even finished my tirade. I never saw it coming. Whatever else he was, he was a sneaky bastard. He'd had a small, concealed needler in his palm the whole time. I figured that out later.

When I was on my back, trying to breathe and staring up at him, he dared to loom close.

"You want to know what *I* think?" he asked me conversationally. "I think you're a big baby who didn't like dying in a fight. Worse, you're a bad grow. A mental case. That's lucky for you because I'm going to give you another chance, just like Claver, here. Now, when you wake up, I want you to come upstairs again and give me the best apology you're capable of. One that money can't buy. Do you understand?"

Growling and spitting blood, I reached for his throat. I caught hold of his neck for a moment, squeezing, but I lost my grip. I was gratified to see the shock on his face as my big fingers tore at his shirt and pulled him off-balance.

Then the needler sang again, and my nerves wouldn't obey me any longer. I gargled and twitched for a time before dying. I was happy to see Winslade, panting and leaning up against a far wall, waiting at a safe distance for me to die. There were marks on his neck. Red welts that would turn purple by tomorrow.

I died with a feral grin on my face.

-22-

When I slid out of the revival machine's maw for the second time in a single day, Anne had her hands on her hips instead of crossed under her breasts. Her expression was a mixture of wariness and irritation.

"Well James? Are we crazy again today?"

"Nope," I said, feeling it was true. "Not any more than usual, that is."

She shook her head and sighed. "You really got me in trouble, you know that? I'm up on report for letting you out of this chamber. The only thing that's saving my stripes is the fact you failed to finish off Winslade."

"Pity," I said, sitting up and rubbing my face.

She looked at me sharply, and I grinned back at her.

"Just kidding," I said. "If a man's got to die, what better way is there to go out than trying to kill Winslade?"

"What *is* your problem, exactly?" she demanded.

I explained about Claver being tortured and revived again, and how the same thing had happened to me once. It was something I had trouble contemplating, even now.

She nodded slowly. "You were traumatized in a past life, so you took it out on Winslade. You know, your story does make better sense than his did. Winslade claimed Claver went for his gun, and he had to kill him."

"Did you see the body?" I asked.

"No," she admitted.

163

"Two deaths in Winslade's office in one day? What are the odds?"

She looked troubled. "If he's torturing prisoners to death...well...that goes against Hegemony regulations. He could be in trouble for that. Claver is a citizen, after all, and some of the people back at Central actually like him."

"Yes, they probably do—but Turov and Winslade don't."

Anne nodded. "Okay, so you had your reasons for going nuts. But I'm asking you again, for confirmation: you feel less angry now, right?"

"Yes," I admitted. "There was a white heat in my mind before—I couldn't control it."

"Probably a duplication error in the prefrontal cortex," she said. "That's the part of the mind that manages our responses to surprises and other stimuli. You couldn't second-guess your reactions, you just gave into them. That kind of error in a grow is hard to detect."

"I can see why," I said. "What now? Am I under arrest or something?"

"As I understand it, Winslade is waiting for you in his office."

Frowning, I pulled on a uniform. "Do you know what he's waiting for?"

"Do you remember what he said when you died? He told me about it."

I strained to remember. Things were coming back to me slowly.

"Oh," I said as I remembered. "An apology. He said he wanted an apology."

"Right. A sincere one."

Heaving an angry sigh, I thought it over. It wasn't the worst possible fate. Maybe I should just do it now and get it over with.

But somehow, I didn't want to.

"Anne?" I asked.

She'd already moved on, tending to her strange machine.

"What?" she asked, without looking over her shoulder.

"Come take a break with me, will you? A short one."

164

"You *are* still crazy, aren't you? Do you know how many people are still on my revival list? We've only got one machine."

"So make another bio and hand off the task. How long has it been since you had some downtime? You can't revive the entire legion without taking a break."

Anne stretched and groaned. She looked at the duty roster displayed on her tapper. I glanced over her shoulder. As I'd figured, she'd already been at it for two solid shifts.

In the end, she followed me out. The orderlies shook their heads and gawked after us in bemusement. I tried not to notice.

Over a cup of coffee, she stared at me meaningfully.

"You're just trying to delay your fate, aren't you?" she asked.

"You mean about apologizing to Winslade? I was hoping for more than that."

"What are you talking about?"

"You have the power—the power to set things right, Anne."

She stopped munching on her pastry and put her coffee in front of her mouth to hide her lips. Some of the cameras and drones could read lips, I knew, and I guessed she was trying to prevent that.

"What are you talking about?" she whispered. "Are you about to go ape again?"

"Probably not. But just hear me out before you call security."

Her eyes slid around the place, and finally landed back on me. "All right. Talk."

"Winslade is screwing up, right?" I asked her.

"I don't know—well okay, I guess he is. But we're still alive."

"For now, but those aliens will come again. Maybe there will be ten times as many next time."

"What are you talking about?"

I explained to her what Natasha and Kivi had said about the pods being biological defense systems for the megaflora. That a single plant had generated around fifteen of them in response

165

to our presence. She looked shocked and worried when I finished explaining these things.

"Here we are," I said, leaning across the table toward her, "sitting in the legion's last lifter and waiting around to see what the aliens will do next. What's our goal? What's Winslade's plan? How will he get us out of this?"

"I don't know. He must have a plan. He's in command."

"His plan is to torture Claver for information on the enemy. He may or may not get anything useful. In the meantime, we're close to being wiped as a legion. This lifter is all that's left. *Minotaur* is dead."

"It's a grim situation," she admitted. "But it's not our job to fix it."

I nodded in agreement. "I know. But I also know the stakes are high. Sometimes, you have to take action even if it's not fully sanctioned."

"What can we do about it?"

"Would you rather have a different person in command right now?"

She looked at me thoughtfully. "I guess—sure. Winslade's not the best."

"Right. Here's my point: you and I—right here, right now—we have the power to decide who's in command."

Anne's eyes widened. "Where do you get these ideas, James? And why am I listening to this?"

I smiled tiredly. "It's a curse. I don't like doing things off-script, really I don't. But when you see a disaster coming at you, isn't it your duty to at least try to stop it? Even if it's some else's job?"

Anne sipped her coffee, and she licked her lips. "Who? Who are you suggesting we revive? Do you really think Turov would be better?"

"Actually, she might be. But there's another officer in the chain of command that should be alive right now. Only Winslade's bullshit is keeping him dead."

"Tribune Drusus?"

"Right."

She leaned back and she sipped her coffee. She didn't seem to want to look at me. Her hands shook slightly as she looked into her mug.

"All right, I'll do it," she said at last. "Damn you, James. I'm such a sucker."

"If you are, it's only because you can see the truth. You know I'm right. Drusus or Turov should be running this show. That's regulations. Winslade is playing God by keeping them dead."

"I know."

In the past, Anne had been party to a few off-script revivals. She'd brought me back to life after I'd been sentenced to be permed, for example. Partly because of that, I knew she could be swayed to use her power over life and death if it was for a good cause.

After Anne was onboard, the rest was easy. We walked back to the revival chamber and dialed in the changes to the queue.

There was a scare about fifteen minutes later as we were delivering Tribune Drusus, however.

"Specialist?" an orderly asked Anne. "Primus Winslade wants to talk to you. Have you got your tapper on silent?"

Anne looked at me. She looked guilty and a little scared. "Sorry—I'll take the call."

She stepped away while I toweled Drusus off and gave him a uniform. The orderly looked back and forth at Anne and me, clearly wondering what the hell I was doing in the chamber and what we were up to. But so far, he hadn't asked directly.

"Winslade's coming down here," Anne said. "He wants a fresh Claver."

"A third one?"

She nodded grimly.

Tribune Drusus sat up, bleary-eyed. "What's this about Claver?" he asked us.

I turned toward him and smiled. "Good to see you back among the living, sir."

"Brief me on our status, Veteran," Drusus ordered, "very quickly.

"Gladly, sir."

167

As I talked, Drusus dressed and left the revival chamber. He walked with me toward the upper decks of the lifter. His face grew darker by the second as he listened.

I gave him a fast run-down. He'd been dead for over two days. Winslade was in overall command of the expedition by default. We'd suffered alien attacks and lost half our remaining troops. Conveniently, I left out everything about Winslade and me fighting in his office, but I did mention we'd revived Claver to question him about the fate of the freighter.

"I felt I had to act, sir," I finished. "Specialist Grant shouldn't be blamed for disobeying orders. I convinced her that regulations were not being followed regarding the designated order of revivals."

"Meaning you didn't like having Winslade in charge of the last few members of this legion?"

I nodded.

"Hmm," Drusus said. "I'll have to reconsider your actions when I've got the current emergency under control. In the meantime—thanks for getting me out of purgatory."

"You're welcome, Tribune."

Winslade met up with us before we reached his office. He was coming the other way, probably wondering what the hold-up was down in the revival chamber.

When he saw Drusus, Winslade's eyes flashed wide, showing the whites for a brief moment—then he had control of himself again. I don't think there were two people he would have been less happy to run into right then.

His left hand clasped his right, making a single popping clap of happiness. A false smile flickered over his mouth.

"Sir! Tribune Drusus! I'm so glad to see you up and about! I am so glad that we've finally gotten past the combat troops and into the upper brass revivals. Great news, that."

Drusus gave him a flat stare in return. "Let's take a little walk, shall we?"

I stopped following them then. Winslade took a moment to glance back at me. His eyes were full of venom, but I didn't care.

He hadn't gotten an apology out of me, and as far as I was concerned, he never would.

168

-23-

The third version of Claver lasted longer than the first two. I supposed that was due to the fact Tribune Drusus had taken over the interrogation.

Drusus invited me to the festivities. I was there because I'd heard Claver's story the first time, and Drusus wanted a fact-checker. Winslade, due to his excesses, wasn't allowed in the room at all.

"Let's go over this carefully," Drusus said. "You know of these creatures. You call them the Wur. You've dealt with them, and you know their points of origin."

"Not exactly," Claver said. "I know they plague the squids. That's how I first found out about them. They're like a cancer in the Cephalopod Kingdom. Forgotten worlds, wilderness planets—they start right in the midst of your territory like a deadly fungus quietly growing in a city park. They expand insidiously, covering an entire world with their vegetation."

"So, are you saying this forest we're in is all part of an alien biomass?"

"Yes. Exactly. The small mobile creatures they spawn— they're only a defense mechanism, like the white blood cells in our bodies. The gigantic plants themselves, the things you might erroneously call trees—those are our alien opponents."

It was hard to fathom. I was used to thinking of plants as mindless and fairly harmless. The idea I was sitting even now at the foot of an evil thinking being, one that couldn't move but which could *grow* things that moved for it—the concept was alarming, to say the least.

"I'm still unclear as to the nature of your interaction with these aliens," Drusus said. "How did you come to make a deal with them? Why did they chase and attack you?"

"Hold on a minute, boss," Claver said, chuckling. "I didn't make any deals. I just happen to know a few things about them from the squids, that's all."

Drusus shook his head and glanced toward me. "I'm beginning to understand why Winslade lost his patience with this man."

Claver's eyes narrowed. "Is that a threat, sir? Are you planning to torture and kill me just like your primus? Come to think of it, he might have been acting under your orders... Maybe this whole rescue routine is part of your grand plan, cooked up to trick me into giving you information I don't have. Well sir, let me warn you, Central is going to hear all of this eventually. Central will hear me out!"

Tribune Drusus seemed unmoved.

"Yes," he said. "I am threatening you. Cooperate, or you'll wish you had."

Claver kicked up his foot and stuck out his bare toes, spreading them wide.

"Start blowing them off, then," he said. "Just like Winslade did—at your orders! Fiends, the lot of you Varus people."

Drusus smiled. "That approach didn't work for Winslade. And for the record, he operated without my consent. But...his results were still instructive. I've got a different fate in store for you, if you should refuse to cooperate."

"Refuse to..." Claver sputtered then he cranked his neck around and looked at me. "Are you listening to this? I'm counting on you as a witness when Equestrian Nagata takes down the full report. Abuse, distrust, accusations without grounding—McGill, you'll back me up in court, won't you?"

I stared at him for a moment, thinking. When I had my thoughts lined up, I answered. "I didn't like the way Winslade treated you. In fact, I tried to kill him for it."

Claver brightened and gave me a fierce grin. "You went for Winslade? I love it. Boy, I owe you one for that."

170

Drusus looked uncomfortable, but I pretended not to notice. I didn't like Winslade, and I'd reacted while in a less controlled state of mind. All that didn't mean I was in love with Claver, however.

"Don't get any big ideas," I told the prisoner. "I'm not going to save you from every legionnaire that wants a pound of your flesh. You should know that my parents were in the crowd when your ship smashed down into Earth. They were permed out there at the spaceport."

Claver licked his lips. "I'm sorry," he mumbled, "but that wasn't my fault."

Drusus cleared his throat. "Do I have your attention, Claver? Good. Here's what will happen if I'm unhappy with your responses from here on out—"

"This ought to be good," Claver interrupted, sneering.

"Hegemony made an agreement with you," Drusus said, "which allows you to share in the trading rights for resources mined on Gamma Pavonis. It's stipulated in that agreement that criminal actions void the contract. I will move to declare your contract null and void, and I'll strip you of your transportation and trading rights, which under—"

"Whoa, whoa, whoa!" Claver said, eyes bulging. "That's just plain mean! What's more, it's counterproductive and illegal. I'll fight you, every step of the way. You don't have the authority to—"

"No? You forget, sir: I'm in command of this expedition. This task force has been granted punitive powers. I could easily execute you permanently—but there might well be another Claver out there somewhere, still operating. No, the best way to gain your cooperation is to attack your source of wealth. Are you listening now?"

"Yes, Tribune," Claver said, glowering defiantly.

"All right then. Let's hear that story again. This time, make me believe it."

I had to hand it to Tribune Drusus. He knew this scoundrel well. Claver would rather die than give up incriminating information. But when faced with the loss of his most lucrative contract, he'd buckled.

"First, I want assurances," Claver said. "I want your word my contracts will continue, at your recommendation, if you find my story credible. No matter how happy or unhappy the truth makes you."

Drusus considered for a moment. "Agreed," he said at last.

"Okay then, good," Claver's said. His voice shifted suddenly, and I was under the impression he was speaking plainly and truthfully—perhaps for the first time.

"Here's the deal," he began, "I traded with these plant-people. They're weird, but they understand payment and the delivery of goods. I found out about them from the squids, just as I said. I thought to myself at the time that I shouldn't be a bigot, just because they're plants. These fellows might turn out to be good customers. After all, they operate like rebels inside the Cephalopod Kingdom. So, I contacted them and offered them titanium."

So far, I believed his story. Claver always had a nose for deals. He'd trade with anyone—or anything.

"You see, they *need* metals," he continued. "Most of the planets they inhabit are like this one, low-metal worlds. Most species don't like low-metal worlds as they don't make good colonial homesteads. But these plants—they don't need metals .Except, that is, for one thing."

"Starships," Drusus said.

"Exactly! Starships. They need metal to build them, to escape a world they've overgrown and move on to the next. No one can reach escape velocity from a world with cellulose, acids and organic gasses alone. They need more powerful chemical reactions. Things that can only be contained in the best of metals."

"Trading with such beings—that's a treasonous offense all by itself," Drusus pointed out.

"Hold on, hold on. Remember, they weren't inside the boundaries of Frontier 921. They were in the squid kingdom. They were beyond the frontier, outside the Empire. So...I made some perfectly legal deals. I ran metals to their secret worlds, the ones the squids had yet to stomp out. It's been giving the squids fits, by the way. In a manner of speaking, I'm a misunderstood hero, sir, and that's the God's-honest truth."

Drusus seemed amused. "Could you explain your thinking on that point?"

"Well, I've been supplying our worst enemy's enemy with critical supplies. Why do you think they haven't flown to Earth and wiped us out yet? Fear of the Empire? Hardly. They have problems of their own. Their ships are busy. I've been helping to keep them busy."

"Everything you're saying makes a strange kind of sense," Drusus admitted. "But I fail to see why these beings chased you to Earth and tried to destroy you if you were their benefactor."

"Yeah, that part. Well, like I said, I was doing business with them inside squid territory. But then they wanted me to make a secret delivery inside the borders of Frontier 921. At first, I thought they wanted to meet out here where squid patrol boats wouldn't pick us up. Imagine my shock when I saw they'd colonized a world right here, in the midst of Imperial space!"

Drusus nodded. "So, you refused to do the deal?"

"Essentially…" Claver said, eyeing both of us. He shrugged. "I turned my ship around, went into warp and pulled out. They chased me to Earth. You know the rest."

The whole scenario was clear in my mind now. Claver had been scared to find a colonized world near Earth. He'd run out on his trading partners. Enraged—probably because they'd already made payment—the Wur had chased him to Earth and destroyed his freighter.

Drusus' hand fell on Claver's shoulder. Claver flinched in response, but Drusus didn't strike him.

"Claver," he said, "I'm going to accept this version of events. I'm sure you've edited the story heavily in your favor. But a deal gone bad—I can buy that story. I can also buy that you'd deal with an alien menace so dangerous it's seriously damaging an interstellar neighbor of ours."

"Why, thank you kindly, sir—" Claver began.

"—but," Drusus continued, "I want you to understand that your actions still border on treason. None of these dealings have been sanctioned by Earth or the Galactics. You're operating outside the law. You're aiding and abetting a threat to this entire region of space. These beings will never be content with a few forgotten worlds among the stars, will they? They have clear ambitions to take this region of space for themselves."

Claver shifted uncomfortably, and Drusus removed his hand from the man's shoulder.

"That said," Drusus went on, "a deal is a deal. You're free to go."

"A deal is a deal!" Claver agreed happily. "I'd prefer to be dropped off on Machine World, where I have associates waiting, if it's not too much trouble."

"You misunderstand me," Drusus said, his eyes dark and unblinking. "You're free to exit this lifter. To walk among your megaflora friends."

"What? You're kicking me off this ship? They'll—they may not be very understanding, Tribune, sir."

Drusus nodded. "That's possible. But that's not my fault now, is it? In the future, should we meet again, I would suggest you keep local Earth officials apprised of discoveries of this magnitude. Are we clear?"

Claver sputtered and complained, but in the end, he was kicked off the lifter and out into the forest. We gave him supplies, a vac-suit and a snap-rifle—in my opinion, that was more than he deserved.

I watched as Claver wandered off into the forest, casting dark glances over his shoulder toward the curious troops who watched him leave.

"Banishment," Drusus said to me. "An ancient, traditional punishment. If anyone might survive such a fate, it's a man like Claver."

"I think it was a good call, sir," I said.

Drusus looked at me appraisingly. "I'm glad you feel that way. I've studied your case as well, McGill. While I know that Legion Varus has a tradition of accepting off-script behavior from their troops, we can't allow anarchy to prevail. Your actions regarding Winslade and disobeying orders—they're too great to be ignored."

My heart sank. I felt certain I was about to learn my fate today as well.

"I understand, sir," I said standing tall. Whatever he was going to say, I'd accept it. I had a level of respect for Drusus that was greater than any officer in the legion—with the possible exception of Centurion Graves.

"Good," he said. "Here's your mission—or punishment, if you prefer to think of it that way. You'll gather your squad. Together, you'll follow Claver discreetly. Use buzzers to track him in the forest. Find out where he's going and what he's up to. There are so many things we don't understand about this planet and Claver's interactions, such as how he talks to giant trees in the first place. Your job, from now on, is to learn those details."

My mouth hung open. "Uh...but what about the Wur, sir?"

"You'll deal with them. You have my utter confidence. Report in daily, and try to stay out of sight."

"Right...uh, sir? When do we return?"

Drusus gave me a thoughtful glance. "I'll review your reports. Possibly, I'll make the decision that your reconnaissance team is worthy of a rescue effort. In the meantime, I'm taking this lifter out of this region. It stands to reason the Wur pod-walkers will attack this camp again, and I don't want to be here when they do."

I nodded numbly. Then I had a thought.

"But sir...why punish my whole squad? They didn't do anything wrong."

"That's another lesson. As a commander of troops, you must always be thinking of the people who are following you. They will pay for every mistake you make. It's called responsibility. You might want to look that one up on your tapper."

"I'll do that, Tribune."

"Good luck, McGill," he said.

Then Tribune Drusus turned around and mounted the ramp into the dark hold of the lifter. I watched him go, feeling like a man who'd been exiled.

Because that's exactly what had happened.

-24-

In distant Roman times, banishment had been a common form of punishment for society's rejects. Sometimes it was suffered by a family member who no one could stand, or an entire household cast out of their homes by their fellow villagers. Nations sometimes rejected whole tribes, exiling them and commanding them to leave for the wilds. It was a fate that had been suffered by many in history.

I stood at the edge of the encampment. My grim-faced band of soldiers was arrayed behind me. The officers were watching from behind the safety of the lifter's blast-glass. Winslade had called our mission a "deep patrol" for the benefit of the squad, but I knew the score. We were being sent on a suicide mission. Even if we did make it back, there wouldn't be anyone here because the lifter was leaving without us.

We stepped over the still smoking bodies of the Wur. I entered the forest with no illusions. This was "Death World."

At the rear of our procession was a revving drone, a pig loaded with everything we'd need for several weeks. That fact had my team in a bad mood. They weren't dumb. They could count, and a large amount of supplies meant a lot of marching around in these deadly woods.

"What the hell is this all about?" Carlos demanded when we'd left the main camp behind. He craned his neck this way and that, peering into the undergrowth for other squads. "Deep patrol? I don't see anyone else marching off to their deaths in these ferns. What makes us so special?"

"Haven't you heard?" Kivi asked. "McGill went ape and shot Winslade. The bio people in the revival room are all whispering about it."

I glanced at the two of them in irritation. "I didn't shoot anybody."

"Then why did you take *two* trips through our revival machine today, Vet?" Kivi demanded.

"Bad luck, I guess."

Refusing to explain any further, I led them deeper into the quiet forest. This planet was probably the quietest place I'd ever visited. Normally, there was wildlife peeping and howling in a landscape like this. But we heard very few sounds of that nature. No insects buzzed. No animals screeched or growled. The forest was dead, in a way. Only the profusion of gigantic plants, an alien species that had invaded the planet fairly recently, showed we were on a living world at all.

My squad grumbled and engaged in wild speculations. I figured it was a good diversion for them. They didn't know that we'd been sent off to die out here while the lifter took off for greener pastures. I was a little worried about a breakdown in discipline when they figured out that part.

"Vet?" Kivi asked after a half-hour had passed.

"Yes, Specialist?"

"I recommend that we remove our helmets, or at least open our faceplates."

"Why's that?"

"You hear that hiss in your suit? That's the air-conditioning, and it's wasting power. If we want to be able to fight a prolonged engagement, we should reduce consumption. The oxygen levels in this atmosphere are nearly double that of Earth. There won't be any problem with breathing."

I looked at her for a moment. Kivi was my tech specialist. I would have traded both her and Carlos for Natasha, but Natasha had moved up to support Graves and wasn't part of my squad directly. She hadn't come with us on this trip. I'd felt both good and bad about that. We could sure have used her, but I was glad to spare her from my punishment.

My eyes shifted to Carlos. "Bio? Do you agree with Kivi on this?"

He nodded. "We'll save power with the faceplates open, except during peak heat. As to toxins, we've yet to identify any in the air. The plants are dangerous, even the ones that don't march around. But we can breathe."

I gave the order. Soon, we were all more comfortable, walking with heads bared.

Our helmets were new, and in my opinion, superior in design to the previous models. They were no longer solid titanium casings. Instead, they resembled a series of concentric shells. They could be folded up into what looked like a crescent moon when not in use and stowed in our rucks. We stashed them away and breathed clean air.

"Feels good, doesn't it, Vet?" asked Lau. The rookie had come up to the front of the line to march with me.

Feeling a sour frown growing on my face, I struggled to stop that response. I fought an urge to smack the boy down. That's what Harris would have done, but I felt that while many of Harris' behavioral habits represented wisdom on his part, others were born of plain orneriness. I forced a half-smile and nodded to the kid instead.

"Sure does, Lau. Night's coming, and the temperature is dropping. I'm drying off sweat that I thought was permanent. It's enough to make you look forward to darkness."

"Vet?" Kivi called. "My buzzers have made contact with someone ahead of us."

I rushed to her position and looked at a tiny screen.

"That's got to be Claver," I said. "Squad halt! Everyone shut up."

Crouching, a few curious heads crowded around. I didn't push them back. They were going to find out what was going on sooner or later.

"Claver?" Kivi asked in a hushed voice as she recognized the hiker that her buzzer was tracking. She looked at me. "Is that what we're doing out here? Following Claver?"

"Yes," I said.

"Why didn't you just tell us that, Vet?" Carlos demanded.

I glanced at him. "Because I didn't want anyone tipping him off."

That statement was partly true, but mostly, it was bullshit. Telling them we were following Claver wasn't going to stop their questions. They were going to pile them on now.

Sure enough, Carlos and Kivi were already frowning. I wondered if I'd somehow spawned two more James McGills: underlings that questioned everything you did.

"McGill?" Carlos asked in a whisper. "Why are we following Claver? Why not just arrest him, or better yet, shoot his ass?"

"The brass thinks he might lead us to something. We'll follow him and keep out of sight. Just have one buzzer on his tail at a time, Kivi, at a safe distance."

"Got it. He's moving again, about two kilometers ahead of our position. We should veer about twenty degrees west."

We followed Kivi's directions, and eventually the sun went down. Claver kept on walking, so we did the same.

Along about midnight, when my soldiers were beginning to complain about the long march, Claver finally stopped and made camp.

I noted with interest that he didn't light a fire or pitch a tent. He didn't even cut down a fern to make a bed. Instead, he crawled into the ferns and wove the leaves together making a sort of nest around himself.

"That's weird," Kivi said, watching on her tapper while chewing her rations. "Why do you think he's doing that?"

"Hmm," I said. "I think he's going to great pains not to tear up the ferns. Maybe he knows something we don't know."

"Yeah?" Carlos said, laughing. "I think he's some kind of eco-freak. I hate these ferns. They never stop lashing me in the face."

So saying, he unleashed a force-blade, extending it from the forearm of his suit. With a single deft motion, he slashed down a big branch from the nearest fern. The smell of burnt plant material tingled in our noses.

"Dammit, Carlos," I said. "Don't mess with the plants unless I give you an order to do so! Got that?"

"Sure, Vet," he said, organizing his kill into a bed of sorts. "But do you mind telling me why not?"

I walked over and hauled him to his feet. "Because," I said angrily into his surprised face. "They might not *like* it."

He gave a nervous laugh, which I ignored. I released him and walked away.

"You mean they might grow pods or something?" he asked. "I doubt that. The pods came from the big trees, not these ferns."

I sat on a root the size of a truck and looked at him. Kivi began to explain before I could.

"Look," Kivi said. "McGill's right. We don't know this world. What we *do* know is that these plants have complex defense mechanisms. They might do anything—grow a pod, whatever."

"But this is just a fern, right?"

"Yes, but remember that according to Galactic records, nothing lived here a few centuries ago. The ferns and the trees—they don't belong here. They've been transplanted, seeded here. I don't trust anything that grows here."

Carlos studied the fern branch he'd bedded down on with concern. Finally, he got up and dragged it away. Then he came back and lay on the dirt.

"This is bullshit," he complained. "I bet Claver knows about the buzzer. I bet he's just screwing with us on purpose."

"Maybe," I said. "Why don't you test your theory? Chop up a few plants and make a log cabin out of them. If you're fine in the morning, we'll all know it's safe."

"Just like the rockfish back on Dust World, huh? No thanks, Vet."

I chuckled, set up a watch order, and fell asleep.

* * *

When I was awakened, it was by a panicked Kivi.

She was shaking me, talking rapidly. Behind her head, the sun filtered through the thick canopy of green growths. The light was gloomy, but it was clearly morning.

180

"McGill! Wake up!"

"What's wrong, girl?" I asked, heaving myself up and clawing at my rifle.

She put a hand on my arm. "No, you can't shoot your way out of this one."

Frowning, I turned back to her. She looked at me suspiciously, worriedly.

Glancing around the camp, I noticed I was the only person she'd awakened. It was dawn, and most of my troops were still sleeping. It was her watch, the last one of the night. The nights were short here on Death World as were the days. The planet's rotational period was only about twenty hours long.

"What's wrong?" I repeated.

She brought her tapper up to my face. I looked, and then I knew.

On screen, the lifter was departing. The feed was live. The ship was taking off right now, leaving us behind.

"I didn't order you to leave a buzzer back at camp," I said.

"You didn't order me not to, either."

She had me there. I looked into her brown eyes. They were angry, scared and a little bewildered. I felt a bit bad.

"Sorry," I said.

She punched me then. I didn't have a helmet on, and although I twisted my head to one side, she caught me with the knuckles of her gauntlet. Blood dribbled down from my ear, but I didn't strike her back. I didn't have the heart.

"I *knew* it," she said. Then she proceeded to go into a marching, kicking fury. Curses and leaves floated around the glade until the others woke up.

"What the hell—" Carlos demanded, then he looked at me. "Hey, you two didn't sleep together last night, did you?"

Kivi threw him an angry snarl. "No, we didn't. And that's never happening again. McGill didn't screw me this time—he screwed all of us!"

To understand my squad's behavior, you have to understand our culture and lifestyle. As a team of interstellar troops, we weren't quite like the professional armies of the past. Oh yeah, we were good soldiers, don't get me wrong. We could fight better than most humans ever could since we kept dying and coming back young and strong. We had more combat experience than our counterparts in days gone by—but we had a different flavor to our social interactions, too.

Sex among soldiers wasn't frowned upon as long as it was consensual and both parties were relatively close in rank. Kivi and I had, for example, been intimate on a number of occasions over the years. More recently, Carlos and Kivi had maintained an affair that had lasted throughout our campaign back on Machine World. It seemed to have died out on Death World, I realized now. I hadn't seen them together for weeks.

That was par for the course, unfortunately. Our personal relationships tended to die after a while. The worst part was the lingering feelings afterward. In some ways, these ghosts contributed to a breakdown of discipline, but they seemed to be unavoidable. When you placed both sexes in tight quarters for decades, it was only natural and inevitable that love affairs would come and go.

In effect, we acted like old married couples sometimes. We were friends, we were war-buddies…we lived, screwed, and died together. At other times, we got on each other's nerves so badly we drove one another to the point of murder.

I threw up my hands, eyeing my squad. They were all standing now, looking at me for direction—for answers.

"Okay," I said. "Let's put this on the table. We've been assigned to tail Claver. He's headed out into the bush, exiled by the brass as part of a deal he cut. The reason he was released is because he claims to have had dealings with these plant-aliens. He can supposedly talk to them. He understands them. It's our mission to discover how he does this and to learn what these aliens are up to."

"A deep patrol?" Kivi demanded. "That's what you called it? It's a death warrant!"

"Hold on," Carlos said, bemused. "Okay, so the assignment sucks, Kivi. Why are we all going to die?"

"Because, you idiot," she said, "McGill is lying. The lifter has taken off. We've been abandoned just like Claver. I've tried to contact the crew—nothing. My ID has been blocked. Me, a tech—*blocked*. We're all blocked."

"What?" asked Carlos, his voice cracking on a high note. He checked his tapper then fell back onto the ground again, staring up at the green canopy overhead.

"The lifter took off?" he asked from the ground. "We're screwed. Totally screwed. Oh God, why did I join this shit legion? I don't believe this."

I ignored Carlos, who was prone to dramatic displays. I frowned at Kivi instead. "We're blocked? No net traffic?"

"Nothing."

"Huh..." I said thoughtfully, poking at my tapper. It appeared she was right. "How are we supposed to report in our findings?"

Kivi came at me then, and I really thought she was going to punch me again. I flinched a little, but she just stood close and stared up at me, eyes blazing.

"Because, you big idiot, they frigged us. Maybe Winslade took over again, and he's getting revenge. Or maybe he revived Turov to trump Drusus, and she decided to screw us. Does it matter? We've got *nothing*. We're on this rock in a forest full of hostile monsters, and we can't even eat them."

"These plants are poisonous, huh?" I asked.

"Very."

Nodding, I heaved a sigh. Kivi had a pretty ironclad case against me.

Right about then, Carlos kicked up his act a few notches. He took out his sidearm and pressed it under his chin. Still lying on the forest floor, he gazed up at the giant trees without blinking.

I walked over to him and loomed into his field of vision.

"That's a violation, Specialist," I said.

"I don't care, McGill. You never care about the rules—why the hell should I?"

"Come on, Carlos. Don't off yourself here. That's bullshit."

"I'm doing it. If you want to get eaten and shit out by one of these monsters, you go right ahead. I already did that and once was good enough for me."

Having known Carlos since the day we both signed up together, I knew he was serious. He was about to do it.

183

Normally, Carlos was all fun and games, but today he just didn't feel like laughing. I didn't blame him.

I felt a pang of sympathy for him, but I didn't let it show. Killing yourself to get out of duty in Legion Varus—that was unacceptable. Sure, if you were badly injured and a burden to your unit, you could get away with it. But blowing your brains out because you didn't like your assignment? No way.

"I can't guarantee you'll be revived," I said.

"I know that. We're blocked. We're all as good as permed anyway."

Thinking about levers I could use to motivate him, I could only come up with one thing.

"Okay then, Specialist," I said. "If you discharge that weapon, I'll pull your stripes."

Carlos' eyes rolled to look up at me. "That's bullshit, McGill. I worked hard to get specialist."

"This tantrum you're throwing is bullshit!" I roared, doing my best imitation of Harris. "I'll have your stripes, I swear. Now get on your feet, holster that weapon and march, soldier!"

Carlos growled with frustration. He scrambled up cursing, and he put away his gun. He didn't want to look at me after that. Neither did Kivi.

"Nothing like a fine morning in Legion Varus!" I shouted, clapping Lau on the back.

The kid looked as green as a pod-monster. He'd only died once in combat so far, and I could tell this wild behavior by his noncoms was freaking him out. I gave him a hearty laugh and took point.

We marched after Claver who, according to Kivi, had been up an hour ago and moved on.

-25-

We'd only marched about a kilometer farther when we ran into something odd. We were up on a ridge, a rise in the land created by a massive root. Consequently, we could see a few kilometers across the forest floor. Up ahead were more ferns—but unlike the other ferns, these were moving, rippling like a field of wheat.

Now, you have to understand these ferns weren't your standard-issue Boston ferns you'd find back on Earth. No, these things were like trees in their own right. Their fronds were like palm fronds—only bigger. They swayed and gyrated in a pattern, like they were doing a line-dance.

"Is there wind up ahead?" Carlos asked.

"Nope," I said. "See the foliage on the tree above the ferns? Nothing's moving."

"It's got to be a pod-walker," Kivi said. "I'll send a buzzer down there to see."

"Everybody take a knee and keep quiet," I ordered. "Kivi, send in a bug to check out the ferns. And give me an update on Claver. What's he doing?"

"Nothing special," she said. "I've been watching him. He's pretty far ahead now, and he's moving faster than before."

"Is he past that strange zone among the ferns?"

"Yes. He's way beyond that. He's on the other side of the next big tree-trunk on the right."

Normally, being one tree trunk ahead of my squad would've meant a man was right in our face. But the scale of this place—it was amazing. Some of the trees were effectively the size of small mountains, and Claver was on the other side of the next one in line ahead of us.

One of Kivi's buzzers leapt from her arm and vanished into the ferns. I watched as it flew, thinking that its carefully designed camouflage technology was wasted on this world. It'd been built and programmed to behave like an insect—but there weren't really any insects on Death World, at least none that we'd discovered thus far. There was no way anyone would mistake a buzzer for anything other than what it was on this planet.

I moved to Kivi and watched her tapper. She was flipping back and forth between the streaming video of Claver, and the buzzer gliding toward the restless ferns.

"How do you keep that thing from running into all those ferns?"

"I don't," Kivi said. "It's on automatic. The AI is quite good when it comes to navigation and evasion."

"You're in the windy zone now, aren't you?"

She nodded. The ferns on the vid feed were in motion, rustling and shivering. From a distance, the effect had resembled a windstorm. But up close, you could tell it wasn't wind. The ferns weren't moving in the right pattern. They were shivering and thrashing as if someone was shaking them.

"That's really weird," I said. "What's going on? A localized earthquake?"

Kivi looked up at me. "Maybe. Or maybe the tree the ferns are growing near is shaking."

That was a thought. I stood up, dug out a scope and stared into the distance. I wanted a close-up of the massive thing we were calling a tree.

"If it's moving, I can't see it," I said. "The branches and foliage are as still as a grave."

"What about the roots?"

"Send the buzzer up that way. I can't see the roots through the ferns."

"Vet?" Carlos asked. "Are we done here? Don't you think we should start marching again?"

I gave him a glance. "You want to take point? You got it."

Grumbling, he started down the side of the hill. Kivi stood and followed, stumbling over every obstacle. She was watching the feed from her buzzers as much as she was watching her feet. That was an occupational hazard for techs, I guess.

"Hold it," she said after another dozen steps. "I found something, McGill."

Frowning, I walked up to her and waved for the others to halt.

She showed me the feed. At first, I really didn't know what I was looking at. It appeared to be brownish surface scored with orange-white streaks. The streaks were oozing some kind of fluid.

"What's this?"

"It's a root. An exposed root on the surface. Those slashes—I think Claver cut them before he left the area."

I could see what she was talking about now. Slices had been taken out of the base of one of the tree roots. Big cuts, a meter long and at least two centimeters wide.

"Do you think he did that to trigger the defensive instincts of the plant?"

Kivi nodded. "It stands to reason. And that means he must know we're following."

"How would he know that?"

"My buzzers, probably," she admitted. "They make noise. A distinctive sound that doesn't naturally occur on this planet. I'm sorry. I tried to keep him from knowing I was tailing him."

"It's all right. You were following orders."

I waved the squad forward, but Carlos hesitated on point.

"Hold on, Vet," he said. "Shouldn't we go around? I mean, if we avoid this region entirely, nothing bad can happen, right?"

"Maybe, maybe not," I said. "We don't know how long the defensive growths take to form. We can assume that the first pods grew because of the broadside attacks. Or maybe it was the burning exhaust of our lifter when we landed. In any case, the enemy can't generate a pod instantly. Claver is already losing us, and I don't want him to get farther away."

"Yeah, but just to be safe..."

I frowned at Carlos. "Chicken? Now? You were trying to off yourself just a few hours ago."

"I'm only thinking about the rest of my squad. I'm the medic, here. You don't have another. Normally, bio people don't take point."

He was absolutely right about the role of a squad medic. I'd put him on point because I was tired of his crap from earlier on.

Taking in a breath, I tried to think tactically. Getting our medic killed out of spite didn't seem like the wisest move.

"All right, who volunteers?"

Everyone slid their eyes from one to the next. The experienced troops—they kept their mouths shut.

"I'll do it," Lau said, stepping forward.

"That's the spirit," I said, giving him a nod. "Take point, Lau."

We marched on, right into the zone with the shivering plants. It was weird being in their midst. Whatever had them moving, I couldn't feel it. There wasn't an earthquake under my boots, localized or otherwise. There wasn't any wind, either. What else could make a plant move like that—on its own?

"Carlos," I said, "did you see any of those nano-fibers inside the fern plant you cut down last night?"

"You mean that corn silk stuff? The strings Natasha said were muscles?"

"Yes."

He thought about it. "My cut was clean. The force-blade burned the plant. I suppose there could have been a few strands hanging from the end... I'm not sure, really. I didn't inspect it or anything."

"Roger that, well...let's pick up the pace, people."

We began to trot rapidly through the ferns. I was getting a bad feeling. One thing they'd taught us in training was to listen to feelings like that and act on them.

We hadn't gone a hundred meters before Kivi shouted to get our attention. I veered to her position, rifle at the ready.

She was standing in an open area where a huge root loomed. I jogged up and look at the spot she was examining. Cut, orange-white lines were bleeding sap.

"Claver did this," I said.

"He sure did. Notice the cuts? They spell something, but it's hard to make out."

Frowning, I eyed them carefully, then I busted out laughing. The cuts were long and tall, and they formed the dripping letters of my name: MCGILL.

"I don't think it's funny at all," Carlos complained. "He knows we're after him—what's more, he knows who is after him. That's bullshit. Someone must have tipped him off, and I'm not talking about your nosy buzzer, Kivi."

That idea made some sense, and it stopped my laughter.

"Well," I said. "If he knows we're coming, he probably won't lead us anywhere good. We might as well catch up with him and end this."

Carlos lit up with a smile on his face. "You mean..." he said, making a slashing gesture across his throat.

"If it comes to that, but I hope it doesn't. That's not our mission. We're to gather intel not execute him. We could have done that back at camp."

"We should have. Claver is just toying with us."

"This is a wild goose-chase," I admitted, "and Claver is the craziest goose in this forest."

We pressed on, but Kivi stopped us about ten minutes later.

"What's going on now?" I demanded.

"He's stopped. He's at the next tree. Notice the one with the split trunk? He's in there, underneath it."

"What do you mean, underneath it?"

"There's a natural dip in the ground—right there, see? A bowl surrounded by roots and roofed by the tree itself. It's like a cave...a big one."

"What the hell is he doing in there?" I demanded, looking at her video feed.

I saw for myself that Claver was sitting with his legs crossed and his eyes closed. He had the look of some kind of meditating monk.

"I don't know," she said. "Maybe he's trying to talk to the aliens."

We were past the zone of moving ferns now, just barely. That made me feel a little more confident. After all, nothing had jumped us yet. If the megaflora was generating a defensive growth, it apparently took a while. I'd been looking for pods on the trunk, but I hadn't seen any yet.

"We'll hold here then," I said at last. "We'll watch him and see what he does. This is exactly the kind of thing we were ordered to observe and report on."

"McGill," Carlos said, "I'm just going to say one thing."

"Promise?"

He waved my words away. "Look, if he knows we're here, and he knows we're watching him, why the hell would he stop and start some kind of séance with the plants?"

"I don't know," I said, "but I hope to find out. We'll watch him for an hour, that's all."

The hour passed while my people milled around and pissed and watched the landscape nervously. They reminded me of a pack of nervous housecats, but I couldn't fault them. This world was a weird one, even by my standards.

At last, I stood up.

"Time's up," I said. "Let's go get him."

Lau scrambled to his feet, anxious to take point again. I let him, and I found myself liking the kid more all the time.

Unfortunately, this wasn't his lucky day. He fell to the ground not a dozen paces ahead of our position, grasping at his throat. He convulsed a few times before relaxing. He looked dead to me—and I've seen a lot of dead folks.

"Squad halt!" I shouted. "Nobody move!"

We all froze, looking around and panting.

"We should burn these plants," Carlos said. "Burn them all to the ground!"

"Good idea," I said, "but right now, we've got troubles."

"What killed him, Specialist?" Kivi demanded, looking at Carlos.

"You're asking me?" he demanded. "How the hell would I know? He's too far away to examine."

"Then go examine him," Kivi suggested between clenched teeth.

"No," I said. "Nobody move. Kivi, send a buzzer down there and check the corpse. Pipe the feed to our tappers."

She did as I asked, cursing and fumbling with her equipment. A tiny drone flexed its wings and flew to Lau. It landed on his collar and examined his face.

The magnified close-up on my tapper was disturbing. Staring eyes. Protruding tongue. He was as dead as yesterday.

"I don't know..." Carlos said. "There's a little foam, and his tongue is out. I think it was respiratory—but I'm only guessing. Gas, maybe."

"Helmets on!" I shouted, and everyone hastened to obey. They unshelled their helmets and secured them as quickly as they could.

But it wasn't quite fast enough. Gorman fell to his knees nearby. He was the closest one to Lau, the second man in line.

"Gas," he managed to get out before he pitched onto his face and died.

The rest of us engaged our filtering systems then shut out the atmosphere entirely.

"It's got to be a nerve agent to work so quickly," Carlos said. "Something heavy, something we can't see. Notice the two victims are farther downslope than the rest of us?"

Sargon came up close to me then while I studied the dead men, wondering what to do. His belcher was banging on his shoulder, and his expression was grim.

"Vet, maybe we should start burning these ferns. Any of the ones that are moving around."

"Not a bad idea," I lied, "but I think we should leave them alone. I think Claver cut that root to trigger them to release gas. That's a biological defensive system. If we burn the ferns, God only knows what will happen next."

Sargon shrugged. "I don't like this. I prefer a stand-up fight."

Knowing just how he felt, I nodded thoughtfully. "We've got to get out of here. We'll circle around to the north by walking up that ridge."

"That's a root, Vet, not a ridge," Carlos pointed out.

"I know that! Every rise of the land in this region is a root."

We hustled up the root. I took point, not having the heart to order another to do it. On my tapper, I marked the spot and declared Lau and Gorman dead. As our tappers weren't hooked to any wider area network than our own local squad command channel, it didn't mean much. But if someone found us later on, at least the deaths would be confirmed, and they would be cleared for revival.

It was a longshot, but I felt I wanted to play this little adventure by the book from now on.

"Claver's gone," Kivi said when we'd climbed upward a hundred meters or so.

"What do you mean, gone?" I demanded.

She looked at me guiltily. "I've replayed the vid file. The space under the tree was confined, and the buzzer, well, it's programmed to get closer to targets if they're sleeping or at least holding still. Claver nailed it. I guess that's what he was really doing—luring in the AI on my buzzer."

"Well then, send another one after him!" I shouted.

"I did, I did."

"Where is he?"

"So far, no contact. He's fled the region. I've got the drone on a spiraling search pattern going out from the tree in widening circles."

"I know what a frigging spiral is," I growled. "Shit."

What made me the maddest was that we'd been outsmarted by Claver. He was a slippery man, probably the slipperiest I'd ever encountered. He'd been playing us from the beginning, setting traps and seeking to lose our pursuit.

Right then and there, on the graves of Lau and Gorman, I vowed to catch the man. We might all be as good as permed on this poisonous deathtrap of a planet, but I was going to get Claver before this was over.

-26-

We pressed ahead, traveling in the direction we hoped Claver had gone. Soon, we came into a region full of a new variety of plant. We'd never seen the like of it before. Instead of ferns and massive trees, there were vines here, vines with heavy pods hanging from them. The pods dragged on the ground like ripe fruit.

Now, when I say there were vines, a person might mistakenly envision a sweet little beanstalk. Something a few meters high with bright green leaves. That's not the kind of vine I'm talking about. First off, the leaves were crackling and brown as if they were dying. They were much bigger than any vine back on Earth, about ten meters high on average. The pods hanging from these vines were a dark, waxy green. Sort of like cucumbers, gargantuan cucumbers the size of SUVs that lay on the bare earth, growing fat and shiny.

"Don't touch any of these things!" I ordered.

My squad didn't need much encouragement in that department. They warily avoided contact with the scary-looking vegetation as we walked into the garden.

My admonishment turned out to be a good idea. There were spines on the pods, we learned as we got in among them. Red, hair-thin spines that glistened with some kind of clear liquid.

"I think we should roast this whole field," Sargon said. "We've got some grenades and incendiary agents. If we light them up, they might all burn."

"Might be a good idea," I admitted, "but then again, they might all hatch and eat us instead."

"I've got him!" Kivi said suddenly. "I've picked up Claver again!"

I trotted gingerly around a few spiny cucumbers to her position. "Show me."

She did, and I experienced my first grim smile of the day. Claver was in the center of this vast field we were attempting to cross. He was at a central nodule, a nexus point where all these vines came together. He was walking around the spot, examining it carefully.

"What do you think he's looking for?" I asked Kivi.

"I've got no idea," she admitted.

Thinking hard for a second, I turned back to Sargon. "We're going to try your idea."

"Great!" he said, clapping his gauntlets together and digging in his pack. "I'll set them up on a timer. Everyone give me all the phosphorous you've got, grenades too. We'll retreat to the edge of the field long before—"

"No," I said.

"No what?"

"We're not retreating. We're advancing. Set up the firebomb behind us. We'll head for Claver's position."

"Are you sure about that, Vet?" Sargon asked. "You might burn us all alive. See these brown leaves? Notice the high oxygen levels? This will burn *hot!* Hell, even the breeze is heading toward the center of the field."

"I know all that. We'll move fast, and if Claver hides or doubles back on us again, there will be a fire right behind us he can't escape. He's not getting away again. If we don't get him, the fire will."

No one looked happy with my plan. Kivi walked up and put a hand on mine.

"James," she said. "That's not what we were ordered to do. We were ordered to follow Claver and find out what he's up to."

"Oh yeah? Well, let me clue you in: that's never going to work. He knows we're after him, and he's not going to lead us anywhere but to our deaths. He'll just keep setting up traps for us."

"How do you know that, McGill?" Carlos demanded.

"Because I've dealt with this man on three planets. You don't just let Claver loose and expect him to do what you want. That's never going to happen. Drusus doesn't understand what we are dealing with."

"What do you think he's really up to out here?" Kivi asked, watching her tapper again.

"Honestly?" I asked. "I'm not sure. But I *am* certain it involves getting all of us killed. If we keep following him blindly, he'll figure out a way to do it. Only at that point, if he feels like it, will he go and talk to his plant friends."

They looked scared and uncertain, but no one openly argued with me.

"Okay," I continued, "build your bomb and set it up, Sargon. The rest of you spread out and advance—but try not to touch the spines. Armor or not, I don't like the look of them."

Ten minutes later, we were advancing in a line, trotting through the vines. Behind us, a short fuse was ticking. Sargon had tried to set it for half an hour, defeating my entire plan. Fortunately, I'd checked his work and reset it to ninety-seconds. That got the squad moving.

A blast of heat and light loomed behind us before we'd gone a hundred meters. Maybe I'd set it wrong, or maybe a minute and half just wasn't all that long under these circumstances. We couldn't move quickly enough through this field, picking our way from plant to plant.

"Show me Claver!" I ordered when I levered myself back up off the ground. Burning bits of vegetation were raining down on us. That part made me happy. I hated these plants.

Kivi piped in a view of Claver. He was no longer toying with the central nexus of the vine plant. He was up and rushing around, looking for something.

Then suddenly, he loomed close to the camera position. I got it then. He was looking for the drone. He came up to our faces, snarling.

"You dumb-asses!" he shouted at the camera. "You just killed us all!"

195

I felt a chill run through my bones, despite the steamy heat of the planet. I could tell he meant what he was saying.

He went to smash the buzzer, but he missed. The drone went straight upward as Kivi was driving it higher on full power. I heard a distant popping sound. Was Claver shooting at it?

"Do you still have him?" I asked Kivi.

"I think so. He found that buzzer like a pro. But I hid it among the spines on a pod. I bet he might have caught a few of them when he tried to smash it.

"Serves him right," I said.

Looking over my shoulder, I saw the flames were licking the dry fields eagerly.

"Let's pick up the pace!" I ordered, and we charged deeper toward the center.

Now and then I was forced to slash a vine or stomp right over a pod in my metal boots. That wasn't as dangerous as it sounded as we were wearing armor. But what I didn't like about it was any possible effect it might have on the pods themselves. So far, they hadn't displayed any form of defensive capability. But that was far from conclusive as we'd only just started damaging them directly.

When the pods finally did react, it was in a big way. The pods didn't like getting burned, apparently. When the flame reached them, they woke up—or whatever was growing inside them did. Creatures loomed out of those waxy, oblong cocoons. They were instantly wreathed in flame and therefore difficult to identify.

Blinded by fire, the large, squatty creatures clawed and staggered as if they were sleeping animals rudely awakened into an inferno. Standing around five meters tall, their alien bodies weren't shaped like men at all. They were more like spiders. Multi-legged monsters with spiny hair that burned merrily as they died.

"Holy shit," Carlos breathed. "Do you see those things, McGill? Are all these pods ripening with monsters like that?"

"I would expect so," I said. "Keep moving before the ones around us get the word."

196

My orders came too late. The message seemed to have been telegraphed up the burning vines to all the pods we were marching past. One broke free to my right, making a squelching sound like a man shoving a foot into a wet rubber boot. It was right in the middle of my squad, and we couldn't go around without getting closer to the advancing flames.

This spider wasn't on fire yet, so I could see it clearly. It had the same orange fronds, the same kind of sensory organs that I'd seen on the creatures born of the trees. The fronds were immediately alert. They scanned and spotted us quickly.

"Cut it down!" I shouted, and we opened up with our morph-rifles.

Most of us had our weapons set up for close-assault mode, and we lashed the monster with fire, but it didn't go down easily. Taking two staggering steps into a storm of bullets, the thing flipped over, thrashing. It got back up, but we blasted it back down again. We had too much firepower pouring into its body for it to struggle up a third time. It was still heaving and steaming when we marched right over it.

"I've got to hand it to you, McGill," Carlos said. "No one I've ever served under could come up with a better way to get his squad killed."

"Shut up. We're not dead yet."

Miraculously, Carlos *did* shut up. Maybe he was saving his breath to run.

We had to kill three more spiders before we reached the nexus. The last two came on together, converging on us from both sides. Sargon caught one with his belcher, nailing it right in the belly. The weaponeer had been knocked flat and was lying on his back at the time, aiming up into its guts—but still, it was a beautiful shot. The thing gushed out thick hot liquids and died.

The last spider also got in close—too close for rifle fire. We hacked it apart with force-blades. It was nasty work, and we lost another trooper, but we won past it.

Behind us, our squad's pig wasn't so lucky. All this time, our ox-sized drone had been trotting dutifully in our wake like a faithful pet. But the vines were a problem for its navigational software. The doomed thing hadn't been able to keep up.

One of the spider-beasts came out of the burning perimeter and charged close, sensing the drone somehow, despite the fact the spider was on fire itself. Maybe the drone's heavy, vibrating tread had given it away.

Whatever the case, the spider jumped on the supply drone's back and rode it down to earth. Tearing at it and ripping sacks of supplies off, the spider began making a kind of shrieking sound. Maybe it was happy to get a little revenge, I don't know.

"Shit!" Carlos called out. "Oh *shit*, we have to go back! That thing has all our gear—our food!"

"Be my guest, Specialist," I said.

"Dammit, McGill. I'm not going to be a taste-tester when we get out of here. You can just forget about that."

"Wouldn't dream of asking," I said. "That's Kivi's job."

Kivi hadn't been listening to our radio chatter, but she heard her name mentioned.

"Keep them moving, McGill," she said. "We're almost there. The center of this garden is dead ahead."

We broke through the twisting field of vines and came out into the open. Instead of being like curtains in our way, the vines were now strung up high, like power wires hanging from pylons.

There, we found a squat central mass. It was in the center of about a hundred vines, each of which radiated out to a long line of pods.

The big central nexus reminded me immediately of those barrel-like cacti they had in Earth's deserts. Round, but not a sphere, it stood tall and was almost as thick around as it was high. More striking than its girth, however, was its vast collection of spines.

While watching Claver poke around this thing on video, it hadn't looked like much. But now that we were up close, I could see the spines were each the size of a sword. They were more than meter long and tapered to a perfect point. The core of the plant wasn't anything a man could mess with easily.

"What do we do now?" Carlos demanded. "I don't see Claver."

"You want me to blast that thing, Vet?" Sargon demanded.

"No, hold on. Circle around and look for Claver. Kivi, did you see where he went?"

"My buzzer is still searching the area. He has to be here—but I don't have him on my vid stream right now. The smoke..."

The smoke was getting heavy. We'd outrun the fire, but it hadn't burnt out. I had the feeling it was going to consume the entirety of this spider-growing patch before it was through. The surrounding undergrowth of the forest itself was a lot wetter and probably wouldn't burn—but this dry patch was toast.

We spread out and looked all around the glade. Claver had vanished. The smoke got thicker, and I was getting desperate.

"Dammit," I shouted a minute or so later, "he must have given us the slip again. I can't believe it!"

"Vet?" Sargon called.

I glanced over at him. He aimed his belcher at the central nexus meaningfully.

"I guess you might as well blast it," I said. "We'll destroy this thing and then move out of the patch on the far side before the fire gets here."

Sargon sighted and cranked his aperture to a narrow beam. He planned to punch holes in it, I could tell, and I approved.

"STOP!" roared a voice.

We all spun around and stared.

Claver stood up right in our midst. He'd been buried, I guess, under our feet. The big cactus-thing had gripped our attention and we'd walked right over him in our haste to enter the center of the field.

Dirt dripped from him, and his face was lit with a gleam that I might have mistaken for madness. But I knew Claver...he always had an angle.

199

-27-

Claver walked up to me like he hadn't a care about what I might do to him. A wall of fire wasn't a hundred meters behind him. A throng of dying, burning, screeching spiders was out there too, in the fields all around us. On top of all that, he had a dozen rifles aimed at his chest. Any one of us could have cut him down with the twitch of a finger, but he didn't care.

He approached me with an angry air, like he was an officer who'd just found the dumbest recruit in the legion and planned on a giving the boy a thrashing.

"You," he breathed, staring into my faceplate. "I should have known. No one else could have screwed this up so thoroughly. What's wrong with your brain, son?"

"They say it's genetic," I said, "but I don't believe them. My parents were more or less normal."

"Listen," Claver said. "We don't have much time. You've caught me—that's what you wanted, right? Just leave the nexus alone, and we'll move out. We can still make it out of here."

I glanced over my shoulder at the massive, barrel-like plant. "What's so special about this giant cactus?" I asked.

"That's one of them—one of the megaflora."

"I thought the trees were the megaflora."

He shook his head. "We don't have time for this—"

I reached out with my rifle barrel and tapped him meaningfully on the chest. "We have enough time for a few more answers. We can outrun these spider things. They only wake up when they get lit on fire."

Claver's eyes rolled up in his head. It was an expression of disbelief and exasperation. I'd seen it countless times before, but usually on the faces of women I'd dated.

"I don't even know what they'll do—this is unprecedented," he said.

"In that case, you'd better start making sense," I said. "Sargon over there has an itchy trigger finger. Since you seem to care more about the cactus than you do your own life, you should probably talk faster."

Claver's eyes went to Sargon then back to me. "All right. I didn't think you'd go this far. I guess I'd forgotten that Legion Varus is the scourge of the known galaxy."

"That's us."

"Can we at least start walking out of here?" he asked.

I considered. "All right. Squad—move out. Walking pace."

Claver clearly wanted to move faster. He began to trot every dozen steps, but I reached out and yanked him back to a walking pace. I figured it was an incentive to get his facts straight.

"Okay," Claver said, "this is big, McGill. Bigger than a patch of alien spiders. You've done a lot of damage out here, but we still might be able to convince them that you didn't know who you were dealing with. We might be able to get out of this alive."

I shrugged. "I've died before."

"No, I'm not talking about individual deaths. I'm talking about the death of our species, not just you and your squad. You see, this nexus isn't just operating a few spiders and spiny plants. This is a brain. A central node in a vast nervous system that covers most of this planet."

I frowned at him, not entirely understanding.

"A brain?" I asked. "Since when do plants have brains?"

"These creatures are cellulose, mostly, and some of their forms do use photosynthesis. But they aren't plants as in our classic definition. They don't just sit around and soak up sun all day. They can move—and they can think."

"Okay," I said, "I'll buy that after what I've seen them do."

"Right, they coordinate. They organize. They can build things too, if they want to."

"Like spaceships?" I asked.

"Yes, even that," he said. "But that's not what you have here. This is a brain node—think of it that way. This central node has been spawning smaller directive creatures to handle others. Think of them as shepherds that herd flocks of dumber plants."

"You're talking about the spiders, right?"

"Yes, exactly."

"Why didn't you tell us all this back at the damned lifter?" I demanded. "This information would've been more useful at that point."

Claver laughed. "I told that fool Drusus just enough to get thrown out of his camp. Why would I tell him more? He didn't pay for more."

"Then why are you telling me?"

"Because the situation has changed, and you're screwing up my plans. If you destroy a nexus, well, God help us all."

Frowning, I kept walking with him. The fire behind us reached the edge of the central nexus. A few more spiders were caught up in the flame and died horribly.

"Uh..." Carlos said, walking up to us. "I don't want to interrupt you two lovebirds, but that nexus thing is about to get roasted."

"Nah," Claver said. "It'll be okay. The vines already ripened on this field, see, and it's stopped distributing water to the pods. That's done to trigger the spiders to hatch."

"What the hell are you talking about?" Carlos demanded suspiciously.

Claver shook his head and spoke carefully as if Carlos was a slow child. I knew the feeling. "That big central thing you call a cactus? It's full of water, and that means it's too green to burn. Nothing right around it will burn, either."

Thinking back, I had noted a large barren area without pods growing in it around the plant. Maybe Claver was right.

"Okay, keep talking," I said. "My inclination is to turn around and blast that cactus to fragments. Tell me why I shouldn't do it."

"You *can't* do that," Claver said. "Seriously, McGill, I know you're a man of limited intellect. But that doesn't mean you're completely incapable of logical thought."

"Thanks," I said, narrowing my eyes at him. "Let's give my substandard brain a workout, shall we? You said these plant aliens like to seed forgotten star systems such as this one. You described them as rebels in the Cephalopod Kingdom. Was that story bullshit too?"

"Not entirely. They do live among the cephalopods. But I did withhold one critical piece of information about their conflict."

"What's that?" I demanded.

"The cephalopods are losing their war with these creatures. These plants are winning. That's why I don't want to off-handedly kill one of their brains. They don't have billions of brains among them—only a few. Are you capable of comprehending the distinction?"

I wanted to punch Claver. Hell, I wanted to shoot him dead. He'd set traps for us, insulted us, and he'd gotten Earth into God-knew-what kind of danger.

With a growl in my throat, I turned to Sargon.

"Weaponeer?" I called out.

"Vet?"

"You see that cactus-looking thing behind us? There's a lot of smoke, but it's a big target."

"I see it," Sargon said, squinting and putting his belcher up to his shoulder.

"Hey, hey, hey!" Claver said, reaching for Sargon.

Sargon, wearing powered armor, batted him away easily since Claver was in a light, smart cloth suit.

"Take aim and punch a hole into that cactus for me, weaponeer," I said. "I want to see what a plant-brain looks like on the inside."

"With pleasure, Veteran McGill!"

203

-28-

The belcher hummed and the air crackled for an instant. A bolt of energy leapt from Sargon's weapon to the big nexus brain. An uneven hole opened with a puff of what looked like steam. Liquid poured out. Claver had said it was full of water, but the stuff that came out was more of a thick, discolored goop.

"There you go, Vet," Sargon said. "One plant-brain, cooked to perfection."

"Excellent."

Claver fell to his knees. I wasn't sure if that was from Sargon smacking him down or due to shock. He stared, slack-jawed at the nexus thing. More and more goop kept flowing out of the smoking hole in its surface.

Walking up to him, I proudly surveyed my weaponeer's work. Claver seemed to be beyond words.

"I thought you said they were full of water," I told him. "That looks more like snot to me."

Claver turned to me, his face displaying vast disbelief.

"You *idiots*," he said, almost as if he was out of breath. "Not since Napoleon fired a cannon at the Sphinx…you have no idea what you've done. You're like children playing with matches, unaware the town is burning."

I grabbed him and hauled him to his feet. I gave him a shaking that made him look like a kid's ragdoll.

"If that's true," I said, "it's your own damned fault, not mine! You've been full of crap every word, every step of the way. If you ask me, you're too clever by half for your own good. Now we're marching out of here. You can come with us, or sit in this cactus patch and play with the spiders."

I left him there, and I didn't much care what he did. I'd had enough of Claver and this weird, deadly planet. If we ran into any new menaces, I planned to blast them first and ask philosophical questions later.

Eventually, Claver followed us. He walked as if in a dream.

Sargon came up to me and voiced his concerns. "Claver seems to be taking this hard," he said.

"Yeah, well…he'll get over it."

"I mean, he seems dejected and even a bit nuts."

Glancing back, I could see what Sargon meant. Claver was staring at the ground—and talking to it.

"I figure he's probably overwhelmed by the strain of being alone on planets like this one," I said. "Imagine living without the joy of human companionship for so long."

Sargon gave me an odd look. "Are you joking, Vet?"

"Yeah."

"I thought so. What if the crap he was spouting is true? What if we just started a new war with these plants? We can't just keep doing that kind of thing without paying the piper eventually."

"Listen," I said, "don't let Claver get to you. Remember what Turov did? She blasted this planet with *Minotaur's* broadsides. That flattened an area the size of Connecticut. What difference does one cactus make in comparison to that?"

Apparently, Claver had been listening to our talk. He snapped out of his reverie and rushed to catch up to me. He reached for my arm, but I twisted away from him.

"What do you want?" I asked dangerously.

"That's it!" he said. He was smiling now. "I can blame it all on Turov. That woman is a bigger fool than you could ever be."

"I can't argue with that," I said, "but what are you on about now?"

Claver turned and trotted off into the ferns. We'd passed the edge of the spider-pod field and now marched through the endless undergrowth of the forest again.

"Halt!" I said authoritatively. I drew my sidearm and aimed at Claver's legs. "I'll put you down if you take another step."

One side benefit of blasting aliens you weren't supposed to was that people tended to take your threats seriously. I'm not sure if I would have shot Claver as he ran off into the forest—but then again, I might have.

As it turned out, I didn't have to make that choice. His pace faltered, and then he stopped.

"Get your butt back here," I demanded.

"What's the point? You're all as good as dead—and me with you if I stick around."

His comment made me eye the wild land around us with fresh concern. Then I turned back to Claver. I took careful aim.

"Explain why, and maybe I'll let you go," I said.

He turned around to face me with a calculating look in his eye. I'd seen that look before, and I knew it meant he planned to bamboozle me. That didn't worry me at all, though. Every time I'd met up with Claver, he'd pretty much had that same plan in mind.

"All right," he said, coming back to me. He walked right up to my gun barrel, as if he didn't have a care in the world. He might be a liar, a thief, a schemer, and a general scourge on the soul of humanity—but Claver was no coward.

"Talk," I ordered.

The rest of the squad halted and gathered around, listening. Some looked amused, some worried, and some were pretending to be bored, like Kivi. But mostly, they were interested in what Claver had to say.

"The broadsides Turov fired didn't hit any of the nexus nodes like this one. Her guns knocked out their construction yards. That's where I usually come to do business. To trade metals and other refined goods with the locals."

"Okay then, tell me this: why would shooting a nexus be a bigger deal than blasting apart a large section of the planet?"

"Admittedly, destroying a valuable facility from space is an attack. But invading this world and executing a gestating nexus just as the pods are ripening—that's an entirely different level of evil according to their way of thinking. You see, the megaflora you keep calling 'trees' are less than sentient for the most part. They're like animals, just intelligent enough to fulfill their orders. The nexus is what gives those orders. Killing one of these cactus-looking creatures is a much bigger deal. It's like the difference between cutting down your neighbor's rosebush and shooting his wife."

I could understand what he was saying, but I frowned in confusion about a number of other points.

"Okay, I get that," I said. "Maybe I acted hastily. But why the hell did you lead us here without explaining yourself if it was such a big deal?"

"Leading you here wasn't my intention. I did everything I could to evade pursuit. But not even I can survive forever on Death World without gear. I had to get help, to cut a deal with one of the nexus brains. So I came here to make that deal— then you showed up and began burning the place down!"

"Hmm," I said. "Look, Claver, I appreciate that you probably had a lucrative contract going with these beings. But the last I heard, they followed you all the way to Earth, running you down and knocking your ship out of the sky. How does that make you their best buddy?"

Claver scowled. "That was a misunderstanding. They wanted metals, so I brought them metals. Unfortunately, they could tell that my ship had more cargo aboard. They demanded it all. I tried to explain that it wasn't all for them, that I had other deliveries to make. They didn't get it and tried to take the remainder by force. I resisted and ran. The rest is history."

"Okay…" I said, thinking it over. It did make a kind of sense. If there was ever a race of aliens that might take things the wrong way due to cultural differences, it had to be these plant-creatures. "I can see that, but then how did you plan on making things nice with them here? Our ship hit them, and they can't be in a good mood after that."

"In their minds, you and I aren't the same. You represent the Empire. I represent a free-trading consortium of enlightened individuals. Therefore, *I* didn't attack them. The Empire did. My plan was to blame the lack of a full shipment on your violent kind. It was working, too. The nexus was pissed after the broadside attack and ready to blame anything on your ship full of aggressors."

"You managed to make contact then?" I asked, eyes narrowing. "How?"

Claver waved his hand dismissively. "A translation device of no importance. What matters is that—hey, get off me!"

I grabbed him almost as fast as Sargon did. Despite his threats and complaints, we searched him thoroughly. Nothing special could be found.

Afterward, he stood there with his smart cloth suit down to his knees. The fabric rustled and shivered as a result of the violation. I knew it would reknit itself in time, so I didn't worry about it.

"You lied," I said. "There's no translation device."

"There's nothing internal, either," Kivi said. She'd been scanning him with more sophisticated instruments, using buzzers with emission-detection gear. "He couldn't have one, anyway. We just revived him, and we certainly didn't bring down this phantom translator on the lifter."

"No, no, no," Claver said irritably. "You people lack any kind of imagination. The translator runs on my tapper. That's why it was reconstructed along with my body. My translator is an app, not a physical device—morons."

Kivi stepped forward and grabbed his arm. She scanned his tapper carefully, browsing menus and plugging in a more powerful computer she kept in her ruck. All techs had access to computer systems that were far better than a man's tapper.

"Good encryption software—but not good enough. You've hacked this device, Claver."

"Like any pro would. Look, don't tear it up. I'll share the app just to save time."

He did so, and Kivi looked intrigued. "It appears to use liquid injections and scents—disgusting."

"That's how you talk to a plant-creature. You generate the right organic molecules in the right sequence, and it responds. A few droplets of blood and spit are all you need. The program takes what it needs and dribbles out words. The process takes a long time, unfortunately. These plants don't have an efficient, brief means of communication like we do."

Curious but a little grossed out, I examined the program and what it directed a person to do to communicate. I could see why Claver needed time to talk to the nexus and work out a deal.

"Okay," I said at last, letting go of his arm. "I believe that you have a way to talk to them. You had a dodge worked out to blame us for the attacks. But now that deal is blown because we shot the nexus. What's plan B?"

"What's next? Claver laughed. "You tell me, ape. You shot my plans in the head. Now do you get it? Now do you grasp just how screwed we all are?"

Unfortunately, I did.

Kivi discovered something else as she examined all the data she'd pulled off Claver's tapper. She learned that his tapper, unlike our own, hadn't been disconnected from the Legion's network.

When she informed me of this, I gave a little war whoop and laid hands on Claver again.

"What the hell?" he complained. "What, didn't you get enough fun the first time you pantsed me?" By now, his smart cloth had covered him again.

"Arm out, man. You have something we need."

He looked confused, but held out his arm. Kivi went to work on it immediately, hot-linking us to his unit then using her more powerful machine to boost the signal.

"We've got a connection!" she shouted within three minutes.

"You really are the squad's tech," I told her. "Not even Natasha could have done better."

She beamed with pride, and I relayed a message to the one man I knew I could trust to give me real information: Centurion Graves.

"The rest of you stay off the net," I told them. "They've shut us down before, and I don't want them turning off our little work-around until I've had a chance to report in."

"But you're signaling Graves," Kivi said. "Tribune Drusus is the one who sent us on this mission."

"Exactly. Maybe old Drusus decided to cut us off after watching us wander off into the bush. I know Graves didn't order that, so I'm playing my best odds."

"Are you sure you know what you're doing?" she asked suspiciously.

"You think you're better at dodging and bullshitting than I am, girl?"

Kivi shook her head seriously. "Only Claver might be—no one else that I know."

I took her words as a compliment and kept trying to get Graves on the line. It took a while, and I began to worry. What if Graves refused to talk to me? What if he was asking Drusus what to do next?

After a full minute, which can be a very long time when you're sweating and staring at a spinning icon embedded in the skin of your enemy's arm, the connection was finally made.

"McGill? Is that really you or is it some tech having fun?"

"A little of both, I guess, sir," I said.

His face slid out of view to the left and right. I could tell that he was checking to see if anyone was within earshot. The camera in his tapper wasn't perfect, and neither was the signal. It was coming from a long ways off.

"Talk," he said. "Quickly."

"Sir, somehow we've been cut off from Legion Varus, but I came up with a way around that technical problem. I'm reporting in."

Graves chuckled. "Same old McGill. I know it's you now. You're full of shit."

"Thank you, sir. Do you want to hear what I have to say? I've got critical intel from the field."

Graves looked like he was seriously weighing his options for a second. I didn't like that. If he shut me down then told the techs to block this channel—well, we were pretty much screwed.

"All right," he said at last. "I'll bite. How many have you lost so far?"

"Only three, sir."

"Pretty good. How many enemy villages have you laid waste?"

"Uh…just one, actually. But sir, we caught up to Claver as he tried to make contact with the aliens. We have a translation system in our possession that will allow us to converse with these plants. It's an app on our tappers now."

Graves frowned. "Really? Show me Claver's face."

I angled my tapper. Claver stared at us sourly. We'd tied his arms to his sides by this time. I didn't want him to be fooling with his tapper and making edits of his own.

"I'll be damned," Graves said. "I'm going to have to admit, I'm losing a few credits on this one."

"You bet against me, sir?"

"Absolutely. Once Turov ordered you disconnected from the legion's net, I figured it was curtain-time on the James McGill show."

"Turov?" I asked, but even as I did, I began to figure out what had happened.

Before I'd left, I'd pissed off old Winslade pretty good. I'd gone over his head by reviving Drusus. My move had ended his command position.

So, what would a conniving little weasel do in response? Why, trump my trump, of course, with one of higher rank. He'd revived Turov and made his case to her. Being her favorite teacher's pet, she'd apparently upped the ante on Drusus' banishment and ordered my squad disconnected and abandoned.

"That's right, I said Turov," Graves continued. "She was the one who ordered your IDs blocked. Right now, you're all as good as permed. Lost on the surface of an unknown, hostile world without tapper connections? No way to tell who lives and who's dies? We could never have revived any of you legally."

"Quickly then," I said, "before we're cut off, let me give you the identification codes for my dead troopers."

"Those really don't matter," he said. "But thanks for the thought, McGill. I'm going to disconnect, now. I wish you all the—"

"Sir!" I said loudly. "Hold on, man! You can't just leave us out here to rot. Bring us in. We're not even sure where the Legion is! You can't—"

"Shut up, McGill. You're already on your way back home."

The signal cut off, and I stared at my tapper, frowning.

Then I got it. A cold feeling came over me, and I looked this way and that, studying the megaflora canopy of greenery overhead.

"I don't get it," Carlos complained.

"What kind of bullshit is this?" Kivi breathed. "I can't connect again. We're blocked. What the hell are we supposed to do now? I can't believe Graves would do this to us."

Claver nudged me. I looked at him in annoyance.

"Are you going to tell them, or am I?" he asked.

I shook my head. "Don't bother. There's no point."

"What are you talking about?" Kivi asked suspiciously.

"Squad!" I said loudly. "I want everyone to huddle up on my position. Stand right here, circle tight."

"Vet, have you gone crazy?" Sargon asked. But he and the rest of them walked toward me frowning in confusion.

"Follow orders, troops," I said. "All will be well."

Right about then, Kivi caught on. She squawked, dropped her pack and started to make a run for it.

My foot snaked out catching her ankle, and she went sprawling. I felt kind of bad, but I knelt with my knee on her back, pinning her down.

"Tech down!" I said loudly. "Gather up! Help me get her to her feet!"

"McGill, you fucker, let me run!" Kivi said, struggling and snarling.

"It's best this way, Kivi," I said calmly. "It really is. It will all be over within a second."

"We might be permed!"

"It's our only chance of getting home. At least, it's the best one we're going to get."

"All this marching around in the trees was for nothing!" she shouted. "Why'd we even bother?"

"We learned a lot," I said, "and we caught Claver. He's going to die with us. That's good enough for me."

Breathing hard, she finally relaxed and closed her eyes. I helped her up, and the rest of my squad fussed over her in confusion.

I could hear the missile now. It was coming in low from the east. If I had to take my best guess, I'd say it was homing in on my tapper which I'd left in acquire-mode as it tried to reconnect with the legion's net.

At the very end the missile screamed, as did some of my troops. They tried to scatter—but it was too late. Way too late.

We were blown to smithereens. Fortunately, I could never recall the details afterward. I think it was a clean death for all, but I couldn't swear to it. Some of us might have crawled around in the forest, dying—I guess I'll never know for sure.

-29-

When the revival machine unloaded me into a tray some time later, I felt weary. I figured I'd probably died more times on Death World than on any other planet I'd ever visited. I was tired of dying and frankly, I hated the place.

A bio I didn't know went to work on me. She was a big woman with big, wet, strong hands. She did everything but lift me up in the air and slap me on the ass. After poking and prodding for a full minute, she declared me a good grow and rousted me off her gurney.

"Back at 'em, Vet," she said. "We've only got a few hours before it's go-time."

I blinked at her uncomprehendingly. "Go-time?"

"Back to your unit. They'll explain everything—or not."

A man with a veteran's rank wasn't supposed to be depressed by a death, but I was feeling a bit down. It'd always bugged me when my own officers killed me. It just didn't seem right somehow.

Marching down the passages of the lifter to the ramps, I wandered out into a camp I'd never seen before. The ground around it was a burnt wasteland rather than the lush green of the forest. The biggest shock was the glare of the orange sun overhead. I'd never seen the sun directly on Death World. There'd always been one branch or another of megaflora in the way. But today, it was clear skies and sunshine as far as I could see.

The lifter had been moved out of the forested region so that it couldn't be easily ambushed by the pod-walkers. To get to us now, they'd have to march across miles of open, blasted land.

The landing ship stood in the dead zone that had been created by the broadsides Turov had fired when we'd first arrived. The tree trunks were still there, but only as smoldering broken towers of charcoal.

In the distance, what had to be five kilometers away, was the living wall of the forest. The edge of it was scorched and blackened in places, but the farther away you looked, the greener it was.

I found Graves with a loose knot of his officers around him. Leeson, Harris and Toro were all there.

There must have been a dark look in my eye because Leeson stepped into my path and planted his hand on my chest plate.

"Welcome back, McGill," he said. "What can I do for you?"

"I'm just here for the briefing, sir," I said. "Could you get out of my way?"

"I need an assurance. I've heard some bad things about your recent behavior. Now, I know you're a hothead, and I can normally accept that. But today, we're committed to action—very soon. I need to know you aren't going to mess with our schedule."

My eyes, which had been focused on Graves all this time, finally slid to Leeson.

"You're asking if I'm going to kill Graves for whacking out my entire squad with a missile, is that it?"

Leeson nodded seriously.

I sighed. "I've been thinking…I can understand why he did what he did. He couldn't afford to send anyone out to pick us up."

"That's right," Leeson said. "You were over two hundred kilometers out. Our only flying vehicle is the lifter itself. He didn't like losing your equipment—but he needed to get you back here, pronto. If he hadn't acted, you might well have been lost in the woods forever, and probably permed."

"I get that, sir. Can you let me in on the briefing now?"

Reluctantly, Leeson stepped aside. I walked up and joined the circle. Harris looked alarmed at my approach. He frowned at me like I was an invader. I ignored him and stared at Graves.

"McGill?" Graves asked when he saw me. "It's about time you showed up… Why are you looking at me like that? Don't tell me you're about to start whining about a bad death."

"Never felt better, Centurion."

"Good. Keep it that way. All right people, it's go-time in less than two hours. The target can't be permitted to get away, and we can't afford to damage it. Therefore, no missiles, no heavy weapons—not even belchers. This will be carried out entirely with small arms and infantry. We must seize the target vehicle intact. Unit, dismissed."

Even though I had no idea what the target was, I was game to capture it. Since I'd obviously missed most of the briefing, I hung around as others moved away to marshal their troops.

The group of officers and noncoms broke up, but Harris and Leeson lingered, eyeing me with suspicion. I wasn't sure if I should take that as a compliment or an insult. It was a little of both, I guess.

"McGill," Graves said, "walk with me."

We took a stroll around the lifter. Leeson and Harris stared after us, but they didn't follow.

The pigs had dug a new ring of trenches in the scorched ground, but I could tell the trench lines were tighter than they'd been before, almost under the shadow of the lifter. Also, the anti-personnel turrets were open and ready for business.

"James McGill," Graves said slowly, chuckling to himself. "I have to admit, I didn't think you'd make it back."

"One missile did the trick."

"I sent three, actually. I wanted to be sure."

"That was mighty thoughtful of you, sir."

"Smart ass," he said, smiling. "Do you want to know why I brought you back and insisted you be revived immediately?"

"Tell me, sir."

"Because you have that translator app. We might need that. Any knowledge of how these weird aliens operate will be helpful in the upcoming operation."

216

"Are we talking about attacking a vehicle of some kind, sir? I pretty much missed the briefing, and I'm in the dark concerning the details."

"We found one of their ships," he said. "It's just a transport, not a starship. It's lying right at the edge of this blast zone. It might be damaged, we can't be sure."

Nodding, his statement provided another reason why they'd moved the lifter to this damaged region of the forest. I'd thought they'd moved just to put some distance between the pod-walkers and our last remaining forces, but now I realized they'd found something interesting here.

"You see," Graves continued, "all this used to be a manufacturing area. A special zone on the planet that worked metals and built high-tech gear. God knows how a bunch of plants work metal, but they seemed to be able to do it. Most of the region has been destroyed, but one assault ship survived."

"How did you detect it, sir?"

He shrugged. "The techs did that. As I understand it, the task wasn't difficult. It's a low-metal world, and an object of refined titanium stands out among a mass of sensory data."

"Got it. Uh...what's the ship for, sir?"

"We plan to fly it up to *Minotaur* and retake her. That's why we have to capture it intact."

"Why not just fly up in the lifter we've got right here?"

Graves shook his head. "That's what I wanted to do. Tribune Drusus, too. But Turov overruled us. She didn't want to risk everything on a single throw of the dice. If we can use a vehicle that we captured, well, the stakes aren't as high. If we fail, we can start over again down here on the ground. We haven't lost everything."

I thought about that, and it did make a certain amount of sense. Still, the plan sounded iffy and overly cautious to me.

"But sir," I said, "what if we *can't* fly this alien craft? What if we're wasting time trying, and in the meantime *Minotaur* is destroyed, or fortified for use by the enemy? Hell, they might be figuring out how to fly our own ship right now, and maybe they'll figure that out faster than we can figure out how to fly theirs."

"Excellent points, all of which I've made publicly. You know what all my objections bought me?"

I frowned for a second then brightened with inspiration: "A front-row seat on this mission?"

"Bingo. Our unit will be leading the charge. It's our lucky day."

"Thanks for the private briefing, sir," I said. "Is that all you wanted to tell me?"

"No, there's one more thing. I wanted to warn you to stay away from Turov. I know you might harbor ill-will toward her, but you need to swallow that emotion like a noncom is supposed to."

Confusion spread over my face until I got the message. Graves thought I might go ballistic and attack Turov for having disconnected our tappers and leaving my squad out in the bush to rot. Sure, the thought had crossed my mind, but I wasn't going to act on it.

Everyone seemed to think I was some kind of hothead. I supposed, after some of the things I'd said and done in the past, a man had to expect to gain a certain reputation.

"Message received, sir," I said.

"Excellent," Graves said. "Gather your squad as soon as they exit the revival machine, piece together spare equipment for everyone, and get ready to march. Dismissed."

-30-

Go-time.

We didn't wait for dawn. We didn't wait for dusk, either. We suspected a bunch of plants didn't care much whether it was light out or not.

Less than a day after legion techs had discovered the wreck, five full units of troops marched toward the site. We wore determined expressions but carried substandard gear. After the pod-walker attack, the bio people had managed to rebuild our numbers from a few hundred up to a full cohort in strength. But we didn't have enough guns and armor to go around.

For the most part, all the troops were from Winslade's cohort. He'd been given overall command of the operation as well. I don't think he was happy about that. He'd probably rather be back at the lifter sipping a cool beverage, but he played it straight enough.

"Listen up, Legion Varus," the primus' voice buzzed in my helmet. "I know we're supposed to be heavy infantry but only half of you are wearing armor. Be glad I managed to get everyone a rifle at least. The units we're leaving behind at the lifter have been stripped bare. There was talk of sending us off with every other man using force-blades alone, but I squashed that idea."

His words were alarming. The trouble was we'd been sent down to the Death World fully equipped, but most of us had died. In many cases, we'd lost our equipment. My squad, for example, had lost everything. Many of the ill-fated troops in the drop pods had lost their weapons as well.

As a result, my squad's load-out was definitely less than optimal. It'd been decided that anyone not specifically designated as a line-combatant was to be given a smart-cloth tunic and no armor at all. That really upset my specialists—especially Carlos. You would've thought they'd cut off his left nut.

"This is too much," he said, starting up again. "First, Graves blasts me to paste after humping it over half the planet. Then as a reward for faithful service, they shaft me with a snap-rifle and a gunny sack full of med gear. What am I supposed to do if one of those pod-walkers catches my ass again?"

"Same thing you always do, Carlos," Sargon answered. "Die squealing!"

Sargon seemed to think this was extremely funny, and he laughed long enough to get most of the squad laughing along with him. People were tired of Carlos' complaining, and I couldn't blame them.

"Look at you, muscle-brain," Carlos said, talking to Sargon. "One breastplate and a pair of boots. The rest of you is wearing fancy pajamas. Half a suit of armor isn't much good against spines and acids."

"I've got a belcher," Sargon said, "and I'm happy with that. Some weaponeers are carrying rifles like the rest of you pukes. I can't imagine the shame."

The chatter went on like that, but I tuned it out. I didn't much care what they said as long as no one got mad enough to blast another squad mate. I couldn't allow that.

"How much farther, Kivi?" I asked.

As my tech, she was watching the map displays on her tactical system. My helmet-based system only reached so far. Hers could scan the entire planet if she was hooked to the legion net—which she was now.

"I'm looking at five to seven kilometers—depending on whether we march straight through or circle around."

We were pretty close to the tree line now. Marching over scorched ground that sent up choking clouds of ash as we passed by. The trees were like a mountain range directly ahead of us. The massive plants were daunting. Their trunks were somehow more imposing when you could visually compare them to flat, open land.

As we walked into the gloom under half-burned branches, I felt an oppressive coolness steal over my body. The blackened skeletal claws of the megaflora clutched at the skies overhead. It was the ultimate haunted woods.

"I hate this forest," Carlos said, deciding to complain about something new. "It's unnatural. We're like beetles crawling among redwood giants."

"Yeah, but bugs are quieter," I commented, but it didn't seem to faze him.

"Five kilometers in—that sounds like Turov missed a bet," he continued. "She should have kept firing and destroyed everything."

"If she had, maybe we'd be stuck on this planet forever," Kivi pointed out.

"Are you kidding? You've got to be joking, right?"

Kivi gave him a disgusted look. I could tell why their short-lived relationship, which had flourished on Machine World, had quickly petered out. Carlos just couldn't help but rub people the wrong way, even his ex-girlfriend.

"What's your point, Ortiz?" Kivi demanded.

"My point is, buttercup, that this mission is going tits-up already. We're not going to take over some damaged landing craft built by plants and fly it up to *Minotaur*. The whole idea is laughable. It's got to be Turov's dumbest plan to date. No, if we don't die capturing it, we'll die for sure trying to get it to fly."

Kivi hated it when he called her "buttercup" which was a nickname that he had apparently begun during their brief time together. Her weapon rose up and aimed at his back—but I was ready for that. I grabbed the barrel and tipped it toward the sky. She only had a snap-rifle, but it was equal to Carlos' own gun. As they weren't armored, any conflict between them was likely to turn deadly real fast.

221

Holding onto the barrel, I gave Kivi a grim shake of my head. She sighed in frustration and aimed her weapon away. I let go, and the march went on.

We ended up circling around to approach our target from the forest side. Soon, we were walled-in by greenery. Most alarming of all were the pods we saw hanging from the trunks.

"We should kill every one of these we encounter," Carlos said.

"I agree," I replied, for about the tenth time.

"Then come on, just do it."

"Can't. I already asked—request denied."

Carlos came close to me. We were beyond the region of radioactive ash so we'd taken off our helmets. Breathing the local atmosphere wasn't entirely safe, but it saved power and our air tanks.

"Don't listen to Winslade," he whispered loudly. "When have you ever listened to him, anyway? Where's that old McGill magic? Come on... He won't do anything. He's a pussy."

"I'm fresh out of magic at the moment."

He pulled his head back like a turtle and peered at me. "Damn, I never thought I'd see it with my own eyes."

I frowned at him. "What?"

"You—turning into a stiff. Since when did you decide to play Boy Scout? I've never seen you refuse to take action to save your squad. It's like one of these aliens transplanted your brain or something."

"Listen up, Specialist," I told him. "I'm *not* refusing to take action. I'm just unsure what the right play is in this case. Attacking these pods might be a good idea, or it might needlessly set them off. Remember the spiders back at the field around the nexus? Burning them got them to wake up. If we'd walked past quietly, they might never have done a thing."

"Maybe, but then again, they might have come after us later in a massed swarm if we hadn't burned them first."

I shrugged. "See? Uncertainty. We just don't know enough about this world to go second-guessing all the techs and bio people in the legion. They've been studying the matter a lot longer than we have."

Carlos steered away from me again, shaking his head. "I'm feeling a little sick, here. James McGill, a stiff. A rule-following member of the shepherd's flock. Makes me want to puke."

"You're in rare form today," I told him. "Clear off and move to the rear of the column. Maybe you can wrap up someone's stubbed toe."

Grumbling further, he did as I asked. It was a relief to see him go. Sometimes, I wasn't sure how I'd managed to stay friends with a man who often irritated the living hell out of me. That was a mystery that I'd probably never figure out.

After he was out of earshot, I wondered about his words. Was I becoming dull and predictable? A rule-follower who didn't question his betters? I didn't like the thought of that.

Fortunately, fate didn't give me much time to ponder. About three minutes after my talk with Carlos we came into sight of the fallen craft, and Winslade ordered us to encircle it.

The ship itself was…*strange*. It didn't match anything I'd seen before. Empire ships were usually squared off and built with complex geometric pieces layered together. Squid ships tended to be oblong and rounded, like giant zeppelins from Earth's past.

This craft wasn't like either of those basic designs. The ship looked to me like an insect. There were legs on it, thick struts that tapered up from the padded feet to the body itself. The back had a fanned set of wings that appeared to have been drawn inward against the body and folded on top of the upper hull. I guessed the wings were there for atmospheric travel. The front of it—at least what I thought was the front—was a bulbous module with a tongue that seemed to spit down to the floor of the forest.

"You know what that looks like to me?" Kivi asked.

"Yeah…a fly, maybe?"

"Close. It's a mosquito. A thickly-built mosquito."

"You're right. How odd. They chose a design that matches nothing on this world."

"It's an efficient, ancient design," she said. "There were mosquitos eating dinosaur blood back on Earth, you know."

Harris and his squad had been trailing us. Now that we were hunkering down along a ridgeline, they came up behind us and stared at the ship, just as we had.

"Looks like a bug," Harris said.

"A mosquito," I suggested.

"Yeah...you're right," said Harris. "That long tongue-thing that comes out of the head and touches the ground—that would make quite an impression if it stabbed into a man." He laughed, but no one shared in his mirth.

Della came up next, and she threw herself down beside me, hiding among the ferns.

"I don't like that thing," she said. "Is it true such monsters exist on Earth?"

"Mosquitos? They're real enough. This ship *does* look like one, if you magnified it about ten thousand times."

"A terrifying image of evil," she breathed.

I chuckled. "Plenty of people in Georgia would agree with you."

"What's wrong with the ship?" Della asked.

"What?"

"They said at the briefing that this ship was disabled. That it had survived the broadsides—but I don't see any damage."

She was right. I contacted Kivi, who answered back quickly.

"We're working on that," Kivi said. "We don't know the answer. The initial images showed damage—but the vessel looks perfectly operational now."

"Well, I like mysteries," I lied. "How long until we run up that thing's tongue and take a look inside?"

"Tongue?" she asked. "If this craft's design is based upon real insects, the correct term would be proboscis."

I rolled my eyes. "Whatever. How long?"

Soon. The techs are all chatting about it. They're recommending caution, but Winslade has overruled them."

"Uh-huh," I said. "I figured that was coming."

"There's something else, James," Kivi said in concern. "Did you know that we've been designated to take the point on this attack?"

"I'd been meaning to bring that up," I said apologetically.

"You really are a bastard. You know that don't you?"
"So I've been told…"

-31-

The assault began about thirty minutes after we first reached the mosquito-ship. The more I got used to it, the more the insectile vessel looked like it belonged here. Where else would a giant mosquito fit in, after all, than in the midst of a forest full of trees that were over a kilometer tall on average?

Graves marched in the lead of our lonely unit as we approached the ship. I had to give the man credit—sure, he was a heartless bastard with soul of a stone, but he had guts, too. He often led from the front without any concern for his personal safety.

Winslade, by comparison, was way back in a headquarters bunker he'd had the techs dig for him using drones. The bunker was behind the trunk of the tree nearest to our position. I imagined him hiding back there, using a bunch of specialists as an excuse and as protection.

He'd ordered the rest of us to capture the ship on foot. All around me were people from my unit. Della, Harris, Johnson and Leeson—we were all marching in a widespread formation. We kept our distance from one another, hoping we'd be harder to take out if the ship suddenly lit us up.

I was of the mind that we should up and charge the thing, but that hadn't been the consensus. A heavy infantry group in exo-armor can move very quickly across a field like the one we were in, but the trouble was not all of us were in armor now. If we tried a quick assault, we'd be strung out depending on who had working legs that could auto-run and who didn't. To keep the line coherent, we'd been ordered to march together.

So far, the ship had just lain there quietly.

It really *did* look as if a giant bug with gossamer wings of titanium had just landed on the forest floor to take a break.

We reached the ship without incident. Walking up the tongue-like ramp made everyone uneasy—except possibly for Graves himself. He walked up that uneven slanted surface as if he was mounting the steps outside the Mustering Hall back home.

"One at a time," he said. "I'm wondering if we're looking at a vehicle manned by a smaller variety of alien. This ramp is pretty narrow for beings as large as these aliens tend to be. Input, Natasha?"

"What, Centurion?" she answered as if startled.

"Weren't you listening? What kind of being would use this type of ramp?"

I glanced over toward her, and I felt a surge of sympathy. She wasn't enjoying this adventure. Not at all. Her face was white, and I could see her eyes rolling around in her helmet as the dark maw of the ship yawned wide up ahead.

"Uh…I don't know, sir."

Centurion Graves laughed. "Don't tell me this thing has you spooked? I can tell you haven't seen enough alien craft yet. Some of the designs are downright weird. You should see a Mogwa's personal pinnace, for example. They look like rifles, and you enter through the muzzle. The first time I did that, I thought it was going to blast me to kingdom-come."

Natasha and I exchanged glances among ourselves. We had no idea what he was talking about, but we were impressed he'd been on a real Mogwa ship at some point in his long career.

Graves stepped over the final lip at the top of the tongue and into the strange mouth of the craft beyond. He vanished like a swallowed morsel. Only his suit-lights gleamed faintly to show where he was.

"Hmm," he said. "There are no internal light sources. No windows, either. Turn on your lamps, people. And make sure your faceplates are closed and locked."

Those who had forgotten to button-up adjusted their suits in a hurry. Visors were slapped down, and they clicked as they locked into place.

We advanced into the craft, shining our suit-lights into the bowels ahead. The ship was simplistic in design. There were only three decks, and the bottom deck was the biggest of the three. That space was filled with egg-shaped nodules that lined the floor, walls and ceiling. The eggs were in what looked like a honeycomb of hexagons built with secreted resins. There were fleshy leaves surrounding each egg, and what looked like roots or veins growing between them. Graves ordered us to stay out of there. The eggs were clearly some kind of alien life-form.

The middle deck was full of equipment. Strange-looking devices that seemed to produce carbon dioxide and generate power.

The top deck was the control system. Fortunately, it was unoccupied. The accommodations were very large, however. Whoever was expected to pilot this ship was clearly a giant.

"Has anyone ever seen a being that might operate this kind of control system?" Graves demanded.

I looked at the controls, baffled. Paddle-like devices lined the floor. They looked rubbery and almost organic. Two or three meters above the paddles was an uneven surface—call it a table or a board—encrusted with strange growths. The techs analyzed the paddles and determined they gave the pilots feedback as they were hooked to external sensors. Instead of visual gauges or read outs, the feedback systems consisted of tactile nubs and tips. These things squirmed when you made contact with them.

Out of all of us, only Natasha seemed more fascinated than disgusted. She became increasingly excited as she examined the alien technology.

"This is unbelievable," she said. "So different from Imperial standard. I can only guess at the details, but this thing that looks like a seashell has to provide a reading of speed—or maybe navigational data. The pilot sits here, next to this pineapple thing, and he must have to remain in contact with the mobile data readouts. Then, using these paddles way down here—"

"Are you serious?" Graves asked in disgust. "Nothing Imperial standard at all? There's no way we'll ever figure this out."

"Well, it's not a familiar interface, naturally. But given enough time, Centurion—"

"We don't have time. I'm going outside to report back to Winslade. This mission is a bust."

Graves strode out of the ship to stand on the tongue. Those of us left inside looked at one another, relieved and worried all at once. After all, nothing had attacked us yet. But on the downside, we weren't going to be getting home inside this strange ship.

Graves contacted us moments later on the unit-wide channel.

"We've got a problem," he announced. "We've been out of communication while we've been in here exploring. Those pods hanging from the trees we passed on the way to this ship have begun tearing themselves open. Walkers are massing up between our position and the lifter. This whole thing might have been a trap all along. In any case, Winslade has ordered us to stay here and defend our captured prize at all costs."

"I don't believe this," Leeson said to me. Then keyed his mic and talked to everyone. "Centurion, did you tell the primus this ship is impossible to figure out and full of alien eggs, sir?"

"We have our orders," Graves said. "Take up defensive positions and remove those eggs in the main hold. I want them all tossed overboard."

Leeson and I looked at one another. Neither one of us wore a happy expression.

"Leeson," Graves continued as if he could see our faces. "Stop crying and get your platoon on it. Clear out that hold."

Closing his eyes and shaking his head, Leeson let out a long sigh. "All right, you heard the man. Let's move out!"

Trotting down the nearest ramp, he vanished in the direction of the hold. I followed, with Harris and his squad behind me. Profanity echoed from every wall all the way to the bottom.

We soon stood in a knot among the alien eggs nestled in their honeycombs. There had to be a thousand of them—maybe more.

"I say we burn them," Carlos said. "That worked last time."

"That's a solid idea, Ortiz," Leeson said, "but we can't do that. We might damage the ship. The whole point is to take this ship for ourselves, not to burn it up."

"Graves himself already said we can't fly this thing. Maybe we should have an accident to speed things along."

Leeson eyed him for a moment. I couldn't tell if he was considering doing it or shooting Carlos for being mouthy. It might have been a toss-up.

"You've been following McGill too long," Leeson said at last. "I'm going to recommend an assignment change after this mission. You can be Harris' medic next time we deploy."

"No reassignment is necessary, Adjunct," Carlos said.

"I say it is. You two have been rubbing on each other in the same squad for years. Don't you want to get away from McGill?"

Carlos gave him a funny look. By funny, I mean stressed and uncertain, not like he was about to laugh or anything. I realized right then that Carlos didn't want to be separated from me. He'd been by my side for years, just as Leeson had said. Despite all our adventures, mishaps and downright disasters, he wanted to keep it that way.

"I was just talking big, sir," he said. "No changes in the rosters are necessary."

Leeson snorted. "All right then. How about you shut your mouth, get down there into that hexagon of bug-spit, and carry the first egg out?"

Carlos set his teeth. He glanced at me, but I didn't say anything. I knew what Leeson was thinking: if Ortiz didn't want to get transferred, he could damned well start doing more work and less complaining. Leeson was testing him, and I couldn't honestly fault his methods.

Resignedly, Carlos moved to the nearest of the hexagons and stepped inside. There were hundreds of these large indented regions on the floor of the hold and more on the walls and ceiling. About a meter deep, these hexagons didn't have water in them, they had eggs instead.

The eggs were kind of kiwi-shaped. They were roughly scaled on the outside and they had vein-like roots running in between them.

I was immediately reminded of the cocoons we'd found back in the forest with the nexus plant. Could these eggs be like those things? Pods, full of some kind of new life-form?

As Carlos approached the nearest egg, moving slowly so as not to step on any of the hose-thick roots that ran between them, I looked all over the hold. Where were these roots going?

"Get on with it!" Leeson shouted.

Carlos hesitated. Harris and his team had gathered up behind us. They were all grins, nudging one another and pointing at Carlos with glee. They were enjoying the scene.

Carlos had always had a big mouth. Over time, that tended to irritate a lot of folks, and in our unit he'd pretty much irritated us all.

But still, I felt an urge to defend him.

"Adjunct, sir?" I said.

"What now, McGill?"

"That's my one and only medic you're endangering out there. He hasn't got a strip of armor on, either."

"You want to take his place?"

"Yes sir, if I may."

Leeson stared at me with narrow eyes. "Request denied! Carry on, Ortiz, and hurry up or I'll start kicking those eggs over one at a time myself."

"Maybe he should carry two at once, sir," Harris suggested.

"Shut up. One man, one egg. If Ortiz lives, you'll all get your chance to carry plenty of them."

Harris retreated hastily.

Carlos took in a deep breath, knelt, and put his hands around the lower, fatter end of an egg. He then straightened, using his legs to do the lifting. Even so, he struggled with the weight of it.

"Heavy, sir!" he managed to grunt out.

"That's cuz they're all attached with those hoses. Put it down, fool, and cut it loose first."

231

Blinking with the strain and fear, Carlos put his egg down. He then produced a knife and slashed the vein-like roots that interconnected the eggs. He was sweating, despite the fact it wasn't all that hot in here.

A hissing sound erupted as he cut the hoses. Liquid gushed out and pooled around his boots. A vapor arose, like white smoke.

"That looks like the stuff we met up with on *Minotaur*," I commented. "Is that acid?"

"By the look of it," Natasha said, "it must have a highly unstable pH."

"Pick the damned thing up, Ortiz!" shouted Adjunct Leeson. "Time's wasting! If your boots melt, well, we'll find you new ones."

Everyone knew what that meant. The only supply of fresh boots was back at the lifter in the lockers near the revival rooms.

Carlos knelt again, gripped the bulbous egg and lifted. It came clear, but it sloshed and dribbled more liquids.

"Natasha said these plants use stinks and liquids to talk," Harris said. "Maybe it's trying to talk to you. What's it saying, Ortiz?"

"It says you smell like your mama's purse, Harris," Ortiz called back.

Harris growled something I didn't catch. I had to hand it to Carlos, there he was carrying an alien egg dripping acid all over his shoes, and he was still smarting off to his superiors. I had to admire his dedication.

Carlos almost made it out of the hold. The trouble came when he reached the edge of the honeycomb he was in. I reached down along with Sargon, and we hauled him out—at least we tried to.

Unfortunately, the egg-thing, or pod, or whatever you want to call it, tipped too far and spilled liquid all over his pants.

That white smoke billowed and hissed like hot rocks hit with cold water. I could hardly see for a second, and although I tried to haul Carlos up onto the higher deck with us, he stayed down there as if glued to the deck.

"Have you got him, Sargon?" I asked.

232

"I think so."

"Carlos, what's wrong?"

There wasn't any answer.

"Carlos? Dammit man, drop the egg. Let's get you out of there."

"No!" Leeson shouted from behind me. "I don't want to see Ortiz without his frigging egg!"

"One more pull, Sargon."

We reached down, braced ourselves and pulled hard. We each had one of his elbows and were pulling on his arms. I couldn't tell what was wrong with him. There was white smoke billowing all around all three of us. I could hear the sounds of leaking fluids.

Suddenly, I lost my grip. Sargon gave a whoop and held something up into my face.

Confused, I stared at Sargon. He was just an outline in the vapor. "Did you get him?"

"Sort of," he said. He showed me what he had.

It was an arm—Carlos' arm. The rest of him...well, that was missing.

-32-

"Damn!" Leeson shouted when we showed him what was left of Ortiz.

Sargon thrust the bubbling arm up into Leeson's face, making sure the adjunct got a good, close look.

"Should we go in there and fish the rest of him out?" Sargon demanded. "I think there might be some more parts that haven't melted down to foam yet."

"You're crazy, weaponeer!" Leeson said. "All of your men are crazy, McGill."

"You ordered my man into that pit sir, not me," I answered.

Adjunct Leeson nodded, still staring at the arm. "So I did."

The smoke had cleared somewhat, and we could see that a discolored soup lay around the egg, which looked rather deflated now.

"McGill," Leeson said in a lowered tone. "I'm asking for your expert advice, here. How do I disobey a direct order from my superior and get away with it?"

I blinked at him for a second. It seemed odd to me that my adjunct was asking me such a question. In addition, I found it equally strange that everyone thought I was some kind of wizard when it came to going off-script.

Still, I felt his question was heartfelt, so I attempted to answer as honestly as I could. "There's no need to get any more troops killed, sir. Ask for Natasha's analysis first."

Leeson ordered Natasha to join our huddled group. She checked over Carlos' remains.

"Acid," she said. "Probably the same stuff that ate into *Minotaur* when the aliens attacked. It makes good sense, if you think about it."

"Let's pretend we're all dummies," Leeson said. "Explain it to us."

"These eggs—they're baby ship-invaders. Remember the monsters that ate through the walls of our ship? They must have started off like these eggs. When fully formed, they're able to burn their way into the hull of a ship."

"Then why the hell don't they burn their way through the walls of *this* ship?"

"The first layer of defense is the egg-casing itself. Many acids only work on either organic or inorganic surfaces. Some of the most deadly ones will eat skin and metal but leave wax or glass alone. Look at the deck in this hold. There's a rubbery layer coating it, a membrane that protects the metal. These hoses or veins, they're embedded in that semi-transparent membrane."

I could see what she was talking about now. What I'd mistaken for roots or hoses were really vein-like growths in an almost transparent skin that coated the inside of the hold.

"A hold full of baby ship-invaders..." Leeson said. "I think I get it. This ship isn't exactly like a lifter. I bet it drops these invaders, seeding them out in space like land mines. The plant-creatures like the ones that attacked us originally when we entered this star system—they amount to a defensive system."

Liking his chain of logic, I nodded in agreement.

"Stands to reason, sir," Natasha said.

"Will fire destroy these things safely?" Leeson asked her.

"Destroy, yes—safely...I don't know."

Leeson's eyes sought mine. "My helmet is beeping. Graves wants a progress report. What's my next step, McGill?"

"Your tech has now given you valuable intel," I said. "That's what you'll tell Graves about when he finds out you didn't do as he asked. Always distract with an interesting detail."

"Okay, I got that. What next? Should I answer this call?"

"No, that will establish a timeline you can't afford. We have to move fast. Burn up the eggs."

Leeson looked worried, but after a moment of indecision, he made his choice.

"Harris!" he shouted.

"Sir!"

Harris, who'd been lingering near the exit after the suggestion he would be the next to go on an egg-hunt, suddenly joined our group.

"Harris," Leeson said, "is it your opinion that these eggs represent a clear and present danger to my men?" He pointed at the mess in hexagonal chamber.

Harris frowned then looked over the situation. He caught sight of Carlos' arm, which Sargon was still waving around like a baton.

"Holy shit!" Harris said. "Yes sir, I agree wholeheartedly with that statement."

"Then I order you to destroy this danger. Now."

Harris grinned. "With pleasure, sir!"

That was it. We broke out every plasma grenade and incendiary device we had with us. Standing back at the entrance, we burned them all down to the metal.

Unfortunately, some of the acid got through the egg-casings, the membrane, and the flames. Then…it burned through the lower hull of the ship we were supposed to be capturing.

Leeson was cursing and crying about that, but we had to abandon the ship before we could do anything to stop it. The fumes, heat and blinding corrosives were melting our suits.

Stumbling out into sunlight, falling off the mosquito's tongue and gasping for air in the clear, I was never so happy to have abandoned a ship in my life.

Graves was the last man to exit the ship. He came down the tongue at a walking pace, just as he'd done when first boarding her.

At his approach, we scrambled to our feet and stood at attention. Graves walked among us with a grim expression on his face.

He stopped in front of me, and he drew his sidearm. He aimed it into my left eye socket.

"McGill," he said. "You see that gutted ship behind me?"

I glanced toward the mosquito. It was on fire now, stem to stern. The belly was a burning hole with acid, flaming alien eggs and only God knew what else falling out of it.

"Yes, Centurion."

"That might have been our only way off this planet. You just might have permed us all, Veteran. For that—"

"Sir!" Leeson shouted.

"What is it, Leeson?" Graves asked, his gun never wavering from its target.

"Sir, McGill did not start the fire."

Graves turned his head slowly toward the adjunct. "What did you say?"

Leeson began to explain. He mentioned the death of Ortiz, the analysis of Natasha and the back-up determination by Harris that the eggs were dangerous. Leeson managed to tell the story right, but he screwed up badly on the last part.

Not all men are born equal when it comes to the subtle arts of misdirection, embellishment and general weaselry. Leeson simply wasn't up to the task. In retrospect, I figured I should've coached him on exactly what to say—but there just hadn't been enough time for that.

The basic problem was he was too damned honest for his own good. Sure, when a man lives by his word, he should commit himself to the truth. But the time and place for honesty had long since gone by the wayside. The fact was Leeson had disobeyed orders. Lying about it afterward, in my opinion, was a relatively minor offense. One that was downright required if you were going to get away with the original crime.

"So," Graves said, his attention fully upon Leeson now. "*You* ordered these men to destroy this captured vessel because you lost your nerve?"

"It wasn't like that, sir, I—"

"Answer the question, Adjunct. Yes or no."

"Well, I...I guess that's so, sir. I'm sorry. It was an error in judgment."

Graves nodded. " Indeed it was."

237

The centurion turned to Harris. "Veteran, as the most senior noncom in this platoon, I'm temporarily elevating you to the status of platoon leader. Are you ready to take on that responsibility?"

Harris looked from Graves, then to Leeson, confused. "Well sir, I think the platoon already has a good leader. I don't—"

Blam!

Grave's sidearm had gone off. Leeson toppled forward onto his face, his helmet a smoking ruin.

"I repeat, Veteran Harris," Graves said in a perfectly even, calm voice. "Are you ready to assume command of this platoon?"

"Absolutely, sir!"

"Good. Now, gather up your troops. We're marching back toward Winslade. He's gotten himself into some kind of trouble."

That was it. Leeson was gone. We stripped his body of whatever useful equipment he had, and we left him lying there on the ground. I felt bad about it—but damn, that man needed to learn how to stretch the truth properly if he was going to pull off stunts like this.

As we marched double-time back toward the giant trees, Graves moved to my side and trotted there beside me.

"Sir?" I asked him. I couldn't help but glance at his sidearm. Fortunately, it was back in his holster.

"McGill," he said, "I still smell your signature brand of bullshit on this fiasco. If I learn that you had a lever on Leeson, that he confessed to save your sorry skin, I'll—"

"Sir, it was the damnedest thing. Leeson just up and lost it, I swear. Before any of us could stop him, the whole place went up. In his defense, though, those eggs were pretty creepy. He might need a psych eval when he gets revived."

Graves' slid his eyes to meet mine for a moment. He shook his head. "Sometimes I don't know if you're smart, dumb, or just a smart-ass."

"My grandpa used to say I was one part genius and three parts retard, sir."

"That sounds about right. I can only commiserate with the man."

He moved off then, and I sighed heavily releasing a lungful of tension. Sure, I'd sold out Leeson. But he'd already been executed in the field. With any luck, that wouldn't amount to a perma-death. Graves usually forgave a man after meting out his own particular brand of harsh, instant justice.

-33-

It had been a long while since I'd served directly under Veteran Harris. We'd often had trouble getting along, but we'd always pulled it together when push came to shove in a combat situation.

Today was no different. Harris looked at me, and I looked at him. We veered toward one another, and he gave me a nod.

"That should have been you back there, taking the bolt in the face," Harris said.

"I disagree. Leeson made his own choices."

"You coached him in your special brand of chicanery and look what happened."

"His choice, Harris," I repeated. "He's a full-grown man."

Harris looked at me sidelong. "You think you could have gotten away with destroying that captured ship, don't you? You figure you're above the chain of command. What makes you—"

"Two o'clock, Vet!" I said, pointing.

Harris dropped his bitching about my behavior and unlimbered his morph-rifle in a single, smooth action. He adjusted its structure into a long-range configuration.

"Enemy sighted!" he shouted, engaging the unit-wide channel.

There they were. Towering monsters the size of redwoods themselves. Their long, dangling limbs bent in curves rather than angles. I'd done battle with pod-walkers before, but this time seemed different. It took me a moment to figure out what it was.

"Command?" I heard a breathless female voice in my helmet. It was Kivi. She was in the rear of our formation, running with those of us who were unarmored. "The pod-walkers are being herded. See those smaller creatures at their feet? That's what you have to kill."

Graves spoke up next. "McGill, has your team seen those spiky-looking things before?"

"Yes sir," I said. "I reported them just before you brought us home with a missile barrage. Claver explained they're direct servitors of the enemy brain-plants. We call them spiders, sir."

"They do look spidery... So, it's their job to get the pod-walkers to charge in a single mass, is that it? Makes sense. I never did figure out how the walkers were able to coordinate. They don't seem too intelligent alone."

The walkers were encircling Winslade's position. The sound of the action was reaching us now—snaps, whines and ripping noises like distant thunder. I could tell a terrific firefight was in progress. The sound of the weaponry was intermixed with the howl of the enemy.

"Okay, here's the plan," Graves said. "We're going to dive into the thicket of ferns to our right. Try to stay together, don't straggle. We'll swing around under the cover of the undergrowth and hit the aliens right in the butt, pinning them between our guns and Winslade's."

I swallowed. Graves' plan had its merits, but it was going to take us close to the enemy. I'd been hoping that we'd engage them from range with our rifles and belchers. I'd figured we'd distract the walkers and help Winslade that way.

Graves was planning a much more direct and aggressive play. We were going to be under their feet, in the thick of it.

Harris was still running near me. Resignedly, he reconfigured his rifle again, turning it into a short, stubby carbine weapon. I did the same. This was going to be a close-assault action, so we needed our guns to operate with a high firing-rate.

We soon dove into the thicket of ferns. We would normally have been running at speeds only an Olympic runner could match, aided by our exo-skeletal legs, but we couldn't do that this time. Too many of our troops didn't have armored leggings to propel them along. Already, I could hear our lighter-equipped troops puffing. The rearmost were struggling to keep up.

"We should slow down," I told Harris. "We're losing our lightest troops."

Harris shook his head. "Wrong. We'll plow in at a dead run. Let Kivi and the rest fall behind—they'll last longer."

Thinking about it, I nodded in agreement. Harris was right. Why endanger our most vulnerable troops right off the bat? Might as well give them a fighting chance.

The more I thought about it, the more I liked Harris' manner of bending his orders. I figured I still had a thing or two to learn from him. Not just in adjusting orders but also when it came down to tactics. He got the job done any way he could. If he won the fight, the officers weren't likely to complain just because he'd done it his own way.

The ferns were thick now, slamming and lashing us like palm fronds in a hurricane.

"McGill," Kivi called on a private line. "I'm over a hundred meters behind you. If you don't slow down—"

"Squad," I said, overriding her voice and all the rest of the chatter among my people. "When the foremost elements engage, halt and find a good firing position. Engage at will."

Sargon answered me then. "I like that. Thanks for the clarification, Vet."

I knew what he meant. The rest probably did, too. I'd just edited our orders a little more. Graves had wanted us to hit hard as a single shocking strike, but what was going to happen now would be a more spread out force, all firing together, but not physically close to those deadly, stomping feet.

There wasn't much more time to think. At first, we caught a few glimpses of the enemy, looming over us like trees that were bending and then straightening up again.

What could they be up to? It looked like…

"Centurion?" I called. "It looks like they're throwing rocks at Winslade's troops. Is that right?"

"I wish, McGill," he called back. "They're throwing things, all right. They're throwing living pods. Winslade's men are on the receiving end. They can't keep a coherent line because the enemy keeps smashing those pods right into their midst."

I got it then. The big pod-walkers were picking up and throwing the smaller creatures. We closed in fast and broke out into the open. The whole battlefield was laid out before my eyes.

There were pods—greenish black things that reminded me of the eggs we'd seen inside the invasion ship.

But these pods were much bigger. They were about three meters long and two meters thick. They must have weighed a ton each. The pod-walkers bent, picked them up and threw them like pinecones into Winslade's line.

As a counter to this action, Winslade's people were lashing the walkers with a storm of small-arms fire. As I watched, a pod split open under withering fire and green-white liquid drenched the walker that had lifted it above his head. A pall of white smoke rose up from the walker's head-section as the acid went to work.

Sargon took careful aim and fired his belcher. He shot for a pod raised high, not for the walker. He opened up another pod before the walker could throw it, copying what Winslade's people had done.

"Score one for our side!" Sargon whooped as the walker fell thrashing.

"Good shooting, Weaponeer!" Harris shouted. "Platoon, engage!"

We opened up with our morph-rifles, advancing at a walking pace into close range. We sprayed a deadly hail of bullets right up into the butts of the nearest walkers, who didn't seem to know we were there until that moment.

Stupidly howling with pain and surprise, the towering giants turned on us. One stood right over me. He lifted a pod high, like a primitive man with a rock lofted in both hands.

I thought it was over. It was a shame, really. I'd only just gotten into the fight.

But when the walker smashed down the pod, it didn't strike me dead, it crushed Harris instead. Acid exploded, spraying my armor and burning through my smart cloth where I wasn't wearing any armor. The newly hatched creature inside shivered and rose slowly from the shattered pod.

Cursing and dancing away, I didn't bother to look for Harris—he had to be dead. No one could take such a blow and live. Even if the hurled pod hadn't broken his spine, the gush of deadly liquids would have finished the job.

Nearby troops blasted the acid-dripping alien apart. It was indeed one of the same kind that had invaded *Minotaur* when we'd first entered this star system.

"Advance!" I shouted, realizing I was in command now. "I want concentrated fire on the walkers that turn to face us. Ignore the rest."

Again, I was editing our orders. Graves had told us to light up all the walkers to distract them—to keep them from overwhelming Winslade's line. But I figured that plan was flawed. If they just turned around and killed us all quickly, we wouldn't be doing much to help our fellow troops. No, I wanted to kill as many of the enemy as I could, one at a time, if possible.

The walker that had killed Harris went down fast. We tore it apart with hundreds of rounds at short range.

Two more walkers turned on us, pods held high. Sargon beamed one's head off, and it threw its pod right into the back of the other walker. I had to grin at that, we'd caught a break. They both died before they could do much else.

I took a moment after that to survey the battlefield. I didn't like what I saw. The other two platoons in Graves' unit weren't faring quite as well as we were. Tactics or luck had failed them. I checked my tactical displays—we'd lost all our officers except for Graves himself. Half our troops were dead, and the enemy didn't appear to be dying as fast as we were.

We'd broken a hole in the enemy line, but it wasn't enough to call a victory yet. There were at least ten walkers hunting down and destroying Toro's platoon one man at a time.

"Harris?" Graves called.

"Harris is down, sir," I answered.

"All right, McGill. I need your platoon to support Toro's right now. Flank right, attack immediately."

244

I marshaled my people, and we advanced toward Toro's group.

As I watched, a big hand dipped down and scooped up a fleeing trooper. I think it was a bio, judging by her light gear. The walker crushed her with a convulsive squeeze of that many-fingered hand. Dropping the limp pulp, it reached for another.

We began to light them up, one after another. After half of the enemy was down, the rest turned and made a lumbering charge toward our position. I knew as they stumbled toward us that we couldn't take them all. Not when they were focused on us single-mindedly.

I tried to contact Graves for clarification, but he was dead. I was on my own.

There wasn't much time for thought, but I had one burning question in my mind: Who'd ordered these walkers to act in a coordinated fashion? Scanning the battlefield, I saw them—a dozen or so spiders up on the back of a high root behind us. Overlooking the region, they were quiet, calm, and deliberative.

"Platoon, disengage!" I roared. "Follow me up this root structure. Double-time! If you don't have powered legs—well, hide someplace!"

To tell the truth, I don't quite know why I gave the command. Tactical ingenuity? No, not entirely. Rage was more like it. I wanted to kill the spiders who'd ordered the death of my entire unit.

They sat smugly up there on their high root until they saw what we were doing. Then, like cowards, they began to dive off on either side. We reached them seconds later and tore apart the slowest spiders with ripping blasts of fire from our guns.

Turning back to the walkers, I'd expected to find them charging up the root after us. But they weren't. They were milling around searching for prey in random patterns. Without the direction of the spiders, they'd broken off their attack.

Up on top of the ridge-like root, we found stacks of unopened pods. A big pile of them in a bowl-like area. The pods were big ones, juicy and ripe with corrosives.

My troops were firing down the steep sides of the roots, tagging the spider commanders in the ass, but it wasn't enough. Many were getting away.

"Roll these pods after them! Move people, move!"

My last dozen troops hastened to obey. Sargon was still with me, along with a few others I knew: Della, Sladen and Marquis. We worked in teams of three, rolling the pods over the sides of the root. Dropping pods and shooting after the spiders, we caught a few more and watched them die. Then we rolled the rest of the pods into the face of the walkers that were closest.

That's when things changed on the battlefield as a whole. The walkers had been operating as an organized formation of troops, but now that we'd killed most of their commanders, they were bereft of intelligent leadership.

Some stood dumbly, swaying and looking around, confused. Others charged blindly at whatever enemy they saw. They stopped throwing pods and marched directly into Winslade's guns. They were cut down with focused fire.

A few more tried to get to us up on top of the root, but we were ready for that. We rolled pods down onto them, burning away their limbs with acids and blasting them with concentrated fire. As the root was relatively narrow for walkers, they were only able to approach one at time.

After a few minutes passed, they were all dead—every one of them. Not one of the enemy walkers had retreated. None had asked for quarter.

That suited me just fine as I wasn't in a merciful mood, anyway.

-34-

Long after dark, my squad marched back to the lifter bone-tired but feeling victorious. Sure, we'd lost the ship, and the walkers had killed half our troops. Despite these realities, we'd managed to defeat the enemy and kill some of their commanders.

When I got to the lifter and we passed through the outer defenses, the troops in the ditches eyed us in concern. We must have looked a sight. We had tarnished, half-melted armor, dirty faces, and plenty of wounded troops.

A runner came down the ship's ramp before my squad made it half-way through the camp.

"Veteran McGill?" he asked me.

I recognized him then. It was none other than regular trooper Lau. How many times had this poor bastard died on Death World, mostly under my command? I didn't even want to start counting.

"What is it, Lau?" I asked him.

"Graves is out of the oven. He wants you to attend an officers' meeting, upper deck."

I heaved a sigh. "What the hell for?"

Lau shrugged. "I guess because he died and didn't see the end of the battle. Winslade is up there, too. Both of them missed it, but they know you were there."

"Right. Okay—thanks Lau. Get some food and rest. That goes for the rest of you, too."

247

Kivi, Sargon and a few other survivors of the long day moved tiredly toward the chow line—which was long, but not as long as it should have been. We'd lost a lot of people today.

Kivi walked up to me, put a hand on my shoulder, and gave me a worried look. "Don't let them blame you for anything, James," she said in a low voice. "You fought well. You did the best job you could have done today."

"Thanks Kivi," I said, "but I doubt they're angry. Hell, we're the ones who broke the attack in the end."

"That's the spirit," she said, and she walked away to join the chow line.

I looked after her with a frown on my face. She was a tech. That meant she had a special line on inside rumors. Techs chatted and texted one another all day long like birds on a wire. What could she know that I didn't?

Resolutely, I mounted the ramp and marched up to the upper deck. When I got there, a tight group of officers were sitting in chairs, chatting. Graves was there but not Leeson or Toro. So many people had been killed they were reviving just one top officer from each unit and building up the rank and file regulars first before popping out the adjuncts. Someone had to man those trenches outside, after all.

Notably missing were Turov, Drusus and Winslade. I knew Winslade had died—but the other two should be here.

I didn't have long to wait. I found a Danish and shoved it into my mouth, then gulped some sewery coffee when everyone jumped to attention.

Drusus walked in and ran his eyes over the crowd. "At ease."

I chewed fast, gulped, and put my cup down. Drusus walked right up to me, which I hadn't been expecting.

He looked me over. "McGill..." he said, as if he were looking at a puzzle. "You lived through the battle, didn't you?"

Nodding, I dared a brief smile. The tribune didn't return it. Instead, he made a sweeping gesture toward the rest of the group present.

"Do you realize that none of the others present here today made it to the end of the action in the forest? They were all either killed, or they didn't go on the mission in the first place."

Glancing around, I noticed for the first time that no one else looked like they'd been sweating in the mud all day. There wasn't a scratch or any sign of oily sweat in the group. Fresh revives and loungers, the lot of them.

"Huh," I managed. "That's against the odds, I'd say."

Tribune Drusus nodded, eying me closely. His stare wasn't an accusatory one. He just looked at me thoughtfully.

"That's what I thought at first," he said. "That your survival was against the odds. Unlikely, even. However, I now believe it was due to an enemy tactic."

I hardly had time to absorb what he was talking about before Imperator Galina Turov showed up next. She looked as pissed as a short-tailed cat. She put her fists on her hips and stared at us.

Everyone jumped up again, standing at attention. We didn't salute because we were in a combat-zone. All that was normal, but what surprised me was that she didn't tell us to stand at ease.

She walked among the group, eyeing us like we'd all screwed up. Finally, she stopped in front of me and aimed a finger into my face.

"This man," she said, "has shamed you all. That's what's going into my after-action report. You died like rats in a ditch. It was a grand embarrassment for the lot of you. On top of that, Graves managed to burn up the only other functional transport on this planet. I'm disgusted."

Eyes wide, I tried not to look at her disrespectfully when she turned around to glare at the rest of the officers. Keeping my eyes high and locked was always hard for me to do when Turov was around. We'd had a few inappropriate encounters in the past, and she was looking mighty fine today.

Sometimes being revived and given a young body again was confusing when it came down to appearances. In Turov's case, it was worse than usual. She was far older and more politically dangerous than she looked. She held the rank of Imperator, which meant she could command multiple legions in the field. The ancient Roman rank was the equivalent of a two-star general in the pre-empire armies of Earth.

Dangerous, powerful and manipulative, she was also a rather petite woman with calculating eyes, short hair and a finely shaped rear end. After her last revival, she'd come back looking like a twenty-year-old. That was a disturbing appearance for any high-level officer under the best of circumstances.

"That's right," she said, running her eyes over me speculatively. "While the rest of you died out there, or didn't bother to go, this country bumpkin *lived*—and not by hiding under his desk in the lifter."

"Sir?" Graves said. "May I say something?"

"If you must, Centurion."

"You're mischaracterizing the situation. We fought hard on the battlefield. McGill lived, but I agree with Drusus. He survived due to enemy tactics, not some innate virtue on the veteran's part. By saying that, I don't mean to lessen the importance of McGill's role, but I feel we should clarify things."

"Nonsense," Turov said. She put a hand up to silence Graves, who was about to speak further. "Yes, I know about the theory that the spider-creatures that command the enemy forces targeted our officers purposefully. I'm not entirely convinced that's true—but I am convinced that McGill targeted *their* officers in return and broke the enemy by doing so."

I blinked and looked around the room. She was right, of course, but I wasn't sure how she'd analyzed the details of the battle so quickly. We'd only just returned and made preliminary reports. There were suit-cameras, of course, but going through all that data took time.

Turov made a gesture indicating we should be seated. We all found a chair and sat down—there were plenty to go around with so many people still stuck in the revival queues.

She began to strut around the tactical display table while we all stared at her.

"This situation is intolerable," she said. "It's only a matter of time before the enemy marches out here in strength and finishes us off. It's my firm belief that they're reluctant to leave the shade of their forest, and that's the only reason we're still breathing."

She tapped at the tactical display system, and it sprang to life. The lifter had been set down in the center of the region destroyed by the broadsides. The forest appeared as a green half-crescent around our position with the sea at our backs.

"If I'd known when we first arrived in this star system what I know today," she said with feeling, "I would have flattened every inch of the forest without mercy."

No one said anything as she tapped here and there on the table. Red shapes appeared. They were oblong blobs representing enemy troop-masses. There were an alarming number of blobs.

"Thousands," she said, "more pods are hatching every hour. Our buzzers are working overtime just cataloging them all. We're detecting numerous varieties of enemies as they hatch: walkers, the smaller acid monsters, spider-commanders and other types we've yet to encounter in battle. Some of them fly, a few even swim."

More blocks appeared behind us in the sea. I'd been of the opinion that was a safe zone for us, a last-ditch area to retreat. Such hopes were quickly dashed as she kept tapping and revealing more enemies.

"I now wonder if the assault ship was set up as some kind of decoy," she said. "It really doesn't matter at this point. We're going to be wiped out within the next hundred hours. They could probably overwhelm us much sooner, if they all decided to march at once. But they've demonstrated some degree of caution since their first encounter with the lifter's defenses."

"How do you suggest we defeat them, Imperator?" Tribune Drusus asked. He'd maintained a quiet presence this whole time.

"Since the moment when I was finally revived," she said, giving him a dark look, "I've been dedicating my strategic thinking toward that end. My first thought was to retake *Minotaur*. That's why we attempted to capture their invasion ship. Although we lost that gambit, at least we destroyed their flight capacity. If we regain control of *Minotaur* now, we control this star system. They will be at our mercy."

251

"You're certain they don't have any other ships?" Drusus asked.

"Yes. The techs have used suborbital drones to sweep most of this planet. As far as we can tell, they don't have any more ships nor do they have another shipyard facility. We destroyed their colony base, their factories, their refineries, etc. We crippled them. Unfortunately, we've also crippled ourselves with losses. We have only one lifter and half a cohort of troops."

Drusus cleared his throat. "We can still launch this lifter up into space and take back *Minotaur*. If we win the assault, we win the campaign."

She nodded briefly. "This is true, but I still think it's too risky. Failure means utter destruction for the entire legion. For now, I've ruled out such a direct approach."

Several of the officers present squirmed in their seats. They clearly didn't agree with her but were too cowed to speak up.

"Well," Drusus said, "if surface-to-space assault is off the table, what other options are there? They continue to grow new pods every hour. We can't revive troops fast enough to keep up. Additionally, our ammo and equipment levels—"

"I know all that," Turov snapped. She turned to point at me again. "McGill has given us the answer."

No one in that room could have been more surprised than I was at her statement. I swallowed and put on my best poker face. Every officer gave me a flat stare—except for Turov. She gave me a fleeting half-smile.

"That's right," she said. "Crazy McGill may have saved us. Observe."

She began to play vids then. I recognized the clips. First, she showed a shot of me burning spiders and ordering Sargon to shoot the cactus-like nexus in the deep forest. The officers watched with interest. Some winced as Claver explained the dangers, but I killed the plant-brain anyway.

After witnessing this, several officers looked at me in astonishment. This was their first exposure to my performance in the field. My butt seemed to want to crawl out of my chair, but there was no escape for either of us.

"Next clip," Turov said, "this one is from today's action."

She played another vid, again from Kivi. I suddenly understood why Kivi had been trying to warn me I might be in trouble. She'd probably been ordered to surrender these clips to Turov and had surmised I was to be investigated.

This clip showed our final, valiant charge up the root to kill the spiders.

"Impressive," Graves said. "You attacked with the ferocity of soldiers who know they're about to die and yet want to strike one final blow. I see in your troops no hint of breaking morale. They followed you up there knowing they would probably die. By doing so, they took the initiative from the enemy without hesitation."

I nodded. "My squad is the best, sir."

Turov pursed her lips and froze the clip on the singular image of a spider, dying and curling with acid and bullets destroying it.

"This then, is the essence of my plan," she said. "We need to take the fight to the enemy—the real enemy. Those who are making the strategic decisions. Claver calls this varied species Wur. Like a hive full of social insects, they have several forms, and all of them serve a purpose."

As she spoke, she displayed examples of each of the aliens we'd encountered. "These plants have a critical weakness," she said. "Most of them don't possess much in the way of a brain. The hierarchy goes something like this: at the bottom are the ferns, which are consumed by the mobile creatures. Next up are the trees. The purpose of the trees is to produce pods and provide a livable environment for the rest. Above them, the spawn of these trees are pod-walkers and other stupid creatures. Commanding the spawn of the trees are these spiders. They are local, tactical leaders."

The group followed her presentation, nodding with interest. It was compelling. I'd experienced most of what she was talking about, but I hadn't spent a lot of time figuring out the details of the ecosystem or the enemy's social structure. I'd been too busy trying to stay alive.

"At the top," she said, "are these brain-plants."

Here, she displayed the cactus thing I'd had Sargon blast open.

"Claver refers to these growths as nexus plants," she continued. "We've sent flying drones to locate them. This one was attacked by McGill. See how it fared after McGill's action?"

More images followed, aerial shots this time. The field of vines and spiders was burnt, dead. The brain-plant had perished, and everything around it had died as well. There were no further signs of activity in the region.

"You see?" Turov asked. "Simplicity itself. While surveying the world and searching for ships, we've located six more of these fat cactus-like bastards. They're the beings that tell the trees to grow pods and which type to produce. They make the strategic choices about when and where to attack. They're the true enemy we must destroy to win this conflict."

Drusus cleared his throat and leaned forward. "I assume you want to fire missiles at each of these locations?"

"That's right. All at once. We'll strike them all over the planet at the same moment."

"Are we sure the spiders won't drive the walkers to attack afterward for the purpose of revenge?"

Turov looked thoughtful. "Some might, but I doubt it will be a coherent mass-attack. Recall when McGill killed the spiders. Some of the walkers nearby attacked his squad. But most wandered aimlessly as if they'd lost their way. My best xenologists say these aliens operate as if they share a large, distributed mind. If you destroy the higher level creatures, the rest will become confused."

"That's why they targeted our officers," I said suddenly. "Maybe they thought we operate the same way. Maybe they thought they could destroy our army by killing our leaders."

Turov gave me another half-smile. "It could be," she said.

Graves spoke up then. "Imperator," he said. "What does Claver think of this approach? He knows them better than the rest of us do."

"Claver is a fool, a traitor and half-mad," she said with conviction. "He is self-serving, and I don't care what he thinks about anything."

With that, the meeting broke up. There wasn't really much of a discussion. The battle plan had been drawn up. The targets were being located, confirmed, and slated for destruction in the morning. We were to launch a precision strike across the planet all at once.

I had to admit that if Turov's plan worked, it would be a stroke of genius. I sincerely hoped that it would.

-35-

It was night time, and the only illumination came from our suits and the landing lights of the transport ship itself. This made for a shadowy atmosphere.

Dead set on getting some food into my belly before they closed down the line, I headed for the tables and tents they'd set up in the area under the lifter itself. Leaving the meeting, I made a bee-line for the chow tent, but I didn't make it before a dark figure accosted me. Claver stepped out from behind one of the thick titanium struts and got into my face.

"I knew you'd come this way," he said. "I've got to talk to you, McGill."

Glancing at him, I shrugged. "I'm getting a tray of food right now," I said. "You can join me if you want, but stay on the opposite side of the table."

Claver chuckled. He followed me in the food line, choosing an apple off the fruit tree. Our meals always included fresh-grown fruits and vegetables. We had special trees that grew whatever was selected the night before. The cooks had selected apples today, and there were plenty left.

I loaded my tray with two heaping plates. I started off with a layer of rice on one plate and a layer of potato-paste on the other. On top of both, I ladled a meat and gravy mix. It tasted like pork—but we all knew it wasn't.

While I chowed, Claver talked.

"Listen, McGill," he said. "I know we've had our differences in the past. But this is important. You have to hear me out."

Chewing and shoveling, I gave him a nod. I figured as long as I was going to eat anyway, time spent listening to him wasn't wasted.

"Okay, glad to see you're willing to hear me out at least," Claver said, leaning forward. His hand slid across the table toward me. He had a small, black device in it.

Thud! My fork came down in front of his hand, blocking its progress. He yanked his hand back, but left the device. There was blood trickling from his thumb.

"Dammit, boy," he said. "You're so sensitive. It's just a spy-blocker. Settle down."

I looked the device over. It could have been a bomb or anything else. I flicked it back toward his side of the table with my fork then went on eating.

"Talk fast," I told him. "I'm almost done with my first plate."

He leaned forward again, switching the device on. "Okay, here's the deal: I know about Turov's plan. Her plan to destroy the enemy brain-plants."

"She indicated she'd talked to you about it. I take it you don't like the plan?"

He shook his head. "It will start another war, pointlessly. It's one thing to have a conflict with the Wur. It's another to kill all life on one of their colonized worlds. Just think how humans would react to the destruction of a planet full of our kind."

"We aren't going to kill them all," I said. "We're going to eliminate a certain variety of plant. That's all."

"Oh yeah, right," he said with an unpleasant laugh. He picked up a table knife and held it up between us. "How about I lobotomize you with this?"

"How about I break your neck with these?" I held up my hands.

Claver rolled his eyes. "I'm not threatening you, clod. I'm making a point. If you cut up a man's brain and send him home to his relatives, they won't be happy. What Turov proposes will leave a mindless colony on this world. It might even die of neglect, just like an idiot left wandering in the wilderness."

Frowning, I nodded. I had to concede his point. From what I'd seen, we would be crippling this world. Was that an appropriate response? Sure, they'd come to Earth and shot down one of our freighters. My parents had even died in the process. But from their perspective, they hadn't done this to attack our world. They'd run down a pirate ship—Claver's ship—and destroyed it. Looking at it this way, Claver was just as responsible for the loss as the Wur.

"You're telling me this is all a misunderstanding," I said. "One that you caused, by the way, with your failed attempts to trade with them."

"At least my intentions were honorable," Claver said. "There are often misunderstandings when two new species meet one another. What I'm advocating is a measured response and hopefully a negotiated peace. Remember, they're strong and they're plaguing our enemies."

Thinking about that, I nodded. "Okay, keep talking. What can I do about this?"

"You can talk to Turov for me. I've tried, I've done my best, but she's not interested. Maybe you can make her see reason before she does something that can't be negotiated away."

"Hmm," I said thoughtfully. "You want me to convince her? How the hell am I going to do that?"

"If anyone can, it's you. Not even Winslade is as good at slick salesmanship as you are."

I snorted in disbelief and pushed away the last of my food. I'd wiped out seven eighths of it, but somehow Claver had put me off the last bites. I heaved a deep sigh and shook my head.

"I'll think about it," I said. "But you overestimate my hold over the imperator. She's got a mind of her own."

"Don't I know it," Claver said. "You should give it your best shot if you want that kid of yours to keep breathing."

He stood up, and I did too. I reached a long arm across the table and grabbed his tunic up in a wad.

"Is that some kind of threat, Claver? I could have permed you six ways from Sunday by now."

258

"No threat. I'm talking about cold realities. These aliens will come for us some day if we keep pissing them off. Some species out here fear the Empire, while others are just too busy right now—but they'll all come eventually. The Empire is falling apart."

I let go of him, and he pocketed his spy-blocker. I stared after him as he disappeared into the shadowy evening. I wasn't even sure why he wasn't in chains or dead. The only reason I could come up with was that he'd managed to talk Turov into letting him have his freedom. Maybe he had some dirt on her.

Heaving a big sigh, I mounted the ramp into the lifter. A few checkpoints later, I found myself activating the touch-chimes on Turov's quarters.

"Enter," she said.

I stepped inside and was immediately surprised. I'd been in lifters in five different star systems, but I'd never seen a chamber like this one. It wasn't sumptuous, mind you, but it was well-appointed considering it was merely a room inside a lifter.

The curved walls were covered in silky fabric. The ceiling was relatively high, higher than the usual rooms that often forced me to duck my head. Possibly most startling of all was the chandelier. That's right, there was an honest-to-God *chandelier* hanging from the ceiling in the center of the chamber.

Turov came from the back, which I assumed was a bedroom of sorts. She pushed aside a sheet of cloth that separated her private space from the rest of the room. The curtain curled away from her fingers then folded itself back so it hung perfectly straight and still.

"Smart-cloth," I said, marveling. "You've decorated this whole place with smart-cloth."

"Well," she said, "there wasn't much aboard in the way of luxury items when I was revived."

"Where's the chandelier from, then?"

"The former captain," she said. "He didn't mind if I borrowed it."

Blinking, I gave her a small nod. Her answers had created more questions in my mind than anything else, but I decided they were questions best left unasked.

"Why are you here, James?" she asked.

I slid my eyes around the room and landed them back on Turov. Despite the fact everyone considered me to be a man full of guile, I was feeling a little uncertain.

While I thought about my response for a second, she stretched against a wall, which enhanced her curves.

"Uh, I don't know," I said, smiling. "I just thought there was something different about you today. I thought I'd come find out what it was."

She smiled.

Bingo, I thought. She was an attention-seeker, through and through. It wasn't always in a sexual sense. She liked to exhibit her prowess in public in any number of ways. The woman was very good at manipulating her way through life any way she could.

"You find yourself attracted to a superior officer," she said. "I understand. It's a common enough occurrence. In this case, although I'm flattered, I have to deny your unspoken request. It wouldn't be appropriate."

That had never stopped her in the past, but I was willing to let it go. However, this meant my original plan had just evaporated. I'd come here to see if I could make a connection with her before giving her Claver's hard-sell. Now, it looked like that wasn't going to happen.

"Well sir," I said, standing up and towering over her. "I guess you're the better of us. I'm sorry to disturb you, I'll be—"

I didn't make it to her door. She came around the tiny table that squatted beneath her out-of-place chandelier and touched my chest with soft fingers.

"Sit back down," she said.

She sounded a little annoyed, but I clumsily did as she asked. She shook her head and tsked at me.

"A lady can't give in at the first pass, James. Surely, a scoundrel like you knows that. You're supposed to keep trying."

"Oh," I said. "I get it now. How about this?"

I reached up and pulled her down into my lap.

She sighed disgustedly, but she didn't jump off.

"You're the romantic equivalent of a lowland gorilla," she said. "I don't know what it is I ever saw in you."

There was a bottle of red wine on the table. I opened it and poured her a glass. She sipped it and offered some to me. I drank a bit, but it was too dry for my taste.

Still sitting on my lap, she finally melted. The woman was a strange one. Sure, she could be a cast-iron bitch when she wanted to be, but she could also warm up in private like no other.

Soon, we were making passionate love. I learned that she indeed had a bedroom behind that smart-cloth sheet. What's more, a queen-sized bed nearly filled the room. That had to be a first on a military ship like this one.

Afterward we lay together, wrapped in a thin, twitchy sheet. The bedclothes wanted to rearrange themselves over our bodies, but my feet were hanging over the end of the bed and pissing them off.

This was the moment, I knew. I had to make my pitch if I was going to do it at all.

"Galina?" I asked.

"What is it, James?"

"I'm worried about tomorrow. I'm worried about destroying all the plant-brains."

"Why?"

"Because we might be starting a new war—or at the very least, pissing off a species we only just met up with."

She laughed. "Why should you care about that?" she demanded. "You make a habit of pissing off aliens all over the galaxy."

"That's true, but this is different—these plant-brains might be considered civilians."

She lurched up and sat next to me. She stared at me with dark, calculating eyes.

"Claver," she said. "I smell him on you. He sent you here to my bed, didn't he? That conniving rat."

261

"Uh…" I said, caught dead-to-rights. "Listen," I said. "It doesn't matter who I may have talked to. The truth is the truth. Maybe we should reconsider. Maybe we should talk to the plants or at least make the attempt. Everyone has access to the translation app I brought back—"

She gave a hiss of frustration. She threw the sheet off my body.

"Get out!"

I sat up and began to dress. She stared at me with rage in her eyes.

"I should have known," she said. "People are always trying to manipulate me. You're worse than Winslade, sucking up like this for something you want."

"I'm sorry you feel that way, but I don't think I was any more manipulative than you were today."

"What do you mean?"

Shrugging, I spread my hands wide. "You've always been a beautiful woman, Galina, and you use that mercilessly on the male officers."

She grabbed up a handful of her squirming sheets and pulled them over her lovely breasts.

"That's a low thing to say, James," she said. "It's rude, in fact. I think you're obsessed with women's bodies. To suggest that I've misused my personal attributes—"

I put my hands on my hips. "Oh come on," I said. "You look great and you use it. That's all I'm saying. Lots of people do that."

She looked at the wall in obvious irritation for about ten seconds. Then she sighed.

"All right," she said. "You're forgiven. Just don't bring up any more bullshit you hear from Claver. He's got some kind of scheme running, that's all it is. Don't get caught up in it. Now get out of here, I need sleep, and if I let you spend the night, I know I won't get any of that."

I left a short time later with a smile on my face. Sure, I'd failed to convince her that Claver was right—but I'd enjoyed the failure, all the same.

-36-

When I reached my bunk at last, I found another woman sitting cross-legged on top of it.

"Natasha?" I asked. "What's up?"

She looked me up and down while I removed my breastplate and boots.

"I've been waiting for you," she said at last.

"What for?"

She didn't answer right away. Instead, she gave me a reproachful look and crossed her arms.

"I had no idea you were still making visits to Turov's quarters."

Denials sprang to mind, but I rejected them all. Instead, I sat on my bunk beside her. She scooted away to the far edge and frowned at me.

"What about it?" I asked. "What can't wait for tomorrow's attack?"

"Not bothering to lie about it? At least that's an improvement."

"Yes," I said, "I visited Galina tonight, and I'm willing to own up to that. Are you willing to admit you spied on me to figure out where I went?"

She shifted uncomfortably. "I'll admit I accessed the personnel tracking system. That's part of my job as a tech."

I snorted and put my head back against the wall. I closed my eyes.

"Gave you a workout, did she?" Natasha asked.

"Come on, Natasha. I fought a battle today and marched across miles of blasted land. Give me a break."

"Okay. You're right, I'll try to forget about Turov. I'm here because someone among us is sending off-world messages."

That statement got me to snap my eyes open again. "Who?"

"If I knew, I would have said."

"What kind of messages? Sent where?"

"I don't know. They're encoded, encrypted. But someone is doing it. Whoever it is, they're sophisticated enough to set up a shield-bubble around themselves. A barrier that keeps me from knowing who they are, or precisely where they are. I can only guess that it's one of our techs. Who else would have the skill?"

Climbing off my bunk, I rearranged my tunic and teased the nanites into sealing my breastplate into place again.

"Can you give me a hint as to the source?" I asked.

"The general location is inside or around this lifter. Sorry, that's pretty vague, I know. They aren't transmitting right now, and I doubt they're sitting at the same spot waiting to be caught anyway."

I looked at her. "Why are you telling me this? Why not one of the officers?"

She chewed her lip. "Because I thought it might *be* one of the officers—Turov or Winslade. Remember Tech World and Machine World? They've made back-channel deals before."

Understanding her concerns, I nodded. "If one of our top commanders is the guilty party, it will be very difficult for a noncom to accuse them."

"Do *you* think it's Turov?" she asked.

"Give me the exact times of the transmissions."

She gave me the times, and after thinking about it, I was able to personally vouch for the imperator's innocence. This didn't please Natasha, but she understood.

"That leaves Winslade," she said. "No one else could have access to this kind of sophisticated equipment."

"You're forgetting about one other possible culprit: Claver."

She stared at me. "Isn't he in the brig?"

264

"Maybe he should be," I said.

Leaving Natasha behind, I went in search of Claver. I asked around and finally found him outside the ship, sleeping in the trenches.

That puzzled me. I crouched over his sleeping form, my boots sending crumbled bits of dirt into the trench. Why was Claver outside? Why not wrangle a bunk in the lifter? Either the officers had tossed him out here, or he'd exiled himself.

"You going to shoot me or strangle me this time?" Claver asked.

He didn't look like he was awake, but he was. I wasn't surprised. You didn't live a long life as a rodent like Claver if you weren't alert to danger at all times.

"Lovely night out here," I said. "Plenty of fresh air, soot...and just a touch of residual radiation."

Cautiously, Claver unfolded himself from a sleeping position and sat up. He eyed me from the bottom of the trench.

"How did Turov take my recommendations?" he asked.

"She hated them."

He chuckled. "Why am I unsurprised? What did you do, just walk in there and tell her 'hey, Claver says to change around all your plans'?"

"Something like that."

He sighed heavily. "I thought you were a smooth operator. I thought you knew how to push a lady's buttons."

"I did my damnedest."

He cocked his head, climbed out of the trench, and looked me over. "You slept with her, didn't you?" He laughed uproariously. "Good job then. I take it back. You did your best. That woman is almost impossible to sway. Pity."

"Why are you out here, under the stars?" I asked. "Why not sleep in the lifter? You're a civilian, but you still have special status as a trader."

"Because I knew I couldn't count on you. It would have been so much better if I could have. I had to take action. Now, events are in motion, and they're out of my control."

I looked over my shoulder at the lifter. The silvery skin of the ship reflected the bright stars of the region. Here and there, floodlights illuminated patches of the scorched ground beneath the transport, but most of the landscape was black.

"Someone or something is going to hit the lifter," I said. "That's what you're telling me, isn't it? Is that what you arranged?"

"Nonsense," he said. "I'd never do that. You're paranoid. A good trait for a Varus legionnaire, I get that, but wrong nonetheless."

He started to climb out of the trench, but my hand shot out and pushed him back down.

"What?" he sputtered. "You trying to arrest me again, boy? On what kind of trumped-up charges this time?"

"I know about your transmissions. I know you've been sending off-world messages."

Even in the dim light, I could tell he looked startled.

"That's crazy-talk," he said. "You're clearly delusional, Veteran. Don't worry though, it's just death-lag. Happens to a lot of good men. You get a little funny in the head after a rough battle and a revive."

"I didn't die out there," I said. "And I don't get traumatized by death in battle, anyway. Not anymore."

He looked me over appraisingly. My eyes were uncompromising, and my grip on his arm was unbreakable.

"Look, McGill," he said. "You can arrest me or even kill me if you want to, but it won't do you any good. Let me give you a piece of advice: all that matters in the real universe is who holds who's leash. Remember that."

My thoughts swirled around in my head. I was seriously considering shooting him on the spot. I could try arresting him instead, but it seemed pointless. If I shot him right now, though...that might change the future. Unknown disasters might be averted. Maybe not the calamity he'd summoned this time, whatever it was, but possibly the next one.

"Back on Tech World," I said. "You were my prisoner. You tapped on your tapper and summoned an unholy army of the Tau to assail my legion. That was a dark day, and you were full of excuses as to why you did it. I think you're going to have to answer for your sins one day, and maybe, just maybe, today is that day."

"I'll come back," Claver said confidently. "I always prepare for a death. I'm ready for it."

"You might be prepared for a regular death," I said, "but I'm not talking about that. Have you ever permed a man, Claver?"

He blinked at me. "Accidentally, maybe. Like the Tau back on—"

"No," I said. "I'm talking about a human. A man who's accustomed to catching a revive now and then. Someone like a legionnaire, or a Mogwa. You ever permed such a being?"

"No," he admitted, looking at me curiously. I clearly had his undivided attention. "I can't say that I have."

"I've done it," I said. "Not officially. Not because I was ordered to. I did it on my own initiative. I know it can be accomplished, and I might be moved to do it again someday."

Claver squirmed. "You aren't a tech," he said. "You're not a bio, either. You're just a weaponeer with an extra stripe. In short, I don't believe you."

"You doubt my will to take such an action?"

"Not at all. You're a killer through and through. A brute of a man who'd as soon wash his hands in blood as soap and water. But you don't have the skills."

"I've done it," I repeated, "and someday, I'm sure I'll do it again. I might not have fantastic technical skills, but I have something you don't."

"What's that?"

"Friends. Friends with the power to do things I want done."

We stared at each other grimly in the dark. Finally, Claver blinked and looked down.

"Maybe we should talk then," he said.

"I think we should. Who did you contact?"

"Business associates," he said. "Powerful ones that can deal with the problem Turov has created. They'll be here soon—and don't bother to ask about postponing their arrival. They won't turn back now. Not even if you put a stake through my heart this instant."

A frustrated growl escaped me. "Why the hell do you care so much about these plant-brains?" I demanded. "You're selling out your own people for a bunch of fancy vegetables.

267

They're *freaks*, Claver. These aliens would kill us all in a heartbeat. What's wrong with *your* brain?"

I was losing it, raising my voice. In response, Claver gave me a smug smile.

"You're missing the point entirely, and I can't say I'm surprised by that. You're as dumb as the stick you write with McGill, and that reality is showing through again today. Really, I'm shocked you've managed to give me so much trouble in the past."

"Insults don't help get a man out of being permed," I told him. "You didn't answer my question."

"My apologies. I'm struggling to come up with a way to explain a complex topic to a man of your intellect. It's quite a challenge."

Feeling myself losing my temper, my grip on his arm tightened. As I was wearing metal gauntlets, the pressure exerted was painful.

"Claver, I swear, if you don't start talking plainly, I'm climbing down into this trench and if that happens, you're never getting out of it."

"All right," he said. "I'll make the attempt. To start with, you have to understand my perspective. I don't want all-out war. I want a balanced conflict. I want the various sides in this part of the galaxy to maintain a sort of equilibrium. No one should ever be defeated or declared the victor. Except for the Empire, that is. I want them to lose this war and get out of our space for good."

Shaking my head, I tried to grasp what he was saying. "You don't want Earth to kick these plants out of our territory?"

"No," he said. "Of course not. Look, as long as there's a healthy war on, I can sell materials to both sides and make a handsome profit every step of the way. Peace? That means no trade. Victory? Defeat? Refer back to peace. They're all the same result from my point of view."

I stared at him for a few seconds. I was starting to understand how he thought, how he looked at a situation. He was fantastically self-centered—but it went beyond that. He'd actively participated in political events to stir the pot of war. He *wanted* endless conflict without a break in sight.

"How does that goal jibe with protecting the brain-plants?" I demanded.

"The Wur are vulnerable due to their centralized intelligences. They can be defeated that way, but I don't want them to be defeated. Can you understand that?"

Standing up, I took in a deep breath. The night breezes were up, and the air didn't taste half-bad.

"You're a monster," I said. "That's what I get. But at least you're true to your principles. Sleep in your trench, Claver, if you can. We'll see who wins in the morning."

I left him there and walked back to camp to find my bunk. I didn't bother to report to Turov or anyone else. What would be the point? Claver was either truthful or full of crap. Either way, we'd know by morning.

I never glanced back at the man in the trench. He could have run off or shot himself—I just didn't care.

-37-

The squids showed up the next day. It was a fresh disaster for Legion Varus, piled on top of a long list of them.

"James?" Natasha called me, sounding out of breath. "Come to my location. It's an emergency."

I grabbed my morph-rifle and followed my tapper to her location. She was sitting under the lifter's ramp in the cool shade beneath the ship.

"What's got you?" I demanded, seeing her sitting there.

She was staring at her tapper. She didn't look hurt, but she did look upset.

"Sit here," she said. "Look at my tapper and listen closely. I don't dare turn it up."

Frowning, I moved to her side. I'd been expecting an alien attack, at the very least. This business of hiding under the ramp was a disappointment.

But Natasha was nothing if not reliable. If she thought her tapper was displaying an emergency, then I knew it probably was.

The vid I saw streaming on her wrist was alarming, I'll give you that. It displayed the face of a cephalopod captain. He was decked out with one of those golden collars they liked. It had a lot of pressure points all over it, like buttons. I watched as he ran the tip of various tentacles over those points, causing transmissions to be sent.

"You will submit or be destroyed," the alien captain said.

The squids always talked like that. They were slavers by trade, and they only understood dominance and submission. The idea of diplomatic negotiations as trusted equals—that just didn't compute in a squid's brain.

His words got me to thinking about what Claver had said the night before. Something about leashes and who had captured whom. That must have been a hint, I realized now. A line like that could have only come out of the mouth of a squid.

I heard Turov's voice next, although the streaming vid kept displaying that vile squid.

"Captain Torrent," she said sternly. "You're in violation of our treaty. This system is within the boundaries of Frontier 921. You have no right to order an Earth ship to do anything here."

"Technically, you are correct. At this moment, a state of war does not officially exist between us, and our two species have made certain agreements regarding Gamma Pavonis. However, a situation involving the honor of the Cephalopod Kingdom has arisen here on this planet. A situation that we cannot ignore."

"You must be talking about the infection of alien plant life we've discovered here," Turov said. "Have no fear, it will be excised soon. You do not have to take any action to support us."

"Your statements are so disorganized as to be rendered meaningless," Torrent said. "We do not want you to harm the plant species resident in this system. The fact that you have clearly already done so might be sufficient grounds for the war you so richly deserve. I can only go back to my superiors after this world has been scrubbed of your taint and hope they will see things with a clarity matching that of my own six eyes."

"I don't understand," Turov said, sounding concerned for the first time. "If you're in conflict with this nomadic species why would you attempt to stop us from destroying them?"

"Our motives are our own! Your ship and your invasion forces are being monitored. You will *not* fire missiles at the nexus plants. Any attack upon the nexus plants will be construed as at attack upon this vessel."

271

Turov was quiet for a few seconds. I wasn't sure if she was conferring with her officers, or if she was just confused.

"Don't listen to that slime-bag!" I shouted at the tiny screen. "My legion doesn't take this kind of bullying from anyone!"

Natasha gave me a wry glance. "I can see why Turov didn't invite you to speak with the cephalopods this time."

I stared at her tapper angrily. "We've got to get back into space. It sounds like Torrent hasn't figured out yet that *Minotaur* is crippled. If he knew that, we'd probably be toast by now."

Turov informed the squid she would consider her options and then broke the connection. Natasha lowered her tapper and looked at me.

"What are we going to do, James?" she asked. "With that squid ship up there—they could destroy us at any moment. We can't even use *Minotaur* to defend ourselves."

"There's only one squid cruiser up there, right?" I asked.

"As far as we know."

Nodding, I felt the sick sensation of a missed opportunity. If we had taken *Minotaur* already, we'd be in the clear.

"Turov was wrong," I said. "We should've launched an all-out attack on *Minotaur* with the lifter yesterday. Do or die, we had to retake our ship. In a space battle, one imperial dreadnaught is worth several squid ships."

She shrugged. "That doesn't matter now. It looks like we're at their mercy."

"Squids don't even know what mercy is. Can you track down Claver for me again?"

She did so, and we followed the signal out to the mess tent.

He was in line for breakfast, talking up a couple of young, female recruits. They were smiling and shaking their heads at his outlandish compliments.

My hand closed on his shoulder, and I yanked him backward right out of line. He wheeled around staggering, eyes big. When he saw it was me and Natasha, he snorted.

"You had me worried," he said. "I thought one of these girls had an ape for a boyfriend—but lookie here, it's just

McGill. What's the matter, boy? Don't you get enough tail on your own?"

Manhandling him toward the ramp, he came along willingly enough until he realized I was taking him up to the officers' deck.

"I don't want to talk to Turov," he said. "There's no point."

"That's not your choice," I said. "I should have dragged you to her last night."

When we marched together into the conference room, only Turov, Winslade and Tribune Drusus were present. None of them looked happy to see us.

"What is the purpose of this intrusion, Veteran?" Turov demanded.

"Claver here called the squids," I said. "He confessed to me."

Imperator Turov cocked her head in an entrancing way. She managed to look cute and dangerous all at the same time.

"Did he now?" she asked, stepping toward Claver. Then she stopped and looked up at me, frowning. "How did *you* know the squids were here?" she demanded.

Before I could answer, she looked at Natasha, who appeared to be embarrassed.

"Spying again?" Turov asked her. "You techs are all the same. Get out before I take your stripes!"

Natasha hurried away. Turov looked over her shoulder at the others. "Winslade, downstairs. Prepare the action we discussed."

"I'm not sure that would be a good idea," Tribune Drusus said.

"I'm well aware of your objections," Turov said. "Do you want to interrogate Claver or not?"

"What will we gain from that?" Drusus asked. "Time is short. We must marshal our forces. We must appear to comply with the cephalopod captain's wishes. Let's use our last lifter to retake *Minotaur* while we can."

"I've heard your arguments, Tribune."

"I feel I must restate them because they're critically important. It's only a matter of time until the cephalopods

273

realize we're not in control of *Minotaur*. Once they do, they'll stop giving ultimatums and start firing salvos."

"We don't know that. This Captain Torrent is talking big, but they always do that. We'll call his bluff."

Tribune Drusus fell into a tense silence. Turov turned to Claver and I, who were listening in with interest.

"Sounds like Drusus has a pretty good plan there, Imperator," I said.

She twisted her lips into a grimace. "When I want your advice, McGill, I'll—forget it. That will *never* happen."

She eyed Claver like he was a bug on a plate.

"You," she said. "You're worse than these plants. At least the Wur are loyal to their own kind. You disgust me."

"All life is my kind, Imperator," Claver said spreading his hands open wide. "Have an open mind, for pity's sake."

"Pity? No, there shall be none of that for you. Are you aware I've come up with a way to perm insects like you? Even if you have a clone, a back-up, an automated revival system somewhere—I can have you erased."

Claver cleared his throat. "McGill mentioned something about that. Let me make an appeal. Let me suggest a solution that will get us all out of this unfortunate situation."

"By all means."

"Here's my idea: let me talk to the plants. Send me to negotiate with the biggest central brain in the forest. I can convince it to let us go in peace. To let us trade with this species."

"A central brain?" Turov asked. "What are you talking about?"

"The plants don't operate as a committee," Claver said. "One brain is in charge of this entire planet. It's hidden, and it coordinates all the others."

"Hmm," Turov said, walking around the two of us thoughtfully.

We watched her pace for about thirty seconds before she made up her mind.

"All right," she said at last. "McGill will go as your watchdog. Tell the plants we'll kill all their brains if they don't pull back their forces and make a deal with us."

Claver's grin was broad and a little predatory, I thought.

"That's perfect," he said. "I know these creatures—they'll deal. They want trade for metals. They understand the concepts of equitable give and take...for the most part."

After the meeting, we went our separate ways. Turov followed me and approached me in the hallway.

"Sir?"

"McGill," she said, looking up at me speculatively. "Do you like these plant aliens?"

"Hell no."

"Do you think the Wur will make good trading partners for Earth?"

"I think they'd make a better salad, sir."

She smiled. "Then you and I are in agreement. Go with Claver. Let him lead you to his brain-plant, the biggest of them all. When you find it...kill it for me."

I stared at her for a second, then I nodded. "Yes sir, Imperator. Can I take my squad?"

"Yes, and take Natasha too. Her spying is getting on my nerves."

"Will do."

She quickly looked both ways up and down the passage, and when she saw the coast was clear, she gave me a little kiss on the cheek. She had to stand on her tip-toes to do it, and I had to lean forward to help out.

We parted after that, and I went outside to marshal my squad.

Claver looked over the group with misgivings. He had his hands on his hips, head shaking from side to side.

"This won't do. Too much weight."

"Too much weight?" I asked. "What are you talking about?"

He laughed at me like I was the biggest dummy on the planet. "What? Did you think we were going to *walk* through that trackless forest over there? Our destination is hundreds of kilometers away and walking would take weeks, dippy. Here's the plan: we'll reconfigure a pig into a flying platform. That can be done in a few hours. Ask your tech, here."

I turned to Natasha questioningly.

"Well, yes," she said. "Drone pigs have repeller plates built in, like that surfboard table-thing you built back home, James. They have to so they can run with a heavy load over rough terrain. But rebuilding one is against—"

"Since when does McGill give a shit about regulations?" Claver demanded. He turned to me. "Veteran, do you feel like walking into that forest with a couple thousand hungry pod-walkers chasing your ass around?"

Thinking about it for a second, I shook my head.

"Good. And here I thought you were as stupid as one of these plants. Let's go."

It took a little wrangling with the quartermaster, and a few calls for support from the brass, but we got it done. The resulting platform was like the floater I'd built back home, but it was bigger and faster. As Claver had suggested, it wasn't big enough for my entire squad. I had to choose only four people to go along with me.

In the end, I took Natasha, Carlos and Kivi. Claver made the fifth man. I wanted to take Sargon, but I figured bringing a weaponeer on a peace mission might give away my intentions.

Before we left, I quietly loaded extra explosives and detonators onto our flying pig. A whole rucksack full of them.

-38-

When I'd been told we could build an aircraft out of a drone, I'd visualized something like a flying carpet. Instead, we ended up scudding over the forest floor on an uneven platform that looked more like a homemade raft than anything else.

Just hanging onto the damned thing when we had to swerve to miss a fern branch was difficult. Claver wanted to fly the contraption, but I didn't let him. I had Natasha do it instead as she'd supervised the rushed conversion process. She knew best what her hay-wired vehicle was capable of.

We weren't an hour into the journey before we were all questioning the wisdom of the entire adventure.

"It's obvious, isn't it?" Carlos demanded. "There aren't any officers on this little jaunt. You caught the significance of that, didn't you? This is a suicide run. A joke in poor taste."

My eyes slid over to him then back to the forest, which was as endless and green as ever. We skimmed along at a good clip, covering a couple kilometers every minute.

"You've got a point," I said.

"Damned straight I do. Here's their bullshit excuse: 'We wanted our best to save the day! That's why we're sending *you* clowns to certain death.' Sure, right... You want to know what I'd have asked our grand Imperator, McGill? I'd have demanded to know if *she*, our glorious leader, was willing to go along on this mission."

One thing that made Carlos possible to listen to, if you didn't take him too seriously, was his tendency to answer his own questions immediately after he asked them. That made him tolerable as long as you weren't the type who got annoyed quickly.

"Why isn't Turov here horning in on the glory this time?" Carlos asked Kivi. She rolled her eyes, but he answered his own question anyway. "Because we're all as good as dead, that's why!"

He kept complaining, and I kept scanning the horizon. The worst part of the trip so far had been the first moments after we hit the cool green gloom of the forests. The walkers lurking at the edge of the tree line had tried to catch us, reaching up with impossibly long arms that went on and on.

Hundreds had shambled after us, but only one had gotten close. It managed to snag one of the skids of the undercarriage with a finger that was as thick as a baseball bat, but we hacked it off and kept on humming.

Now, in the deep emerald gloom of the rolling land, we seemed to be beyond their reach. Only rarely did we see any of the enemy. When we did, it was always a lone spider or lost walker. They barely had time to register our approach before we were gone, doing about seventy knots over the whipping ferns.

"You're not even listening to me, are you, McGill?" Carlos demanded at last.

"Nope."

"The next time I get the chance, I'm going to let you die."

"Same here."

He finally shut up after that. Ten minutes later, I scooted myself carefully over the lurching, vibrating surface of our make-shift vehicle and joined Claver and Natasha in the front. Natasha was driving while Claver navigated.

I noticed, as I approached them, that the front end was taking on more fern-strikes. They slapped and rustled as they beat against the prow.

"Dammit, McGill," Natasha said. "I can feel the whole nose dip down when you come up here. Hold your position in the stern, please."

I scooted my butt back to the rear of the ship and used my suit radio to contact her instead of tapping on her shoulder. The drone's engine buzzed under our butts, generating a level of noise that was close to that a helicopter.

"How's it going Natasha?" I demanded. "Is Claver bullshitting you, or are we really headed somewhere that looks promising?"

"I'm not sure, actually," she said. "As far as our scans go, the region he's taking us to has no contacts at all. No spider-fields, no walkers—nothing but ferns and tree trunks."

"That's just grand."

"The good news is we'll be there in less than an hour."

Time crawled. Over the next hour, we grew tired of the novelty of traveling on our flying pig.

Finally, as we neared our destination, Claver carefully climbed his way back to me. He had Carlos go forward to balance out the ship—I can't say I was sorry to see the specialist move out of earshot.

"McGill," Claver said, looking at me seriously. "We need to talk."

"Go ahead. I'm listening."

"I need a favor," he said. "I need you to give me a shot at communicating before you do anything nuts."

Shifting uncomfortably, I gave him a shrug. "Sure. Negotiate away. That's what we're here for."

He eyed me distrustfully. "I'm not an idiot, McGill. I wasn't born yesterday, remember? In fact, I was born almost a century ago. You remember how I was called Old Silver before you got me killed and brought back a few times?"

I smiled at the memory, although it was probably rude to do so. Claver had been called Old Silver when I first met him because his body was physically about fifty. That was very unusual in the legions. He'd worn his silver hair like a badge, proudly showing the world he hadn't died for a long, long time. Actual gray hair in the legions was almost unknown. People tended to die often. When they were later revived, their bodies were regrown as they had been when they were last stored. Only a man's mind was backed up regularly. The effect prolonged our lives by many years. Claver had gotten his youth back all at once on Tech World—with my help.

"You like being young again?" I asked him.

"Sometimes—but it still pisses me off that I lost my silver hair and my nickname."

I smiled. "Glad to be of service."

He gave me a sour glance. "Look, my point is I'm older and wiser than I look. I know how things are going to go when we get to the nexus plant. You're going to try to kill it. What I'm asking you for is a little time, a fair shot at talking to it first."

My grin faded. His request was a serious one and not entirely unreasonable. Moreover, I was impressed he'd figured out what I was planning to do.

"How long?" I asked.

He stared at me for a second, dumbfounded. "Dammit! I was only fishing. I hate when I'm right! You're honestly planning to kill the biggest brain on this planet, aren't you? Of all the crazy—"

"Why else would Turov send me?" I asked him reasonably. "I'm better at blowing things up than I am at talking to them."

Claver studied his hands, frowning fiercely and muttering curses. He was dejected but thinking hard.

"Okay," he said, nodding to himself at last. "Okay, I have to prove my case to you, that's all. I get that. Maybe I'm lucky it's you. Anyone else would follow Turov's orders blindly. They'd shoot and ask questions later. But you, you've got that independent streak. How many times have officers ordered you to slaughter helpless civilians only to have you refuse them?"

I blinked a few times. I wasn't quite sure if he was playing a game with me or if he really meant what he said. "You're claiming that this plant species is innocent? They killed your whole crew. They permed my folks back on Earth."

"There have been misunderstandings, certainly. That's normal when two wildly diverse species meet up for the first time. They're a hive-minded species of self-mobile plants, for God's sake. But I'm hoping you're a better man than most. A man with a big heart and an open mind."

"Ten minutes," I said after thinking it over. "You get ten minutes to talk to your plant-buddies. After that, I'm making a salad."

"That's not enough time. I can't do it. Just connecting with the plant takes a ritual of sorts. It's like hypnotizing a deadly snake. You don't just walk in there, shake hands, and start jawing like an auctioneer. You have to gain trust, exchange fluids and scents—"

"Okay, okay. How long?"

"An hour. Probably ninety minutes to get a coherent reply. It could take longer, but I doubt it. The good thing is we'll only have to talk to one plant. The top brain has the authority to speak for the others. It won't have to relay the message and request a vote or anything like that. If we can agree on a negotiated peace, we'll know their answer right off."

Heaving a sigh and throwing up my arms, I almost told him 'no' on the spot. Stalling for an hour and a half was going to be nearly impossible. Turov was watching, after all. She knew where I was on the map. She probably had drones searching the area intently. When we got there, she expected fireworks to start. If they didn't, she'd know I was disobeying her orders.

"Listen," I said. "I don't have time for a tea-ceremony. Get in, say your piece and get out. I'm not losing my stripes by disobeying orders to make you happy. You get half an hour, tops."

"Okay," he said quickly, slapping his hands together. "Thirty minutes will do fine, thanks."

He was grinning again, and he seemed excited. He turned away to go back up to the prow, but I landed a heavy gauntlet on his shoulder and pulled him back.

"What the hell?" I asked. "What was all that business about ninety minutes being the minimum?"

"I'm a trader," he said. "I always ask for the Moon and then settle for Delaware. That's my actual motto, in fact."

I shook my head sourly and let him go. He scooted back up to the front of the vessel, chuckling to himself. I'd been scammed already, and I had a bad feeling about the rest of the afternoon.

281

We arrived sometime later and landed at the edge of a gully. Claver asked us to wait on the drone, but there was no way I was going for that.

"Right," I said, "like we're going to sit out here in the car while you handle everything. Start walking, and don't make any funny moves."

"You promised, McGill," he chided me. "Don't forget."

"You'll get your minutes. The clock is ticking right now."

Claver set off at a trot, and we had to move quickly to keep up. I shouldered the rucksack of explosives and grimly brought up the rear of the group.

We walked down a long, curving ramp of black earth. I quickly realized why we hadn't seen anything special in this region. There was a big, deep hole in the ground. At the bottom of the pit, I could see slushy mud. The opening wasn't very wide and was overgrown with those damned ferns. From the air, the buzzers and probes had missed the spot and marked it as nothing special.

"Turov's on my tapper," Natasha said, looking at me worriedly. "Should I answer?"

"Don't touch it!" I said. "Mine's beeping too, and I'm ignoring it. That's why she's calling you now. Listen up everyone, the story we're going with is that we weren't able to get clear reception down here in this hole. Ignore your tappers. That's an order."

"McGill, McGill, McGill," Carlos said, shaking his head. "What kind of a fresh Hell are you leading us into this time?"

"Just keep an eye on Claver," I told him.

We reached the bottom of a muddy ramp and stood in about a half-meter of swamp water.

Claver sloshed forward in a crouch. "You see it?" he whispered.

"See what?"

"That bulb over there, dummy. The one with the spines."

"Oh yeah," I said, feeling like I wanted to belt him one. I resisted the urge and let him sidle forward.

"Better wait here," he said. "She'll get nervous otherwise."

"She?" I asked.

"These plants spawn spiders, and they have a definitely feminine twist to the mind. I think of them as female."

"Whatever turns you on, Claver," Carlos interrupted. "Get on with it. My trigger finger is aching, and I don't care much if I shoot you or the cactus."

Claver gave him a sneer, but he quickly scuttled ahead nonetheless. We watched as Claver approached the plant and caressed a few leaves then stabbed himself with one of the meter-long spines. He allowed droplets of blood to sprinkle onto the leaf he'd touched, which was rustling on top of the water now.

"Is he feeding it blood?" Carlos said. "That's sick. I'm glad I'm not a trader."

"He's gaining its trust," Natasha said, recording the entire affair. "I wonder who told him how to do it. I don't think he's the type who could figure this out by himself."

"I bet the squids told him," I said.

They looked at me in alarm. "The squids?" demanded Carlos. "Are you sure they know how to talk to the plants?"

"The squids are the reason we're on this mission instead of just using missiles to wipe out the brain-plants."

No one knew what to say to that. We hunkered down and watched Claver and the cactus. For a couple of minutes, they exchanged fluids. Claver let the thing burn his arm with acid, then he spit on it and suchlike. It was disgusting.

After that, he sat down in an odd position and tilted his head up toward the shrouded sky. The cool gloom of the gully showed him only in silhouette.

Six minutes passed, then ten more. My team became restive, and I couldn't blame them.

"Let's blow it up," Carlos suggested.

"He made me promise I'd give him a chance."

"He's had his frigging chance. He's been sitting down there in the mud for twenty minutes!"

Realizing Carlos was right, I figured I had to do something.

"Here," I said. "Set up explosives on this ramp and string them around the gully."

"In case spiders show up?" Carlos asked. "I'm on it."

While Carlos and Kivi busied themselves with the explosives, I got up and moved forward in a crouch.

The nexus leaves rustled and slapped the water as I approached. It was weird to watch stuff that looked like it belonged in a giant pumpkin patch moving and shivering on its own.

"Claver, time's up," I hissed.

He didn't say anything. I reached forward and shook his shoulder.

He turned around, smiling up at me.

"So peaceful," he said. "The toxins are poetic at times. When you exchange fluids—you should try it someday, James."

I don't think he'd ever called me 'James' before. I didn't like the change. I didn't like the glassy look in his eyes, either.

"You're high," I accused him.

He nodded languidly. "All part of the package when you talk to the Wur. Call it an unintended perk."

"Your time's up, dammit!"

He laughed and almost fell backward into the mud. Then he got up, staggering a little.

"It's *your* time that's up," he said.

My eyes grew steely as I followed his outstretched hand. I wasn't sure what I'd see. Maybe spiders climbing down the walls or something like that.

But instead, I saw the last thing in the world I'd expected: Squid troopers. Dozens of them were coming down the ramp behind my team. They were fully armed and armored with mesh suits. They carried weapons that looked like snap-rifles, and they were moving with that odd, humping gait they always used when hustling.

My first instinct was to turn and kill the brain-plant, but Claver's hand came up with a single index finger unfolded.

"Ah-ah!" he said, smiling. "None of that, now. The squids are watching. Remember what they said: you can't damage the Wur. That's goes double for this nexus."

"Carlos, Kivi, on your six!" I shouted in my suit radio and threw myself down in the mud.

My team had been busy stringing explosives, as I'd told them to, but they spun around and engaged the squids like the professionals they were.

There were only four of us, but we had better gear. We'd been issued morph-rifles and armor. Our guns were configured for rapid-fire, and we hosed down the first squids and sent them thrashing to the ground.

The havoc these new weapons wreaked on squid troops was very satisfying. Snap-rifles were garbage compared to these guns. Up until now, I hadn't understood the difference as we'd been using them on walking trees.

Flesh is a lot softer than cellulose. Compared to the pod-walkers, which were capable of absorbing a thousand rounds or more before going down, the cephalopod troops fell like they'd been hit by a truck. When shot, pulpy explosions appeared all over the enemy, and less than a second afterward they sprawled limply.

"Short bursts, make them count!" I shouted. "They're on the walls!"

More squid troops were descending all over the walls of the gully. They wormed among the ferns up in the forest, then dropped down into the pit with us on long shining strands of monofilament. It was as if we were being attacked by a hundred giant silkworms all at once.

The multi-legged cephalopods loved the water. Once they were down in the cold muck, they rippled forward as fast as a man could run across an open field.

"Light them up, Carlos!"

He hit the detonator without hesitation. A sheet of fire gushed up followed by steam and calamari. Two dozen squids died. A hot wave went right over my body, and I had to hold my rifle over my head to keep it from getting soaked.

Claver stood back up, sputtering from the mud. "Impressive," he said. "But that was only the vanguard. They'll put you down with snipers now."

True to his word, my armor began to spark orange with snap-rifle hits. The squids had taken up positions around the upper rim of the gully over our heads. They were firing down at us, partly obscured by the ferns that festooned the cliff edge.

I could see we weren't going to get out of this alive. The explosives had been my big play. We'd killed scores of squids, but I suddenly realized there might be a thousand more in the forest above us.

Grabbing Claver like a rat and giving him a shake, I put my rifle against his neck. The hot muzzle burned a mark into his throat.

"I'm killing you right now," I told him.

"That's been factored in," he said calmly. "Checkmate, McGill."

I threw him down with a growl of frustration. Ignoring him, I marched several squelching steps toward the nexus plant.

"McGill!" Claver shouted at my back. "You'll kill your whole legion! The squids won't permit you to—"

What I did next might seem extreme to some. But those that know me well wouldn't have been surprised.

All my life my teachers, my counselors and even the principal of my elementary school herself had never liked me much. By the time I'd hit first grade, I'd been banned from the school bus—for life. When a teacher turned her head toward the vid screens up front, she'd often caught me trying to climb out a window when she looked back. I'd also enjoyed barking like a dog while crawling around on the carpet for laughs. It'd all been in good fun back then.

In short, while I've grown up plenty since my early days, I've never been a man who could completely control his impulses. Today, well...today I was truly pissed off.

It was Claver who'd pushed me over the edge. He'd been pushing my buttons all day. First, he'd gotten me out here on false pretenses. Along the way, he'd hinted I was as close to mental retardation as a man could be without crossing over that nebulous line. As a final insult, he'd flat-out tricked me and gotten himself high as a kite in the bargain.

I couldn't abide the idea of him sitting in the mud, laughing and uncaring about whether he lived or died because he probably had a clone of himself squirreled away somewhere—I just couldn't let that go.

So I marched to that big, spiny plant, reconfiguring my weapon into shotgun-mode as I approached it. I placed a boot

286

up against the thick, melon rind-like base of it. Then I shoved the wide-mouthed barrel of my morph-gun between the spines.

My plan was to apply maximum impact low on the central node—wasn't this plant full of liquid, after all?

Claver tackled me at the last moment. Squid snap-rifle rounds showered my back at the same time.

Shrugging all off, I pulled that trigger, and I held it down. In shotgun mode, the morphing gun could operate with fully automatic action if you squeezed the multi-stage trigger all the way.

I held that trigger down, and I drilled myself a hole.

Boom!
Boom!
Boom!
Boom!

-39-

Stuff gushed out of the hole I'd blasted into the nexus brain-plant. The liquid wasn't warm, like blood. It wasn't slippery, either. Instead, it was thick, gray-green and cold. The closest substance I could think of was pond water—from a pond with too many ducks living nearby.

I staggered as thousands of gallons gushed out over my armor, but I stood tall and grinned.

Claver was ape-wild all this time. He'd been trying to pry my hands off my gun with fanatical strength, but he'd failed. Even without my exoskeletal armor, I doubt he could have stopped me. I was twice his size and angry enough to snap him in two.

Grabbing him by the neck with a steel gauntlet and holding him away from me, I turned around to survey my situation. The tactical display on the interior of my helmet's visor told the tale.

There were four names superimposed on my vision by my armor's computer. Except for Claver, all of the names were blinking red. My squad mates were down and out.

The squid troopers were in the gully now, approaching me warily from every direction. Crouching down low in the muddy water, they looked more at home to me than they'd ever looked on land or in a spaceship. They moved with a fluid grace that was smoother than the motion of any human ever born. Not troubled by bones, their odd tentacles dragged them along with only their upper bulbous bodies exposed.

They all had snap-rifles aimed at me, but they weren't firing. It took me a second to figure out why not, then I had it: the brain-plant was right behind me with a hole exposing the meat inside. Any miss would hit their ally.

I grinned, and I held Claver up to them like a trophy. Gripping him by the collar, I gave him a shake. His attempts to wriggle free were unsuccessful.

"You can have this traitor!" I shouted at them. "You can have your brain-plant, too, but I doubt you can save it."

A score of them approached slowly in two ranks. They were tense, and their slanted eyes blinked and squinted wetly. Bubbles popped in their suckers as they rose and fell, dipping into the muck. None of them spoke, but that wasn't a surprise to me. They probably didn't have translation devices.

I pondered my next move. Kill Claver? Take as many squids down as I could? It had to be something like that. Whatever I did, I wanted to make sure I died in the process. I didn't want to get captured by these bastards.

Squids were slavers. They liked to capture, torment and breed other beings to their liking. Worse, I couldn't ever get revived if I was captured. Without a confirmed death, I was as good as permed, except I would spent the rest of my days living in bondage.

Claver couldn't talk because I had him by the collar and, if the truth were to be told, I had his neck wrapped so tightly he was turning purple. Still, he reached for my face with twisting, dripping fingers.

Holding him farther away, I shook my head. "This is my time now, Old Silver. I'll see you next go-around, if we catch a revive."

"Wait," said a soft voice. "Do not harm yourselves."

At first, I thought Claver had spoken or perhaps Kivi. But it wasn't either of them. Kivi was face down in the mud and dead, having fought to the end. Claver—well, he wasn't even making croaking sounds anymore.

It was Claver's bulging eyes, though, that clued me in. I followed them and saw a squid of a different sort.

Wearing a colorful suit of deep blue with a gold collar, this squid was a fraction bigger than the troops around it. Standing well back from the half-crescent of soldiers that surrounded me, the leader appeared to have a translation device.

"What do you want, you damned squid?" I asked it.

"There's no need for sacrifice. We are honored by your actions."

Frowning, I stared at those surrounding me. They slowly lowered their weapons.

Claver went into convulsions about then. Grunting, I eased up on his collar. A thread of drool slipped out of his mouth and dripped onto the dirty water. His eyes were slack, but the color slowly returned to his face, and raspy breathing began. I lowered him to my side but held on. He looked like a half-empty sack of potatoes.

"You're honored by my actions? What the hell does that mean? Are you happy I killed your brain-plant?"

There was a pause, maybe for translation or for thinking, I wasn't sure.

"Yes," came the response.

That surprised me. I gave my head a little shake. "Well, if you wanted the plant dead, why didn't you do it yourself?"

"We were sworn not to."

I squinted, trying to take that one in. "Okay. You wanted the plant dead...but you couldn't do it yourself. Why didn't you tell us that? We'd have taken care of it, rest assured."

"That would have been dishonorable. We are sworn to protect the Wur. To defend their core beings with our lives."

"Why would you do that if you don't even like them?"

The squid squirmed forward, moving closer. I tensed up in reaction. I'd been jerked around quite a bit lately, and if this was all an elaborate trick to get me to lower my guard and get myself captured—well, let's just say I wasn't in the mood for any more shenanigans.

"Be at ease," the squid said. "I'm Torrent, the Captain of the ship that orbits this world. These are my crewmen."

"That's great," I said. "I understand you're from the ship. What I don't understand is why you're happy the nexus plant is dead. I also want to know what you're going to do next."

"Next? I'm going to answer your questions. But first, creature, I must ask you to swear that this communication will stay strictly between us."

My head turned to one side, then the other. Was this squid serious? His talk of swearing, honor and the like—these concepts didn't match up with the way I thought of the cephalopods.

But then I recalled they were subjects of a Kingdom. They believed in old-fashioned concepts, I supposed. How could you swear fealty to a king and follow his edicts if you didn't have some sense of honor? Maybe it only extended to their own kind, but I could tell they *had* to have honor.

"Okay," I said. "I so swear. I will not tell anyone what you're about to tell me."

"And your suit-recorders?"

"Oh yeah," I said, shutting them off with one of Natasha's illegal apps. "Talk to me. We're off the grid."

"You have given me freedom from my servitude and by the code I am required to assist you, creature of dirt."

"I get that."

"Good," Torrent said. "It is appropriate that you understand the value of this gesture on my part. My ship was assigned to defend the infections in this region of space. I was summoned, and I served my duty."

"Okay..." I said, frowning. "But why does it make you happy that I killed the nexus?"

"I found my duty oppressive. This planet will now die in its entirety, and it's all due to your action. I'm therefore free of a service I never wished to perform."

"I think I'm starting to understand," I said. "A little more information, if you would: Our languages and customs aren't the same, and I'm still confused on a few points."

"You will have plenty of time to learn our ways," Torrent said. "You fought well, and I believe you'll make a delightful slave. In fact, I've decided to capture you personally. I shall breed you to create a new and superior strain of warrior. You will make me wealthy, creature, and you should feel prideful in that knowledge."

"Uh...that's great, Torrent. But how about a few more answers before you break out the leg-irons?"

The squid's tentacles writhed as it considered. "I hope you're not a stubborn beast. Do you like to mate?"

"Oh yeah, I love doing that."

"Excellent. Ask your question."

"You squids—you cephalopods—you're slavers, right? Your culture is all about slaves and masters. Why would you serve as the slave of a plant? I'd think that sort of thing would be beneath one of your race."

Honestly, I expected my question would enrage the squid. That was part of my goal. But instead, it only squirmed and studied me.

"Your question reveals a shameful truth. I will only answer because I'm honor-bound to do so."

"Yeah, well?"

"The plants—they infect many worlds in our kingdom. They have gained possession of many of our queens on their thrones of cold stone. We can't reproduce without our queens—therefore, they're in a position to make demands."

"You mean, they've enslaved *you*," I said.

Captain Torrent's eyes narrowed in a brief moment of hate. "Your insults have earned you pain. Your training will not be easy, I can see that now. I will enjoy watching my beast-handlers break you."

"Slaves and masters," I said thoughtfully. "That's what your culture is all about. See this man here?"

I held Claver aloft. He dripped and slumped. "He's my property," I said. "I own his ass." A broad smile lit up my face then, but I doubted the squids knew what that meant.

"You are mistaken," Torrent said. "You're both *my* property. Now, surrender yourself. You've cost me too many crewmembers already."

I shook my head and chuckled. Using both hands, I broke Claver's neck and dropped him into the slime.

The squids surged forward, but I lifted my hands high. In my right was a plasma grenade. It was already active, and the blue-white glow rapidly grew in intensity.

"Good bye, squids!" I shouted.

My last moments were happy ones. I got to watch about twenty squids go humping and splashing away from me like a herd of jackrabbits crossing a brook.

Then the blue-white flash enveloped my reality, and I stopped existing for a time.

-40-

"We've got anterior fibrillation! Clear!"

Vaguely, I felt several hands let go of my limbs. There was a hum and a snap, followed by an instantaneous bolt of pain.

The hands came back to grab hold of me. I struggled, but I was as weak as a cat.

"One more?"

"Hold on. I think...he's back. He's stable."

The hands relaxed, and one of them patted me on my bare chest.

"Get suited up, McGill," Anne said. "You're wanted upstairs."

"Are we back on Earth?" I asked in a croaking voice.

Anne chuckled. I still hadn't opened my eyes more than a crack. What little I could see was washed out and full of glare. Despite this I caught her smile, and I smiled back.

"I wish," she said. "We're still on lovely old Death World."

"How did I catch a revive?"

"It was tight. Fortunately, Turov sent out long-range drones to your location when your squad didn't respond to calls on their tappers. They provided us with a vid-feed of that firefight with the squids. It was quite dramatic, right to the finish."

"Glad you liked it. What about my heart? Are you going to recycle me now?"

She helped me up, still amused. Her delicate touch made me remember some good times we'd had a year or so back.

"No such luck," she said. "You're a good grow, you just came out with an erratic pulse. We've fixed that. Get dressed."

"You're kicking me out already?" I asked. "How about another date?"

She looked slightly pained. "I thought things were over between us."

"That fellow who broke your heart was another James McGill," I said. "He was a right-bastard from what I hear. I'm an entirely different breed."

Shaking her head, she guided me to the lockers and fitted me with a uniform. "Get up to the officers' deck. They want a full report. They saw what happened, but they don't understand all of it."

"What about Claver?"

She shook her head. "He's on ice, for now. No revive until authorized."

"That's probably for the best."

Once I had my clothes on, I made one more pass at her. "How about that date? We could do a picnic on Green Deck for old-time's sake."

"You don't give up easily."

"Never have."

She looked down at the deck for a few moments. "I'll think about it," she said at last.

"I'll take that to the bank!" I said, marching off in a good mood.

The events that had transpired out in the woods hadn't gone as expected, and I wasn't sure how my superiors were going to react to my story. But at least I had my priorities straight. I had a date to look forward to.

There were only two people waiting for me upstairs. Imperator Galina Turov met me with her head cocked to one side, like she didn't quite know what to make of me.

Winslade, on the other hand, appeared to have made his decision. He studied me with a mixture of disgust and anger—to him, I was some kind of walking dog-turd.

"At ease, Veteran," Turov said.

Taking her suggestion to an extreme level, I took a seat in a comfy chair and stretched out in it.

"I'm a bit foggy," I said. "Sometimes a revive leaves a man with cobwebs in his head."

"Maybe you need to be recycled a few more times to clear that up," Winslade suggested.

"Shut up, Primus," Turov told him without taking her eyes off me.

While Winslade pouted, she walked over and stood near me. That provided me with an excellent view. She really was a sight for sore eyes.

"You did *something* out there..." she said. "Something you weren't supposed to do. Maybe several things."

Shrugging, I gave her a half-smile.

"Look," I said, "I think everyone got what they wanted. The plants are dying, aren't they?"

"Yes. Slowly—but they're dying. They don't seem to be able to think coherently. The xenobiologists think they normally communicate through scent signals, like ants, and they aren't getting signals they can comprehend. No new pods are being grown. The mobile creatures that remain wander like feral beasts. They no longer feed, and they'll become gaunt in a week or two."

I spread out my hands. "See? Everyone's happy."

"I'm not happy," Winslade snapped. "I want to know what you said to the cephalopods. You talked to them quite a while before you killed yourself. Our drones zoomed in and caught the action—but not the words."

"They did most of the talking," I explained. "The captain said he wanted to capture me, to breed me. He said he could sell a line of new warriors with my DNA."

"You'd like that," Turov commented.

"The idea had its appeal," I admitted. "But, as a man of duty and honor, I took the hard way out and tried to blast them all to Hell and back instead."

Winslade snorted and clasped his hands together. His eyes were half-shut with suspicion whenever he looked at me.

"James," Turov said, "it's vitally important you make a full and complete report to me concerning your interaction with the enemy. Something small, even a minor detail, might be valuable to Earth intel."

For the first time since I'd walked into her office, her words troubled me. I'd planned to wake up and go back to my old routine, all the while staying quiet about what Captain Torrent had said. But Turov had a point. The squids were our enemies, and they'd given me information, whether I'd promised Torrent to hold onto it or not.

"Hmm," I said. "What do you think of a promise made as a matter of honor, sir?" I asked her seriously.

Turov frowned. "You promised to stay quiet? You promised this to a cephalopod officer?"

"I was in difficult circumstances," I pointed out.

"Ah, then such a promise is not ethically binding. Is that not right, Primus Winslade?"

He looked us both over, shaking his head. "I can't believe you're even taking this seriously, Imperator. Order this disrespectful noncom to brief us on what happened. Anything less would be conduct unbecoming."

"Answer my question, Primus," Turov said sternly.

"About the ethics of the situation? Of course it works that way. You can't torture a man into a confession and have it be legally binding—at least not in a civilized society. You can't extract contracts or promises from a man under any kind of duress. That isn't honor, it's force."

I thought such words were ironic coming from Primus Winslade, the torture-master. But even so, his points made sense to me. I was still a bit troubled, but I decided to tell them what had transpired.

They listened closely as I described my interactions with Captain Torrent. They were particularly interested in the details of how and why the cephalopods came to be committed to defending the Wur.

"Very odd," Turov said. "They don't like the Wur. In fact, they're in a state of war with them. But still, they continue to protect them."

"I don't think that's quite what's happening," I said. "I think Claver lied about the war between the squids and the plants. That war is over—and the plants won."

I explained further about Torrent's description of the squid queens, captured on their thrones.

"Back on Machine World," I said, "do you recall that giant squid we found in a cold tank down in the lowest tunnels?"

"Of course," Turov said. "Your idiot friend, Ortiz, blew it apart."

"I believe that was later determined to be a matter of self-defense."

Turov rolled her eyes. "Yes. That lie was in the report, as I recall. Well, what about the giant squid?"

"It was female," I said. "All the others we've met up with, every soldier, officer, you name it, have been male."

Turov squinted at me. "Are you saying it was a queen?"

"Makes sense to me."

She moved to her desk and leaned her butt up against it. I caught Winslade eyeing her from behind. I couldn't blame him.

"That means the queens—their females—are rare," she said thoughtfully. "Anything necessary and rare is important. Could the plants have won the war by capturing critical members of the cephalopod species?"

I shrugged. "Could be. It's certainly worth reporting to Central. If I don't miss my guess, the xeno-freaks back home on Earth will get the shakes over it when they hear these details."

"Right," she said. "Good thinking, James. I'll make sure to deliver that information personally."

That was Turov in a nutshell. She was going to deliver her findings—my findings—all prettied-up with a bow on top. She'd take the credit and reach for more rank. It was her standard operating procedure.

But I didn't care. I wasn't much of a rank-climber myself. What I was happy about was the probability this tidbit would get her off my back.

The central display began beeping as did Turov's tapper. She frowned, but answered the call.

"What is it?" she snapped. "I gave orders that I wasn't—"

"Imperator, the cephalopod Captain is attempting to open a channel to your office—"

Turov's butt flew off her desk. She worked the screen, and a moment later the ugly, gold-collared Captain Torrent flickered into being in all his glory.

She gave me a stern glance. "Stay off-camera—and stay quiet."

I nodded. Even I knew Torrent might not be thrilled to see me in the background during any negotiation.

Captain Torrent's eyes swept the scene, but I positioned myself where the cameras wouldn't pick me up. I could see his wet, pinkish-brown skin was pock-marked with wounds. He'd been injured. One of his eyes was drooping and weeping a bit, too. Probably, my plasma grenade had picked up grit, turning it into needle-like shrapnel and blasted him with it. As far as I was concerned, it couldn't have happened to a nicer alien.

"Imperator Turov," he said. "An accident has occurred. The nexus Wur on this planet has ceased to function."

"A pity."

"Your odd word translates to 'a small matter.' We do not agree with your assessment. This matter is a significant one. A dishonorable failure for our species."

Turov nodded. I could see the wheels turning inside her head. She was trying to come up with a way to gain an advantage in the situation, but she was also being cautious.

"What action will you take next?" she asked.

"You have no right to demand such information."

"I didn't mean to—"

"However," continued Torrent, "in the spirit of investment, I'm willing to share information with inferiors such as you, beings that might yet prove useful to the Kingdom. We're leaving this system. Please inform your crew and all the other slave-candidates awaiting our leadership on your homeworld. The Wur garden that once enveloped this planet will wither and die without nexus guidance. Therefore, there is nothing left here to protect. Our mission has ended."

"A most unfortunate accident," Turov said. "We offer our condolences for your loss."

Torrent looked at her quizzically. "Your words have no meaning. We've suffered a loss, but there is no translation for the concept you connected to that fact. No matter, we will be your masters in the end. This discussion is at an end."

Torrent disconnected abruptly.

"What a dick," I said.

Turov looked at me and Winslade thoughtfully. "Did you notice? They have no words for pity or condolences. You're right, James. They're truly unpleasant creatures."

"Did you see his eye?" I asked proudly. "He took a hit there. I'd bet my bottom credit it was shrapnel from my grenade that did that."

She looked at me closely. "You *did* kill the nexus as I requested. What's more, after talking to the cephalopods, you sent them packing into space. I'm quite impressed, McGill."

Winslade squirmed uncomfortably. "That's like thanking a cat for pissing on the curtains," he said. "McGill only did what came naturally to him. Deceit, violence—such things are all in a day's work for—"

"Conceal your jealousy, Primus," Turov uttered the words without looking at him. "You're embarrassing yourself."

Winslade got to his feet, looking annoyed. "Permission to get back to my duties, sir?"

"Granted. Pack up your cohort. The squid ship is gone. The plants are dying. Correspondingly, we're going to board and retake *Minotaur* in the morning."

Winslade looked startled. "Is that wise, sir?"

"I said it, didn't I?"

He fidgeted, but then he nodded at last. "We attack in the morning. May I make one suggestion?"

"If you must."

"We should leave the revival machine here, along with a protective unit. Just in case the assault force is lost. They could rebuild the legion if things went badly. That way, Varus wouldn't be wiped out."

Imperator Turov looked at him suspiciously. "And who would you recommend be left in command of this unit on the ground?"

"Well sir, I wouldn't want to delegate such a critical mission to amateurs. I'd be willing to take on the assignment myself."

"Of course you would. Dismissed."

Winslade left, and I was glad to see him go.

Smiling an odd smile, Galina came to me and sat in my lap. When my hands came up to reach for her, she slapped me a hard one across the face.

I looked at her questioningly.

"You're becoming insolent," she said. "I wanted to shoot you when you sprawled yourself out in this chair like a child. Winslade knows we're having an affair. It's affecting his performance."

I scoffed. "I think you'll find *my* performance hasn't diminished in the least."

My arms came up again, and this time she allowed them to encircle her. She squirmed a little, but she let me touch her. Things progressed quickly as they always did with Galina. After making doubly sure the desktop display was turned off and not recording anything, she leaned on it and let me have my way with her, right then and there.

After we were finished, she walked primly around to the other side of the desk. Her clothes reknitted over her as I watched. I was sorry to see her soft skin vanish under cloth.

"That was the last time, James," she said.

My jaw sagged. "Really?"

"Yes. People are beginning to talk. I find that annoying. Please don't be distraught."

I felt an urge to laugh at the idea that I would cry about losing her, but I knew enough to hold that back. Sure, I liked our get-togethers, what man wouldn't? But I'd never been one to fool myself into thinking she seriously cared about me. The best I could hope for was an even break now and then.

"I'm surprised, not hurt," I said. "Women don't dump me all that often. Not without good reason, anyway."

"Yes," she said. "Usually you forget about them and wander off. Just as often they catch you cheating and become angry. Don't you think it's better for both of us to end it this way instead? As adults?"

Thinking, I stuck out my chin and nodded. "Good enough. I guess I'll be going, but there's one more thing, Galina."

"What is it?"

"Did you mean what you said? About being impressed by my actions in the field?"

She met my eyes evenly. "Absolutely. Compared to you, Winslade is a worm under a rock."

I knew she was right, of course. But hearing it from someone in command was good for the spirit.

Galina Turov was as ruthless as they came, and she didn't pull any punches. That said, I felt I could count on her to say what she thought was the truth most of the time.

Happy with her honest praise, I smiled all the way out of the lifter and back to my squad.

-41-

The next morning we launched an all-out assault. *Minotaur* had been squatting in space over Death World for about a week now. In all that time, it hadn't shifted orbit or responded to transmissions other than in the most rudimentary, automated fashion.

Fortunately, the dreadnaught was far enough out in space to stay stable. The orbit hadn't decayed, so it wasn't in danger of falling and crashing yet. The techs had already calculated we had around two years before that happened. But we weren't interested in waiting around any longer than we had to.

We loaded up four hundred troops, carrying the best of the gear we had left. We left Winslade and about two hundred troops behind, camped on the endless green expanse of grass that had begun to grow over the scorched land. Turov had assigned him a single combat unit, which was made up of poorly equipped recruits. They had a few bunkers and drones and of course, the revival unit.

Winslade was all smiles and waving as we took off and left him. You'd have thought we were loved ones going on a cruise.

Anne, Natasha and most of the other non-combatants were left planet-side with Winslade. There would be time enough to ferry them to *Minotaur* later—assuming that we were able to recapture her.

All attention turned toward our goal once the cloud cover enveloped the world below us. I was up in the command center with Turov, Tribune Drusus and Captain Graves. That was quite an honor for me. I didn't know why they'd taken me up there, unless it was because there was plenty of room. The briefing chambers were meant to hold all the officers in a full cohort.

Turov, as usual, spoke first. "I want to tell you all that I have the utmost confidence in the highly-experienced troops Legion Varus has left," she said, looking from one centurion to the next. "I'm only sorry that we could not bring more troops. It would take months to revive the whole legion, and this lifter is only capable of transporting a single cohort."

A centurion named Martinez spoke up. She was a stocky woman with her hair pulled back so tightly her eyebrows were half-way up her forehead.

"We could have waited one more week, at least," she said. "Then we'd have a thousand troops rather than four hundred."

Turov looked at her flatly. "Yes. But we don't have guns for that many men. In that same period of time, we don't know how much stronger the enemy aboard the ship might grow. They might even gain control of the ship and maroon us here."

Tribune Drusus cleared his throat. Turov glanced at him and nodded.

"Now," she said, "I'm going to turn planning over to our master tactician, Tribune Drusus."

She stepped away from the central console and Drusus stepped forward. The officers relaxed visibly. Drusus was far more experienced in this area. I considered it a wise move on her part to relinquish control.

"Thank you, Imperator," Drusus said. "I've been studying this problem since we first learned *Minotaur* had been overrun. Here's the ship in detail."

He brought up a three-dimensional display of the vessel and spun it around with his fingertips so that we were looking at the stern region.

"As best we can tell, the enemy pierced the thick hull surrounding the engine core. This took time, but when they finally made it through, they were able to do enough damage to poison the atmosphere of the ship."

As we watched, a simulation of poisonous gas flooded the ship. The decks were each displayed in their appropriate color: gold for the command level, green for the central exercise zone and blue for the bio level. These decks were sealed at first, but with the help of the invading aliens, the gas spread from zone to zone until the entire ship was affected.

"This scenario is supposition, of course," Drusus said. "But we know from models that it could have happened this way, especially given the alien capacity to excrete acids that burn through metal quickly. Taken by surprise, most of our troops would have succumbed to the radiation and poisoned air. The rest were probably killed by the invaders themselves."

We watched in grim silence as deck by deck, the ship was invaded and all resistance extinguished. I felt a fresh surge of hatred for the Wur, and I had to wonder how many desperate troops had fought to the death on *Minotaur*. Cut off and dying, I was sure our troops had done their damnedest—but it hadn't been enough.

"That's all history," Drusus said, watching our grim faces. "Here's the plan to retake the ship. We'll start here, at Green Deck. The upper dome is shielded with a heavy blast-dome, but we can disable that from the outer hull and get the clamshell dome to open. After that, all we have to do is puncture the inner transparent bubble and enter the ship."

There were surprised looks all around. Martinez spoke up again.

"But won't that release the atmosphere, sir? Explosive decompression will result. If there are any survivors..."

"If there are, we doubt we'll find them on Green Deck. Think about it. These are plants. Where do you think the Wur are most likely to have taken up residence? Moreover, the atmosphere inside the ship has been compromised already. We'll have to release it all anyway to begin the clean-up process."

Martinez nodded. She retreated a step and said nothing more. I understood how she felt. The situation was terrible. All this time, down here on the planet's surface, we'd been too busy to think about how the rest of our legion had fared. But now, we were going to be confronted with the gruesome realities.

There had to be thousands of dead. They'd been left rotting for a week inside our ship. Even if we could retake *Minotaur*, we were going to have a hell of a time making the ship livable again.

There wasn't much argument after that. People got their assignments, and they left one by one to brief their teams. Each unit got a specific mission, either to capture a critical zone of the ship or to search and destroy enemy combatants.

"McGill?" Drusus said at last.

"Here sir," I said. I'd been hanging back in a shadowy region near a curving bulkhead. There were only a few people left in the chamber, so I walked up to the central console.

"There you are. It's not like you to hide."

"No sir. What can I do for you?"

Drusus eyed me strangely. "I've got a special mission for you. I want you to get to Gold Deck and secure this area."

He leaned over the table and zoomed in on the map of the ship. A region blinked red. It was part of Gold Deck, way out along the starboard side.

"Storage locker six, sir?" I said, reading the label that popped up between us.

"That's it. There should be something useful there or right near that location. A combat vehicle."

It was about then that I noticed Turov. She was staring at me from her seat in a chair behind Drusus. She looked like a cat eyeing a bird on the wrong side of a plate glass window. That look on this particular woman's face made me nervous.

"Uh...a combat vehicle, sir? You mean a dragon?"

"That's right."

"I thought we left all the dragons—"

"McGill, are you refusing this mission?" he asked.

"No sir. Not at all. I can see how a dragon might be useful. I accept the mission, sir."

"I'll inform Graves."

306

That was it. I walked out, headed to my squad in the hold, and sat down with them. Sargon was the first one to notice that I had an odd look on my face.

"What's up, boss?" he asked, frowning.

"Nothing," I said. "But we've got a special op coming."

I explained it to him and the rest of the squad. They were left scratching their heads with me.

"Let me get this straight," Carlos said. "Your girlfriend sent you to Gold Deck to get her shoes, is that it?"

"Shut up, Specialist," I said.

Kivi perked up at the mention of the word "girlfriend." She looked from me to Carlos and back again.

"Girlfriend? On Gold Deck? McGill, don't tell me you've been fooling around with Turov again. I thought you'd buried that evil relationship back on Tech World."

"Think again!" Carlos said unhelpfully. "Actually, I can't believe you didn't already know, Kivi. You need to get online more. There are chat-line reports and even a few blurry snaps taken by suit-cameras."

"What?" I demanded. "Of all the dirty, underhanded—"

"Luckily they aren't underhanded," Carlos said, showing me his tapper. "At least you have your clothes on. Turov's hair looks a little funny in this shot, though, as you two are coming out of her office together. That's a dead giveaway, McGill. Unprofessional."

A blurry shot of me kissing the Imperator was displayed on Carlos' arm. I had no idea who'd taken it. Hell, it might have been a buzzer on the wall for all I knew.

"That's the trouble with pinhead cameras flying around everywhere," I complained.

Kivi's face pushed between us, and she got a good look.

"Dammit," she said. "You're a fool, that's all I have to say. You're not going to get anything out of that relationship other than friction with everyone in the legion."

"Ha-ha!" burst out Carlos. "Friction! McGill's all over that."

"There's no relationship, Kivi," I said, but that sounded weak, even to me. Still, I had to try. "We're not seeing each other anymore. It was just a weak moment caught on camera."

"Oh, so you admit that you *were* seeing her?" Kivi asked, shaking her head.

"Hey," Carlos said, nudging me, "check this out."

Knowing I shouldn't, I saw him swipe to a brief vid. This one showed me coming out of the Imperator's quarters, not her office. This time neither of us was entirely dressed, and she had a beverage in her hand.

"Shit," I said.

"Look at it this way, McGill," he said, "at least she's smiling."

I grabbed his arm and tapped the delete button while he chuckled. A few moments later, he showed me he had it back again.

"What the hell...?" I demanded.

"It's on a server somewhere. In a cache, floating on a cloud—whatever. Give it up, McGill. You're famous. The good stuff never dies on the net."

Knowing he was right, I sat glumly for the rest of the flight. I decided to ignore them. After all, I'd done it, and they couldn't be expected to let it go. Sometimes there were things that superseded the chain of command. I couldn't squelch their fun without turning into a raging dick, and they didn't deserve that.

So, I suffered the ribbing until it died down then turned to business, giving out tactical assignments.

"I don't have to remind you all that this is do or die," I told them when I had their full attention again. "We're sitting in the last lifter. Our legion is over ninety-percent dead. The enemy strength is unknown, but it was enough to kill everyone aboard when they invaded."

They began to sober up as they listened to my words. The odds were bleak.

Legionnaires, particularly those who had the misfortune to sign up with Legion Varus, aren't strangers to death. But that didn't mean we *liked* dying.

-42-

The opening stages of the boarding action went smoothly enough. *Minotaur* hung in space, a derelict. Emergency flashers along the hull blinked slowly, showing the ship was in distress.

Even more ominous was the constant pinging tone that hit our headsets every ten seconds. It was on every channel—a powerful signal that rhythmically informed us the ship was in dire trouble. No one aboard had bothered to turn it off, and as we weren't aboard yet, we couldn't either. It was the best evidence yet that the entire crew was dead. Who would have let that signal continue beeping for a solid week without acknowledging and canceling it?

As we got closer to the ship, the tone pinged louder. It set my teeth on edge, and I had my crew lower the volume of their headsets' general channel and increase the volume on the squad channel. We could still hear the distress call, but it no longer interfered in our conversations.

Our lifter spun around and began braking, setting up to land on the massive dreadnaught's hull. The lifter was the most vulnerable at this stage of the game. If the enemy had gained control of the anti-ship weaponry—well, we were all as good as dead.

Gritting our teeth and listening to that incessant pinging, we waited until the transport came to rest on *Minotaur's* hull. We felt the transport shiver as clamps were applied.

"We're down, and we're good!" Graves announced to the unit.

His words were met with a ragged cheer. All around me, troops clutched their morph-rifles and double-checked their suit integrity.

"All right," Graves said. "We're pumping all the air out of the lifter now, storing it in tanks for later. Prepare for hard vacuum."

I could already hear the steady hiss of escaping air. It grew in intensity, and it seemed to me that I could feel cold spots inside my armor. I don't think a spacesuit has ever been made that didn't have hot and cold spots in it under extreme conditions. Some of our suits were pretty banged up, and they didn't always work perfectly. My armor, for example, liked to pool up water in the lower left corner of my visor while in zero G. It was really sweat and steam from my exhalations and not overly dangerous, but it did demonstrate that the dehumidifiers weren't operating at a hundred percent.

"They tell me from the bridge that the outer clamshell controls have been accessed from an external port," Graves said, relaying what he was hearing from the brass channel. "We're working with the AI to convince it to open up. That could be difficult if the transparent dome over Green Deck is compromised. The AI is programed to prevent decompression."

"No shit," Carlos said to me. "Next, he'll tell us the whole plan to break in through the glass is tits-up. Then we'll have to go in using those acid-holes the plants bored through the hull. You see if I'm—"

"Shut up, Ortiz," I said.

For once, he did as I asked. No one wanted to hear about all the crap that could go wrong. We weren't on our first mission in space. We knew it was the most deadly environment any man could have the misfortune to fight in.

A rumble went through the ship. Everyone put their right hand on their buckles and gripped their rifles with the left. Carlos looked at me, and I could see he was scared.

"Remember the first time they pumped the air out of a lifter on us?" I asked him, smiling.

"Oh yeah—how could I forget our first shared death experience? Graves is still a cold-hearted bastard. How can he maintain such a grim life after all these years? I mean, wouldn't you get tired of it?"

I waited for a second, but he didn't answer his own question.

"I expect it gets into a man's blood," I told him. "After a few decades, it's all he knows."

Carlos looked down at the deck. Debris floated around us. Discarded ammo. Dangling straps and wires. What looked like perfectly secured environment on the ground was rarely clean in space, once everything started to drift in the air.

"You think we'll end up like Graves?" he asked. "Not caring if we live or die?"

Frowning, I strained my brain for a few seconds—but as luck would have it, I didn't need to come up with an answer.

Yellow flashers began rotating. The ramp was going down.

"Legionnaires," Graves said in our headsets. "We're going to move out in an organized fashion. Double-check your magnetics. If I see a man floating off with one of my last full sets of equipment into deep space, I'll shoot him in the ass."

The ramp lowered into the silence of space. The atmosphere was gone, so while we could feel the motors with our butts, we couldn't hear them with our ears.

The harsh starlight of L374 shone in like a beacon as the ramp lowered. When the ramp was fully deployed, we slapped the central button on our safety belts, and they fell away.

We got up en masse, but at first, we could hardly move. There were lots of troops ahead of my squad this time. As close as I could figure it, we were going to get off the lifter in the very last wave.

Up ahead, troops exited in a steady stream, scrambling into the glare of the local star. The reflections from their helmets were dazzling.

"Is that clamshell open?" Sargon asked. "I never heard Graves say—does anyone know?"

"It's clear," Kivi said. "The embedded techs are talking. Lots of techs have buzzers out now. Should I deploy one, Veteran?"

311

I glanced at her. I knew she had twenty of them, but sending one out early was technically a waste. In open space, they couldn't use their wings. The tiny drones had to expend puffs of fuel to fly, and they had a very limited supply of that.

Opening my mouth to deny her request, I had a second thought. For purposes of morale, it would be good to see what we were going up against.

"Fly one," I said. "Just one, mind you, and pipe the feed to everyone in the squad."

She hurried to obey. A few seconds later my tapper displayed an over-the-shoulder view of the lines of troops. The image slewed and moved rapidly.

With sickening speed, it zoomed past the helmets of a hundred troops and out into the open. I watched my tapper in fascination.

Open space. There wasn't anything around other than *Minotaur* and the colorful disk of Death World itself below us.

I could see the clamshell, drawn back and displaying the inner layer of hardened polymer that kept the cold void outside the ship. Along the rim of the dome, a growing throng of soldiers spread out. They were walking oddly, using their magnetic boots to keep them anchored to the metal hull.

As we watched, a weaponeer in the lead squad fired his gun at the polymer sheet the troops were encircling. The effect was immediate and alarming. The ruptured surface exploded outward like a massive sheet of glass in slow motion. I could see air and water vapor escaping into space like a geyser. The mix frosted into a trillion ice crystals and began to coat the onlookers who stood too close to the edge.

Up until that moment, everything had gone exactly according to plan. We'd flown up from Death World to *Minotaur*, docked, opened the clamshell and punctured the dome. Honestly, I'd begun to hope that despite everything we'd recapture the ship without a loss. *Minotaur* looked to be devoid of any life at all. What if the radiation had killed the Wur as surely as it had killed the legion and the crew? That would be a best-case scenario, and up until now, it had seemed possible.

But then, as the air vented and the troops fell back from the fury of the blasting gasses, I felt a rumble beneath my feet.

Through Kivi's drone, I could now see what it was. The two halves of the clamshell dome—the blast shields that normally covered Green Deck—were beginning to close again.

For about a second, no one reacted. The two metal half-domes rolled up. The motion appeared to be slow from the point of view of the drone, but to people out there on the hull, it was moving pretty fast.

Two figures were lifted up and tossed into space. They tumbled, ejected by the force of the moving dome. A few other figures were even less lucky. They were entangled in debris, and as the metal crescents rose, they were crushed to a pulp.

"Emergency!" shouted Graves. "Everyone out of the lifter! Board *Minotaur* now—anyway you can. That's an order!"

We surged forward. The organized, shuffling mass of troops turned into a wild flood. I glanced one last time at my tapper to glimpse the view Kivi was relaying from her drone. Troops were throwing themselves into the geyser of escaping gas, fighting against the pressure to get inside. The geyser was visibly weaker now, but with nothing for the invading troops to push against, they were having a hard time overcoming that gushing current.

Meanwhile, the clamshells were still moving, shutting themselves at a steady rate. I could tell from the look of the choked up group ahead of us that we weren't even going to make it to the exit before *Minotaur* closed up again.

"Squad!" I shouted. "Everyone release your magnetics and jump up! Climb on the ceiling, hand-over-hand!"

They hesitated until they saw me do as I'd ordered. Then they followed my lead.

Moving as fast as I could, I dragged myself over the ceiling, which was webbed with storage nets and the like. Employing this tactic, we at least made it to the ramp. Behind me, I could see others adopting my approach. The ceiling of the lifter was thronged with troops who were moving like spiders.

"What do we do when we get out into the open?" Carlos demanded from behind me. "Just throw ourselves out into space?"

"Yes. Launch yourselves like you can fly. When you're over the dome, open the external venting valve on your secondary air tank. Make sure the nozzle is aimed toward open space opposite your angle of flight. Use it like propellant. Remember that trick from vac training?"

"Hell no," Carlos answered.

"Well, it will work. Open up your spare tank, and let it push you downward. That's an order."

They grumbled, and I could hear a lot of rapid, almost panicky breathing over their microphones. No one liked the idea of expending their limited air supply as a propellant, but they didn't openly refuse.

I launched first as I was the man in front. I think, in retrospect, I kicked off *too* hard. It was like pushing off from the wall of a pool and gliding forward. Only in space, there was no water to slow me down.

Soaring like a bird, I flew over the heads of a hundred struggling troops. I could see ahead that the dome was more than half shut. The jaws of the blast shield were coming together, and soon whoever was caught in them would be crushed.

Up high, the two halves of the dome were farther apart. I glided into this space, and the light of L-374 was shut out immediately. Stark shadow enclosed me, and I could feel the cold of it right through my suit.

A steady hiss began as I employed my spare tank. I fired it behind me and a little upward. The force began to push me down.

Still, I could see I wasn't going to make it. I was moving too fast. Before I could slow down, I was going to fly right out the other side of the closing dome.

"Squad, deploy that tank early!" I shouted. "I might not make it! My tank isn't providing enough counterthrust!"

"I'm in," said Kivi. "I can see you, McGill. You're too high."

Cursing, I struggled and looked around for a solution. It's hard to think while spinning. Worse, my helmet blocked much of my vision. I couldn't look over my shoulder, and I could barely see down into the dome.

Finally, I came up with a plan at the last second. I opened my main tank.

That did the trick. I shot down into the clamshells, and they closed silently over me, shutting out the light of the star and most of our troops. I quickly closed both tanks and checked the oxygen levels.

I thudded gently into the closed dome and pushed off it to sail down toward the others. They were peering down through the breach into the dark unknown that was Green Deck.

Joining them, I took stock of my situation. We were officially aboard *Minotaur*, but that's where the good news ended.

Half my squad had been left outside, along with two thirds of all our invading troops. Even better, I was down to three hours of air, tops.

-43-

Vac-suits provide good protection against radiation. They have to, because open space is full of exotic particles and dangerous flares of invisible light.

Accordingly, one of the first things I checked when I stopped spinning around was my suit's radiation counter. *Minotaur* was ticking hot, but the dose was far from lethal.

"Looks like the evacuation of the atmosphere worked," Graves said. "Radiation levels are down. Let's have a headcount. Who made it in here?"

We sounded off by squads, and I gathered my people while maneuvering toward the broken spot in the dome. As the pressure had just equalized, it was no longer firing a geyser up into our faces. Looking down, I didn't see a forested area like I'd hoped to. First off, it was dark down there. Secondly, the trees I could make out looked dead and stripped down to the bare wood. Had the plant life eaten them?

"Hmm," Graves said. "We're out of touch with seventy percent of the unit. After checking with members of the other units, however, I've found they did even worse. As I'm the senior officer present, I'm taking over tactical command until this action is over or until someone higher-ranked manages to get inside the hull."

No one objected to the idea of Graves taking command. In fact, we were happy. Graves was a good man to have behind you in an unknown and possibly grim situation. If Turov had made it into the dome instead, I'd have been worried. Her record wasn't the best in tough tactical actions.

Graves marshaled us quickly. He sent a few scouts down to the floor of Green Deck, then folded squads and platoons together. It soon became apparent there was only about a combined unit's worth of legionnaires inside *Minotaur*. Only a hundred or so of us had made it through the closing blast shield alive.

Harris was one of those who hadn't made it. Della was one of the few members of his team who had made it in, and she was folded into my squad.

Of my original group, I had Carlos, Kivi, Lau and Gorman. The rest had been too slow getting inside the closing dome—or they'd died trying.

When we were organized, Graves contacted me directly.

"McGill? How'd you manage to get your people in here?" he demanded. "I put you at the back of the bus so you wouldn't cause trouble."

"I've never liked the bus, Centurion," I said. Then I quickly told him how we'd done it.

He was amused. "Never heard of a man so eager to get himself killed," he chuckled. "I like that. Take point, madman."

For a moment, I debated telling him about my oxygen supply situation, but I passed on that. I had a few hours left, after all, and reporting my technical difficulties before they stopped me from following my orders seemed weak. Instead, I dove for the ragged opening, and my hodge-podge squad dove after me.

We sailed down into stygian darkness. Dead leaves, corpses and even globules of ice floated around us.

"Look at our stripped trees," Carlos said. "The alien plants must have eaten them. Disgusting freaks. They're like an army of giant slugs."

"The balls of ice are beautiful in a way," Della said. "They must be from the lake in the center of the artificial forest. It's so strange to see it frozen into balls and left floating in the dark."

"The ship's plumbing system automatically sucks most of the water down into holding tanks before battle," I told her.

"But this time, they clearly didn't get it all. Della, can you dive into that empty pond and see if there's anything alive down there?"

She was the fastest troop I had, even in zero G. There was something about growing up on a barbaric alien planet that made a person tougher than usual. I couldn't help but admire her form as she grabbed a tree branch and swung around it like gibbon.

Before she could push off however, the branch she was on snapped. It was brittle with cold, but she managed to get her legs around the trunk. The rest of us watched as she shimmied all the way to the ground and then darted over a cliff wall, vanishing.

We waited for about ten seconds. Then another twenty. I'd just begun to frown and open my mouth to ask if she was okay, when she radioed back to me.

"There's nothing from Earth down here," she said. "Even the water plants are dead."

When she first said that, I naturally assumed that she was talking about algae and the like, but when I launched down and joined her, I was in for a surprise.

The whole lake bed, some hundred meters across, was full of alien pods. Every inch of the sandy bottom was replanted with hulking, bulbous growths. Fortunately, they all seemed to be as dead as the Earthly plants were.

Around the lake bed there were still trees from Earth, but all of them were stripped to bare wood like looming skeletons. The plants that were in better shape resembled those I'd seen back on Death World.

For some reason, the sight appalled me. I'd always liked Green Deck. It pissed me off that these damned aliens had taken it upon themselves to uproot our greenery and replace it with their own. It just didn't seem right.

"Centurion Graves?" I transmitted. "McGill reporting. The enemy is here, at least in pod form. The pods appear to have been frozen to death by depressurization, however."

"Say again, McGill?" Graves asked. "Do you see enemy troops?"

"No sir, not exactly. We're surrounded by alien pods and vines, and I'm certain we didn't plant them here. Fortunately, they're frozen stiff."

"Interesting. It sounds like the radiation released from the core didn't kill them, but the hard vacuum did. I'm bringing the rest of the unit down to your position."

We poked around for a time as the unit formed around us. We had to use our hands to pull ourselves around on the dead vines until we found a big iron pipe. We figured it must have been the one that drained the water while *Minotaur* was in flight. Walking on it with our magnetic boots activated, we managed to reach the main exit.

There, we were in for another surprise. The exit had been sealed.

"Weapons at the ready, soldiers," Graves said, hand-over-handing it along our line to the front. He grabbed each man's helmet or air hose and pulled himself over our heads.

It was a strange way to move, but it worked well. He used his gauntlets to grab onto our suits and pull himself along. In zero-G training, we'd learned a number of techniques, and we were using them all now. Another trick was to use our magnetic boots to walk on another man's armor. There was a lot of titanium in our suits, but there were steel components, too.

Graves inspected the exit, which looked like it had been welded shut.

"Is Natasha here?"

"No sir," I said. "Turov left her back on Death World."

"Great. What have we got in the way of techs?"

A few came forward. Graves recognized Kivi and selected her. He directed her to inspect the edges of the metal and give an expert opinion.

I could tell right off Kivi was nervous. She'd only been a tech for a short time, and her background knowledge didn't extend much past whatever it took to get through tech school. Natasha, on the other hand, had been a hardcore science-geek her whole life.

"I'm not sure..." Kivi said after letting her light play over the strange, weld-like fusing of metal that ringed the exit. "If I had to guess, I'd say they used their secreted acid. Maybe they're able to apply it lightly over two surfaces, melting them together. Then they might chemically neutralize the reaction. That would cause the metal to fuse like this—but it's only a guess."

"Good enough," Graves said. "Weaponeers, destroy this door. Everyone else, take hold of something solid. There's likely to be a blast of gas if the corridor beyond is pressurized."

Those of us who were near the door hastened to get out of the way. Three belchers emitted lances of fire the moment we were clear. The door turned white-hot in an instant then melted into a burning, incandescent radiance. The metal burned like a giant sparkler, and a hole opened up in the center.

A gush of released gas flowed out of the hole, but it wasn't as powerful as when we'd opened Green Deck to space.

"McGill, give me a quick recon."

I scuttled forward, and once I'd stepped through the white hot breach, I felt weight return to my limbs. That was a relief. The passage didn't provide anything like a full G of gravity, but it was enough to keep me on the ground.

Behind me, my squad hurried to keep up. We had our rifles up to our faceplates, ready to tear up anything we saw.

"It's a mess inside, sir," I said. "Empty spacesuits, dead plants, debris—I'd say there was a fight in here, all right."

"No sign of active resistance?"

"None, sir."

"Unit, forward!"

We pressed on. The one thing that surprised me was the lack of bodies. There were a few, but not as many as I'd expected there to be. What's more, when we investigated those we found, we discovered they were empty suits and not dead men at all.

"Where are all the bodies?" Carlos demanded. "What did these green bastards do with them?"

"Why don't you find one and ask him?" Kivi suggested.

Carlos turned to frown at her, and there might have been an argument if Graves hadn't called to us over the unit-wide channel.

"Unit, halt. The central passageway appears to be clear. I'm going to switch over to our original invasion plan. Each unit with specialized orders will now carry them out. Graves out."

"What the frig?" Carlos said loudly. "Is he crazy? There's only about a hundred of us left, and he wants us to break up and get lost in the ship?"

"Our mission is to recapture this vessel," I told him. "Our original operational orders were designed to do just that. Gather up, people. Our squad's target is Gold Deck. We'll take this duct leading upward as a shortcut."

In addition to powered lifts, there were tubes with ladders in them to allow access between decks. We found one that went up. We slung our rifles on our backs and shimmied into the tube one at a time. Leading the way, I emerged on another level of the ship.

Gold Deck was eerie. I'd been up here on a number of occasions, and there'd always been a pack of staffers bustling around in perfectly creased uniforms. Now, the place was deserted.

"Spread out," I directed my squad as they popped out of the tube behind me. "Search and confirm we're secure."

"Vet?" Kivi asked in a hushed voice. "Shouldn't there be some dead people? There were a few in the passages, but…"

"Actually," I said, "there were none. The corpses we saw were really empty suits of armor. The bodies themselves are all missing."

She gave me a worried glance. I headed for the central consoles, and she stuck close behind me. We tried to engage the power couplings, but failed.

"No juice," Kivi said. "The power cables have been cut off somewhere between here and the generators."

"Where are the generators?"

"Engineering."

No one had much to say to that. Engineering, or Red Deck, was where the breach had originally occurred. Most of Graves' troops were headed there now. We all had visions of high radiation, holes in the core shielding and hard vacuum that couldn't be easily sealed off.

Reluctantly, I contacted Graves. "Centurion? McGill reporting. We've reached and secured Gold Deck. It's a ghost town. The bad news is we've got no power up here for the control systems. Any chance of getting a feed from Engineering?"

"Negative, McGill," Graves said. "We're nowhere near reaching our target yet. We've encountered a lot of damaged areas of the ship: Debris, exposed radioactives, collapsed passages, you name it. We might have to space-walk to get there at all."

"Okay then, sir," I said. "Should we hold our position here until you can get through?"

"No, I've got a better idea. Take your squad down to support Adjunct Toro. She's trying to get into Blue Deck, and she's having some kind of problem."

"Will do, sir."

We almost left before I remembered my special orders from Tribune Drusus and Turov. They'd ordered me directly to take this part of the ship. In fact, they'd asked me to locate a specific locker on Gold Deck.

Clanking to the spot, I opened the locker. Sure enough, there was a spanking-new walking vehicle we called a dragon inside.

"Looks like it's in good condition," Carlos commented.

"It is," I said thoughtfully.

I mounted the dragon's back-plate and got a surprise—the dragon wasn't empty. There was a body inside.

It had to be the first intact dead body I'd seen since I'd boarded *Minotaur*. The shocker was that the corpse was none other than Imperator Turov herself.

"Carlos, get up here," I ordered.

Carlos scrambled to my position and looked her over.

"She died in the pilot's harness," he said. "She doesn't have a respirator. Looks like she was overcome before she could seal up the dragon."

"Yeah..." I said thoughtfully. "What I don't get is why she didn't mention during the briefing that this was where she died."

322

"Maybe she doesn't know how it ended," he suggested. "The ship's systems were failing all over the place. Maybe her final moments aboard the ship weren't recorded. Anyway, let's pull her out of there. I'll drive the dragon for you, Vet."

I glanced at him and snorted. "Fat chance. I'm driving this thing."

It felt strange to handle Galina's corpse. After all, I'd made love to this woman a number of times over the last few days. But here she was, dead as a doornail and frozen stiff in the vacuum.

We set her aside gently, and I climbed into the dragon and reached for the controls that would fire up the vehicle. But then, I remembered something and stopped.

Galina had possessed a very valuable item. An artifact that was quite possibly unique in all of Frontier 921.

The Galactic key.

-44-

The Galactic key was a forbidden tool. It was a piece of technology that set our alien masters apart from all the lowly beings that eked out a living along the rim of the Empire. The key could enable or disable any Imperial-approved, alien-made device. Anything that was built by one world for use on another had to include a bypass system that only the Galactics were supposed to be able to use.

Physically, the key didn't *look* like a key. It looked more like a seashell. But that appearance belied its power. In the Galactic Empire, any technology that was worth having was traded between worlds. Once a given star system exhibited they had the best version of that item—such as a snap-rifle, revival machine, or even a starship—they had the exclusive rights to market it in their region of the Empire.

That was all well and good, and these simple trade laws made the Empire work even with thousands of diverse cultures. However, the races known collectively as the Galactics were special. They lived in the Core Systems and they were our masters. To maintain their dominance, they liked to keep a few tricks up their sleeves. One of these tricks was their keys.

Using a key, a Galactic like one of the Mogwa could bypass security and operate anything they liked, even if they didn't own it. That meant they could board a starship like *Minotaur* at will—or even fire her guns, if they felt the urge.

Looking down at Galina's dead body, I couldn't help but wonder. Could she have the key on her?

"Oh for God's sake, McGill," Kivi said with her hands planted on her hips. "Don't tell me you're losing it over this woman's dead body. You've seen *me* dead often enough."

Carlos chuckled. "Kivi's right. I've never seen you look this broken-up over her corpse. Not even when it was fresh."

Kivi slapped at him, and then she glared at me.

"Uh…" I said, trying to think.

The trouble was I couldn't tell them about the key. They didn't know it existed. It was a secret that only Claver, Turov and I shared.

The reason I was staring at the corpse had nothing to do with grief. I was wondering if Galina had died with the key on her person. Had she sent me here, hoping I'd find it for her? If that was the case, why hadn't she told me that was the nature of my mission?

Uncertainly, I leaned over and began to search her pockets.

"This is disgusting," Kivi said, misinterpreting my actions.

"Shut up, Specialist," I said. "I'm trying to see if she has the activator for the dragon on her."

"You don't need that," she snapped. "The dragon will recognize you. It's got a computer inside, you know."

Then I found it. A bulge in her left hip pocket. Fishing in there, I tried to pull it out while hunkering over her body to hide what I was doing. The damn thing was stuck in her pocket.

"McGill, you're mental," Kivi said.

She stalked away, but Carlos hung around.

"You want me to get you two a room?" he asked.

"Shut up, man," I said. "I've got special orders."

"I bet you do."

"Give me your knife," I said.

"Sick puppy," he said, but he handed me his belt knife anyway.

I slashed Galina's hip pocket open and immediately saw the problem. The key was a small device, but she'd secured it in her pocket in a pouch of some kind. It was tied down so she couldn't lose it accidentally. I cut the cords, and then I stood up, thinking hard.

"What's that thing?" Carlos asked.

"Nothing. Shut up."

"That's like the third time you've told me to shut up in the last minute. I think you're trying for a record."

"Why aren't you shutting up, then?"

Frowning at me, he watched suspiciously as I climbed into the dragon and closed it up behind me. Sure enough, Turov had turned on every piece of security the vehicle had. I was forced to provide voice samples, a password and badge identifications. Even then, the engine wouldn't turn over. She'd set the dragon up to operate only for her.

Cursing, I looked out the front visor at my troops. If I climbed out now in defeat, I'd have to face even more probing questions. My squaddies weren't very obedient outside of a battle, and they weren't dumb, either. They knew something odd was going on.

Then I remembered the key. Making doubly sure the tiny cockpit was sealed, I took the key out of its pouch and touched it to the console.

I wasn't sure it would work. I knew that the dragons were Dust World's product, and they were trying to sell them to other planets, but they hadn't gotten a full patent on them yet. Still, if they wanted to get approval at all, they would have to have—

The big, hydrogen-burning engine thrummed into life. Smiling, I knew I was in business.

My troops had been standing around outside the dragon, looking up at me sourly. But now that the machine had come to life, they retreated rapidly. That was a good thing for them, because I had some walking to do.

Not three minutes later, I was in the primary passages on my way down to Blue Deck. In my wake trotted a dozen soldiers like baby ducks following mama.

"McGill?" Graves called, his signal weak and crackling, "Toro is still requesting assistance. Get to Blue Deck immediately."

"We're on our way, sir," I said. "We've got a dragon with us, too."

"A dragon? Oh right, Turov keeps one up there. Paranoid woman. Well, you may have to use it. Toro made some kind of strange report about finding a lot of bodies. Now she's not responding to my calls."

My good mood evaporated. Graves had a way of making that happen. We hadn't seen a body except for Turov's and she'd been sealed up in a dragon. Why would there be a lot of them on Blue Deck? I couldn't think of a pleasant reason.

"On it, Centurion," I said. "Proceeding to the first hatch."

To control a starship, there were really only two zones that were critical. Engineering was one since you couldn't fly the ship without controlling the drives. Gold Deck contained all the piloting and navigational equipment, not to mention sensors, making it the second most important target.

There were, however, two other regions that any sane commander wanted to capture before he tried to fly a ship anywhere. These were the tactical control room, which operated the broadsides—and Blue Deck.

One might think that possessing what amounted to an advanced medical facility wouldn't be at the top of the priority list—but it was. The revival machines were there, and they were the most valuable equipment aboard any legion ship.

To begin with, they cost almost as much as the starship itself, but that wasn't the only reason they were prized. They also decided who lived and who died, literally. In any struggle to capture a ship, they had to be secured.

Hatches led deeper and deeper into Blue Deck, and they were all blown and hanging wide. The deck was pressurized and heated, but we didn't feel like removing our helmets, even though our instruments said the air was safe enough to breathe. In fact, it registered as warm and radiation-free.

That was probably because the entire deck's air volume was exchanged, heated and filtered every three minutes during normal operations for safety's sake. But I didn't trust the atmosphere. Just because the atmospheric indicator lights were green didn't mean they were going to *stay* green. We kept our helmets sealed just in case.

327

The first sign of trouble came in the form of three floating bodies. There was no active gravity here on Blue Deck, and we'd seen lots of empty suits—but these three weren't empty.

"Am I seeing this?" Carlos asked. "The limbs on those suits—where are they?"

He was right. They'd been torn off, plucked free. They were floating torsos with helmets attached, but no arms or legs.

"Squad at alert," I said. "Toro? Adjunct Toro, are you here? Veteran McGill reporting. I've brought a squad to render assistance. Come back, please."

There was nothing but a gentle hiss in my headphones. The bodies were freshly killed, that much was obvious. Red blood ran from the missing limbs and pooled on the walls, ceiling and floor in the odd way that liquids spread out in zero G.

"McGill to Graves," I said, but I didn't hear a response. "McGill to Graves—I don't seem to have you on my active contacts list anymore, sir."

Nothing came back from him, either.

"We're in some kind of communications blackout zone, McGill," Kivi said. "Nothing is working on my kit either. This smells like a trap to me."

"Roger that. Circle up tightly on my tail, people. Toro didn't have a dragon. We might—"

That was as far as I got before we were attacked.

I'll be the first to admit that I was surprised when our foes finally showed themselves. In fact, I gave a shout of horror and dismay that was almost as high-pitched as the noises made by the rest of my squad.

We'd been expecting plants. Maybe those walking tree-things we'd seen before on the ship and later down on Death World. But that wasn't what came at us.

Instead of acid-spitting trees, we were assailed by the bodies of our own dead. They didn't look exactly like our people anymore, but we could tell that there was human flesh and bone mixed in with the horrific things that launched out of every door, every closet and every alcove of Blue Deck to overwhelm us.

These things were *strange*. As they flew toward us I could clearly see they had vegetation sprouting out of them every which-way. Orange, floating sensory bulbs drifted around them like flowers. Tubers had lengthened the feet, turning them into gnarled root-like masses. Twisting vines came out of their mouths and eye-sockets—sometimes they even stuck out in-between exposed gray-white ribs.

It was disgusting and dangerous all at the same time. Some of these monsters were armed. They carried our own rifles, randomly folded into shotguns or automatic carbines. These weapons sprayed explosive bullets at an alarming rate. They shot their own kind as often as they hit us, but they outnumbered us in the extreme.

My squad opened fire in return. The carnage was terrific. We were all clenching our teeth and squeezing triggers. I lofted two grenades from my dragon's chest-cannons straight down the corridor ahead of me. These flashed and blasted apart the reconfigured bodies—but more kept coming.

We shouted until we were hoarse. We fired until our magazines ran dry. In the end, I let my last surviving troops fall back and run for the exit to contact Graves and tell him what we were up against.

But my dragon didn't retreat. I marched it forward, breathing in hissing gasps between my teeth, as I squelched through hundreds of floating dead things.

Using grippers, I kept tearing their flesh apart until they were all destroyed. Every last one of them.

Then, when it was over, I climbed out of my dragon and opened my visor just long enough to barf on the floor. I told myself the stink had overwhelmed me—but I knew better.

-45-

I thought that after I'd been so critical in the retaking of Blue Deck, I'd be hailed as a hero—but I'd thought wrong. A call startled me as I surveyed the carnage.

"McGill?" Graves said in my headset not two minutes after the last infected corpse stopped flopping around. "Are you still screwing around on Blue Deck?"

"Yes Centurion," I said. "I'm flirting with the bio girls right now. You can sound the all-clear."

"Very funny. Turov wants a status report on the revival machines."

"Did you say Imperator Turov is aboard this ship, sir?"

"Yes. She brought in the rest of our troops from the outer hull using the holes the aliens burned into the warp core. They retook Red Deck. There were some strange abominations down there—half human and half plant. Now she's moving up to Gold Deck to try to get *Minotaur* operational again."

At about that point in the conversation, I realized that our communications were working as they should again. Could I have accidentally killed whatever it was that was providing radio interference? I didn't know, but what I did know was that these aliens were easily the weirdest I'd yet to encounter.

"Strange abominations, huh?" I said. "I've seen lots of those. Blue Deck was full of them when we got here. They brought in all kinds of bodies and—"

"That's great, McGill. Turov wants information about the revival machines, and she wants it yesterday."

"Uh..." I said, squinting through my canopy and rotating the dragon's upper body from side to side. I spotted a revival chamber a hundred meters off. "Just a second."

I marched with a heavy, clanking tread toward a hatch. The metal hinges were melted and fused, and the door was hanging askew—not a good sign.

Inside, I found a mess that was worse than what I'd imagined. In my mind, I'd conjured up a burned, stabbed and generally slaughtered revival machine with its guts spread all over the deck. That would have been a pretty sight compared to what I actually did discover.

The revival machine was in the chamber, all right, and it looked like it was still alive. The maw was steamy and hung open like the jaws of a prehistoric beast. The strange part was it had tendrils growing right out of it. These tendrils led to a string of pods lying on the floor, pods of a nature I'd never seen before.

These bulbous shapes weren't like cucumbers or peppers. Instead, they looked like hairy, orange-colored kiwis. The skin of these pods was thin as if they'd over ripened. Many had split open in spots. I had no idea what these freaky growths were, but they were obviously linked by vines to the human bodies all over the floor and to the revival machine itself.

There were at least thirty of these pods. They also grew into the dead, shrunken corpses of our bio people. This pissed me off. It was obvious that the specialists and orderlies had fought to the death to defend their equipment, and now they were being used as fertilizer to grow fresh enemies.

As I watched, the revival machine's maw sagged open a little wider. A round pod, coated in slime, rolled out and plopped onto the deck. A fresh green strand led to the stem, connecting it to the chain of the pods and corpses.

Could this be how the aliens had been reproducing? By using our bodies for fuel and corrupting revival machines to create fresh pods? It was weird, and it was beyond disgusting.

My grippers came up automatically. I didn't have any ammo left for the chest-cannons—but I did have the power to tear these things apart.

"McGill?" Graves asked sharply.

I'd often thought Graves had some kind of ESP. He seemed to know when I was about to do something unsanctioned.

"Bad news, Centurion," I said. "The revival machines seem to be corrupted, converted over to alien production. There were at least a thousand human corpses on Blue Deck altogether, and those that were capable of attacking us have been destroyed. There are more, however. Let me link you to the vid."

I set up a stream and piped it to wherever Graves was on ship.

"Holy shit," Graves said heavily as I panned the room, giving him a good look at the scene. "What a mess. Where's your squad, McGill?"

"I sent the survivors to the exit. Do you want me to destroy this enemy infestation, sir? We can't possibly—"

There was a buzzing sound as someone cut into our private channel.

"McGill?" demanded Turov's voice. I could tell she was pissed from her tone.

"I read you, sir. Go ahead."

"You're not to touch any of those pods under any circumstances. I've been monitoring your vid stream. They've become symbiotic with the revival machines. If you cut them off from the human raw resources, the shock could kill our machines."

"Hmm," I said thoughtfully. "If you say so, sir. What do you want me to do?"

"Stand guard until I can get to your position with techs and bio people who know what they're doing."

In my heart, I seriously doubted any of our specialists had experience with an infection like this one, but I did as I was told. I withdrew to the main corridor and shoved deformed bodies out of the way to make a path. I would've started disposing of them, but I had my orders.

When Turov and her team finally arrived some minutes later, I could tell that none of them were happy. They were horrified and disgusted.

"A vid stream just can't do this justice, can it?" I asked them, trying not to look too smug. "If you people would like to get to work, the first corrupted machine is in chamber six. It's still making new pods, even now."

Turov ordered her team into the chamber, but she didn't follow them inside.

"Get that revival machine back into operating condition," she ordered. "I don't want to hear any excuses."

Watching them go in there, I mentally gave them no more than ninety seconds before the first one barfed. Sure enough, it happened in just under a minute.

All that time, Turov stood with her hands on her hips next to me. She had her lips curled back to show her fine, white teeth. I figured she was grossed out by the guts that were glued onto the chassis of my dragon.

"Let's get out of here," she said. "We have things to discuss."

I marched down the passageway behind her, and we exited Blue Deck. Getting out of that slice of alien hell relieved my mind and spirit. Watching Galina's posterior all the way down the corridor didn't hurt, either. That woman could walk like she had high heels on, even in combat boots.

It wasn't until I came out into the central corridor that ran along the spine of the ship that I finally got an inkling that something was wrong. Perhaps I'd been lulled by the view. Or maybe I was still too mentally stunned by my ordeal on Blue Deck to think clearly.

Whatever the case, when I walked out into a ringed formation of some thirty armed heavy infantry, several of them weaponeers, I was surprised when they leveled their weapons at me in unison.

Even better, Winslade was leading them. He had a nasty grin on his face, and I figured it was meant for me.

"Primus Winslade?" I asked. "I thought you were babysitting the bio people down on the planet."

333

"I'm overjoyed to see you, too," he replied. "The lifter is bringing everyone up now."

"James McGill," Turov said loudly. "I'm placing you under arrest. Now, get the hell out of my dragon this instant!"

-46-

I'm by no means inexperienced when it comes to being arrested. I'd go so far as to say I've deserved most of my many arrests, punishments and even a few of my executions. But usually, I knew damned well what the charges were when arrests happened.

Today, I was baffled and a little pissed off.

"Hold on," I said, rotating the dragon to survey the group. I noticed about then that none of their faces were familiar. Turov had made sure to utilize troops who weren't from my own unit.

"What's this about?" I asked. "I just got done clearing Blue Deck following your orders, sir. Did I do it incorrectly?"

"Yes you did," she said. "I never instructed you to rob my body. You've stolen valuable technology and used it without authorization. I have witnesses to that effect and supporting vid files."

"Oh," I said, catching on. "You're talking about the key, aren't you?"

"Shut up," she hissed.

"Why?" I asked. "Seems to me that I'll be needing some witnesses and vid-streams of my own today."

I rotated the upper chassis of the dragon to address the crowd. The group tensed, aiming their rifles at me. Apparently, they'd been briefed about the power of a dragon up close—and probably about my reputation as a mean dragon-rider as well.

"You boys rolling your suit cameras?" I boomed, cranking up the external speakers. "I've got something important to show everyone."

"Damn it, McGill, come out of that vehicle and surrender!" Turov demanded.

"I'd be happy to, Imperator," I said in a reasonable tone, "if you would please state the charges for me in detail."

"I already have! You stand charged with grave-robbing. You stole the personal effects of a dead officer—me."

"Right, right, but if you could only describe what it is I'm supposed to have stolen, that'd be very helpful. You see, I don't recall anything of the kind, and I have to know what it is if I'm going to give it back to you."

Her eyes traversed the circle of faces quickly. They were confused, but ready to act on her orders. I had no doubt that thirty troops could take one dragon, particularly one that was out of ammo. Sure, I'd probably manage to kill a few of them in the process, but I was certain they'd kill me in the end.

The most dangerous members of the platoon were the weaponeers. They were aiming their plasma cannons at my dragon nervously.

Turov could give the order to fire at any moment—but I knew she wouldn't. The trouble was that the weaponeers would have to use their belchers to penetrate my armor. And if they did that, the key might well be destroyed in the process.

Turov was doing the same calculations that I was; I could see it in her eyes. I took a clanking step toward her, servos buzzing. She skipped back in alarm, and her troops lifted and half-pulled their triggers, taking a fresh stance.

"My," I said, "everyone's sure jumpy today."

"McGill, you climb out of that machine and give me my property, or I swear I'll have you executed for this."

"I've got a better idea," I said. "Order your hit squad to stand down and leave us alone. After that, I'll happily make the exchange in private."

She glared up at me thoughtfully. "What if you decide to kill me?"

"Then you'll pop out of a revival machine hopping mad," I said. "No one wants that. Look, all I'm asking for is a breather.

I just retook your ship for you, and I think it's the least you could do."

She bit her lower lip then waved her arm at the assembled troops. "Primus Winslade, withdraw. McGill and I will handle this situation personally."

Winslade seemed surprised and confused. He didn't know about the Galactic key, but he was weasel-smart. He knew something was up, something he didn't understand.

"Is that safe, sir?" he asked.

"Probably not," Turov admitted. "But you have your orders regardless. Withdraw!"

Winslade ordered his goons to lower their weapons. With a look of suspicion and curiosity, he marched them away. The troops filtered past, glancing over their shoulders at me and the Imperator. Lord only knows what they were thinking.

The Imperator and I walked off in the opposite direction, toward Gold Deck. When the troops were out of sight, I laughed aloud.

"What's so funny?" she demanded.

"The looks on their faces were priceless. The stories they'll tell tonight—I'd love to hear them."

Imperator Turov wasn't often in a good mood under the best of circumstances, but I'd be willing to wager I'd rarely seen her in a worse temper than she was today.

She stopped, drew her sidearm, and fired a bolt into my face. It didn't penetrate the armor, but it did make me wince, and it dazzled my eyes a little despite the light-filtering effects of my visor.

"Hey, what's that for?"

"James, you have enraged me to the point that if you weren't in that machine, I'd execute you right now."

"Galina," I said, "you're an ungrateful woman. All I did was borrow the key and use it to operate this machine. I had to bypass your excessive security to get it to run. By doing so, I was able to destroy the alien infestation on Blue Deck. Would you rather have lost *Minotaur* to the enemy?"

She continued to point her gun at me. "Give me my property," she demanded.

"All right, all right, I will. But what do I get in exchange?"

Her pretty head cocked to one side. "What? You're making demands?"

"I'm just asking."

She took a deep, hitching breath and let it out slowly. She closed her eyes and let her gun sag down.

"All right," she said. "I'll give you rank. Adjunct—that's it, don't ask for more. Graves has already put in the paperwork. I've been sitting on it, but I'll approve the promotion when we get back to Earth."

This was a stunner to me. I'd been thinking about a romantic interlude—hell, I might have even settled for a passionate kiss. But rank…?

At first, I almost rejected her offer. I didn't want rank to come that way: through backroom deals and dishonest leverage, but then her words slowly sank in.

"Graves has already put in the paperwork?" I asked. "That means it's legit."

"You are mistaken. What will make it real is my signature."

I struggled to think. If there was anyone in the legion who wasn't a pushover, it was Graves. He'd never recommend me to be elevated to an officer's rank unless he honestly thought it was the right thing to do.

"You've been sitting on this?" I asked. "Is that what you said?"

She shrugged. "Your conduct isn't always the sort of thing we look for in our officers. Not even in Legion Varus. Surely you can see that, can't you?"

"Yeah, well, you've got a point there."

"Then we have a deal?"

"I guess that's a pretty good offer," I said, "but there's just one more thing—"

"You're kidding!" she interrupted. "You're demanding a personal favor as well? I told you our relationship was over with!"

"Uh…" I said, vaguely. "I'm just asking for a kiss. The kind of kiss a vid hero is supposed to get from a lady when he saves her butt."

She looked at me speculatively. "All right. Let's go to my office. I've had the techs working to clear out every taint of those horrible aliens for the last hour."

We walked the rest of the way to Gold Deck. Under the watchful gaze of a dozen surprised staffers, I escorted the Imperator into her office and shut the door.

"Could you put that gun down for a second?" I asked.

She smirked but did as I asked. I climbed out of the dragon quickly, just in case she was planning to pick up her weapon again in a classic double-cross.

But instead of greeting me with the barrel of her gun when I turned around, she met me with tight smile. At first I thought she was happy to see me—but then I followed her eyes downward and realized she could see the seashell shape of the Galactic key in my hand.

"It's right here," I said. "Told you."

"Give it to me."

I stepped forward, but I didn't put the key into her hand. Instead, I snaked an arm around her waist and drew her up close.

She resisted a little at first, but then she warmed up, and we kissed for about a minute. She was breathing hard by the end, and I'd have to admit I was doing the same.

She looked into my eyes.

"All right," she said. "You can have me one last time."

Smiling, I put the Galactic key on the desk, but I didn't put my hands on her. She looked shocked when I took a step toward the door.

"I'm sorry," I said, "I just wanted a hero's kiss. Like you said, we're broken up, and that's for the best."

She sputtered, grabbed the key off the desk and kicked me out of her office. I didn't mind. I was getting tired of her ungrateful behavior anyway.

-47-

The aliens had really done a number on our ship. Patching the holes in the thick hull around the warp core took the longest. It took more than a week for us to clean up and repair the ship. As soon as *Minotaur* was operable again, we made preparations to travel back to Earth.

During the long hours of working on the ship, I'd had no more contact with Imperator Turov. Our brief rekindling had died out, and I wasn't sad to see it end. We'd always had an odd relationship, anyway.

When we finally did power out of orbit and engage the Alcubierre warp drive, I think every tech on board was holding his or her breath. They gritted their teeth and quickly engaged the drive with their eyes closed, like someone ripping off a band-aid.

After a bit of hesitant shivering, the warp bubble formed and enclosed the ship. We slipped away at a velocity that was effectively greater than the speed of light. I joined the techs in a ship-wide sigh of relief.

When we left the L-374 system I was on Green Deck. The weirdest thing happened when we went into warp. Normally, a holographic image of moving stars crawled overhead when we were inside the bubble-effect. The imagery was projected on the dome over Green Deck creating the pleasant illusion that we could see the universe outside and watch it drift by.

For this voyage, such unnecessary systems hadn't been repaired. While breaking into the ships, our troops had damaged the dome and pretty much destroyed the projectors that made the simulation work.

Overhead, instead of the blackness of space dotted with crawling pinpoints of light, I saw a uniform surface of throbbing whiteness.

"Kind of looks like a soap-bubble," I said to Anne.

"You're right," she said, "it does."

We were finally having our promised date on Green Deck, much delayed though it was. We'd both been too busy up until the launch to engage in anything like romance. She'd been trapped on Blue Deck, cleaning the chambers and reviving troops. Likewise, my squad had been given countless tasks to help the damage-control crews.

"See there?" I asked, pointing aloft. "That shimmer of light—it's mostly white, but sometimes it shifts into a multi-hued ripple, like a rainbow. Beautiful, isn't it?"

"Yes," she said thoughtfully. "It's lovely. I guess we really don't need to watch fake stars, even if they're comforting."

I heard a strange note in her voice, and I looked down to see what she was doing. She had a flake of ash in her hands. Unfortunately, that was most of what was left of Green Deck.

The trees around us were white skeletal sticks, shorn of bark and leaves. The rocks were scorched and chemically burned. The grass was gone in most places, but we'd managed to find a spot that had a few fresh, green blades to sit on. Most of the organic matter that had once made this place attractive had been destroyed or consumed by the aliens when they controlled our ship.

"Are you sad about Green Deck?" I asked Anne. "Don't worry. It'll all grow back soon. They say by the next time we ship out, this place will look as good as new."

"No," she said, "that's not what's troubling me."

"What is it, then?"

She met my eyes at last. "James, do you know what the bio people are talking about?"

"Uh…no."

"You and Turov. That's all they whisper about. You didn't even *try* to hide your lust for her. You couldn't even manage that much, could you?"

My face froze. I hadn't been expecting this. Sure, now and then one of my girlfriends got wind of another. That was only to be expected. But Anne had said yes to this date. She'd come out here for a picnic without cluing me in that she was upset about anything.

"Well..." I said. "I'm not going to deny I had a few moments with that woman. But let me assure you, she's not my girlfriend now. She wants to shoot me dead most of the time."

Anne snorted with laughter. "Yes, I bet she does. Sometimes I feel the same way. Let me explain myself: I came to this spot with you to tell you I'm done going out with you. Okay? Whatever our relationship was—it's over."

Nodding slowly, I didn't say anything. What was there to say?

"Look," she said. "I know who you are. And I know we haven't been together for a long time. I don't feel like I own you, James, but I also know that no matter what happens between us, your eye will always wander. Even more importantly than that, you've got a family of your own to worry about."

"You mean Della and Etta?" I asked. I wasn't used to thinking of them as my family.

"Of course. Even if you don't have much of a connection with them now, you should at least give it try. I can't let myself get in the way of that."

"Okay...I guess."

She gulped her wine after that, stood up, and walked away. I didn't get a goodbye kiss—nothing. She kept her head down and didn't look back. I noticed she walked kind of fast, too.

A pang of regret struck me as I watched Anne leave, an honest pang. I'd had a thing for her for a long time. Now, it looked like that wasn't going to work out.

After she left, I drank the whole bottle of wine I'd spent a lot of credit on. Laying down flat on my back on our small patch of dry grass, I took a much-needed nap.

I woke up an hour or so later—but I didn't do it naturally. Someone had given me a light kick me in the head.

"You're going to get radiation poisoning out here," Carlos said. "You know that, don't you?"

Catching his foot, I twisted, and we rolled around wrestling. That stopped when we were out of the green patch and into the ash itself. We got up, dusting ourselves off and spitting.

"Why the hell are you kicking me awake, Specialist?" I demanded.

"You do it to me all the time."

"True enough."

Carlos picked up my bottle of wine but made a grunting noise of disappointment when he realized it was empty.

"Where's your date?" he asked.

"It didn't work out."

"Too bad," he said.

I gave him a quizzical look. "Since when do you care?"

"Well, I came looking for you to ask if you would mind if I chased Della."

My face must have changed because he put up his hands in a surrendering gesture.

"Whoa, hoss!" he said in an exaggerated country accent. "Don't go cracker on me! I'm just asking. She's not even out of the revival machine yet."

Della had been with my team on Blue Deck, but like a lot of my people, she'd died there. She hadn't been revived yet as the brass had decided those with technical skills were more important than fighters.

Thinking over Carlos' question, I shook my head. "I guess I do mind. In fact, I've got to have a serious talk with Della when she comes back. I've been sort of avoiding her since we left Earth. You know, it seems like I have a hard time with serious personal issues when I'm out on a campaign."

"I know what you mean," he said. "It's like there's this life, the one we have in space, and then there's life back on Earth. I don't like mixing them together much. They're too different."

343

It was an unusually thoughtful statement for Carlos. I clapped him on the back, and we walked through the ship's guts toward our unit's module.

For the next week or so, we all worked double-shifts repairing and cleaning up the ship. It was a Thursday afternoon, technically, when Della finally came back to our module and found me waiting for her.

"Hey," I said when I saw her, "you okay?"

It was the kind of question legionnaires asked one another after a death and a rebirth. Sometimes you could shrug it off—other times, it hit you wrong somehow.

"I'm fine," she said.

I wasn't entirely convinced by her tone, but I took her word for it.

"Good," I said. "I wanted to talk to you about something. I wanted to suggest we fly out to Dust World and see Etta. I'll even pay for the tickets."

She stared at me fixedly for a few seconds. "I was revived less than an hour ago, and you have to spring this on me now?"

"Sorry," I said, taken aback. "I thought you might be happy."

She walked away down a passage toward our sleeping quarters. Sighing and figuring I'd screwed up somehow, I followed her.

"Della...?"

She didn't walk into her squad barracks as I'd expected. Instead, she walked to my room. I followed her inside, and she shut the door.

"All right," she said, "what's this all about?"

Her arms were crossed, and her eyes were narrowed.

"Just like I said, I'd like to meet Etta."

"All of a sudden? Without your parents to goad you into it?"

"That's right."

"I've been dead for two weeks," she said, her voice sounding haunted. "I've never been gone for so long before."

"Oh...yeah," I said. "I know that feeling. I've been there before. That's a weird one. The key is not to think about it."

"Seriously? That's your best piece of advice?"

"Yes, absolutely. There's no better way to handle these situations. Complete denial is the best policy. Lock your mind down like a jail cell. Keep that up until you forget about the whole thing. That routine works like a charm for me, every time."

She looked doubtful, but she did smile a little. "I'll keep that in mind," she said dryly.

"Well? What about my idea? You want to go back to Dust World with me?"

"I'm not going to try to stop you—but I'll pay my own way, if you don't mind."

"Okay, sure...so you'll go with me, right?"

"Didn't I make that clear enough?"

"Just checking."

Della sighed and rolled her head around on her shoulders. I could tell she was trying to relax and think clearly.

"Yes," she said at last. "I'll accompany you, James. If I have to, I'll even escort you around the rocks and see you don't get lost. My father will be anxious to interview you."

"Fair enough," I said.

I was trying to sound cool, but I felt a fresh worry growing in my mind at the mere thought of Della's father. He was the leader of the colonists on Dust World. They called him the Investigator, and he was a strange guy...strange as in kind of scary.

-48-

When we finally got close to Earth, my heart grew heavy. Everyone else seemed excited. They were watching the forward observation view screens every night as old Sol got bigger and brighter. Finally, we could make out the white specks of planets as we came out of warp.

Earth herself, blue-green and wreathed in white clouds, was lovely. But I didn't feel like celebrating.

My planet was still there, but my family wasn't. Sure, I'd teased myself with fantasies. Maybe the casualty estimates were exaggerated. Maybe my parents had been lucky and found a bunker at the last minute....

But I knew the odds of such things were astronomical. That's why I didn't bother to check the news vids, search the net, or anything like that during the final hour or so of our approach.

Up until that point, due to relativistic effects, we'd been out of touch with Earth. Except for the very expensive use of a Galactic deep-link service, there was no way to communicate at a speed greater than light, other than using a starship for a courier service.

Instead of messing with my tapper, I packed my gear and hiked down the ramps alone. My solitude didn't last long. Della swooped out of nowhere and fell into step beside me. I smiled at her gratefully. I was glad to have a friend with me as I exited the big ship. Part of my mind was thinking about funeral arrangements, but I kept telling myself that must have been done by now. My relatives would have handled it. Facing grandparents and the like—that was going to be tough.

Della seemed to be in a cheerful mood. She talked about places she wanted to visit with me when we went to Dust World. She claimed there were caverns with edible wild life that I simply *had* to experience. I did my best to match her mood.

"James," she said, tapping me on my shoulder. "Your parents should be out here, somewhere."

I frowned. Had she only just thought about that? Had it never occurred to her that this moment, returning home to Earth, was likely to be crushing to my spirit?

She continued tapping me, and she pointed off into the crowd. Still wearing a long face, I followed her gesture.

It took several seconds for what I was seeing to sink in. When it did, I stopped walking down the ramp and stared, jaw sagging.

"How could they...?" I asked. "Did they get revived?"

"No. Didn't you read your tapper? They sent us both a message an hour ago."

I stared at Della, and she stared back.

"You mean, you didn't know?" she asked.

"Uh..."

I started walking again. What else could I do? My legs felt numb. It was silly when I thought about it. Here I was, a man who'd died a dozen times in all sorts of violent encounters, stunned by the simple fact my parents had mysteriously survived.

Now that I was out in the open on the spaceport puff-crete pavement, I could tell they'd been working hard to repair the place but hadn't quite managed it. The dark hulk of the spacecraft had formed a new hillock about where the old terminal building had been.

As far as I could see, the aliens had managed a direct hit on the spaceport. Even the puff-crete pavement had been damaged. The area I was walking on right now was clearly fresh-poured and had the mottled pinkish white texture to prove it. Aged puff-crete tended to get dirty and turn gray over time.

I broke into a trot and started grinning. By the time I managed to fight through the crowds to my folks, I was laughing like a loon. Sweeping them up in my big arms, I lifted them both in the air. My dad was a big fellow, almost as big as I was, but gravity couldn't hold him to the Earth.

"Wow," Mom said, "that's the most enthusiastic greeting I've ever gotten from my son!"

"Same here!" my dad said. "Who stole my sour teenager and made him a happy man?"

Staring at one of them and then the next, I shook my head. "I thought you two were permed for sure," I told them. "How did you get revived? You must have had your data stored somehow—but for civilians, that's not cheap. I don't get it."

My mom looked at my father reproachfully. She slapped at him, and he shrugged, putting his hands in his pockets.

"I told you we'd never fool him," she said. "Your father thought we could just greet you here and act like nothing had happened. I knew that was never going to wash."

Confused, I frowned at them both. My mom moved toward Della, who looked wary, but she allowed herself to be hugged. Hugging wasn't a typical social activity on Dust World. Della had never looked comfortable with hugs, but she'd learned to tolerate them.

We all walked toward the parking lot. Around us, the crowd was melting away like frost on an April morning.

"I guess I have to explain," my father said at last.

"That's right, you do," Mom said.

"Well, you see, it was like this. After you left us at the gate, we were supposed to go up to the stands and listen to the speeching and clapping for the next half hour while your legion stood at attention in the sun."

"That's exactly what we were *supposed* to do," my mom interrupted, "but we've never actually done it."

"And it's a damned good thing this time, isn't it?" my father demanded.

"Hold on," I said, interrupting. "Are you two telling me that you weren't here when the ship crashed into the spaceport?"

"That's right," Dad said. "And for that, I'm a hero, as far as I'm concerned."

"What you are is impatient," Mom said. "Just like James." She turned to me, and her face softened. "Your father has never been able to sit still long enough to watch a ceremony—any ceremony. He would've walked out on our own wedding and taken a nap in the car if I'd let him. It's disgusting. Every time you leave Earth, James, I wonder if you'll ever come back, and this man prevents me from seeing you one last time!"

"You *always* leave?" I asked them, still incredulous. "Every time?"

My father squirmed visibly. "Well...there are like ten thousand troops out there, you know, all lined up. There's no way we can even pick out your face in the crowd."

Suddenly, I laughed. I laughed long and loud. My dad *was* just like me. An impatient, rule-breaking, corner-cutter. An expert truth-bender who covered things up to protect other people's feelings.

On the drive home, I thought about all the moping around I'd done on this voyage. There'd been plenty of quiet moments in my bunk at night, soul-searching and grieving. It had all been for nothing.

But I didn't care now, because I had my family back. I was happy for the first time in months.

* * *

Several happy days followed. My mom spent most of that time planning our trip to Dust World. Della stayed with us again, and we got reacquainted. All in all, it was a great homecoming.

On the first Monday morning after returning home, however, a knock came at my door. Della wasn't with me as she usually spent the early hours wandering the woods out in back of my parents' place. She loved the earthly wilderness.

349

Being from Dust World, she was very much the outdoor type, but she was accustomed to deserts with small oases of exotic life. There wasn't anything like the swampy terrain of southern Georgia where she was from.

I opened the door, yawning. Of all the people I expected to see, the face that greeted me in the bright white light had to be near the bottom of the list.

"Claver?" I asked. "What the hell are you doing sneaking around in my swamp?"

"Can I come in?" he asked.

Frowning at him, I moved to block the doorway. "Tell me what this is about first."

Claver looked over his shoulder, one way then the other. "I don't know if it's safe out here."

"What's this all about?"

Claver sighed, realizing I wasn't going to let him come inside. "All right, I'm going to tell you, and you'll have to make a big decision. Try to make the right choice this time, for all our sakes."

Feeling a rumble in my belly, I was annoyed. It was too early in the morning for one of Claver's twisted schemes. Heaving a sigh, I nodded. "Talk. Talk fast."

"You and I have enemies, McGill."

I chuckled. "You mean *you* do. Like everyone who lost a family member back at the spaceport, for instance."

"A gruesome tragedy, I'm sure," he said, but he didn't sound like he cared at all. "But that's not what I'm talking about. Think back: who did you piss off on Death World?"

Squinting, I tried to recollect the list. It seemed to be long and distinguished.

"We talking about my personal relationships? Or how about aliens? Do they count?"

Claver made an irritable motion with his hand, erasing my words. "No. I'm talking about your superiors. People who can actually avenge themselves upon you directly."

"Hmmm," I said, rubbing my chin. "Well, Turov was angry on and off, but I think we reached an understanding. As to other officers, I know Graves wasn't happy about—"

"I'm talking about Primus Winslade," Claver interrupted impatiently. "You two killed one another. He almost got the last laugh, but Turov stopped him."

"Yeah, that's true," I said, scratching disinterestedly. "What about him?"

"He's made his move. He's taken out Turov."

Finally, at long last, he had my full attention. "He *what?*"

"He found out about the key. He must have seen you use it or something—anyway, Turov turned up dead, and the key is missing. That's all I know."

I stared at him for a long second while the gears in my head clicked. It was a painful affair before my first cup of coffee.

"I remember now," I said. "Back when Turov ordered him to arrest me. She wanted the key back—but I wouldn't give it to her. He couldn't figure out why she was putting up with me. I saw the confusion and suspicion on his face. Galina and I were hinting around about a deal, and I gave it back to her in the end, after she made a few concessions."

Claver snorted. "I heard about that. You're a goat in the woods, boy."

Shaking my head, I denied his accusation, but I could tell he didn't believe me, so I switched subjects after a few minutes of discussion.

"Okay, okay," I said. "You think Winslade killed Turov and took her key. I get that. What do you want me to do about it?"

"Do? What do you think? We have to go see him. We've got to cut a deal with him."

"A deal?"

"Yes. He knows that we both know about the key, fool. That means we have to die."

I stared at him. "We have to die? Why's that?"

Claver rolled his eyes at me. I hated that. "I've got an air car," he said. "We can be up at Central in two hours. Are you coming or not?"

"I don't think I need to go anywhere. I don't think you're telling me the whole truth."

"Why not?"

"Because you never have, you old snake."

Claver shrugged, knowing I had him there. "All right," he said. "I'll handle this myself. If I do it badly, you and your folks and your woman and the baby—they can all fend for themselves after that."

"You're threatening me? Right here on my own property?"

"I'm giving you a friendly warning, boy. Winslade is the threat, not me. He's not like Turov. He's a better officer in some ways, but he's got a mean streak in him. Remember what he did to me in that chair? Remember what he did to you?"

Nodding slowly, I had to admit that Turov had never tortured anyone to death. Hell, I'd pulled a gun on her at least as many times as she'd pulled one on me. We had a working relationship. It wasn't based on trust, exactly, but we did understand one another.

"You've got a point," I said. "If I had to choose between Turov and Winslade—I'd take Turov in a heartbeat."

Claver gave me another dirty grin. "There's another reason I can think of: you won't be getting any fringe benefits out of the deal with Winslade in charge."

"Fine, I'll go," I said, and I went back inside to get a few things.

I heard something strange when my back was turned. It was something like a squawk, the kind of noise a surprised chicken might make.

Stepping back outside and shrugging on a jacket, I froze.

Claver was face down on the muddy path leading to my parents' place. A foot was planted on the small of his back, and a naked blade was drawing a red line on the back of his neck.

"Della?" I said. "Girl, why are you mistreating my guest?"

"He's not a guest here," she said. "He never will be. He's a villain, James. Can't you see that?"

"Yeah, he sure is. But today, I have business with this villain. Can you let him up or have you already severed his carotid?"

Reluctantly, Della let Claver up. He climbed to his feet and brushed himself off.

"Where the hell did you come from?" he demanded. "I didn't see a thing."

"You weren't meant to," she said.

352

"Why the hostility? I haven't done you any harm."

"You threatened my daughter and James' family. I listened to it all. I'm already regretting my decision to leave you alive."

He looked at Della in concern. For me, it was all in a day's work, but I could tell Claver was spooked by her. It did my heart good to see it.

"You keep strange company, McGill," he said.

"Della's always been a free spirit," I explained.

"That's what you call this murderess?"

"Normally, I'd be offended," I said. "But she has killed me several times in the past, so…"

"Are you coming with me or not?" Claver asked. "Time is wasting."

"Take me too, James," Della said. Since letting Claver onto his feet, she'd kept her knife aimed at his left eyeball, with her arm cocked back for a thrust. He didn't dare pull a weapon.

"Nah," I said. "Why don't you stay here and protect my folks for me? Just in case this is all some kind of scheme to lure me away from home and leave my folks unprotected?"

Della glanced at me with a fresh worry on her face. "Do you think that's possible?"

"Anything's possible when you're dealing with Claver."

"Thanks for that vote of confidence," Claver said, grinning.

A few minutes later, I climbed into Claver's air car and was whisked away into the skies. I had no idea what was really in store for me. I figured I'd just have to play it by ear when we got to Central.

-49-

Claver knew that Winslade wouldn't just let us march up to his office in Central and start chewing him out. So, he used what he always did in these situations: money.

In my era, unfortunately, Hegemony had more than its share of corruption. The core of the problem seemed to stem from the flow of too much credit through too few hands. When the government awarded a trillion credits to Hegemony and ordered them to build a fleet, it was damned near certain that a few hundred billion of that digital currency ended up in questionable places.

There were the small time grifters: Tribunes and the like who bought their family members fancy new air cars and paid for them with bribes offered by contractors. Then there was the big kind of thievery: sectors paying off officials to place new facilities in their territory rather than the other guy's. It was my guess that this kind of thing had always gone on in large organizations throughout time.

With all that wealth flying around, you'd think people would have had an easy time finding honest work—but they didn't. In my world, every mistake a person made was tracked by some computer or another. Vids were stored in the data cores forever and universally available on the net. That meant there were a lot of people who couldn't get jobs—so they had to survive by other means.

Claver had found such a person. An ex-hegemony veteran by the name of Jonathan Sloane. He'd done something wrong that he couldn't erase, and he'd been kicked out of the service by none other than Primus Winslade himself. We picked him up in Wilmington then pressed on toward Central.

"You're sure you can fix the security systems?" Sloane asked Claver for about the tenth time.

I kept my mouth shut, partly because I didn't really know what Claver was capable of. I'd seen him perform some pretty amazing stunts before—but then again, we were talking about Central itself this time. I couldn't blame Sloane for having doubts.

"Of course I can," scoffed Claver with absolute certainty in his voice. He sounded like he was offended that Sloane would even dare to doubt him.

We glided in on a regulated approach-corridor toward a mammoth building. Central was as impressive a sight as ever. The three of us dropped lightly onto a spur of puff-crete that stuck out from the side of the mountainous structure. The landing pad looked like a hand lifted palm-up toward heaven.

Sloane was sitting in the passenger seat with his arms crossed. He was becoming nervous now that we were actually here, I could tell.

"I don't like this," he said.

"Look," Claver said, "I told Winslade I'm flying in to show him how to use a new piece of hardware he's acquired. You'll just have to wear the belt, and it will make you look like me. When you get in there, do your business and get out fast."

"And why, again, should I trust you?"

Claver grunted in annoyance and tapped at the belt Sloane was wearing. "Turn it on. Let's test it."

Sloane looked at the belt suspiciously. He thumbed the button, but didn't push it.

"Come on," Claver said. "What do you think? It's a bomb? I'm not trying to blow us all up!"

Reluctantly, Sloane pushed the button.

The effect was immediate and amazing. He transformed into the spitting image of Claver himself. Even the clothes were right—everything.

Claver chuckled. "Check the passenger-side mirrors."

Sloane did so, and he whistled long and loud. "I *do* look exactly like you!" he said, marveling.

The belt and the box were, of course, from Tech World. The people known as the Tau on that planet wore these devices instead of clothing. They could project imagery that made a person look like they were dressed in any color or fashion they liked. Claver had clearly tampered with the box to make it project his own face on top of Sloane's.

"I'm impressed," Sloane said. "This will get me into his office—but why don't you just march up there and shoot him yourself if you hate him as much as I do?"

"Hold on," I said from the back seat. "Who said anything about shooting Winslade? I thought we were going to shake him down, to get him to return—"

"You thought wrong," Claver said, throwing me a glare over his shoulder. He shook his head at me slowly, indicating I should shut up.

My lips twisted up in disgust. Claver was a schemer, and I'd been caught up in his crooked plans before. He clearly didn't want me to talk about the Galactic key in front of Sloane. I fell silent, deciding to wait to see how things played out. The idea of having Winslade running around with the key in his possession worried me a good deal. He was worse than Turov, in my opinion.

When I shut up, Claver's face transformed into a sly smile. He turned back to Sloane, who was eyeing the two of us suspiciously.

"Think about it," he said. "We all want this man dead, but none of us want to pay for the crime. By wearing my face, you shield yourself from the vid cameras."

"And why won't they just arrest you?" Sloane asked.

Claver pointed at me at this point. "You see McGill, here? He's another Winslade-hater from way back."

I nodded, because it was pretty much true. Winslade and I had never gotten along.

"He's my alibi. He and I will parade ourselves in front of as many cameras as we can over the next ten minutes. You see? That way you're covered, I'm covered, and he's covered. We three are the most likely suspects—the cops will know that. But when they investigate, they'll realize *none* of us could have committed the crime because we weren't here."

Sloane squinted at each of us in turn. He pointed a finger at me.

"Why don't you have him do it?"

Claver laughed. "Debts are so quickly forgotten! Did that little matter of six hundred thousand much-needed credits slip your mind already, Sloane?"

Claver handed him a gun then. It was a weird-looking thing, fashioned into the shape of a bar of soap. You'd never know it was a weapon, except for the black, oval button on the back of it.

"This thing contains almost no metal. The outer shell is organic, inert material. All their scanners will be fooled."

Sloane eyed the weapon, hesitating.

"Not interested?" Claver said. He made a tsking sound. "I thought you had it all, Sloane: motive, guts and a healthy desire for easy credit. I guess I was wrong. You can play McGill's part. It only pays a hundredth of the fee, but it's a lot safer."

Claver turned toward me, passing the disguised weapon in my direction. "McGill, I guess you're getting rich today. Could you hand McGill the belt, Sloane?"

Sloane licked his lips, then reached out suddenly and took the gun.

"Changed your mind, eh?" Claver asked. "Okay then...go!"

Still looking like Claver, Sloane climbed out of the air car and walked quickly toward the guard post that oversaw the landing site. It was technically a violation to land here unless you were on official Hegemony business, but the guards didn't usually check IDs until someone tried to enter the building.

Claver watched his twin hustle toward security. There was a worrisome pause as they IDed him—but he passed.

Claver's smile was an evil thing to witness. It gave me pause. His plan seemed elaborate, but it appeared to be well thought-out. That didn't completely put my mind at ease, though. Claver's schemes routinely resulted in disaster for everyone but him.

I watched Sloane disappear on his mission of assassination. I'd come to feel sorry for the guy over the brief time I'd known him. He was just a fellow down on his luck and there were countless examples of his kind in the world.

"Come on," Claver said, rapping his knuckles on the dash. "Let's move. He's inside."

"Move?" I asked. "Where are we going? To find some cameras to parade in front of?"

Claver looked at me like I was the biggest dummy this side of a ventriloquist's knee.

"You *bought* that crap?" he asked, laughing. "Sometimes, McGill, I wonder how lonely your brains must be inside that big skull of yours. Come on, we don't have much time."

I felt like belting him one, but I climbed out of the air car and followed him toward the waiting guards.

"Tell me what's going on, Claver," I said, "or I'm tipping off security right here, right now."

Claver looked at me. "You won't do that."

"You want to try me?"

Claver gave me that evil smile again. "You're not the same man any longer, McGill. I've got your number. You've got a kid, a woman—she's nuts, but she's still a woman. Then there're your folks. They seem nice. Did you know that before I came to your door, I knocked on theirs and had a nice little chat with your mom?"

That was it. I hit him. A sucker punch from a man that outweighed him by thirty kilos—that's never an easy thing to shrug off.

Claver spun around and fell to the ground.

"Don't you ever—" I began, but I was interrupted from my intimidating speech.

The guards were running toward us now. They had their hands on their pistols and blood in their eyes. They'd been watching us act weird out here on the puff-crete landing zone for a long while, I guess, and they'd had enough.

"McGill," Claver said, not bothering to get up. "You're determined to screw up everything, aren't you?"

"I'm known for that."

The pounding feet of the MPs came closer, and I looked up at them. When I looked back down at Claver again, I blinked, and my face registered shock.

The man at my feet wasn't Claver. Not anymore. It was Winslade.

But then he smiled, and I knew that evil smile too well. It *was* Claver. It had to be. He must have used another one of his boxes to change his appearance.

When the guards arrived, they recognized Winslade.

"Arrest this man for striking an officer!" Claver said, doing a fair imitation of Winslade's voice.

They grabbed me, and the Winslade look-alike got up, dusting himself off. He followed along behind me looking stern while I was hustled toward the entrance to Central.

I consoled myself with the knowledge that I'd at least gotten to punch Claver one more time.

-50-

We headed directly to Winslade's office. I don't mind saying I was a little freaked out. What was Claver's plan? I'd decided to play it cool. Trying to convince the guards Winslade wasn't Winslade wasn't going to wash. They'd seen me punch him, and they were all business at this point.

What didn't help was that I was from Legion Varus, a known band of ruffians, while Winslade was from Hegemony. Hogs and independent legion people rarely saw eye-to-eye. From the point of view of the police, it was extremely believable that a noncom from a disreputable outfit would take a poke at a Hog officer. It happened frequently enough.

"Could you open my door?" Winslade asked one of the guards. "I seem to have dropped my fob during this buffoon's clumsy assault."

"Certainly, Primus," the man said, touching his hand to the lock plate. The door shot open, and a very shocked looking figure that looked like Claver stood there, staring at us.

Only it wasn't Claver. It had to be the hapless Sloane.

I could see the surprise in Sloane's eyes. Maybe he'd been lying in wait for Winslade, but he hadn't planned on him coming with the cavalry and me too.

Sloane looked at me, and I could see understanding flood into him.

"They caught you, huh, McGill?" he asked. "Well, I still say it was worth it."

He raised his bar of soap and aimed it at Claver, I guess he thought it was Winslade. I could hardly blame him for that.

Claver knew he was in trouble and dove behind one of the confused guards.

The guards were slow to react. As far as they could tell, a lunatic was aiming something resembling a bar of soap at them.

An invisible beam struck the guard that was shielding Claver. The man's eyes widened, and he fell to his knees then flat on his face. I never even saw an injury, so I wasn't sure how he died. The weapon was clearly one of those alien-made specials that killed in devious ways. Maybe his neurons had stopped firing, or maybe his blood had congealed all at once. There was no way to tell without an autopsy.

The second guard caught on when his buddy went down. He drew his pistol, side-stepped so he was partly obscured by the doorway, and fired three sizzling bolts into the room. I heard an alarm go off somewhere. The weapon's discharge had tripped it.

Sloane caught two of the three bolts. The last one splashed the slanting glass behind him, causing it to smoke and create a melted divot. As testimony to the strength of Central's construction, it didn't cut all the way through.

"Got him!" the guard said proudly.

"Well done," Claver said, still acting the part of Winslade. He quickly stepped past the guard and into the office.

When he got behind the desk, Claver did a double-take. Frowning, he stepped back to Sloane who was being looked over by the man who'd shot him.

"This man is—sir, there's some kind of field around him. A projection of some kind. I'm—"

While the guard had been speaking, Claver had stooped and picked up the soap bar. He pressed it to guard's neck and activated it.

The guard pitched forward.

"What the hell—?" I demanded, stepping forward. "What did you do that for?"

"Bah, don't be a baby, McGill. He'll pop out of the oven downstairs in an hour. Would you rather be interrogated?"

"No," I admitted.

Claver grinned with Winslade's lips. It was a strange sight to see. To me, it was like Winslade was standing there, imitating Claver's mannerisms.

"What are you so happy about?" I asked.

He lifted up an object. It was the Galactic key.

"Where the heck did that come from?"

"Take a look behind the good Primus' desk."

I stepped around the desk and saw the real Winslade lying there. Claver began to work quickly while I gaped.

First, he stepped to Winslade's computer terminal and accessed the data core for the whole facility. He used the key to bypass every log in and biometric identification system. He quickly began shutting things off. Alarms began to go off on every floor then fall silent again as each was shut down in turn.

The cameras died, then fail-safe systems activated to back them up. The fail-safes quickly faulted as well. It was amazing, really. I'd never really thought about what the Galactic key could do to a place like Central, which was full of the best equipment that credits could buy—in other words, alien-made gizmos. In this case, it was the all-important data core that was purchased off-world and therefore had to have breakable security to be legal on the frontier.

Two more confused guards arrived with their weapons drawn before Claver could finish his dirty work. They were breathing hard. They looked at the body-choked office in horror.

"Primus, are you all right?"

"Yes, fortunately," Claver said. "But the attackers have escaped. Would you be so kind as to pursue them?"

"Which way, sir?"

"You don't know?"

"The whole building is off-grid. I'm sorry, Primus. We can't even raise dispatch."

"Unacceptable. I'll be making a report later. Go to fourth level, B section. I believe that's where they're headed."

"Fourth and B? Isn't that the kitchen, sir? I—"

"Veteran. Are you questioning my information or my intelligence?"

"Uh...neither sir. Glad you're all right..."

Claver made a dismissive wave. When the guards were gone, I whistled long and low.

"Wow, I'm impressed," I said. "You sound and act just like Winslade. If this trading game doesn't work out for you, there's always the theater."

He looked up from the terminal, distracted. "We're not done yet," he said.

"No?"

He knelt and went to work on Winslade's tapper next. I walked around the desk and watched, frowning. I saw he had the Galactic key in his hand.

"What are you doing to the Primus, exactly?" I demanded.

"I'm perming him, of course. What else? Did you expect me to give him mouth-to-mouth?"

I grabbed him and pulled him away from Winslade. "There's no need for that. He's dead already. Leave well enough alone."

"He's going to explain what happened here to the authorities. We've erased the vid data and damaged the core, but that's not enough to keep any of these men from testifying against us later."

My eyes crawled over the bodies on the floor. Two guards, Sloane and Winslade. Killing them was one thing, but perming them? That was too much.

"You want to get arrested, is that it, boy?" Claver said in a snake-like voice. "We're on a purge, in case you hadn't noticed. A clean-up mission for our team."

"Our team? Who's our team leader? You?"

"No, my muscle-brained friend. Turov is our leader, naturally. She's going to be elevated to equestrian after all the evidence is in against Nagata."

Looking from Winslade to Claver and back again, I didn't know what to think.

"Nagata?" I asked.

"Like I said, we're not done yet."

"What evidence?" I asked.

"The evidence I'm busy planting with Winslade's computer," he said laughing. "Is there any other kind?"

"Okay," I said. "I know Turov is ambitious. I get that. I know Winslade stole the key, and she wants it back. But why are you perming him?"

"He's got to go. Not because he stole the key, but because he knows of its existence and how to operate it."

"Is that all?" I asked. "I can fix that. Give it to me."

Claver stared at me.

"Let me get this straight," I said. "You're one hundred percent sure you can get away with perming a primus in the middle of Central? That is ballsy, my man. A crime like that is a hard one to cover up. People have memories, you know, that go beyond what's in the data core. They'll never stop investigating this. Give me the key, and I'll fix it right."

My big hand was parked in his face, palm up, waiting. After counting to three—maybe it was four—he finally handed it over.

I went to work on Winslade's tapper. I broke through security effortlessly with the key. Essentially, whenever a screen came up asking for a code or a password or a fingerprint, a touch of the key caused the data to fill itself in correctly. Within seconds, I was deeper into the menus than any normal person could go.

There, I found Winslade's memory backups. Going back a few weeks, I found they weren't held locally. They were stored on a server in Central. Again, the passwords and security checks fell one by one. I was soon able to access his core data.

There it all was. His mind, his body, stored in computers down to the DNA and synaptic connections. Riffling through his past like anyone handling a folder full of files, I erased them one by one. His mind was being destroyed—but only the most recent accumulative backups of it. The system worked by storing changes over time rather than full copies of the entire thing.

I left his body alone, but I erased a month's worth of his mind. It was a strange feeling, like I was playing God. To make myself feel better, I kept reminding myself that Winslade's only other option was nonexistence.

Claver watched me closely and talked over my shoulder about the key.

"Are you sure this will work?" he asked.

"Yeah, I told you. I've done it before more than once. Haven't you ever wondered how I get out of things?"

"Maybe you know what you're doing sometimes," he admitted reluctantly. It was still strange to me to hear Claver's voice coming out of Winslade. "Just make sure he doesn't remember the key. We've already got three people who know about the treasure you're wielding in your hand right now, McGill. You, me and Turov. That's about two over the limit, if you ask me. You can't keep a secret so big with four people—it's not possible. Someone is bound to blab or to attempt to eliminate the others. Winslade took it upon himself to demonstrate this today."

It occurred to me that Claver and I were busy doing exactly what Claver had said Winslade might do at this very moment. But I was too busy to argue about that.

"I got your point," I said. "You still haven't explained why we have to take sides. And if we do, why should we take Turov's side?"

Claver straightened up and put his hands on his hips. "You aren't suggesting we strike out on our own, are you?"

"Hell no. I just don't want to align myself with someone I disagree with."

"Ah," he said loudly. "I see the problem now—you're an idiot. I should've seen that one coming a mile off. Boy, let me explain the ways of the universe to you as some critical realities seem to have slipped by that fine mind of yours."

He was pissing me off, but I just kept working on Winslade's memories. If you could get past enough bullshit and insults, Claver often said something interesting.

"You remember when the Galactic battle fleet showed up in Earth orbit?" he asked. "Back when they filled the sky with alien ships?"

"I wasn't there personally—wait, you're not telling me you're *that* old, are you?"

He chuckled. "I was young, but I was there. Anyway, at that point, Earth had to make a choice. We could suck it up and play ball with these pushy aliens—or we could die. We made the choice we did because there really *wasn't* any choice."

"All right," I said. "But what's that got to do with choosing sides now? We don't have to work for Nagata or Turov."

"That's where you're wrong. You see, people in power don't understand men like us, McGill. They think we're just assholes. We're problems desperately in need of a solution—and the solution is an obvious one."

To make his point, he directed a finger toward the mess on the floor. I looked at Winslade's twisted corpse. I had to admit, Claver was right. When you played with fire, you often got burned.

"So," Claver continued, "nosy, irritating individuals like us need to sign on with the powerful in order to keep existing."

I nodded, understanding his point but not agreeing with it entirely. "What's to keep a ruthless woman like Turov from doing the same thing to you and me later?"

"Nothing," he admitted. "Nothing, that is, if we don't prepare for that eventuality."

"What can we possibly do? She keeps climbing in rank. She keeps becoming more powerful. Hell, she might even be the ruler of the world someday."

He gave me a tight look.

"Don't talk like that," he said. "To answer your question practically, there is a way to keep breathing no matter what in these situations."

"Really?" I asked, honestly interested. "Tell me. I'm all ears."

"Knowledge, my boy, that's the key to a long existence. Learn secrets and keep them to yourself. And always have another secret up your sleeve if the last one gets out."

"Secrets? You've got to be kidding. Secrets can get a man killed. Just look at Winslade."

He shook his head. "He didn't keep his secrets. He tried to exploit them. Winslade, here, he got big ideas and went up against someone more experienced and dangerous than himself. That's not what I'm suggesting you should do."

"Okay," I said, "but I still don't see how secrets—"

"If you'd shut up for a second, I'll tell you," he said angrily, then he paused and started to laugh. "There you go again, proving my point for me. An irritating fellow like you

366

simply *must* plan for the worst. People don't revive a man like James McGill out of compassion. Every time you die, there's a good chance someone will come to their senses and think: 'Hell, he's already dead—let's just leave well enough alone.'"

"That's great thinking, but..."

"Hold on. Let me finish. You've got to set things up so that they *need* to bring you back. That's my method. You need an ace in the hole. Now think, what's the one thing a dead, naked man might have that would compel another person to revive him?"

I looked at him blankly for a second.

He reached up and tapped me on the forehead. I went to grab his finger, but his hand quickly retreated.

"All you have at that point is whatever is in your head, McGill. Nothing else. I'm talking about information. Secrets those in power want to learn. Secrets are the only things we still possess after death. They go beyond the normal churn of recycling flesh and brain. My continued existence is based entirely on knowing things that other people don't. I keep secrets—that's all that matters."

I squinted at him, thinking hard for a second before I shook my head.

"No," I said. "You're wrong about that. Actions matter, Claver. What a man does in this life and the next—that counts. Our actions define us, and they outlive us as well. To me, it's what I do that matters."

He chuckled bemusedly. "Think whatever you want, Mr. Philosopher. But just remember what I told you if you want to keep on existing."

Standing up, I pocketed the key. Claver was instantly on guard.

"What are you doing?" he demanded.

"Returning a valuable item to our patron saint, Galina Turov."

Claver would rather have carried the key, but I didn't let him.

The confusion in the building allowed us to hit the elevators and ride them downward. The shaft went at a slant along the outer wall of the pyramid-shaped building. Outside, I

367

could see for miles. It was a sunny day, even out over the Atlantic.

I had a hard time thinking as we rode toward the exit and Claver's air car. What I really wanted to do was run. Sure, Claver had rigged the security and we'd erased Winslade's recent memories—but there had to be some kind of clue, something that they could trace. It made me nervous to think we weren't escaping but digging deeper instead.

Worse than all that was the feeling I'd been dragged into a dirty business. Claver was amazingly persuasive. He'd talked me into joining this adventure, and I was by no means certain I would live to see the sunset.

-51-

As it turned out, we marched right out of Central under a clear blue sky. The security system had been disabled on every floor down to the landing port level, where we'd left Claver's vehicle. When we boarded the air car and sped away, the whole building was in pandemonium.

Once we were on our way, Claver dropped the simulated appearance of Winslade. I found that he was easier to talk to that way.

"Where are we going now?" I asked, looking out through the back canopy.

"Turov's house. It's a pretty nice place."

"I bet. So—Winslade killed her, but she got a revive?"

"She did, but she did it unofficially. She had standing instructions to come out of a private facility if she was assassinated. Winslade probably had plans to eliminate her, or incriminate her somehow, but he never got the chance to spring them."

Craning my neck around farther, I looked back at Central. The place was crawling with security, and people were evacuating the building in endless streams heading in every direction. What a mess we'd left behind. Of all the disasters I'd run out on, this one ranked at the top.

The big sirens were blaring, and all kinds of emergency people were flying in from every direction. They had no idea why their security systems had all shut down at once. With

369

dead bodies on the floor and evacuation protocols in full swing, it was relatively easy to escape. Hell, lots of cars were zooming by, going faster than we were.

"They probably think it's another attack," I said, "like down at the spaceport."

"You never know when terrorists will strike," Claver agreed.

I looked at him sourly. "Most people don't, but you often seem to. Tell me, what secrets do you have that would interest me? You think you've got something big enough to make me want to revive you?"

Claver grinned. It was a dirty grin, the kind an old man gives an underage girl in a bar. "I know you were here with me today in a front row seat at Winslade's murder," he said.

"All the more reason to perm you," I pointed out.

"Right, but let's say, for the sake of argument, that these facts were revealed a week or two after my death."

"How the hell would that happen?"

Claver laughed. "I can see you haven't been paying attention. I'm nothing if not a careful planner. You think about that, the next time you consider leaving me dead. There won't be much time. You'd best get hopping and revive me, pronto."

I tried not to think about his threats—but I did anyway. I couldn't help it. Claver was disturbing to me. If there was ever a man that I'd never understood completely, it was him.

When we got to Turov's place we landed on the roof. We were permitted to head down into the mansion where we met the Imperator in person.

Turov didn't look happy to see me. "Did you have to bring him here?" she asked Claver.

"He's been helpful up until this point."

She eyed me with new respect. "All right then. He helped retrieve my property... Well done, you two. Central has been cleansed of a dangerous renegade today. You both have my gratitude."

I looked at her in honest surprise. To me, the dangerous people weren't dead; they were in the room with me right now.

"People died, sir," I said, "and this joker wanted to perm Winslade. Was that your idea?"

Turov's attitude shifted again. She looked at me like I was some kind of disease.

"Nothing of the sort has ever been suggested by my office," she said quickly. "You need to get that through your head, McGill, if you're going to be working for me."

"Working for you? I'm under your command at the moment, if that's what you mean, but I don't—"

"That's good enough, I suppose," Turov said. "Let's stick to that approach. I'm in your direct chain of command. Also, it's important for you to keep in mind that there are only a few steps between my position and the very top of the military chain. Do not forget that."

"If you say so, sir."

"Imperator Turov," Claver said, leaning forward a little. "I think you misunderstand me. McGill has been useful, but I didn't say I wanted him to join our team."

We both looked at him in surprise.

"Why the hell did you bring me along then, you snake?" I demanded.

He jerked a thumb in my direction without meeting my eye. He kept his gaze on Turov and her gun. "If I might suggest, Imperator, we have better options at this point."

"What other options would you suggest, Claver?" I demanded. "Perming me too?"

"What I'm suggesting," Claver said, talking directly to Turov, "is that an additional layer to our defenses might be helpful. A culprit, clearly depicted as guilty by altered security vids, would go a long way to creating the kind of closure that comforts investigating organizations. In this case, we happen to have a universally mistrusted individual at hand."

Glaring at him for a second, I turned back to Turov to make my case. What I found was her standing there with a gun on me. Her eyes were dangerous.

I'm not a deep-thinking man, but I could tell that I'd been set up from the beginning. Claver had dragged me along on this string of murders for the sole purpose of pinning them on me by the time we reached the finish line. It made me angry not to have seen this coming.

"I get it now," I said. "Claver's been at this all day. Marching around killing folks—I'd figured you'd be dead yourself before we left here, Imperator, but *maybe* that's not his plan. Maybe he wants to kill me instead. I hereby request permission to arrest him right now."

Galina cocked her pretty head and looked at each of us thoughtfully. Then she held out her hand toward Claver.

"Give me my property."

Claver looked at her hand like it was a tentacle attached to one of those squid-aliens.

"I beg your pardon?" he asked.

"I know Winslade had the Galactic key, and you've taken it from him," she said. "Hand it over before I become angry."

"I'm sorry Imperator, but I don't have it. Install a lie-detector app on my tapper and test me. I'm not lying."

Suddenly, Turov's face became worried. "Who has it, then? Where is my property?"

Her voice was rising, becoming shrill. The good news was her gun had swung to cover Claver, instead of me.

I thought about making a move on her. I didn't have a sidearm on me, but I could draw and throw a knife in one smooth motion if the need was there. As she was distracted and out of practice in close combat, there was a good chance I could peg her to the wall before she could draw a bead on me and put me down.

For about a second, I didn't hear what Claver and Turov were saying to one another. I didn't much care what it was, either. They were two snakes hissing in a basket. Finally, I made my decision.

"Imperator," I said loudly.

She startled and shifted her eyes back to me. "What is it now, McGill?"

"I have your key. Right here."

I pulled out the device and showed it to her.

Claver rolled his eyes

"Shut up, Claver," Turov said. "Let me get this straight. *McGill* retrieved the key? And you allowed him to hold onto it?"

372

Claver shrugged. "I brought the key here. He's just the bearer."

She narrowed her eyes at both of us. "I get it Claver. You tried to play me for the fool at the end. Say what you will about McGill, he gets the job done, and he doesn't hide things—at least, he's not good at it. James, I almost always know what you're thinking."

"Thank you, sir—I think."

She nodded to me and without another word shot Claver in the gut. He fell, gasping. He rolled onto his back, eyes bulging in shock.

Claver gasped and made sounds of vexation. "You idiot, McGill. Why didn't you move when I had her distracted? What kind of a thug are you, anyway?"

Turov stalked forward like a huntress and stood over her victim. She shot him again, but it wasn't a fatal wound. He was in shock, I could tell.

"You're not dead yet," she said to him. "But you must give me a reason not to finish the job and then perm you."

Claver's lips quivered, running with blood and spit.

"Throne World," he said, coughing.

She shook her head. "Not good enough. I know about that planet. I know where it is. I know everything—"

She stopped as Claver's trembling hand came to rest on her calf. It squeezed there, and he struggled to speak.

"You don't know everything," he said. "You just think you do, you bitch. You don't know how to take it. How to use it..."

Turov's eyes narrowed. She stared at him for a second longer then shot him in the face.

Watching him die, she put out her hand toward me. "Give me the key."

"What are you going to do?" I asked.

"What should have been done long ago."

Instead of doing as she asked, I put the key on her desk. When she reached for it, I grabbed both her wrists and held them firmly.

"Don't tell me I shot the wrong man," she said in a sudden rage.

"Look, Imperator," I said, "I don't understand everything that's going on today, but I'm not in the mood to let you perm him."

"I'm not going to do that, fool," she said. "I need him."

"You believe all that stuff he said about the squid home world, do you? Throne World, I think he called it."

"That's not why I need him," she said. "I need a scapegoat. You should be happy I chose him instead of you for this purpose."

"All right, but tell me one thing: why should I let you get away with all this? Why should I let you engineer murders all day long? Why not go to the authorities and—"

"Because you were running around assassinating people today, McGill. You and Claver—not me."

I thought about that, and I sighed. I had no evidence that she was involved. Her enemies would suspect the truth, of course. They'd believe my story, but in the end, a noncom would have a hard time bringing down a slippery top officer. Especially when the noncom was from Legion Varus, and the officer was a part of Hegemony.

"I can see your wheels turning," she said. "Now, let me go."

Looking at Claver's corpse, I felt reluctant to let go of Turov. She might do anything.

"What are you going to do with him, exactly?"

"I'll take the last few hours of his memories then let him be revived. When the evidence of his guilt is shown at his trial, he'll suspect something odd happened, but he won't know the details."

Shaking my head, I sighed and let go of her. "Claver may have met his match today."

"Yes," she said as she took the key, knelt, and went to work on Claver's dead arm. "I believe he has."

* * *

374

Nagata hauled me back to Central the very next day. I went with dread in my heart. I just knew that he'd figured out I was involved in the disasters Claver had initiated.

Still, I played it as straight as I could. Caught red-handed, most men would confess. That was always a mistake in my book. Maybe Nagata knew, and maybe he didn't. But even if he *did* know, that didn't mean he could prove it. Why give him my head on a silver platter?

I used the ground entrance. Sweating on the way up in the elevators, I tried to relax and enjoy the visit. It wasn't every day a noncom was invited to talk with the brass at Central.

When I got off the elevator car I stepped lightly down the carpeted hallway, whistling as I walked. There were clean-up crews and technicians doing forensics. They were checking every optical filament that led to the pinhole cameras in the ceiling. In general, these people all looked pissed off. They eyed me with suspicion as I passed by. I told myself it was probably because I was the only man on the floor without the blue globe patch of Hegemony on my shoulder—not because they recognized me.

Reaching up to touch the door chime, my hand didn't even make it to the pad before the door swept open. Inside was Nagata, sitting behind his desk.

"Veteran McGill," he said slowly. "Come in and stand at ease."

I did as I was invited. The door swept closed behind me and I clasped my hands behind my back.

Nagata was looking at his desk again, tapping at it. He had a pistol there, I saw, and something else…

My eyes fixated on the second item. It was familiar to me. It looked like a bar of soap with a button on it, but I knew what it was—a deadly weapon.

Forcing my gaze to shift to the view over Nagata's shoulder, I put a slight smile back on my face. "Nice day out there, sir."

"Indeed."

"The funny thing is," I said in a conversational tone, "this building is so tall, the weather is different up here than it is on

375

the ground. I never get over that. Reminds me of the megaflora back on Death World."

"Shut up, McGill."

"Yes, sir."

I waited while he tapped around on his screen for a moment longer. Finally, he managed to bring up what he was looking for. He spun the image so it would be correctly oriented from my point of view, and he beckoned me to come forward.

There, on the screen, was a slightly blurred image of a large man in motion. I couldn't see his face, just his heavy chin. His fists were rising in the shot as if he was about to attack someone.

Now, this normally would've been of only slight interest to me, except that I recognized the uniform the man was wearing. It was mine. There was a Wolfshead patch on the shoulder, plain as day. The rank insignia of a veteran was visible too.

"You were amazingly thorough," Nagata said while I stared at the image. "But there's always something if you keep digging. In this case, an image was left in a buffer on a man's suit-camera. The man didn't survive the encounter, unfortunately. Neither did his memory when we revived him last night. Equally disturbing, every image his camera transmitted to the data core was destroyed. Only those stored on the mobile unit itself remained."

My eyes flicked up to Nagata's face, and he met my gaze. His voice was easy-going, but his expression was that of a man smoldering with anger. Interestingly, there was another emotion there: curiosity.

Most men might have broken down at this point, but I continued to play it smoothly.

"Interesting shot, sir—but kind of blurry," I said. "Too bad we can't see the face."

Nagata stared at me for a long second.

"How'd you do it, McGill?" he finally asked me.

"Do what, sir?"

"Break into Central, perform a rash of assassinations and escape every security system and guard we have? It was an amazing feat, really. I have to congratulate you."

"Oh now, hold on, sir! You're not suggesting—"

"No, no! Don't be so modest, man! You're gifted. It's the only way I can explain it. When I first met you, I thought you were some kind of thuggish buffoon. Imagine my surprise at this moment."

"I'm not sure what you're..." I began.

"Not clear on what I'm talking about? Perhaps I should show you more."

He proceeded then to flash up a series of images and short vid-clips. Dead men lay all over Winslade's office—including Winslade. I recognized the scene, naturally, but I feigned shock and dismay.

"This is unbelievable!" I said loudly. "Was it a commando raid? Aliens, perhaps?"

Nagata shook his head in disbelief. "Winslade told me you wouldn't confess. I have here in my hands enough evidence to put you away for life. Can you comprehend that?"

"Sir," I said, "I'm not the man you want."

Nagata smiled at last. "That's the first thing you've said that I'm willing to believe. Now, tell me who I really want to prosecute. Who *should* be executed at dawn, McGill?"

I knew what he wanted, of course. That had been obvious from the moment I'd walked in. He wanted me to implicate Imperator Turov. He'd set up this entire confrontation with that in mind.

It was with some reluctance that I did what had to be done next. I reached down to my belt and touched the box there.

Nagata, for all his feigned state of relaxation, moved very quickly indeed. I had to take it as a compliment that he thought I was extremely dangerous, even though his security people had checked every nook and cranny I had for weaponry.

He snatched up the pistol on his desk and put it into my face—only, it wasn't my face anymore.

I'd activated one of Claver's altered disguise boxes from Tau Ceti. Instead of aiming his gun at me, he was aiming it into a mirror image of his own face.

I smiled at Nagata's reaction, and I flipped the box off again. He stared, eyes bulging.

"Alien tech," he said. "The image—such resolution. Very clever."

For my own part, I was starting to like Nagata. I wasn't accustomed to having officers think I was some kind of genius. Removing the belt slowly, I set it on his desk and nudged it in his direction.

"I heard about what happened here yesterday," I said, "but I wasn't here. Someone else was, someone using my face."

"Who?"

"It could have been a lot of people. There are billions of Tau who own boxes like this back on Tech World."

Doubt was in his mind now, I could see it. For the first time since I'd walked in, he wasn't one hundred percent certain he had the guilty party. It was time to press that advantage.

"There are a lot of adjectives people ascribe to me, sir," I said. "But clever with technical wizardry? No sir, that's never been on the list. I'm not going to deny that I could kill a roomful of guards under the right circumstances, but the rest of this attack was way beyond me."

Nagata slowly nodded. A seed had been planted. Now, the trick would be to redirect his suspicions on a new path.

"The list of people who could pull this kind of thing off is a short one," I continued. "But on the top of it is a man named Claver. He had to be involved in some capacity. Hell, he's the one who altered these boxes in the first place to make them do tricks like this back on Tech World."

Nagata put his gun down slowly. He picked up the belt and inspected it closely.

"This device," he said, "combined with a weapon wrapped in purely organic matter—and they're both alien-made."

"I would expect so."

"You're claiming that it wasn't *you* who performed the assassinations here yesterday? That it was some kind of body-double?"

"That's the long and the short of it, yes sir."

He put the box down and leaned back in his chair, thinking hard. "Alien gear...murder in the heart of Central...these things are disturbing. But the most frightening aspect is the fact that someone can walk in here and erase our computers."

I nodded. "That's damned peculiar, sir."

He looked me over, squinting at me as if I made his eyes sore—who knew? Maybe I did.

"What do you know about Throne World, McGill?" he asked.

"Sir?"

"The cephalopod capital."

Happy to change the subject, I related to him a number of things I knew about that distant planet. Most of them he'd already gleaned from reports, but he was interested to learn that I'd encountered one of the squid queens in person. I'd been present when we'd discovered the data globe that helped pinpoint where in space the enemy homeworld was, too.

"You know," Nagata said thoughtfully after listening to me, "I think I've been sitting behind this desk too long. We're going on a mission next year. You and I, together."

"Well now, hold on, sir—" I began.

"Don't worry. You'll stick with your unit. And it won't be just me lifting off into space. Not this time. Thousands of Hegemony troops will be going. Every legion and ship we can scrape together. There's something big going on out there among the quiet stars, McGill. If we sit here on Earth, the aliens will keep coming. Eventually, they'll wipe us all out— even sneaky bastards like you."

I wasn't sure what to say, so I kept my mouth shut.

Nagata got up, walked to his window and stared down that rain-streaked wall of puff-crete and glass at crawling ground traffic around the base of the pyramid.

"We're surrounded by enemies and unknown technologies," Nagata said in a haunted tone. "That plant-race you encountered? They're a cancer in the Cephalopod Kingdom. That's the squid weakness, you know."

"How's that, sir?"

"Haven't you wondered why the cephalopods have yet to come to Earth and wipe us all out? They should be able to do it, inferior ships notwithstanding, but they have their own problems with the Wur eating away their star systems."

"I have wondered about that," I said. "There's a lot we don't know about our place in this galaxy. But the Empire should—"

Nagata released a bark of laughter. "The Empire is declining and weak. It's like an old man with a chill, shaking in a blanket. How can we rely on them for protection from the wild aliens beyond the frontier? The Empire technically controls most of the star systems in this Galaxy—but far from all of them. We're on the very edge of known space. All sorts of things lurk beyond our borders."

"I see your point."

Nagata paused then. We both looked outside at Earth. I wondered what he was thinking about. As an upper level officer, he knew things of which I had no inkling. I found his somber, almost melancholy mood disturbing.

"McGill?" Nagata said at last.

"Sir?"

"If I let you live another day, will you promise to kill an amazing number of the enemy for me next year?"

"I'd be glad to," I said. "I'm always happy to serve Earth."

He nodded, and then he handed me something. It was a small box.

I stared at the box for a moment, but I hesitated before opening it. Honestly, I thought it might be some kind of bomb. Some kind of final punch-line to Nagata's odd, soul-searching speech.

Instead, when I opened the box I discovered two nano-adhesive pins bearing the single gold bar of a junior adjunct. I took them out and felt their weight in my hands.

"Not what you were expecting, is it?" Nagata asked.

"No sir, I can't say that it is."

"Listen, Adjunct McGill. You understand our enemies. Sometimes I even think you're in league with them. At other times, I think you're some sort of lunatic."

"I can understand that, sir."

"But I've been watching you for quite a while. Ever since you started killing Galactics and getting away with it. That impressed me very much."

His words startled me. I'd thought I'd had him bamboozled, but I'd clearly been wrong. He knew far more than he'd been letting on.

"Taking on the role of an officer," he continued, "that's a new level of responsibility. A whole new zone for a man like you. I want you to take this new rank seriously, if that's not too much to ask."

I nodded, running my thumbs over the bars. They were nano-coated, and they wouldn't even smudge.

"I will sir, God willing."

"Good," he said. "That's all Earth can ask from any of her sons. Dark days are ahead, I'm certain of it. There may be a special mission in your future. A task that will make use of your unusual talents."

"I'm always up for that sort of thing," I lied.

He kicked me out of his office after that, and a few minutes later I was walking the streets that encircled Central. Locating the nearest drinking establishment, I put my new rank insignia onto my collar before I walked in.

The gold bars felt good on my neck, but they also felt heavy. I noticed every enlisted legionnaire I found ordering drinks on a Thursday afternoon eyed me differently because I wore them. They looked at me the way kids used to look at the principal back in my elementary school days.

It had been a rough week. To make myself feel better, I drank one beer after another until I didn't feel the weight of the new rank on my collar anymore—or much of anything else.

The End

More Books by B. V. Larson:

UNDYING MERCENARIES
Steel World
Dust World
Tech World
Machine World

STAR FORCE SERIES
Swarm
Extinction
Rebellion
Conquest
Battle Station
Empire
Annihilation
Storm Assault
The Dead Sun
Outcast
Exile

OTHER SF BOOKS
Technomancer
The Bone Triangle
Element-X
Velocity

Visit BVLarson.com for more information.

Printed in Great Britain
by Amazon